THE PRAISE SINGER

THE
PRAISE
SINGER

MARY RENAULT

PANTHEON BOOKS

NEW YORK

Library of Congress Cataloging in Publication Data
Renault, Mary, pseud.
The Praise Singer.
I.   Title.
PZ3.R2913Pq   1978   [PR6035.E55]   823'.9'12
ISBN 0-394-50273-6   78-53495

Manufactured in the United States of America

FIRST EDITION

3 5 7 9 8 6 4 2

So I shall never waste my life-span in a vain
useless hope, seeking what cannot be, a flaw-
less man among us all who feed on the fruits
of the broad earth. If I find him, I will bring
you news.

But I praise and love every man who does
nothing base from free will. Against necessity,
even gods do not fight.

SIMONIDES

CONTENTS

THE PRAISE SINGER

SICILY

A GOOD SONG, I think. The end's good—that came to me in
one piece—and the rest will do. The boy will need to write
it, I suppose, as well as hear it. Trusting to the pen; a disgrace, and he with his own name made. But write he will,
never keep it in the place between his ears. And even then
he won't get it right alone. I still do better after one hearing of something new than he can after three. I doubt
he'd keep even his own songs for long, if he didn't write
them. So what can I do, unless I'm to be remembered only
by what's carved in marble? *Tell them in Lakedaimon,
passer-by, that here, obedient to their word, we lie.* They'll
remember *that*.

That was the year Anakreon died. *He* had all his songs
safe in his head. He proved us that at the city feast after
Marathon; anything we asked for, there it was. Aischylos
. . . no, he wasn't there, he was in mourning for his brother.
I had sung first, of course. And Anakreon finished with
something new to all of us, fifty years old. You could hear
him too, short of teeth as he was by then. We Ionian poets
are a long-lived breed.

Well, his songs are sung, and will be unless the barbarians
come back again; and the ships at Salamis have settled that.
They sing him; but the young men don't get him right. Just

a word here and there; but it would have grated his fine ear. Men forget how to write upon the mind. To hear, and keep: that is our heritage from the Sons of Homer. Sometimes I think I shall die their only heir. Themistokles asked if I had a secret art of memory; which I can forgive in a man with no education to speak of. Practice, practice, that's all; but who wants to hear nowadays about hard work? Ah, they say, Simonides will take his secret to the grave with him. At eighty-three he can't have much more use for it; but old men get miserly.

Well, I bow to the times. Only last year I recited for some scrivener of King Hieron's my whole stock of Anakreon's songs, for fear some should disappear with me. And having done that, I thought I'd best turn to and make a book of my own, lest book-taught slovens should garble me when I'm dead. I've not yet come down to scratching on wax myself; the boy does that, and I don't let *him* demean himself with fair-copying. He must learn young what is due to us. (Yes, well, I must try to keep in mind that he's turned forty.)

King Hieron will send us a clerk, as he would a physician or a cook. Yes, I'm well-found here, and winter warmth pays for the hot summers. I have not troubled the physician much. *Best of good things, sweet health.* That, every wanderer knows. Now I've done with wandering, give me one day at a time, on a vine-shaded Sicilian porch with a lyre beside me, and memory in my head.

Memory, that's the thing. I've met few men who reached my years, and they were peasants, or else in second childhood. Who knows what each day may bring? Sometimes when all's quiet at night I take my lamp to the book-chest. Once or twice I've even taken a pen in hand, when I've thought of a happier word. If the boy sees my marks, he keeps quiet about it. What a deal of reed-paper poems do take up, that will lie in a man's head as small as a bee-grub in the comb. A dozen rolls. I have had to number the outsides, to know what's in them.

I shall leave my scrolls, like the potter's cup and the sculptor's marble, for what they're worth. Marble can break; the cup is a crock thrown in the well; paper burns warm on a winter night. I have seen too much pass away. So when they come to me, as they do from King Hieron down, asking about the days before they were begotten, I tell them what deserves remembrance, even if it keeps me up when I crave for bed. The true songs are still in the minds of men.

KEOS

1

KEOS IS STERN. You'd not suppose so from the proverb, that it knows not the horse nor ox, but is rich in the gladdening vine-fruit, and brings forth poets. That last had not been added, when I was born. On the other hand, it is a lie that on Keos a man has to take hemlock when he reaches sixty. That was only in the old siege when the warriors had to be kept alive. Nowadays, it is just considered good manners.

Iulis, my native city, is high up the mountain, above Koressia harbor. I used to sit on a rock with my father's sheep around me, looking at the foreign sails and wondering where they came from; they thread the Kyklades from all four corners of the world. I could seldom go down to see. My father was not a man to leave his land to a steward while he sat at ease, nor let his sons go sightseeing. My elder brother, Theasides, got leave from work much oftener than I; not because he was the heir, which would have made it heavier, but because he was good with the disk and javelin and a fine pankratiast, and had to train for the games to do the family credit. He was handsome too. My parents never told me in so many words that they preferred me out of sight, but they had no need. I seemed to have known it from my birth.

Keeping out of sight, one is a good deal alone. But if one

is short of company, one can always make it. I kept, you
might say, the very best company in Keos.

If a fine ship with a painted sail passed proudly by the
port, keeping its mystery, for me it was the *Argo* with its
talking prow and its crew of heroes, going north to the
bewitched Kolchian shore. If a hawk hovered, I saw winged
Perseus poised for his flashing swoop; grasping, like the
hawk its prey, the Gorgon's deadly head to freeze the
dragon. The boulder I sat on had been flung by Herakles,
playing ball as a boy. When I drove my flock to pasture, I
was with Achilles on some great cattle-raid, bringing the
spoils of a plundered city back to camp.

As I dreamed I sang, as far back as I can remember. I
needed only to be alone, among the creatures of my
thought, and the songs would come. Childish, at first;
tunes picked up from the work songs of my father's thralls,
or the women weaving. They satisfied me, till I was old
enough to be taken to the Apollo festival, and heard a
rhapsodist chanting his bit of Homer, and some local poet
taking his choir through a choral ode. I suppose I was nine
or ten.

For the first time, I knew that my secret joy was a thing
grown men could make a life of, even a living. I did not
yet hope that for myself. I only dreamed of it, as I'd
dreamed of fighting at Troy; but on the mountain I
dreamed aloud. When some old ewes pushed up to see
what all the noise was about, I felt like Orpheus, and
wished that Keos had lions to be enchanted. Then I would
go home at night, and be silent in a corner. No wonder my
father thought me a sullen boy. But what could I have said
to him?

Time passed; I was twelve, thirteen; I heard the singing
at the festivals; I understood that these men, happy beyond
imagining, had all once been boys like me, and somehow
achieved their bliss. My dreams turned to wishes; but they

could find no voice, except in secret on the mountain. Soon I would be a man, just one of my father's farm-hands. A poet? I could as soon have told him I wanted to be a Scythian king. I would be lucky if he did no worse than laugh. I began to know bitterness, and despair.

Then came the wedding from which my life was born.

The bridegroom was Laertes, our neighbor Milon's eldest son. He was a sea-captain, his rich father having bought him a ship when he came of age. He had grown rich in his turn, by boldness, shrewdness and luck, trading about Ionia and as far as Egypt, and had stayed unmarried till thirty, mostly for lack of time. There was always a stir when he put in with his foreign goods, his outlandish men and his tales. Theas, who was taken to call with our father, used to save the tales for me.

I had never thought they would take me to the wedding. Any treats I had as a child came always from Theasides. This time they could hardly leave me behind, because my five-year-old sister was going. She was pretty, though, with hair as soft as cobweb and red as fire. Once she had asked me gravely how I came to be so ugly, not believing such a thing could happen without a reason her elders would understand. I told her I had been cursed by a raven from whom I had taken a lamb, which left her satisfied. Hearing her crying as her hair was combed, I wondered they should be troubled with either of us at a feast, forgetting that weddings beget weddings and are times for looking ahead.

At all events, my best tunic came out of the chest; a cast-off of Theasides's though there were five years between us; quite good, but I was outgrowing it in my turn. I looked dismayed at my lean thighs with their dark pelt of hair. But I would have to show enough to frighten the women, before I would get a new one. Keos is stern.

Before the house of the bride was a gently sloping meadow, where the bridesmaids stood with their garlands, waiting to sing. The thrones of the bride and groom were decked with flowers. My parents greeted their hosts, and sought out their friends among the guests, taking Theasides with them. He was plainly dressed (there are laws in Keos against extravagance), but the cloth was fine, and if he had been in rags his beauty would have graced them. I, knowing what my parents would have wished of me, lost myself in the crowd. There was more in this than filial duty. I had marked down the slab of rock where the bard would stand to sing, and the clump of brush near by where I could listen undisturbed. I meant not to miss a word.

Bride and groom took their thrones. Though weathered, he had kept his looks, and his purple fillet from Tyre became him. They made a good pair, for all she was half his age. The girls stood in their circle, hand-linked ready to dance, bright on the grass as another wedding garland. And now came the bard, in his festal robe, its border embroidered in Miletos, his seven-stringed kithara in his hand. He walked to the singing place, and drew his plectrum across the strongs.

> *Happy groom, the favored of Aphrodite,*
> *Now at last you have her, your matchless maiden,*
> *Girdled with violets.*

The garland began to turn, like windblown petals.

He was a smallish man past his middle years; his beard, and the hair under his festal garland, were ash-grey. At that time he can't yet have been sixty; but to my youth he seemed as old as Zeus, and I was amazed he could sing so well. I knew nothing of training, except that it was given to good-looking boys who were chosen for Apollo's choir, and went to Delos, the holy island, for his birthday feast. All I had was a voice to which the sheep would answer; and perfect pitch, which I was half aware of, enough to recog-

nize it in the bard. I knew too that his inlaid kithara
was a masterpiece.

There it hangs on my wall. The embroidered neck-sling
wore ragged, and I had a new one worked in Athens. That's
wearing too, but never mind.

He had been costly to hire, by Keos reckoning, where
most things are paid in kind. You can't offer a sheep or
heifer to us wandering men. I once accepted a mule, which
I had need of at the time; but that's long ago. From kings,
maintenance and gold; from lords, either or both according
to their rank; from others, weighed-out silver. Or one makes
a gift, for the honor of gods or heroes. Nothing between.

He had been ten days on Keos, a guest in the bride's
household, teaching the girls the wedding song and the
dance. Sometimes from up the hill I had seen them dancing, but too far to hear. It would have been as much as
my hide was worth, to leave my flock.

From my lair in the brush, a yard or two from the dais, I
saw only the backs of the bride-maidens, as they faced the
seats of honor. But, as I had planned, I could hear each
note and each word.

The dancers had on their best thinnest dresses, of fine
linen beaten soft upon the river-stones and squeezed, still
damp, into clinging folds. As they passed the bride's
throne, one or another would toss a flower from the wreath
she wore; the lap of the saffron-veiled girl was full of roses.
It was too late for the violets of the song. Their clear voices
rose like birds' at dawn. The bridegroom's friends, bold
young rips for the most part, stood by his throne as quiet
as well-beaten schoolboys, saving their bawdries for the
bridal ride. At most weddings, they'd have been clapping
time and calling out to the girls.

The song was the dance; the bard was its perfect instrument. He sang it lightly but with reverence; none of those
little variations thrown in to flatter the hosts, though they

are sometimes good enough to keep. This piece was sacred, this he handled like a phoenix egg. When already a singer, he had heard the Tenth Muse sing her own song herself. Such things are the heirlooms of the bards. This time it was a family heirloom too; the bride's mother in her trailing Ionian gown was smiling and wiping her eyes. She came from Lesbos, and it had been a gift for her own wedding.

I gathered my childish thoughts as best I could, to make all this my possession. But I was aware, too, that near by on the rock sat the harper's boy.

He was a comely lad, well fed and clothed and washed. His blue eyes were narrowed under his drawn fair brows, as he tried to listen. I knew, from my visits to the festivals, that this was no slave but a pupil, working to learn his art. This was part of his training and reward: a wedding song of Sappho's, a treasure to store in memory. I think I noticed he was shivering, though the breeze hardly stirred the flowers; but my mind was on other matters. Once he looked my way. Poor lad, he was far from home; I daresay he would gladly have changed places, even with me. I eyed him with envy, as a beggar might a prince.

I drank down the song as a thirsty plant does water, freshening and growing, feeling in folded flower-buds the core of fruit. Some of the words I'd seized, and would keep tomorrow sitting among the sheep; some would escape me, and I must patch as best I could. The tune I would remember, but I had no lyre, only my shepherd's pipe; one cannot both pipe and sing. Already the song was done, the dance was over, the girls blew the bride kisses and ran back for their parents' praise. For a little while the rain would nourish me; then would be drought again. Tomorrow the bard would leave; and my parents were looking about to see what had become of me.

I crossed the grass, humming as I went, to fix the song. Theasides was with them; six feet high and hardly done growing yet; wide shoulders and strong thighs; his golden hair cut short across his forehead and hanging down his back, neatly crimped from overnight plaiting in honor of the feast, and crowned with fresh flowers. He was smiling still from the pleasure of the dance. I could not think why our father should have missed me.

Beside my parents stood neighbor Bouselos and his wife, whose small vineyard was near our land. With them was their six-year daughter, picking her nose with a fat finger. As I came up her mother slapped down her hand. She tugged Theasides' mantle, and he turned to give her a smile.

My parents did not scold me for my absence. My father even remarked to Bouselos how I had grown. Bouselos eyed my bare lanky legs, nodded and winked.

People forget their own childhood, or they'd remember a child's long ears. The moment she saw that wink, the child jumped at her father's arm. "Daddy!" she piped. "I don't want to marry Sim! I want to marry Theas!"

There was the pause that you might expect; then the fathers laughed, my mother looked down her nose, Bouselos' wife said, "Hush, naughty girl!" But being a spoiled only child, she stamped and said it again. It distressed my brother, who, though himself a favorite, was sweetened by all the gods had given him.

"You can't marry me," he said, reasoning with her kindly. "You know I'm promised to Hegesilla. You don't have to marry Sim yet, not till you're big; and then you'll like him. He's very clever."

All the parents gazed at him, admiring his good heart, in which indeed they were not deceived. My betrothed looked from him to me; it was, you might say, an epigram. Going fiery red—with temper, not maiden shame—she shouted, "I won't marry him ever! When I'm old I still won't marry him! He's ugly, he's all black, he's got a dirty face."

I had scrubbed it well for the wedding, but had not lightened my swarthy skin nor taken off my birthmark. Like all Ionians who have gone east and mixed their blood, we Keans set store by Hellene looks. It is said that before the war in Troy, King Minos' Cretans had a city where Koressia stands, and sometimes we throw back to them. One thing's for sure, on Keos it is not admired. I had black hair, before it whitened; also, though my beard covers it now, a dark mole on my cheek, as big as a double drachma. If I had been a girl, no doubt they would have exposed me on the mountain. But my father was never one to waste a pair of hands.

He looked put about by the words of his chosen daughter-in-law; but it was Theas who darkened with his rare anger. I think he'd even have given the girl a clip; but her mother, from civility to mine, was first with a box on the ear. She was led off bawling. Little Philomache screamed out after her, "You're uglier than our Sim! You're dirtier too! You smell!"

I did not wait to see how they made the best of it. I slipped through the crowd, not roughly lest anyone else should stare at me, and ran into the olive grove. There I could have wept unseen; but I went on dry-eyed through the vineyards to the mountain. Before sunset I was up above the sheep-grass. I sat on a boulder while somewhere below me a goat-boy piped to his herd, out of tune, and the goats replied, fading away downhill. In clear golden air I looked west over shimmering sea; first the little islet of Helena, then beyond that the purple Attic hills.

I had never been out of Keos; so though all Hymettos stood between, I could believe I gazed on the Rock of the ancient kings: Theseus who redeemed the land from Crete and killed the Minotaur, Akamas his son who fought at Troy, Kodros who went disguised to be killed in battle, when the oracle proclaimed that the King must die.

Till now I had been angry only with the present; at being

reminded I was ugly, though I was used to that; much more at having the song put out of my mind, for nearly all had gone. But now I seemed to feel my fate close in on me. This island, twenty miles by ten, was to be my prison; here I would plod the circle of sour Hesiod's seasons, works and days, works and days, tied to a fool and to her fools of kindred; tasting the food of the god once in five years, maybe, when some bard might chance to call at the harbor, held up by rough winds or the need to sing for his passage-fee. Like Homer's orphan child, I would get the sip that wets the mouth and leaves the belly empty. I looked at Attica, and thought of her kings and heroes, of whom I had sung in solitude.

They had come to me in snatches of Homer, or peasant songs, or old wives' tales; but they had faces and ways of speech for me; I knew their armor, and if they used sword or spear. Child as I was, I thought they asked me for something. I had no blood-libation to give their shades body and voice; yet they seemed to say to me, "We die twice when men forget."

There is nothing like despair to make one throw oneself upon the gods. Helios Apollo was going down over the Attic hills, to plunge his chariot in some distant sea; and as he passed from sight, suddenly a great wing of cloud, which had been grey, flamed like rose fire against a sky as green as kingfishers and deeper than the sea. Come then, he said. Then he folded his bright wing in the mist, yielding to night.

Down the mountain I went, possessed by a daimon that made me run, so that I might have broken my neck had not a bright moon lit me. In the farms and hovels, all folk who had lain down with the dusk were sleeping, and the last of the lamps were going out. I would not be back before our door was barred, and our father would beat me. Why not? Tomorrow was the day for mulching the vines; and there was never a night when he had not earned his sleep.

I was still on the sheep-track when our lamp was quenched. Only one was left shining now. It was in the house of Hagias, father of the bride. It seemed strange, seeing she and her groom were long since bedded at his own fine place, new built from his gains at sea; I had seen the bridal torches threading there from up the mountain. Then I thought, It's the bard who is still awake.

If a mouse had crossed my path, I was ready to see an omen. I took the next fork in the track.

As I came to Hagias' vineyard, his two watchdogs bayed at me. They were running loose, which meant their bite was worse than their bark. Wandering men grow either to hate dogs or to know them; but there are no two ways for a shepherd. I sat on a stone, to let them nose me at leisure; after a while they let me tickle their jaws, and we walked on together. I did not go too close to the house, which, good sentinels that they were, they would not have approved; there was a little plowshed, whose roof faced the lighted window.

I've been a fool, I thought. All I saw was a pallet bed, with a boy upon it. But no one on thrifty Keos sleeps with a lighted lamp, and I looked again. He was fair-haired, with a flush upon him, pushing the clothes about and tossing. This explained the lamp, but was no affair of mine. I was about to start climbing down, when a shadow crossed the window, and a man came into the light, holding a cup, which he lifted the boy to drink from. He was a stiff grizzled man, looking old and anxious, with a blanket caught around him as if just risen from bed. Hagias had many servants, and again I would have gone, but something bright caught my eye; craning, I saw on the clothes-stool an embroidered robe. Against the wall was the kithara.

I sat, and watched, and thought of the god's bright omen, and of where it had led me now. It shocked me. There is no one more just than a child. A stranger, a guest of the land, a pleasant-faced lad who had a look of my brother a few years back; what evil was I wishing him, perched on the shed like a dark kite waiting to feed? Black Sim, the boys in the village called me.

Often I had wished my father dead, and Theas in the master's chair, but had never dared to know it. This was the first time I had looked for gain through death, knowing my thought. It is man's nature to pray for what he much desires; but I had the justice of a child, and I did not pray.

Soon the bard left the window-square, but I knew he was sitting near the bed, because I could see one of his feet. The boy dozed with half-closed eyes showing the whites. Presently I climbed down, speaking softly to the dogs, who suffered my hand, but saw me off as far as the olive grove, lest I should deceitfully take a sheep. They'd have made better soldiers than some men I've met.

When I got home, there was a shutter open. I crept up, and two strong hands hoisted me in. Theas set me down, signed to me to be quiet—he had no need!—and showed me a dummy of rolled sheepskin, which he'd laid under my side of the blanket in our bed. In the great bed our parents were fast asleep, and had never missed me. He took me by the ear and gave me a soft slap on the head. I gave him a soft punch on the belly, which was flat and firm as a shield. We were used to these silent games. When he had hidden the skins and we were both in bed, he went straight off to sleep. He had kept awake to save me from my beating. I warmed myself on his wide shoulders cloaked with long golden hair.

Long after this, when I had made my name, someone from Keos asked how it was I had not come to hate my brother, to whom it must have seemed the gods had given everything, leaving nothing for me. I answered that next to having the gods' gifts ourselves, it is best to honor them.

If not, one must grow to hate them; and, Zeus be my witness, I have seen what can come of that.

2

I WAS UP in the dark next day, before even the thralls were stirring. Going to the shed, I found the best of them just awake. He'd been a smallholder on Kythnos, the next island, who had pledged himself after a bad harvest, having no surety for a loan. Next harvest had been worse; the landlord had foreclosed on him, and, having all the hands he needed, sold him away. Even though he was getting a fuller belly from us than he'd had on Kythnos, I always pity a freeborn thrall. You only find them now in the backward places; in Athens, the good Solon freed them before I was born. I said, "Tell the master I shan't be minding the sheep today." The less he knew, the better for us both. I saw him eye my best tunic; he liked but rather despised me, thinking me poor stuff for a husbandman, and thankful no doubt that I was not the heir. He thought the world of Theas; whom I'd left sleeping, innocent of my truancy. It was only fair; even he was not immune from our father's anger.

At sunup I reached the house of Hagias. He was up and about, and greeted me civilly with a cup of watered wine, boy-strength; though, knowing my father, he was clearly amazed to see me not at work. I had mother wit enough to thank him for the pleasure of his feast, as if sent with this message, before asking to speak with Kleobis the bard.

In this I could hardly claim to be my father's envoy; and Hagias, of course, asked me what I wanted: adding that their guest was sleeping still, having sat up late with his boy, who was sick with fever.

"I know, sir," I said. "So he'll be needing a boy who's well. I want to ask him to hire me."

By now Hagias' wife had come up; she had been bustling about with the women slaves, clearing up after the feast. They both stared at me as if I were off my head. Presently Hagias smiled and stroked his beard; he was a stout good-natured fellow, though rather pompous. "My dear Sim—for so I have heard your kinfolk call you, and I speak as a family friend—boys will be boys and have their fancies, and you'll not find me a telltale. Why, at your age my fancy was to travel south, and fight for the King of Egypt. But my old friend Leoprepes would be grieved, you know, at this prank of yours. Because he trains you on the farm, so that you'll prosper when you come to manhood, you don't suppose he'd let you work as servant to another man? That's all this boy is, no more; carries luggage, hires mules, looks after the lyre and so on." My face must have brightened, for he frowned. "Just a menial, and you are son to one of the first men in the deme. What nonsense have you taken into your head? Do you want to be a poet?" And he laughed so heartily that the slaves all turned to stare.

"Yes, sir," I said.

Till now, he'd just thought I wanted to run away from home, which could have surprised no one who knew our family. Now I had put him at a loss for words. He was still in search of them, when from the room behind him the bard appeared, wishing him good day.

Hagias nodded to his wife to be about her business, and asked after his servant's health. He replied that his pupil seemed a little easier. Then he looked straight at me, and smiled; a spare slight smile, like that between men who will talk about business presently.

Did this amaze me? Not so. I had had my sign on the mountain. It is only to the wise that Apollo speaks with a double tongue.

So I waited while he had a few more words with Hagias; then he said, "Was this lad here asking for me? I was expecting him."

Hagias' face changed in a moment. He could hardly have been more civil if I had been Theasides. It amazed me, I don't know why. That barelegged boy in his outgrown tunic seems as strange to me now as an Ethiop to a Thracian. Yet I was once within him, and his soul has passed into mine. These are mysteries.

"Let us walk," said Kleobis, and led me over the meadow into the olive grove. The pale green flowers were falling, the early sun shone in the leaves. Hagias watched us from the house like a true Ionian. Curiosity is our birthright. What else has made us seek out knowledge and skill?

While I was wondering if he had the gift of prophecy, Kleobis said, "I saw you in the brush, swaying to the music like Apollo's snake. I knew you would be coming. Who is your father?"

I told him, and he said, "I have heard the name. How long have you wanted to be a poet?"

"I don't know, sir. Before I knew what a poet was."

He plucked a spray of olive flowers and held it up to the light. "Go on. It was the same with me."

I spoke as best I could. Not as if to a friend; I had had no friend but my brother; but as if to a god in some small mountain shrine, who I could believe would listen. "You know, sir, how little boys sing who can just run about, and mostly it's like the birds. But I sang in tune, all the songs the women sang at work. Then when I was older and went to the Apollo festivals, I started to make songs myself. Please, sir, hire me. I'll work for nothing, just for my keep. If your boy gets better, I'll do the rough work, and sleep in the shed with the thralls wherever you're staying. I've a sheepskin for cold weather, I'll only need my food. I'll not even ask for music lessons. Just let me hear the songs."

We were now well away from the house. He said, "Sing me one of yours."

For this at least I had come prepared. I sang my most ambitious ode. The temple at Koressia is a healing one, dedicated to Apollo of the Mice. He has his own sacred ones, white with pink ears. After pondering for some time how to make mice sound dignified, I had addressed them as "Bold plunderers of Demeter's hoarded store," which I thought pretty well of. Such was the man's magnanimity, he heard me through without so much as a smile.

"You have grasped the form very well. A good beginning. Now tell me, do you ever sing for yourself alone?"

"Well, sir," I said after a while, "one always sings keeping sheep."

He looked round. Not knowing Keos, he must have found this occupation surprising in my father's son. He only said, "Yes, true. Sing me a shepherd's song, then."

I hesitated, now overcome with shyness. "It's not a real poem, sir. It's just a song."

"Good, let me hear it. I've found stuff in those songs that Homer must have heard. They're like agates on a beach; one picks them up rough, and polishes. Come, sing."

I thought if I warned him I'd made it all up myself, he might think less of it. "It's very long. It's about Perseus, you see."

"Indeed, many things befell him. Give me some part you like."

I had been most of a year at it; if I had ever finished it, I daresay it would have outstretched the *Odyssey*. Shoots have been coming up from it for most of my later life. However, I remembered he had not breakfasted, and spared him the Killing of the Gorgons. "Well, sir, this is what Perseus sings to himself when he's working at the nets on Seriphos, and the King won't let him go away."

The form at least was old; the kind of thing women sing as they twirl the spindle, or tread before the loom. I had lifted it as best I could, to give it a bolder feel, more by ear than by thought. Perseus is longing for wings to take him over sea, to the lands of monsters and marvels. When I sang it on the mountain, I became a fair-haired kouros six feet tall; the sheep had always accepted this transformation. Now I was Black Sim and must make the best of it. The song felt very naked sung like this. I thought I should have dressed it up more, like the mice.

At the end he waited awhile, in case I was stuck, not finished. This made me sure I had disgusted him. Then, seeing it was the end, he nodded two or three times. "Ah. There, now, is a voice."

I felt as women must when told that the babe's a boy. I just stood getting my breath. "Now tell me," he went on briskly, "when is your father coming along to see me?"

I stared. I must have looked like an idiot yokel.

"Does he not think much of your singing? Never mind, he and I will talk."

"Sir!" I cried, finding my tongue at last, "he doesn't know that I sing at all. I could never sing before my father."

He did not ask why; just said, "I see," and stood in thought.

"I've run away, sir. I should be with the sheep; but I did leave them cared for. Please hire me. He only likes my big brother. He'll never grieve."

"Do you always mind sheep?" he asked after a while.

"No, I help with the vines and the olives. I have to do the work of the season. Like *Works and Days*."

"Does he tell you so? He is not quite indifferent to the poets, then."

"Indeed he won't miss me, sir. It's not that we're poor. He has the hired men, and five thralls as well. And the house-slaves, of course."

"Then, even though you Keans live plainly, you cannot have known much hardship. Do you understand the life of a minstrel's boy?"

"It's different, sir, if it's what you want to do. I never heard a real poet before, I know that now. Now I have, I can't bear it here any more."

He smiled; I perceived that bards are human. Then he sank into thought again. Presently he said, looking up suddenly, "I can't be sure I shall need a second boy, if Endios recovers. Perhaps you can tell me, since you know these hills; they say there is a yellow berry with leaves like spear-blades, which is a cure for this kind of fever. Is it of any use?"

"Not the one here, sir. Don't you go picking that. One of our thralls had a child that died of eating them."

I'd answered without a second thought; he did not own he had been testing me till five years later, when he himself had fever and I was nursing him. I remember saying then, "But what would you have done, if I'd recommended the berries? I would still have made the song."

"I greatly doubt it," he said with his dry smile. "The grape tastes of its vineyard. I daresay I should have advised your father to let you study somewhere; so much was due to you. But oh no, I'd have had you nowhere about *me*. Apollo's serpent has a healing tongue. I am not seduced by the dance of the painted adder."

At the time, however, he just put his hand upon my shoulder, saying, "Never mind, the doctor is coming and we will trust in him. Come in, Sim, and let us see if Hagias'

good wife will find us a few barley-cakes. What is the rest
of your name, son of Leoprepes?"

He called upon my father the same day.

Seeing he had promised this, you'd have thought that,
when I got home, I would have said so to escape a beating.
But I was as tongue-tied as ever in my father's presence,
baring my back more readily than my soul. I had never
yet defied him—that would have come with the first
stirrings of manhood—but when, asked where I had been,
I could only mumble, "Over to Hagias' house," he thought
me a liar, and defiant along with that. Theas had known
what would happen, and, having no help to give, had gone
off so as not to witness it. Afterwards I had to carry my
sore back up to the sheep-pasture, resume my duties and
send back the thrall.

Thus I was ignorant that Hagias called in advance to
announce the bard's arrival. When I had folded the sheep
at evening, and come back with the dogs, I was amazed to
find the best cloths and covers set out as if for a guest of
honor. My parents, and even Theas, were wearing their
grandest clothes (grand, that is, for Keos, where more than
an inch of borderwork is against the law); and my father,
seated in the master's chair, looked as aweful as a carved
Zeus in a temple. When their eyes all turned to me, it was
too late to run out and spend the night in the sheep-pen.

"Come here, Simonides." Except when presenting me
to someone of importance, which was not oftener than he
could help, I had never known him use my full name
before. I stood before him rigid with dread.

"Tell me," he said, "have I ever behaved to you otherwise than as a father?"

Since he was my father, and had always behaved like
himself, I answered, "No."

"I have done my best to train you as a son of mine, who

should improve, not waste his patrimony. It has been no pleasure to me; you have shown small diligence and less skill. Yet you have thought fit, for reasons you best know, to hide from me your aptitude for a respected calling, and confide it to a stranger whom, till yesterday, you never saw in your life. Is it too much to ask how I have deserved it?"

I was stunned; most of all by finding I had power to wound him. I was fourteen, and had lived as best I knew how. At last I said, "I thought, sir, that you wouldn't like it."

"Is this not Keos? Have you not been to the festivals like any other boy of decent birth? Have the Keans not their own lodge on Delos, for the singers and musicians we send to honor the god? Do you not suppose that if you had shown ability for anything at all, I would not have furthered it? Yet you have chosen to live like a sullen farm-hand, rather than my son; hiding from me all that would have encouraged my hopes of you, till you could send me news by a passing guest."

I heard in horror. My former lot now seemed Elysium, compared with my promised future. I was to be trained under his eye for poetry, as I'd been trained for farming, works and days; I would have as much song left in me as a bird in the fowler's net; and my muteness would be taken for defiance. I thought with longing of the lonely hills and the sheep.

"However," my father said, "since this man is ready to undertake your schooling, and is of good repute, so be it. I hope you will do more credit to his teaching than you have done to mine."

I had had a long full day, and a beating; my working chiton, which I'd put on to go shepherding, was stuck somewhere to my broken skin. While he was beating me I had hugged my secret and never cried. Now I'd had thrown at me, like a curse, the crown of my desires, it was too much.

I cried out, "Oh, *thank* you, sir!" then clapped my hands
to my face and wept.

I only did as I must; I had no thought to punish him.
Now that I'm old, I see it would have been kinder to rail
or curse him. He would have known how to deal with that.
When he saw me greet with tears of joy the news of my
escape from him, some truth pierced his heart. He lived
long enough to see me held in honor; he accepted our
friends' felicitations when I won a prize. But I always knew
that in the cup of his pride those tears still lingered, like
drops of wormwood. To the day of his death, he never
really forgave me.

3

NEXT DAY I went to my master.

My mother had brought out cloth from her chest, dipped
in the famous red Kean dye, and had one of the women
slaves make me a cloak. She even gave me a good copper
brooch to fasten it, and two new tunics. Though she could
not believe that any talent Theas lacked could be worth
having, she had the family credit to think of. As I stood at
the door with my bundle on my shoulder, she urged me to
behave myself and obey my teacher; my father told me to
work hard, and not try to do anything the easy way. To
his mind, there was something wrong with any instruction
a boy found pleasing. Theas ran after me, out of sight of
home, and gave me a heavy silver double drachma.

"Don't let this man knock you about," he said. "If he ill-treats you, come home. It will be one bad day with the father, and after that I'll take care of you." He was always a peacemaker, and not only when it saved him trouble. Even war, which he excelled at later, he never went into lightly. There are men whom Ares would have reaped on a bloody field, if my brother had not been.

At Hagias' farm, my coming was hardly noticed, the doctor being there to physic the sick boy. When he had gone, Kleobis, who was in need of sleep, left me to tend the sickroom. Endios had been bled, and was looking white; I had heard him cry as the knife went in. When I gave him milk, he gazed for a moment at this new ill-favored face, but was too weak to be curious. He lay with closed eyes; I sat wondering how we would get on when he was better. Soon he began to vomit and purge; he said, as I sponged him, that it was from the physic. I told him, to cheer him up, that it would drive out the evil humors; I had heard the physician say so. But I could not see, myself, that he had got much good from it.

After supper, Kleobis sent me to my bed on the far side of the room, while he kept watch. At first the boy's moaning disturbed me, but it quietened, and I slept with the soundness of my youth, till I felt myself shaken. I thought I was at home, with my father rousing me. But no one rebuked my laziness. Kleobis said, "Go out for a while, Sim. You can come back later." There was a blanket drawn right over the other bed, and no movement in it.

I had never been near a corpse except at funerals. It seemed only a moment since he'd talked to me. Two slave-women came in to wash and anoint his body, since he had no kin there. I went out over the dry summer grass, tasting its freshness after the close air inside. Light slanted over the hill, touching the topmost olive-sprays. I said to his shade—

it could not have gone far yet—"I did wish it; but only for a while, and I never prayed for it. Do not be angry."

Later on, when I came back to Keos, I bought a carved stone for his stranger's grave, knowing I owed it him.

Kleobis came out to me, by the flat rock where he had stood to sing. His face was yellow and drawn with watching; the boy had not died till almost dawn. He said, "I ought to have let him go."

I remembered his good clothes, better than my brother's. "But, sir, he wanted to learn from you, he wasn't poor?"

"Only in talent. He should have gone home, to strum a lyre at the drinking, and give his mother grandsons. But he was strong, and useful, and willing. And his father ransomed me once from pirates. I could not turn him off too soon."

"How old was he?"

"Fifteen, I think. He had a beautiful treble, before it broke. When the choir went to Delos, I heard him sing the solo. Everyone said he looked like the young Apollo. His parents had always heard him praised; I could not refuse to take him."

In the house, one of the slave-women was wailing over the body, from kindness, or remembering grief of her own. Kleobis said, "When I saw in the brush your ugly face, my son, touched by the god, and beautiful, I thought, 'Ah, now's the time. I will buy Endios his passage home, in a good ship, and send word to his father that he has learned all I can teach him.' But too late. The god did not require this sacrifice."

I listened gravely, and ventured no reply. Later, I've asked myself if Apollo's arrow was not shot by his son Asklepios. The doctor had been the best in Iulis; but it did seem to me that the evil humors in the boy had been expelled too forcibly, when they might have left of their

own accord. Truly I owed poor Endios a tomb; he has
saved my life many a time. Some of my best friends have
been doctors, and excellent people they were, most knowl-
edgeable about the minds of men, whom they see when
poets do not. But doctors are taught their laws, and they
keep those laws if it kills you. Some of them here in Sicily
come asking how a wanderer like me has kept such good
health to past fourscore. I tell them this or that. It would
be uncivil to say that whenever in my travels I get a touch
of fever, I go quietly to bed and send for the local wise-
woman.

4

AMONG THE TROUBLES all men are heir to, I have had
good things from the gods. I have been honored by kings
and princes and cities, and by men of my own craft, and
have been pleased with it, more I daresay than men with
less need of esteem. I have rejoiced in what I made: in
making it, in singing it, in getting paid for it, all delightful
things. But brightest of all, after nearly seventy years, shines
in my memory the day I sailed from Keos.

It was a clear morning, just wind enough to fill the sail
and spare the rowers. The ship was new, the eyes on the
prow fresh-painted; the cargo was clean, mostly pots and
figs, and smelled as delicious to me as spices. I shouldered
my master's baggage with as much pride as a knight takes
in his horse. It was the first mark of my new calling.

When the sailors had told me where to put it, and shoved me out of their way, I stood at the rail and looked back at the harbor. It seemed like a foreign port already. I was amazed to see Theas appear and wave. He jumped aboard, paid his respects to my master, and looked about him with wistful eyes. I saw, hardly believing it, that he envied me.

Getting me in a corner where they had finished lading, he put a hand on my shoulder. "We've never talked, not as men. I'm telling you now, never think you can't come back here, and be somebody at home. When you've seen other cities, and how men live there, you'll think we must be poor folk. Well, we're not poor, Sim, and we never have been. Sometime I mean to see the world myself, and I'll not need to work my passage. Nor you. You've chosen a calling with plenty of ups and downs, not that I blame you. But one day there'll be enough for both of us, I promise you that."

He had had thoughts like mine. Like me, he would not own to them.

"I must go," he said. "I've the thralls to mind in the ten-acre. If the father sees them idling, he'll be asking them where I am. Here." He undid a buckle at his belt. "This is for you. You'll likely need it sooner than I would. Don't you be the one to start, that's all."

He held out his dearest treasure, a good knife with silver studs on its horn handle. It had been a prize at the games, for throwing the disk and javelin; I had never seen him without it, except when without his clothes. He strapped it on my belt, and embraced me. Next moment we were both in tears. We had not much thought till now that we would miss each other: I a protector, a hero in whom to trust, and he a worshipper—what man is displeased with that? But we were young, we would not die of it. We wiped our eyes and parted; and Kleobis gave us the long look of a poet getting a phrase for a song.

SAMOS

1

YES, I owed Endios a tomb. In death he was my benefactor.

By Keos reckoning, Kleobis must always have been an easy master. But no one can travel without some hardship; being used to it himself, he had naturally supposed that what he could bear at sixty could not hurt a strong lad of fifteen. He took the death hard, the son of a friend and benefactor. On our voyage out, he kept going over the boy's last days; his getting wet on the ship coming from Ephesos; his climbing up from Koressia in maybe too hot a sun, carrying a bag which was maybe too heavy; his sitting outdoors at the wedding when the fever must have been on him. The upshot of all this was that now when he had got a Kean shepherd lad, tough as a goat, he took all the care he wished he had taken before. I never once slept in an outhouse, unless by mishap he had to shake down there himself; when offered hospitality, he had me received as a guest as well. His own son could have lived no better; and my father's son had never lived half so well.

People think the bond between poet and pupil is forged by the holy Muse. Quite true; but nothing forges it tighter than traveling among strangers. Friends met by the way will soon pass on; on the whole, there are just the two of you. If you are out of tune, it can't last long. But if it wears well,

it will be like father and son. Closer, for me. My blood-
father saw that at the start. Well, I could not help it.

My tasks were a game to me, compared with what I had
done at home. Kleobis, sensible man, always traveled as
light as his purse, only gathering stuff when he could afford
to hire a donkey. We never went without clothing for heat
or cold, and best clothes for a performance; but it did not
weigh so heavy as a three-month lamb on the mountain.

Had I been serving only a craftsman or a merchant, I
would have found things to enjoy: steep islands, still and
dark in a laughing sea; white harbors full of strange ships;
a road creeping small into dark blue mountains; a pleasant
inn in a poplar grove by a river; the terrible filthy inn where
they tried to rob us, and I pulled out Theas' knife. After
that, Kleobis treated me like a man.

I only missed one thing from my former life: for a long
time I hated to sleep alone. My mother took against me
from the moment the midwife held me up to her; once I
was weaned, if I cried in the night her remedy was a slap.
But Theas, who was no more than six or seven, would
creep up softly and take me into bed, as he might have
done a squeaking pup. Soon I would climb in of my own
accord, and like a soft-hearted child with a growing pup,
he let me be. So there I stayed, feeling safe with him like
a dog. For months I felt restless and strange without him,
and would wake in the darkness wondering where he was.

All this was the daily bread of my life. The meat and
wine were the songs.

Excellent men, concerned with the training of youth to
virtue, have begged me to declare that art is the child of
labor. Well, labor must bring it forth, like everything else
that lives. As I tell these people, there are women one can't
get without taking pains, or boys if you prefer them; but
first you must fall in love. After that, the pains take care
of themselves. So don't bring me, I say to these worthy

men, some youth who wants to know what kind of song is likely to win the crown this year; or what everyone else is singing, lest he should feel lonely. If that is all he wants, I've no time left to waste on him. Take him away, and apprentice him to a lyre-maker, where he may even be of use. But if you come upon someone who grabs at song like a child at a bright stone on the shore, who shapes and re-shapes like a child building a sand-castle, deep in his act and lost to all around—then, never mind if his sand-castle leans sideways, just give him time. Don't tell him that this year people are doing, or not doing, or no longer doing, this or that. Send him to me, who will protect him from fools like you, will show him the great shell-beaches and watch him at his play.

Oh yes, I worked. Yes indeed. Looking back on my father's last instruction, not to do things the easy way, I used to laugh aloud. In our calling, once you know where you're going, there is no easy way; you get there, or not. Even if you aim to go no further than four lines on a dog's tomb. Well, for that matter, I have gone a good way in four lines, and further still in two.

However, at that age it still took me ten lines at least to say "Good dog." All I was fit for was to learn, but at least I knew it. I gorged like a calf in a spring meadow; not only Kleobis' lessons, but anything I could browse on along the way. Like every bard who will not let his repertoire go rusty, he would go over it quietly as we walked; and by the time he was ready to give me line by line, I had much of it in my head. I did not know, till he told me, that I had a better memory than other people; I thought one would naturally remember what one had liked to hear. To this day, there are pieces of Homer, or Sappho, or Stesichoros, which I can't recall without some bit of road, or courtyard, or stone fountain-rim coming to mind along with them.

This cornel-wood staff of mine—the old man's third leg,
as the Sphinx said in her riddle—when Kleobis owned it,
I felt it many a time. If I spoke to him when he was com-
posing, he didn't interrupt himself, just gave me a rap. If
I was fool enough to start begging his pardon, he hit me
again, to teach me the virtue of silence. I would then mind
my own business, of which I had quite enough. You don't
master the *Iliad* in a month, or in a year; but every day I
added my few lines, like a bee bringing wax to the hive.

I soon learned I have a certain gift of nature: that what
I have learned by heart, I can call back all at once, just as
one does a prospect seen with one's eyes, not one stone or
tree after another. Some philosopher, it must have been
Herakleitos, once tried to explain to me the nature of this
whole, which my memory hears in a moment though it
would take an hour to speak it aloud. But Herakleitos would
make a mystery of anything.

Of course, a man like Kleobis did not live like some
wandering minstrel, singing in markets for a supper. We
never even slept at inns, unless benighted between towns.
In any city, some house was always open to us, often two
or three in rivalry; he had guest-friends everywhere. If he
sang at a sacred festival, we might be lodged in the temple
precinct. Besides all this, Kleobis had a home.

His patrimony was at Ephesos; a farm let to a tenant, and
a city house kept ready for his return by an old Karian slave-
woman. She doted on him, but scolded him so freely that
it was clear they'd been bedmates once. She was not yet
past jealousy, though not of me; me she favored, because
I was too ugly to be a rival. Getting me in a corner she
would give me a fig or apricot, and try to make me tell tales.
I thanked her prettily, and kept my tales to myself.

Kleobis had a moving little song, about an old man
bidding farewell to Aphrodite. I have known it make
wrestlers cry. But if they thought he spoke for himself they

were much mistaken. From time to time he would tell me
that this evening, to reward my progress, I could play upon
the kithara instead of my practice lyre; he was going to
visit friends and I need not wait up for him. It did not take
me long to observe that this happened in cities polite
enough to have some clean amusing hetairas. He was a
fastidious man. I can't recall his ever visiting a common
stews. Happy to get my hands upon the kithara and sing to
its seven-stringed voice, I wished him a pleasant evening,
with no thought that such things would ever be my concern.

In those years, I hardly knew that I was made like other
men. I had married my art, and kept all my love for my
master. I daresay I had Bouselos' little daughter to thank,
for keeping me out of the street of the women. As I grew
from boy to youth, of course I was importuned as all
travelers are. But each of them in turn I thought would
endure me for the pay, mocking me after with some fellow
whore; she must indeed be the lowest of her calling, to
seek my custom at all. I had no need to master desire, while
I had such thoughts to quench it, and felt only shame at
these solicitations. Returning to my lyre, I would sing of
royal maidens, chosen by gods to bring forth heroes. One
of my lays pleased Kleobis so well that he let me sing it at
an Ephesian supper-party. I got a ring of worked bronze
from the host. My first fee. I have it still.

Nowadays, friends and fellow poets will talk of my ugli-
ness as easily as of my clothes. Mostly it is done as a kind
of courtesy, meaning that I can afford it; and I take it so.
Sometimes malice creeps in, but envy does not hurt a man
like scorn.

When I had been about two years with Kleobis, he urged
me to visit Keos, compete at the Apollo festival, and show
them what I could do. By this time I had sung several
times in public, and even my own songs had been well

received. My voice was well over breaking, settled into a middle tone with a good range; I performed with a growing courage. But still, at the very thought of singing before my father, the soul of a ragged shepherd boy possessed me. I said I was sure to lose, and be shamed before my kindred; and besides, if I went back too soon I might find myself betrothed again. He did not press me. The world was wider in those days. We scarcely knew how fast it was closing in.

Already, though, not all our travels through Ionia were in search of wealth or fame. Sometimes it was for safety we took the road. These were the days of Kyros, King of the Persians.

Years before, he had risen against his overlord the Median King, whose people hated him, and soon handed him over. Kyros spared his life, the man being his kinsman; treated the Medes as their King rather than as their conqueror, and soon won their goodwill. By the time I came to Asia, Persians and Medes were almost like one people, and fought as such.

Later, I've heard Darius called The Great. But to my mind, the barbarians never had a king equal to Kyros. His glory filled the world, when I was young. If he had been a Hellene, what a praise song I could have made him. I have some lines in my head, though they have never passed my tongue.

I wish I had seen him, if only once. But he had gone east to prepare for war with Babylon, leaving his generals to gather the Ionian cities in. Men who did see him, I have talked with: he was one of the fair Persians, with that fine gem-carved face you find among them. He had a great horse, and sat it as if he'd grown there; was distant and godlike to Greeks, but much beloved by soldiers; had his hair and beard curled close and short with the irons; wore embroidered trousers, and a corselet of plaited linen from

Egypt, stronger than mail, and dyed with Tyrian purple.
He was seen to rebuke one of his lords for spitting in public.
That is all I heard first-hand.

When Lydia fell to him, the Greek cities should have
read the omens and allied for war. Together, they could
have given his generals trouble enough. As it was, they did
much brave fighting, here and there; but never all at once,
nor all together. Persians and Medes might like to be Kyros'
men; Greeks like to be their own. From time to time at
some sacred festival Ionians would meet and talk about
their dangers; before long, someone proposed they should
choose one general to lead them all; which each city agreed
to, provided it should supply him. Then they all went home.

One by one the cities fell; some by storm, some by siege,
some just abandoned by the people, if they had a port and
ships. Kyros' chief general was a Mede, called Harpagos,
who had joined him because the Median King had killed
his son. He was very loyal to his new master, as the Ionians
learned to their cost.

After a while, some towns surrendered as soon as his
slaves began to dig his siege-mounds; others, as soon as they
saw him coming; and some sent envoys to make terms
before he came at all. All these were spared, by Kyros'
orders, and given one of their own lords as governor; the
fate of the citizens depended on how oppressive these lords
already were. Cities that had fought were put under
Persian satraps.

When we heard in Ephesos that the Medes were coming,
Kleobis offered to send me home; he would pay my passage
from Miletos, which had made terms already. He would
stay in his own city; but I was a Kean and owed Ephesos
nothing. To that I answered that Ephesos had given me the
greatest gift of my life. We embraced, and I went off to
train with the other young men at spear-fighting and throwing javelins. By then I was nearly eighteen.

On the training-ground I found two or three faces no handsomer than my own, and a good many arms less strong. I had kept my lean shepherd's muscle, and my eye was straight. My comrades thought well of me for not having run home. Making new friends, I almost forgot I might die before I'd made one song fit to be handed down from bard to bard.

After some days, the barbarian army was descried coming down the Silenos river-plain. On this the priests of Artemis took counsel with the lords, and decreed that a pharmakos be chosen, to purge the city.

The young men I trained with said it was twenty years since a scapegoat had been needed, in time of plague; so none of them remembered it. But they knew all about it; and those who were old enough went to the great square before the city, to take part in the choosing. The younger ones, and foreigners like me, watched from the rooftops.

Artemis of Ephesos is not like Artemis of Athens. She is no virgin; farmers and women pray to her for increase, and she is hung all over with breasts. All her priests are eunuchs, by their own choice; some do it themselves in the frenzy of the rites. Soon they appeared on the terrace before the temple porch, winding out through the many columns that surround the mighty sanctuary, as if they threaded a marble forest. They carried their wands tipped with the sacred crescent; their young boys clashed ringing cymbals, to order silence. They had brought their victim with them.

He was a mean shambling fellow, led by a rope—his hands were tied behind him—and scared out of his life. The people shouted and catcalled, as if they thought him well chosen. In a voice cracked with fear, he shouted out that if he had defrauded any citizen, anyone at all, he vowed by the goddess he would make it good to him. Being fairly near, I could see he was crossed-eyed and patched with scrofula. There was jeering; then someone shouted out, "Not him! Choose Hipponax!" And there was applause.

I peered down from my roof, to see if I could find Kleobis in the crowd, but it was too thick. I saw Hipponax, however. Everyone knew him, especially the servants of Apollo. He was a poet; and he was so well known because he never left the city. When first I knew of him, I pitied him and felt moved to take his part, for he was much uglier than I was. There is not much wrong with my body, except that I have no height; but he limped in one leg, which he had broken as a child, so that it was shorter than the other. The foot turned in, and his rocking gait had twisted his whole body, making his shoulders tilted. I thought it no wonder he should be bitter, for princes would not want to see him about their courts, where even I had been made welcome. Knowing he was poor, I asked Kleobis if we might not offer him supper. He looked startled for a moment; then thought, and said, "Ask him, my son. He is a man you ought to meet."

I did my errand respectfully. (I was then only fifteen.) Hipponax replied that Kleobis was suddenly very civil, and he hoped our house would not need to be purified, after a Poet of the Agora had passed the threshold.

That his clothes were dirty, I put down to his having no wife; but I thought that in a city not short of water, he could have washed himself. He ate noisily, and was helped twice; leaving off only to say that men were fortunate who had the art of pleasing princes, "but Truth has Want for a steward." Poor old Metriche, who had been cooking half the day to honor a guest—we lived plainly enough ourselves—was not out of hearing before he mocked at her fat buttocks. This started him on women, his favorite theme. He treated us, unasked, to one of his songs against a hetaira who had said him nay, and whose trade he was trying to ruin in revenge. Not that one had to offend him, for him to cut one up; he only needed to hear anyone praised. Before supper was over, he had accused the city's best sculptor of stealing bronze; the least greedy of the nobles, of being too cowardly to risk a quarrel; and a gentle old priest, gifted with prophecy, of vices I'd never heard of till that night. Such was my first meeting with Hipponax; and Kleobis was right, it had done me good. It showed me that the face of envy is uglier than a birthmark on the cheek.

So, when his name was shouted in the crowd, I wondered what Kleobis was thinking. On the one hand, the man was detestable; on the other, he was one of us. That he had sung against the lords showed courage, which one should honor, even though his spleen was like one of those burning mountains which cannot contain their fires. They were doused now, however. He grinned with terror like a Gorgon mask on a shield. The wretched swindler chosen by the priests (he had cheated even the temple) stood up in his bonds, refreshed with hope.

It caught Hipponax's eye and showed him his salvation.

As all poets know, one can stand or fall by one's impromptus. Hipponax stood. He lived some five years more on the strength of it. As soon as he saw it was a choice between the two of them, he offered no defense; he denounced his rival. After it was all over, no one remembered very clearly what the first man had been accused of, or on what evidence. Hipponax was more memorable.

The man was in Persian pay. He had poisoned a well, near which some people had lately died of fever. His wife was a backdoor bawd who undid good men's homes. He had bargained with Harpagos, for a talent of silver, to open a postern that very night. So that all this could be heard, our Poet of the Agora scrambled up a statue plinth. The statue was of an Isthmian victor; but Hipponax was the victor now. One thing he taught me: that whomever you blacken, there will always be someone glad of it. All men seek esteem; the best by lifting themselves, which is hard to do, the rest by shoving others down, which is much easier.

When he'd done, the crowd turned on the swindler, hating him because they feared the Medes; and it was agreed he had been chosen justly.

They stripped him, and put the ritual offering-cakes in his hands, having to tie them there because he shook so, and led him out to the gate. There they beat him as the rite prescribes, on his tenderest parts till he screamed aloud. Then everyone fell on him as they chose, to purge their offenses which he carried for them, and drove him along with sticks and cudgels till he fell. I don't know if he was dead when they came to throw him on the bonfire. I know I saw Hipponax dancing round it.

I climbed down and went home. Kleobis was sitting with a face of stone. He said, "And now they will surrender." Only the day before, I would have proposed making them a battle song. As it was, I just poured some wine.

Whether or not the goddess liked her offering, when Harpagos' siege-mound was ten cubits up the wall, the lords of Ephesos took counsel. They gave out that the city would ask for terms, and all the people acclaimed them.

The envoys rode out, and in due course Harpagos rode in at the head of his cavalry: a tall Mede with a curled grey beard and a gold-thread scarf around his helmet. He shone like a carp in a corselet of gilded fish-scales. The Ephesian lords, unarmed, escorted him to the council chamber. He sat there till they had dismounted first, and one of them held his horse for him. Peace was agreed; in a few days the Medes rode off again. They had done as Kyros had ordered in his wisdom, and spared a city which had given no more trouble than a couple of slaves shot down as they dug the mound. Three of the lords were to rule it as his deputies. It was said they had been treating with Harpagos long before.

Their first act was to get rid of Hipponax. They did not kill him, lest it should be said they feared something he knew; he was banished, which angered nobody, and warned not to come back.

He did not go far, just north across the headland to Klazomenai. Now and then we would get news of him, or someone would bring back one of his poems, in the trip-foot meter he always used, which went with his limping gait. They grew more savage; we heard rumors of someone he'd caused to hang himself. He did not live very well, however, and came down to cadging from strangers in the harbor, or begging alms from people whose enemies he had reviled. He died, they say, lying in rags in the marketplace, and was put underground like a dog that begins to stink. One or two citizens, I've heard, poured oblations upon his grave, thinking his spirit would do mischief if not appeased.

He would have had plenty to sing about, while Ephesos was settling to Persian rule. The new governors soon got even with enemies of their own, who had been too powerful to touch before. That came to be an old story, as the Ionian cities fell. It was a time of hate and treachery, and feuds began which have lasted ever since. They have lasted my lifetime, which spans three generations, and I daresay they are good for another three. If ever a Greek as good as Kyros comes to undo his work, he will need all his wits about him when he gets to Ephesos with its knot of snakes.

All this disgusted me; but for Kleobis, a citizen, it was a shame and grief. He went to see his friends and kindred; my weapon-drills were over, and I was a good deal alone. I did not seek out my former comrades. I had been considering the scapegoats, winner and loser both. They were evil men, but not the worst in a town as big as Ephesos. No; they were the worst men who were ugly too. How did I offend the gods before my birth, I thought, that I should be born halfway to being hated, before I do anything to deserve it? Song would have healed me, but it would not come; and being young, I thought that present trouble would last forever. I said nothing to Kleobis, who had enough troubles of his own.

One morning I thought, as I lay in bed, This can be the last day when I wake to sorrow. The choice is mine. I walked towards the temple, and mounted its inner stair which goes up to the roof, and stood on the little walk within the parapet. The agora lay below me like a dish crawling with wasps. It will be unjust, I thought, if I fall on a man who never did me harm; from this height it would kill him. But fate has never been just to me. It was making me giddy to look down, and I was not yet ready to jump; so I looked up instead.

Suddenly there was a great space of blue; the whole world seemed to open for me alone. The early sun stood in the east behind me, and touched the sea and the isles. A faint mist was on the water, half veiling it here and there, so that the ships seemed to float rather than swim; and out of it, beyond the strait, stood the tall hills of Samos.

I looked down at the city walls, and could not think why they should have enclosed me. Above me, on the roof-ridge, crouched a bronze sphinx, with the sun glittering on her crown. The work was exquisite, every upcurved feather of her wings shaped perfectly. Whoever made this, I thought, knew that it would not be often seen. He made it for whoever should come, and for the gods.

I went down by the steep stair, finding myself quite careful not to fall. At least the surrender had saved some things of beauty from fire and sack. Yet Ephesos seemed to me now like a dry brittle husk, the shell a moth sloughs off when the summer hatches it. Kleobis was visiting somewhere; I walked the city like a stranger, seeing it as if I had been long away. In the evening, I passed the house of

the hetaira who had shut her door to Hipponax. A crack
of lamplight showed; I thought, Why not? Let us see. She
let me in, cheerful and easy, bolted the door behind me,
and poured me Chian wine to drink while she undressed
beside the lamp; a true Ephesian, heavy-breasted, with a skin
like thickened cream. There was a picture painted inside
the wine-cup, of what we would soon be about. Of course
all good hetairas pretend that you have pleased them; but
at least I don't think she guessed I had never done it
before.

When I got home, Kleobis was back, and taking his bedtime posset. He pricked up the lamp to peer at me; I'd
forgotten the Ephesian's scented oil. "Well, well. Here's
a cat that's been in the dairy." Kindly, he did not add that
I'd been a long time getting there.

"I've been thinking, sir," I said. "Isn't it time we went
to Samos?"

He drained the posset-cup and wiped his beard. "Why
don't you get to bed? I can see you're half asleep. Where
else should we be going?"

2

It's a short crossing from Miletos; but I've never been
so frightened in all my life. If we'd had bad weather, I
would not be here today. We were two hundred souls,
aboard a little Phoenician trader built to carry fifty full-
laden. These people, leaving their homes forever, had

brought all they could carry aboard: mattresses, goats, bride-chests, working-tools, vine-slips, wine-jars, cooking-pots and dogs. There were cocks and hens in wattled coops, piglets swaddled like babies to keep them quiet, and babies no one could quieten. The faint breeze did not fill the sail; the wretched black slaves, whom the Phoenicians buy for old ships like this, sweated at the oars, hardly able to work for the crowd pressed almost against their oar-butts. The stink was enough to stifle you; and as the passengers could not be made to trim the ship, it had a list almost to the water-line. I am a pretty well-traveled man; I've had longer and rougher voyages; but never one when I felt so sure that the ship would sink.

However, as we neared Samos there was enough shipping to have picked us up; so I looked at the city, which we were somehow creeping to. It gleamed with new marble; the slopes of the mountains were clad with woods and orchards, or, lower, terraced for vines. Round the harbor the strait was teeming: once we were passed by a blunt-nosed Samian war-pentekonter, which seemed to flash by with its fifty oars, making a wash that nearly finished us; once I ran to Kleobis—or, rather, struggled to him through the crowd—to show him what was then a wonder, the first trireme either of us had seen. Oh, yes, I can remember when triremes were something new. The tall ships, we called them, and were amazed they did not capsize.

We limped into harbor; the passengers crowded to be first off; water came over the side; the crew beat them back with belaying-pins. We got in at last with an inch of freeboard to spare.

Young men today don't know what the fame of Samos was, in the days of Polykrates. Oh yes, they say, the Tyrant; and think they need say no more. Well, today I can understand it.

I, who have lived four times their span, have seen

"tyrant" shift its meaning, and now it has only one. Kleobis, whose memory went back forty years before mine, said it came first from the Lydians, who needed the word before the Greeks did. But in my youth, it was not yet the name for an oppressor. Indeed, most people thought it better than "king" and very much better than "lord." True, it always meant a man who ruled alone. Power may not change but always reveals the man, and there are cities now who hate with good cause that Lydian word. But it was hated at first only by the great lords. It was nemesis to their hubris, and the better of them suffered with the worst.

The Landsharers, they had called themselves in Samos; the people had given them other names. To own land is one thing, to own your tenants another. Polykrates and his faction promised to see them right. He was a lord himself, like every tyrant I ever heard of. Some use the citizens as a tool while others really care for them; but I never met one yet who was without ambition. Even so, some of them did carry out their pledges; Polykrates did, on the whole. He gave the people more justice than they'd had before; he gave them work, and paid them for it, and brought in slaves to save them from rough labor. He had not pledged that he would not grow rich, or make war, or live like a king, or seize the neighboring islands, or spend his money on boys. That was his side of the bargain. He did a great deal in his life, both of good and evil; but as he did good mostly to the commons, and evil mostly to Landsharers and Persians, most of the Samians were pretty well content with him.

True, soon after he seized power he got rid of his two brothers who'd helped him there, one by exile and one by death; but the people thought it none of their business while he made the city beautiful and great. The barbarians, on the other hand, called him a common pirate. It is true that the glories of Samos were mostly built from loot.

Piracy had always been a Samian trade, and they made

no bones about it. They had stolen treasures sent by kings to kings, needing only to hear that such things were on the sea. Polykrates' own noble father had set up a votive statue to Hera, out of his plunder, a boast he had carved on the base. The son had only to seize the nobles' ships to get himself a navy. Nowadays he dignified his forays with the name of war. He was famous all over Hellas for his wealth, for the works of his artists and architects and engineers, for his hundred warships and his thousand archers; and, more than all, for helping himself to tribute from Persian ships, instead of paying any.

No wonder the Samians all looked pleased with themselves, when a beggarly boatload of foreign fugitives stood gazing at the beauties of their city.

It was a very fine place; it was also a very full one. We were not the first beggarly boatload by a good long way.

Because of the wars, Kleobis had not been here since before the tyranny started, and said he would not have known the place. I was happy to gaze about, but could see this made him uneasy. He had written of our coming to two Samian guest-friends of former days; but there was no knowing if the letters had got through.

As we stepped off the mole—only half built then, but already grand with its cut ashlar and bronze bollards—we met the first of these old friends; only by chance, for it was a Samian pastime to see the ships come in and get their news. He was a stout anxious man, who looked as if he expected bad news only. He deplored the troubles of Ionia; rejoiced at our safety; did not ask our plans, and told us, as soon as he could with decency, that his widowed sister and her three daughters, escaped from Sardis, were living in his house. His brother's family was now expected from Ephesos, and he was at his wits' end to know how he would shelter them. Kleobis in turn condoled, and asked after his other old Samian guest-friend. He, it turned out, had been dead a year. Plainly, we would have to look after ourselves.

In Ephesos, Kleobis had comfortable means; but all locked up in land, which just now was finding no buyers. He had left the town house with Metriche, his old Karian girl. She was in no danger; nor indeed would we have been, had we cared to stay. But we would be now, if we went back there from hostile Samos. We had exiled ourselves, and would have to make the best of it. What money Kleobis had, he had brought along; better, he had his name, and Polykrates was a known patron of the Muses. We kept up our hopes.

Every inn within our means seemed full. After much trudging about, we found lodgings with a lyre-maker, who turned out someone else because he thought we would be good for business.

Next morning, Kleobis got out his tablets, and drafted a letter of compliment to Polykrates, sending respects, and hoping for the honor of praising his name in song.

I did the fair copy from wax to reed-paper. It was Kleobis who had had me taught to write. My father had never thought it worth while, and Theasides had never thought about it at all. He could write the farm accounts, and, at a pinch, a letter to a trader; why give the little brother more troubles than he had? Kleobis, however, had found it tiresome that I could do no written business, and sent me to a scribe for lessons. He taught me a fine square even hand; left to right, or plow-ways, or straight down, I can do them all. As a kind of craft, it even gives me pleasure. When I compose a letter, my mind sees the written words. As for my songs, I could no more sing in writing than make love. It belongs to another part of me.

Since it would never have done for Kleobis to be seen running his own errands, I took the letter, glad of a chance to see the famous palace.

It stands on a mountain spur, a little above the bay. A

massive earthwork and ditch were being dug by a horde of
slaves. Some passer-by, seeing I was a stranger, stopped to
tell me that they were men of Lesbos, which the Tyrant had
lately conquered; a great stroke against the Persians, that
island being so near the Ionian shore. I could not see that
the slaves looked very grateful.

I found my way through to a terrace, with a fine prospect
of the city. Before a columned portico stood two soldiers
in high-crested helmets, holding shields blazoned with
hawks. One thumped his spear-butt; a chamberlain came
and took my letter. I waited, seeing across the bay the
purple hills of Ionia, and wondering if I should ever tread
them more. They seemed more my home, now, than my
birthplace had ever been.

The high oaken doors had bronze trims of lion-heads and
roses, gleaming like gold. They opened, and I was led
inside. The entry hall was patterned with colored marbles;
beyond were more doors, of Egyptian ebony. Beyond one
of these was Polykrates.

I had not dreamed of getting further than his steward;
but this was certainly the man. He had finished his morning's business, and was taking luncheon to music, sitting in
a chair before a table with silver plates and wine-cups. As
I entered, his wine-server was leaning over him; a boy of
about fourteen, lissome and dark. Across his master's
shoulder he was making a face at the corner of the room,
where sat two musicians of about his age, with harp and
flute. Their master was rising forty, a big florid man, not
yet as heavy as he would be later; his hair and beard curly
and dark, his eyes light blue in a ruddy face. He had a
cheerful look. Why not, indeed?

He waved his hand, which had a great emerald on the
forefinger, for the concert to leave off. When the flute-
player ceased to blow, one saw a handsome but sullen

mouth, and green languid eyes. What the lyre-player was like I had no time to see; as I came forward, this youth clapped a hand across his mouth, to stifle a fit of giggles.

Polykrates raised the emerald once again, in a gesture of rebuke. No one looked much alarmed. The wine-pourer was winking behind the chair. As I went on, I could feel the others pulling straight faces. One had a fit of coughing, to cover a laugh.

I had been about the world by now; but I was still quite young, and my childhood wounds were tender. I felt myself go white, which cannot have improved me. Remembering I was my master's envoy on whom much depended, I looked straight before me, bowed, and spoke my piece word-perfect. But as I handed the letter, I saw the paper shake.

No one could say the Tyrant was not civil. He took it with a kindly smile, as if to say, "Ah well, we can't expect old heads on such young shoulders, can we?" He read it nearly all through, and said my master would surely hear from him. He deplored the misfortunes of Ephesos, and said he was glad to offer something which would provide for our comfort here. The emerald waved; the steward, who had waited in the open doorway, ushered me out through the marble hall to his business-room, and gave me a purse of silver. There was a whole coffer of them, each neatly tied and marked with its weight.

Kleobis was waiting at the tavern next the lyre-maker's. By that time I could come up smiling, plank down the purse with a flourish, and make the most of my message. There was no need to tell him what I thought it was worth.

"Excellent!" he said. "Did he name a day for me to sing?"

"No," I answered, doing my best. "He has so much business, I don't expect he knows himself when he will be free, he has to ask his chamberlain. He made himself very pleasant. But I suppose if he goes off on campaign again, everything else will be at a stand. At all events, he was delighted to hear of your coming."

I knew no way to lessen the wrong I'd done him. Five paces into that room, and I'd known I could have made his fortune with a single glance, if my face had offered those pretty boys some rivalry. Kleobis had made a famous song about the love of Zeus for Ganymede. It was Ganymede who should have walked through that door, not I.

It was something, that by now I had grown my beard. It made an ugly man of me, but a man at least. It would have been far worse, on Samos, to be an ugly boy.

A quarter-month then passed, in which we saw the fine sights of Samos, or as many as were free. We ate at the next-door tavern; for the rest, we thought we should be seen only at the good ones, and these cost money.

There were two of especial consequence. At the Peacock, the Landsharers met to exchange their wrongs and plot. One visit taught us that one went there only if invited. The other, the Victory, was the resort of Polykrates' new men. I was surprised to find it so lively, till I became aware that most of them were craftsmen, the best artists from Ionia.

Often some man would pick up the tavern lyre to start a song; but it was clear their skill lay elsewhere. This set me thinking. When we had been ten days without word from the Palace, I went out on some excuse, and presented myself to the host, offering to entertain the guests. It being about noon, he let me try my skill on those who were eating there. I got a plate of stewed squid and a drink, and was taken on to start that evening, at a real Samian drachma.

When I broke this news to Kleobis, who could never have done it and held up his head again, he exclaimed with horror that he would rather starve than accept this sacrifice. He was a man of his generation; to sing for pay at a craftsmen's tavern seemed nearly as bad to him as if I had pro-

posed to hire out my body, supposing there had been a
market for it. Had I not learned by now that since the Age
of Heroes ours was a sacred calling, which princes had not
disdained? Orpheus! Achilles! Solon the Good, even in our
own day! (He meant his, not mine.) How could our praise
songs be desired by kings, if we cheapened ourselves like
mountebanks? Did I want to ruin my future? "Let us sail,
my son, while we have some money left. You cannot do
this for me."

"Truly, sir," I said, "it's different here in Samos. It would
never do for you, of course, with your reputation; but it
won't hurt me. I still need to learn from an audience, and
this is a very good one. If they enjoy it, so shall I." This
was no more than the truth. Much as I loved and honored
him, I looked forward to coming before strangers, for
once, not as any man's pupil, but simply as Simonides.

The tavern had been named after Polykrates' first
trireme; and its host thought more of his own dignity than
I did of mine. He introduced me as a most distinguished
bard, exiled from Ionia; which in those days was the best
passport to Samos. I chose my songs to suit my audience;
and, when I had done, was asked to so many tables that
if I had sat at all of them I would have gone home as drunk
as a muleteer.

After only one evening, I was initiate enough to burst
in on Kleobis with, "Sir! Theodoros bought me a drink!"

Even the free sights of Samos had told him who
Theodoros was. He ran his hands through his hair. "Drink
from a marble-carver! A pupil of mine!"

"I've not told them that, sir; I knew you didn't wish it.
Theodoros said he could tell I'd studied with a fine master,
but I never said a word." I could see him brighten a little.
He'd been out of sorts lately, from the change of air, and
want of use for his skill. I could not tell him that this man's
praise had healed my bruises, left by Polykrates' minions.

Theodoros must have been all of sixty; but his great arm
and shoulder muscles were still hard, and his broad hands
calloused. He could behave like a lord, but he always looked
like a craftsman. "There's always something one has to
take from a prentice and do oneself." The taverner kept for
him his favorite cup, black on white figured Lakonian,
smooth as an egg. When he picked it up, you saw the
delicate touch of those big fingers. Besides marble, he
carved gems. The Tyrant's emerald was his masterwork.
He worked too in bronze. Nowadays he had his marbles
roughed out by his pupils, and only did the finishing; but
he tinted them all himself. I know no sculptor today who
does not use a painter; but he used to say he had the whole
in his mind's eye and did not want it spoiled. Besides all
this, he was part architect of the grand new Hera temple,
going up on the western shore.

"Yes, yes," said Kleobis, fidgeting on his pillow. "A great
man of his hands, no doubt. But don't make yourself
common among such people."

"Court people come to the tavern too, sir. I don't think
it would do you harm to be seen there. It would pass the
time." I was disturbed by the tedium of his days, and his
loss of spirits. For twenty years, before this, he had stayed
in no city except as an honored guest-friend. Now that I
can say the same of myself for twice as long, I understand
his feelings.

At least he no longer had my keep to find; which was as
well, since no summons came from Polykrates. Soon after,
on a day of sun and rain, he made a new song about Apollo
weeping for dead Hyakinthos, drawing a cloak of cloud
over his shining head. It was one of his best; polishing it
kept him happy for two days, after which I could see him
starving for an audience. A cruel waste; for it would be a
great success at the Victory. When Polykrates' friends
honored the house, they often brought along their favorite

boys, who no doubt looked to them as lovely as Hyakinthos, even if not to me.

Life is hard on Keos, and its springtime short. The beauty of our youths is that of first-flowering manhood. I, born without beauty, had looked at it with longing—to inhabit it, not to embrace it. The images of desire change with each new love; but the image in the soul will keep its shape. Beauty to me was my tall brother at seventeen, stripped on the wrestling-ground, his oiled muscles gleaming like bronze.

I could picture him at the Victory, wrinkling his nose at the courtiers' Ganymedes. Several had fathers of some consequence, who you would have thought would be bringing them up like gentlemen; but they were all new men, and had settled for favor at court. If your son was in fashion, sour looks would do you no good; nor, if you wanted to get on, would you prevent him from scenting himself with Persian rose-attar, slitting his tunic up the thigh, or swaying along like a lily drenched with rain.

Nonetheless, here was this splendid song, there was its audience; between stood my master's dignity. I thought, and saw an answer.

"Sir, it's wicked for this not to be heard. Listen: come tonight to the Victory, just as a guest. Sit there with your wine. I'll sing the song. It won't be what you would make it; but it will make a hit, for sure. When they applaud, I shall bow to your table, and say, 'There sits the poet.' Depend on it, word will get to the court."

I had half expected him to start up like a pheasant from the dogs, and was ready to talk him round. But he drew his brows together, and pulled his beard. The truth was, we were getting desperate; it was just that he would have liked to sing it himself.

That evening, I borrowed the kithara, which they had never heard me play. But I laid it by, arousing their expectation, and played some slight thing on the lyre, keeping one eye on the door. I was pleased to see the Ganymedes and their devotees in force that night. Presently, in came Kleobis in his second-best robe (the best of course was for recitals). I looked, started, and bowed, as if overwhelmed by the sight of this famous man. Seeing the server take note and bustle up to him, I felt my heart move with love. He looked more worn, hollower round the eyes, thinner and greyer than when he sailed from Ephesos. At least I might pay him a little of what I owed. I picked up the kithara and tuned the strings.

When he was settled and served, I sang the song, turning his way as one does to the guest of honor. By now, I was getting into a style that was my own; but this was his, and I fell into his style as if it were two years back. When I saw from his face that I had got it true, it was hard not to smile back at him; but that might have cheapened my tribute afterwards.

I ended with a dying fall, and a showy cadenza on the kithara; my own, for he had not yet worked up his concert version. There was a burst of applause. I saw his eyes filled with tears, and not of grief. That moment was like a laurel crown to me. But man's joy is fleeting.

"Expect the unexpected." Everyone quotes me on that; it has become a proverb. Well, that was the day on which I began to learn.

I waited through the hammering of wine-cups on the tables; most of them were of bronze, and a fine din they made. I gestured to catch their eyes. They were already falling silent; Kleobis had disposed himself with a touch more dignity; I had even begun to speak. Then, in the twinkling of an eye, I had lost them. All eyes were upon the door.

For a moment I thought, Can it be Polykrates? This may be our chance. Then I saw who it was.

Three years had passed since last I'd seen him, though

only across a hall. Then he had been awaited, now he was
a god-sent surprise; but the chorus of delight burst out in
a paean. "Anakreon! Anakreon!"

He stood in the doorway, making an entrance from mere
habit; style sat on him like his clothes. A small man, with
hair so bright, his head might have been on fire; a face
pale as new ivory, elegantly carved; light eyes like changing
water. And young; not thirty. Nobody now remembers him
young, but I.

Quietly I caught my master's eye. He lifted his brows
and smiled; he had weathered much change of fortune in
his day. His hand moved slightly, beckoning. I picked up
the kithara and came to sit at his table, joining the audience.
Nobody noticed me.

For some time the noise went on. Then Kleobis said,
"We must greet him," and got up.

Of course he was right; to show my bitterness would
disgrace us both. But before we could move, Anakreon's
flaming head was swooping through the crowd like a hawk
through sparrows.

"Kleobis! Dear old friend! What a joy to see you! When
did you get away, how long have you been in Samos?"

Too long for him not to have had news of us, if we'd had
success here. Well, he was Anakreon. At once he recalled
the last time they'd met, when Kleobis had given a much-
praised Ode to Artemis. It was smooth; it was also kind.
Even I got a charming smile and a graceful compliment,
just as if he'd not scanned all the Ganymedes on his way
across, like a vintner choosing grapes. We exchanged our
news, to the pleasure of all the guests. There was a knot too
in the doorway, of refugee Ionians without the price of
a drink.

Everyone was amazed to see him. His native city was
Teos, north along the coast from Ephesos; one of those
whose people had fled by sea with all their shipping, and

anyone else's which was in port just then, and found empty land to start again; on the Thracian coast, in a place called Abdera. Here they had hewed timber, made mud-bricks, planted their vine-slips and their seed-grain, bred from the few cattle they had managed to bring; all the time fighting off the Thracian tribesmen, who thought it unmanly to grow what they could steal. In time, they found that pickings were easier elsewhere; and the Abderans, though they lost some fine men in battle, still held on. The young heroes' names were known to us already. Their elegies had reached us in Ephesos, along with some charming love songs. No traveling minstrel wasted anything of Anakreon's.

He told us that this was his second visit to Samos; before the war, he had crossed over for the Hera festival. Now he was here to stay.

I had guessed it. Something about his entrance had told me.

"My kin are established," he said. "The Abderans can eat and sleep and rear their children in safety, and not many of them want more. I've given them two years of my life; and, believe me, two years in Thrace are longer than ten in Ionia."

Kleobis said smiling, "We had thought you were still running after that little mane-tossing Thracian filly you'd vowed to ride." That song was already famous.

He laughed and shrugged. "Fillies at fifteen, mares at twenty. Branded ones, too; by now she's been tattooed into her husband's clan. Beauty is thin upon the ground in Abdera. This is a banquet after a wayside inn." Here he looked under his lashes at the most-sought Ganymede. The glance was caught and thrown back before the modest gaze was dropped; certainly, Anakreon knew his Samos. He turned back to us, as easily as if he'd merely beckoned the server, which he went on to do.

"So, as you can suppose, my summons here was welcome.

I have just come from the Palace. What a civil-spoken man! And generous, as I have no need to tell you."

He always had princely manners. If he had known that we'd come as suppliants where he was an invited guest, not a hint would have escaped him.

How simple we had been! A king like Polykrates—he was that, whatever they called him—who sent to Tyre for purple, to Persia for sapphires, to Egypt for ebony and emeralds; of course he had sent, too, for the poets of his choice, not waited for chance to bring them.

"Now that the barbarians have swallowed Ionia for as long as the gods allow"—he turned to me, not to leave me neglected—"Samos is the only place for us artists. For the mathematicians, of course, it's different. Why should they go? The properties of a circle, the shadow of a staff at the meridian, will not change their laws, whoever is making laws for men."

Kleobis nodded. "None have left Ephesos. Well, some of them are impious fellows; but Harpagos won't care if our gods are mocked, so long as his are left alone."

Soon after this we said good night; he would certainly be wishing to improve his acquaintance here. As we parted, he called that we would be meeting soon at the Palace.

He meant it, too. In no time at all he was the darling of the court; appointed tutor to young Polykrates, the Tyrant's heir; a sturdy, curly-haired lad, not bad-looking, and, people said, the image of his father, meaning before his father put on weight. There was a daughter, too, who came to the recitals; Samian women lived with the Ionian freedom. (Graceful and pleasant I always found it, and Athens has lost by its strictness in this later age.) She took after her father too, which in a girl was no great dower; still, she worshipped him, and any artist he admired was great with her.

It was Anakreon, I am sure, who got Kleobis a recital in

the supper-room. Twenty years later he still would not admit to it, from respect for my master's memory. A mean man would not have done it; a small one would have done it and let us know; but he was Anakreon.

Of course, it was beyond his power to get me invited. It distressed Kleobis, who in Ionia had taken me everywhere as a matter of course. On the day, however, he picked up his spirits, ran through most of his repertoire, and asked me which songs to choose. I said he must certainly sing the Lament for Hyakinthos. We discussed a couple of others, which he could give as encores. Then he spent an hour at the bathhouse, before going on to the barber to have his hair and beard trimmed and curled. I always looked after his recital robe. I had shaken it out the day before, aired it, and tuned the kithara.

I had to leave before him, to go to work, but he was dressed already. Not so richly, it seemed, as when last he'd sung, though the robe was just the same. Bright colors and gold thread were the wear in Samos; I had not known that my eye had got so used to them. But he had aged, as well. I embraced him, wished him every good fortune the gods can give, and went off to the Victory.

It was full that night. I was cheered when I came in, which got the best from me. When I broke off, I was asked to several tables; it was Theodoros's I went to. He said, "When I have time, I'll do a bronze of your Perseus, just as you made me see him. The Gorgon's head, now; the snakes we could work in the forge, and weld on after the casting . . ." He ran on, while I sat there as mute as a cream-filled cat. "Now Ibykos, last night at the Palace, *he's* been cried up enough; he should have worked with the tools he knew. A foolish business."

I sat up like a cat drenched from a bucket. "*Ibykos?* But he lives in Sicily."

"Yes, that's where he's from. Landed two days back. Samos is the honeypot now, my boy."

My pleasure in the evening trickled away; it seemed treachery to my master. The great Ibykos, pupil of Stesichoros himself; the singer of heroes. Polykrates had imported another treasure. So tonight's supper would be for often-invited guests, who had tasted all the treats and must be offered a change of fare, even though the dish was simpler.

Youthful and hopeful still, I told myself that if Kleobis made his mark tonight, he would be asked again; thanked Theodoros for his wine, and went back to my singing. After my supper-break, I always gave the late guests something; so Kleobis would be home before me.

He was sleeping when I got back. At least, it was clear that he wanted me to think so. I went quietly to bed, and pretended to sleep myself. When the late guests came in, some had come on from the Palace, and told us all about Ibykos' recital.

His ode had first promised to reject all former themes, and then declared its own: the gifts and graces of the Tyrant's son, young Polykrates, whose beauty he compared with that of the young Troilos, to the Trojan's disadvantage. This was his offering, the gift of undying fame.

The promise was kept, as such promises sometimes are. The song is still given sometimes, and people have asked me who this young Polykrates was. Only Ibykos' name has kept it in the repertoire. Anakreon always said it was the worst thing he'd ever done, notable only for its gross sycophancy. As he said later, "Shameless as a dog, my dear. He must have made it before he'd even seen the boy, who was no fool and knew it. He hardly knew where to look, any more than I did. However, he's the apple of Father's eye, and that's all Ibykos cared for. It's made his fortune in Samos."

For Anakreon, this was sharp. But different men as we were and different artists, we had some things in common. I have never come to want in my calling, I am glad to say; but I have gone where my work was liked as I chose to do it. Neither he nor I were like robe-makers to whom anyone can say, "Cut it this size, and trim it so."

Kleobis did not say much next morning; only that everyone had been very civil, and the fee would be useful till something came our way. Soon he was picking up small engagements at houses of the Landsharers. They would never have been offered to a man in the Tyrant's favor; nor accepted by a man who had any hope of it. He was an old-fashioned singer, who had no more sense than to take on an ugly pupil, and sing of immortal loves where mortal ones were the mode. The court had already forgotten him.

Perhaps he should have stayed in Ephesos, and cheered the citizens in their servitude. The Medes, after all, only required that poets should not abuse them; they could sing about anything else they chose. Here in Samos, it was not what one must not sing, but what one must. Tell a man what he may not sing, and he is still half free; even all free, if he never wanted to sing it. But tell him what he *must* sing, take up his time with it so that his true voice cannot sound even in secret—there, I have seen, is slavery.

I suppose this is hardly just to Polykrates. In his way, he loved the Muses. He paid well for what he liked, and if he did not get it he did nothing worse than lose interest. We had been free to come, and were free to go. Now he is dead and I am old, I can see all this. In those days I was young and bitter.

At the tavern I was making enough to keep us both. But man does not live only by bread and olives. Kleobis' heart was dying in him. His new patrons gave few feasts, so did not invite him twice. Before long, he would depend on my base employment. He blamed himself for it, guessing that if alone I would have moved on by now; but he had lost the will to plan ahead. He talked always about the past, and lived in that.

Where could we go? He was too old to start again in the wild north; Anakreon, young and among his own people, had found he could not bear it. Athens, an old friend to art, was near; but they had had civil wars for years, lords against commons, coast against plain; Pisistratos, the commons' choice for Tyrant, was now in, now out, now back, and would no doubt be out again. By myself, I might have tried my luck in Thessaly. Though some of its little lords were not much better than bandits, and I did not know the country, I was strong, and used to hardship. My master was used to it too, but it had begun to tell. It was for me, the son of his art, to see that he had no more.

I thought of my father in blood. I was a rich man's son, and much good it did me.

I had sent no news home since the fall of Ephesos. They did not know I could write, and I'd trusted to word of mouth to tell them I was alive. My occupation was no fault of mine; but I could not see my father thinking so. However, my pride was no longer mine to do as I liked with. I bought reed-paper; when Kleobis was out, I sat down and wrote a letter.

To Theasides son of Leoprepes, his brother wishes joy. Suddenly I started laughing. I could hear him say, "Sim, by the dog! Whatever did the boy pay to this learned fellow? The street-corner scrivener would have done."

I told him everything. I was not in want, I said, and had no need to beg of our father; but the war had ruined my master's former patrons. Were any feasts or contests being planned in Keos, where he could come and sing? I did not ask Theas to hide my letter; that would come naturally at home.

It was easy to find a Kean ship. Since Ionia fell, two-

thirds of them put in at Samos. It was my luck to see
Laertes, whose wedding had changed my fate, walk into the
Victory. He had carried landless fugitives from half-a-
dozen cities, and found nothing surprising in my present
work. Nor, being a neighbor, was he surprised at being
asked to give my letter privately to Theas. To my father,
I sent respects by word of mouth.

Before I sealed my letter, I added by way of postscript,

> A *horn-handled knife, my brother,*
>   *you won for strength at the games.*
> *Me it won from dark Hades,*
>   *saved by your gift though the sea divided us.*

That was the first time I wrote a poem down. It felt very
strange.

The days passed. I found the uses of memory. What with
my own songs, and all those I'd learned (I had the Sons of
Homer entire), by the time I ran out, I could start again
at the beginning. Meantime I ate and drank and could take
home all my pay. Often I could make as much as an extra
drachma, if a song was asked for by name. And it might
even be one of mine.

Anakreon looked in sometimes, and was always charming. He and Ibykos seemed to have patched things up.
Ibykos, having sung his way into royal favor, had sense
enough not to make an enemy of a poet whom fame and
charm alike had made secure. As for Anakreon, he liked to
please and be pleased; the bile Hipponax lived on would
have poisoned him. Indeed, he resented Ibykos less than I.
In Anakreon I knew a master. I suppose, in my heart, I
thought I could better Ibykos myself.

About eight days after I'd sent my letter, Theodoros gave
a supper for his apprentices; they had just set a new marble
up. He asked me for my Bellerophon, a favorite of his
(though I've improved it since then) and I was singing

to his table, when I was half aware of someone with presence, standing in the doorway till the song was done. I took my applause, and turned. A tall splendid man, gold-bearded like a young Zeus, shouted out, "Sim!" and grasped me in his arms.

After a while, aware of everyone staring, I said, "Gentle-men, this is Theasides, son of Leoprepes of Keos, my brother." It was my proudest moment in that house.

The house enjoyed it. Ionians are curious and love news. We put off private talk, while Theas told how he'd heard of the fall of Ephesos, feared for my life, and so on. You'd have thought, to hear him, that I was Keos' most honored citizen, the ornament of my family. Time fell away, as I felt the cloak of his kindness once more drawn over me.

Theodoros had been eating him with his eyes; soon he pulled a chalk out of his pouch and made sketches on the table. He had lately been employed to sculpt Polykrates' favorite, Bathyllos, the green-eyed flute-player. Like a fish he was all head, and boneless beneath the neck; you could have wound him round a flagpole.

Everyone cried that I must sing something for my brother. I gave them some old favorite with a clapping chorus; then everyone danced. When the party broke up, and we walked into the street, we poured out our news as if we had been meeting every day, except that there was more to tell. Out-side my lodging, he said, "I won't trouble your bard to find a bed for me. I've put up at that inn the pilot's brother keeps, the Vinestock."

"What?" I cried. "Theas, that's the dearest place in town. The rich merchants stay there. They'll seize your baggage if you can't pay. Come, settle for what you've had, and come back here."

He laughed, and slapped a jingling purse at his belt. "All found. I'm here to do credit to the family." I looked at him. He grew serious. "Laertes slipped me your letter in the fields. But he had to tell them you were alive; and he never thought to hide what you were doing. He knows Ionia, thought nothing of it, and said you were one of the lucky ones. But you know the father."

Yes indeed. I should have been singing for the Land-sharers, men of decent birth; that would have pleased him, even more than the Tyrant's patronage. Before disgracing us all at a common wineshop, I should have come home, asked for his favor, and lived decently on the farm. My choice must have spoken for itself; there seemed nothing I could do that did not wound him.

Theas clapped me on the shoulder. "Next time, write a letter we can show off to our friends. No one knows you've become a scholar. But what got into you, not to know what to do? Have you been so long away, you've forgotten the Apollo festival?"

It was true; I had. The moon was waxing now, and it came at the next new moon.

"Only stand up at the contest," he said, "and sing as you did tonight, and the rest will be wondering why they troubled to try."

It had long been out of my thoughts, to sing in Keos. Time and change had touched the boy who had flinched before; the roads of the earth and the ways of men, learning and skill, pride and anger. A man thought now, Yes, I could sing before my father.

I knew it should be now, while the mood and strength were in me. But I knew also that here, at last, was something I had to give. "Another year; not this. Kleobis must compete this time, and I can't enter against my master. He needs to be crowned again."

"Why? How could he grudge it you? He's won a dozen crowns to your one."

"That *is* why. He is going down and feels it, and it's no

fault of his. He is losing pride, and with that he will lose
everything. I can wait; he can't."

He looked at me, in a patch of moonlight. "The old man
took good care of you."

I nodded. I did not say, He has been my father. We never
said things like that aloud. "When you meet him, don't
speak about my competing."

"Very well, Sim. If that's the way of it, you must pay
your debts."

Next morning at our lodging he kept his word. "Everyone
still talks of Laertes' wedding, sir. Your song must have
brought good luck; two boys and a girl, and lively as young
goats. It would be a great day if you came again."

Kleobis smiled, and his eye kindled a little. He sat stroking his beard. Presently he said, "My dear boys, it is part
of a poet's skill to judge occasions. There are times to
compete, and times to present a pupil. When the pupil
returns to his native city, not having yet been heard there,
he will arouse, if he does well, both pride and wonder. In
these the teacher has his share."

Theas looked at me, meaning, "Just what I thought
myself."

I, too, could see the truth in it. It was also true that if
he entered, and someone of note should chance to come
and win, that would be his death-blow; and I thought he
knew it. He had not pushed me when I was afraid, and I
owed him the like return.

"Sir, if I can show Keos even half of what I owe you, it
will be the best day of my life. But only if you are there to
see it." Never mind if I don't win, I thought; if they see
Black Sim, Leoprepes' youngest, do anything at all, they'll
believe his teacher can work miracles.

"You'll honor our house, I hope, sir," Theas said. I
nearly jumped out of my skin; but he spoke with confidence.

Clearly, he had come to be a power in the family; Leoprepes' eldest was already a man to reckon with.

As he left, he said, "If you want me later, Sim, I'll be
at the workshop of your sculptor friend, Theodoros. He
wants to sketch my buttocks, or some such thing." We
exchanged mock punches, as we'd done when we were boys.

What Theodoros really wanted of him was to have him
pose for a bronze of Perseus. He did it, too, staying for some
days as the sculptor's guest. He always liked, he told me, to
see how things were made.

I too enjoyed the making of a bronze, though I'd seen it
once already. It had a kind of magic, unlike the slow
chipping and smoothing of stone or marble. Theodoros
had been to Egypt to learn the art; there, they had been
casting life-size time out of mind, when only little votives
were being made in Greece.

He had a huge yard down by the harbor, full of sheds
and hoists and scaffoldings, all powdered white with marble-
dust that got up one's nose. The noise was dreadful, at least
for an ear like mine, what with slaves sawing blocks or
chipping them down for columns, grinding and polishing
column-drums. There was also a clattering forge where
they were making rivets to fasten wall-blocks together.
Clang-clang went the great hammers, and *tink-tink-tink* the
little ones, as some skilled apprentice made the trims for a
bronze. Hands over ears, I threaded my way to Theodoros'
own workroom, which was swept and polished and had a
great table full of drawings and plans. On a dais stood
my brother, splendid in nakedness, one arm propped up
on a wooden stand. He was to be holding up the Gorgon's
head, and the torso muscles had to show the lift. Before
him stood Theodoros in his working dress, which was a
small apron to keep the grit out of his private parts, and a
great deal of clay daubed here and there on the rest of him.
He had set up the core and was putting on the first surface,

talking with Theas; the touchy part of the work was still to come. Theas used to say he learned enough good stories as Theodoros' model to dine out on for the rest of his life.

Two days later, he could hardly open his mouth without being snapped at. I myself had known enough to come in on tiptoe. Theodoros was washed clean from dust and clay. My brother's face returned me to my boyhood; he had shaved his beard. It was the statue's skin that was being finished, down to the finest touch; the nipples, the hair of head and groin, the face. Its color had changed from clay-grey to a creamy white like alabaster. Theodoros was working upon the wax.

It had been spread with a hot knife over the clay and left to harden. Now he was smoothing it with a warm tool, or graving it with a cold one. Not to be in the way, I went over to the table. At one end were the set-squares and compasses and plumb lines of the architect; at the other, under the window, the tiny tools of his gem-carving, the vise and the treadle-wheel for the drill. A young man came in, and set down softly a hideous white waxen mask. The chief apprentice had been trusted with the Gorgon's head.

"Please, Theodoros," said Theas like a boy at school, "may I go outside?"

"If you must, if you must," said the master, who must have known he was too well-mannered to ask unless he was bursting. "Yes, take a rest, I can finish the ears without you. Look in that tray, Sim, and you'll find his eyes."

It was full of split agates; set on one side was the perfect one, brown at the core with a milky rim, each half curved and smooth. "They don't come in blue," he said, "not with the markings right."

At last the wax was finished; there stood complete a white ghostly man, pierced with rods through body and limbs and head, to tie the form firmly within the mold. Theodoros walked round and round it, making a tiny line with a stylos

upon the eyebrow, or stroking a tendon with his broad
thumb. Then he turned his back on it, and said to his
apprentices, who were watching in dead silence, "Yes.
Get on."

Slaves had dragged in a tub full of wet clay. Into this
slip the apprentices dipped their hands, working it with
fingers and thumbs to test its fineness. One found a grain
of grit, at which they all exclaimed with outrage, and
started over again. Theodoros strode over and rubbed some
between his palms, and said it would do, but let Sesostris
look out next time. On this they scooped up the clay,
which was so soft that it almost ran, and began to smooth
it over the waxen body. Their touch was tender and delicate,
as if they were anointing it; but as they worked, the fine
outlines blurred, and in a while it was clay-grey again.
Theodoros said to us, "Come back in four days. There's
nothing to see till then."

As we walked off past the forge, Theas lifted his voice
to shout, "I don't know what the father will say. I should
be home by now."

All the same, he did not look anxious. Sculptors like
Theodoros don't find their models among men who want
to be paid. You will see peasants strong enough to take an
ass on their shoulders, hardier than soldiers; but they are
not built like the athlete who has had the chance to train,
and shape from his own body a work of art. Our father
would not be sorry to see his heir shining in Samos, in
eternal bronze. It was another thing than singing in a
tavern. For that he would wait a few days longer, to see
what had become of me.

Next day we spent with Kleobis, who had cheered up,
and told Theas about our Ionian days. I hoped he would
soon be putting on flesh again. He had lost his old healthy
tan; his face was almost the color of Theodoros' wax. He
came with us, though, to the workshop to see the bronze

broken from the mold. In any great city it's a common sight today; but when I was young, hollow-cast statues were still a marvel in Samos, and unknown in the rest of Greece. A whole crowd who could not get in to watch the modeling were allowed to enjoy the sight.

Theodoros, I saw, could have done without us all. He enjoyed his fame; but, like most artists, not everything it brought with it. He'd have liked to view the work in peace, complete the finishing, and then show it perfect; and I do not blame him. No one can make me disclose a half-formed song; my mold, my furnace, are safely within my head.

After the smooth slip, the statue had been coated with thick strong clay, turning the waxen man into a clumsy giant with just a head, body and limbs. He was stained with the fire, in which he had been slow-hardened; and pierced with vents, through which his delicate waxen flesh had vanished away. When it had been melted out from him, in its place had been poured the bronze.

Theodoros never had sightseers when that was done. It was an agon, he said, a contest, win or lose all. His chief apprentice, who venerated him, confided to me at the tavern that he went on like a madman, shouting at them all, hitting them over the head, calling them bastard sons of slaves. If the mold was not propped and chain-slung just right above the fire; if a bit of unmelted metal closed a channel within the mold; if a hand or a foot had not been drained of all its wax before the casting, it would be disaster. "It's like childbirth," the apprentice said. "You know what went in at the start, but you don't know what will come out."

The fire-stained mold, holding its heavy secret, had been hoisted with a crane, and laid down on an oaken frame. Theodoros and his apprentices stood round with mallets and chisels made of hardwood. He stepped up to the mold. I saw him close his eyes a moment, and wondered what god he was appealing to: Hephaistos, I suppose. Then he hit the head a few sharp taps down the face, and it split open like a chestnut shell. There was Theas, in all his beauty and even a little more, noble and calm, each curl on his forehead perfect. He was dark from the furnace, his sockets awaited eyes, the tie-rods still stood out from his crown and nape, there was a nick on his brow from a bit of grit in the clay. All that would be mended before the burnishing. Theodoros swore at the nick, and cursed Sesostris, and set about cleaning the ears. The apprentices started on the body.

At last they craned it up onto its feet, for us to see it whole. Even unfinished, you could see it was one of the artist's masterworks. I looked from this immortal to my brother, gazing at it with his head on one side, the only time I could remember him looking shy. I thought of him as a child, crying when our father had his young dog killed for sheep-chasing; or staring open-mouthed at a thrall's wife we had discovered bathing in a stream, then grabbing my hand and running away; or exercising with his javelin, creasing his brow to recall his trainer's instructions. His beard was starting to grow again, and had just reached the untidy state. One day it would be grey, if he lived so long; and here forever would shine this burnished hero. Tears came to my eyes; but everyone was sneezing from the dust of the broken clay, and no one noticed.

He had two days to wait for a ship, in which time I showed him Samos. As we strolled the waterfront, he asked me what song I meant to sing at the contest.

"A hymn to Apollo. But I'll have to work on it, to sing it solo. It was meant for a choral ode."

"Why a solo, then? It's the choral odes people come to hear."

"Dear man, because I have no chorus."

"But you could have one on Keos. How long do you take to teach a song?"

"Seven days; at a pinch I've done it in less. When I had a chorus."

"Then whatever's troubling you? We're citizens, aren't we? Just tell me how many, and if you want men or girls or boys, and I'll have them for you."

"But, Theas, how can you? You don't know anything about music, except what you like to hear."

"Oh, I know that," he answered cheerfully. "But I know where to go, to get it done."

Yes. He was the heir of Leoprepes of Iulis. If he said he could do it, he could. So I agreed; thinking in myself that if once more I was going to take and take and show him no return, I would as soon be dead. Even love cannot cast out pride.

He sailed some days ahead of me, to make smooth my path. Theodoros came with me to see him off, complaining that he had not stayed to see the statue polished and set up. Kleobis had a cold, and stayed indoors.

He was lending me the kithara. It is a costly instrument, which only a master of the craft can make; the money I'd saved for one had gone since Ephesos fell, part of it on a gay Samian robe to do the tavern credit. I could not take that to Keos; even my old one from Ephesos had to have half the border stitched back out of sight.

At the very last, on my sailing day, Kleobis begged off. He said his cold still hung about; would be nothing if he looked after it, but on a ship would most likely fly to his chest. He would stay in Samos, and make an offering for me on the day.

I was sad, but not much astonished. He had lost heart, he felt unlucky; he feared, perhaps, that on Keos he would find himself forgotten. I did not forget how the best doctor

in Iulis had tended his sick apprentice; he could hardly
fare worse in Samos, which had physicians of some renown.
So I embraced him, told him to take good care of himself,
and said that if I had any success, all Keos should hear my
teacher's name.

In some ways it was a relief to me. My father was too
well-bred to insult a guest; but Kleobis was, after all, the
father I had chosen in his stead, and I could not think the
visit would have gone off easily.

I packed up the kithara, as I'd done over the years till I
could almost do it sleeping, in its leather case, the embroidered sling folded around the soundbox, the spare
strings in their pocket outside. "No one but I shall carry
it a step," I said, "till I bring it back."

"Did you pack the wax and the resin? Don't forget to
warm the wax, don't use too much, polish alone unless the
wood feels dry." I promised; I had known it all since I
was sixteen. "Have you a spare plectrum?" I showed him
two, one silver and one bone. "Good, good . . . I was as
near to Sappho once as I am to you. A little dark thing;
not much better-favored than you; which in a woman means
worse . . . *If now she flies you, soon will she follow; Taking
no gifts now, soon be the giver; Wanting no love now, soon
be the lover, For all her striving* . . . I tell you, Apollo is a
gardener who knows how to prune a vinestock. Go gather
your grapes, my son."

"If Apollo pruned me, I know who has fed and tended
me. The grapes are yours." I felt like weeping, and turned
away. "Don't come to the harbor. It's a cold sharp wind,
for all it's sunny. Keep warm indoors."

He laid aside his cloak, allowing that I was right. As I
left, he said again that he would make an offering for me.

Among the people come to see me off I found, with
astonished joy, Anakreon.

"We shall meet again, dear boy," he said, putting both

hands on my shoulders with his head aslant, and narrowing his green eyes. "But I think not in a tavern, except to drink. Come, you know as well as I do, yes? Keos has a surprise in store. I wish I could be there, but my host requires me. Ibykos hasn't come. Now I wonder why, when I reminded him . . . ? We shan't quarrel, my dear. The hatter and the shoemaker don't spoil each other's trade. Now remember, let us see you here again, if only for a celebration."

I was seen off, too, by a young hetaira I had visited once or twice. She had put on her best robe and all her paint; it was plain she really wished to claim my acquaintance in public. I was so touched that I embraced her on the gangplank. Oh yes, I was humble when I was young.

I expected to be met in Koressia by Theas, with a spare mule for me. As we turned the point, I descried his bright head; then, as the sail was lowered and we rowed in, I saw the cluster of men about him. It was like an embassy. And one of them was my father.

Left to himself, I doubt if he would have known me. Till Theas hailed me, he was still looking about. I don't know what he had expected, surely not a shepherd boy in a sheepskin; but whatever it was, he was not seeing it. As for me, it seemed he should have been much taller, and without a bald patch on his crown; he should have made me ill at ease, not causing him to be so. My sins against him would be different now.

He embraced me, which he'd not done when I left home, but which was proper with people watching; and that was just how it felt. I asked after his health and he after my journey. Then he presented me to his friends who had come to meet me. I understood now. Just as Theas had been told to stay at the best inn in Samos, all this had been planned to cloak me in respectability. I found myself thinking, O Zeus, how soon can I escape from all these people and get to work?

I conveyed my master's regrets. Only my father remembered who he was, and that was not for his singing. Theas
was at ease with everyone, a man among the men, and
treated so by our father. He did not break the harmony;
he was a son of the house, part of its riches, like a fine piece
of vineyard. I, such as I was, was my own creation, and that
of a foreign bard. What I brought to the house would come
only from me. He was not used to it. Never mind, I
thought; we are wanderers all, from Homer onward. One
sings, and one moves on.

Our ride to the farm was quite a cavalcade; the friends
had been invited to celebrate my return. I thought, like a
passing traveler, how good the land looked and how small
the house. My mother at the door had aged more than my
father. She kissed me, and said I should have sent word
that I was safe, which I knew was true. As her eyes dwelt
on me, I remembered our father saying once that I got my
looks from her side of the family. Whoever it was he had
reproached her with, dead, I suppose, before my birth, I
must have grown more like him.

While she bustled about with the food and wine, I
slipped inside to find Philomache. She was waiting, dressed
in her best, to appear for the short time proper to a modest
maiden. In these years she had bloomed, with the thin
delicate skin of red-haired beauty; her only defect was that
she was small, like me. She stared amazed at this man who
had come pushing through the curtain; then rushed to me
crying, "Sim! I never knew you! How much better-looking
you are!" She stood back from me, and added, "I mean,
you look like someone important, now."

"Theas says you're betrothed." It had been on my mind;
I did not think our father would have considered her wishes,
if the estate was right. This was so; but by luck she was
pleased with the young man, who it seemed had courted
her prettily, sending her gifts and garlands as if they had

been free to choose. "He's here now," she said, lighting up; I could see she was less shy of him already than she was of me. "Midylos, the son of Bacchylides."

It was the father, I now remembered, to whom mine had presented me first of all at the harbor. He'd not thought to show me the youth with whom she was to spend her life.

"He sent me a dish of apples," she said, going pink, "with a real poem, *written*. It said I was like an apple at the very top of the tree." I did not spoil it by hoping he'd quoted right. Of course, she could not read.

When I sought him among the guests, I found him well-favored and no fool, eager for news about the war. Overhearing our talk, other men came up to learn what was happening in Ionia. Before long I had a good-sized audience. I was used to that in Samos. It was only when I saw my father's eyes on me, that I remembered I'd never been let in with his guests before.

Theas in his wisdom had found me a flautist living in Koressia, and it was there that I trained my chorus. Even so, my brother was at some trouble to bring my father questions about the farm, lest he should come down to oversee me.

Thanks to this, I was happy enough. The flautist had never seen me before; the chorus boys, though all from Iulis, had been young children when I left home. More than half their lives had passed since they had seen Black Sim, if they ever had. I started clear; they were all proud of being trained by a Iulis man, instead of a Koressian as they had been last time.

Though a poet of no distinction, he had not trained them badly. He had even taken them to Delos, where the song, rather than the singing, had lost the prize. They came in together, and you could hear the words.

I'd used for my ode the old story of Apollo and his little brother Hermes, the newborn rogue who crept from his cradle to go cattle-stealing, and crept back there, all innocent, before his lordly brother could trace the herd. Boldly, I had put in two solo passages: a handsome boy for Apollo, and for Hermes, a little treble, bound to win hearts. In those days, breaks in the unison were thought unorthodox. Not long after, Thespis established them in Athens, taking the chief solo himself, from which we have modern tragedy. But Keos is wary of innovations.

The story ends, of course, with Apollo tracking the little thief by the sound of his lyre, which he has just invented. He gives it his big brother in exchange for the stolen cows. Apollo, entranced, forgives him, and tries the new instrument with his divine hand. This is where one shows what the kithara will do.

We rehearsed in the flautist's orchard, a pleasant place. I took care to bring him some gift each time, for the fruit was ripe and of course the boys were stealing it. It is a great mistake to rehearse indoors, when you will perform in the open air.

Once I walked down to the Apollo temple, in whose precinct the contest would be held. True to Kean simplicity, or cheeseparing if you like, it was one of those antique places most cities had pulled down by now, to rebuild in stone. A cottage-sized naos, with the image at one end of it; a roof of thatch, everything else of timber. Apollo, too; and Keos does not excel in wood-carving. He stood stiff as a tree, his arms straight down at his sides, his hair in round curls like sausages; you could say that he had a face, but not much more. Bright blue eyes, bright red hair. The columns had red shafts and blue capitals; woody knots showed on the shafts. I thought of the Artemis temple at Ephesos, the new Hera one at Samos. I gazed, and began to laugh. Not that the god would despise the offerings of simple worshippers. I was just remembering how scared I'd been of performing in this little town, before people whom this had satisfied. I too, as a child, had entered this barn with awe.

Behind the image I found the mouse-pit, the only bit of marble in the place; the sides were polished, to keep the tenants in. "Bold plunderers of Demeter's hoarded store," I said, invoking them with proper gravity. One or two stood up and twitched pink noses at me, in the hope that it was feeding-time.

The flautist—may his shade drink nectar in Elysium!— invited me to his house the night before the contest, to keep rested and fresh, he said. The night before that, my father spent the first half of suppertime complaining he was short-handed for getting in the barley; thinking, clearly, that I could have shortened rehearsals to give a hand. The second half, he went over my list of boys, which he had got from Theas, telling me which of their fathers were of consequence, and ought to be obliged, and which had done him bad turns, making their sons unworthy of any favors. One of these, as it happened, was singing the solo lines for Apollo. I listened in respectful silence.

My mother glanced at me sidelong. I had always been her changeling; now I was double-changed. I knew, though I could not help it, that I was talking like some distant kinsman on a passing visit. I caught Philomache watching me almost with awe. I must tell Kleobis, I thought; it will make him laugh.

Next day I slipped away without ceremony, bidding only Theas goodbye. "I won't ride down with you," he said, "you'll be wanting to think what you're about, and we'll be cutting the barley. He's only short-handed because it's cropped well this year. I offered up a kid for you, at the turn of the moon; but don't tell him, he hasn't missed it." He strode off through the silver olives.

The flautist knew Ionia well; we spent the evening in pleasant talk, and turned in with a cup of warm neat wine, to settle us. Almost it could have been Ephesos. I slept quite well.

The morning was fine, already smelling of autumn. The smoke of sacrifice hung in the air, sweetened with a little incense; Keos is sparing of such things. There were three or four other choirs, all Kean but one, which came from neighboring Kythnos. We poets exchanged homely gossip, as people do at country festivals. The Keans were curious about me, most of them not having heard of me before, even from my family; but they were more concerned with their own affairs.

The choral odes opened the day; the games and the fair would follow. Robed and wreathed now, we poets stood in the temple porch behaving ourselves. The maiden choruses sat whispering, in their strict matrons' charge; the boys dropped beetles down one another's backs, and so on, and were tapped by us poets with our little staffs.

The judges sat on their wooden thrones, brought out from the temple store. There was one, an oldish man, whom the others seemed to defer to. I asked someone why; he murmured that this was a guest of honor from Athens.

The back of my neck tingled. I was to sing before an Athenian.

Despite her wars, nobles against commons, hills against plain, Pisistratos out or in, which made this seem no place for my old master, the name of Athens rang for me, as it had in my boyhood on the Kean hills, looking towards Hymettos. I forgot the Keans, and my worries about whether they would know what I was doing. An Athenian was here.

His name was Prokles. You never hear of him now. But his Lay of Ajax was good, and at one time you heard it everywhere.

I kept my eye on him while the first two choirs were

singing (mine would be third) and at one bad passage I saw him blink. This gave me hope.

So much I remember well. But I've given my Apollo ode so many times, that my ear hears Athenians, Thessalians, Andrians, Euboians . . . At any rate, I was told later that the last choir sang badly because mine had put them out of heart. Well, in my time I have made good music before my betters. Why not? Our art is like a wheatfield, the tallest force up the rest. May I no longer live—not that I shall much longer in any case!—when the shortest want to cut the tallest down.

It was the Athenian judge who crowned me with the laurel. Then the people who'd come up to greet me parted to make way; and I remembered I'd been singing before my father.

I felt for him then, a little. He could not have borne it if his son had failed to win; on the other hand, he'd always hated to be proved wrong. Some of his acquaintances asked him, meaning it quite pleasantly, where he had been hiding me all this time; some said they had not known that he had two sons; and one put so much discretion into it, it was clear he thought me a by-blow. Theas, as usual, sailed in with the right word and got us out of it.

After this, for some days I was taken about to meet people. But one morning, when my father was about his business, Theas fetched me to an outhouse, where his sheep-dog had whelped, to look at the litter and decide which ones to keep. We drowned the runts; the dam seemed glad to be rid of them, and suckled the big ones happily enough. As we flung the bodies on the midden, I said laughing, "That's where I nearly went, I daresay." He went quite white, before covering it with some silly joke. I hastened to share it; we laughed like a pair of idiots. I'd guessed the truth from his face: as a child, he'd heard our parents debating whether to keep me. Perhaps for a long time after, in his simplicity, he'd supposed they might change their minds. No wonder he'd thought the ugly baby, whom only he befriended, belonged more to him than them.

"Well," he said presently, slapping me on the back, "the father wants now to keep you in the family. Don't say I told you; but he wants you to take over the Euboian land."

"*Me?*" I stared at him unbelievingly. "But why? He might as well offer me a ship to pilot. I've forgotten everything I knew about farming; and besides, I've my life to live."

"Cool down! He doesn't want you to farm it. Old Phileas can do it in his sleep; he's been steward for ten years. The father just thinks that a son who does such credit to us all should have a proper estate. All this has touched him in his pride, you know."

"I can see," I said, "that he doesn't want me singing in taverns for a living. Of course I don't intend to. But if one of us is to live like a landed gentleman, with a steward to do the work, it should be you, not me. The gods know, you've earned it."

"Oh, it was I put it into his head. You've never seen the Euboian farm, have you? Nor had I, before you went away." I remembered how the air at home had seemed to lighten, when our father went to visit it. "I've been over once or twice since then. It's good land, horse-pasture mostly, though the olives bear well. The plan is that it's to be your portion, and this place will be mine."

All this was slowly coming home to me. "If you say it's good, it is. But meantime, I'd be caretaking, and I need to travel."

"He knows that. I told him all about it. He's quite willing you go to the festivals to sing—or anywhere else respectable, is the way he put it! You're to draw half the yield from the place in his lifetime; and you won't be skimped on that. Look now, Sim. You'll be a famous man before you've done, that I can see; but even so, you'll live hand to mouth, unless you've something behind you. Only think of all those famous men in Ionia, and yourself for that matter; prospering one day, fugitives the next. If you'd owned some land, would you have hung on in Samos? No slavemaster like an empty belly, the saying goes."

I saw, at last, all he had done for me; and for my master, to whom I could give a home in his last years. My tongue was loosened, and I thanked him as best I could.

He was pleased, as he'd always been when I looked up to him as a child. Why not? If it was a weakness, I loved him for it and was glad to indulge it; it was a small enough return. "You see," he said, "I talked to that judge from Athens, who came to your victory feast. I asked him where a poet would do best, now Ionia's overrun, and he said, 'In Athens, if all goes well there.' He says Pisistratos looks to be settled in the tyranny for life. The people want him, most of the lords put up with him, and he's exiled the few who won't. He hasn't spilled much blood, he governs well. This man says he'll bring back the great days of Theseus."

"So he said to me. But they said the same about Poly-krates."

"Ah. But now you won't have to look for bread. Euboia's so close to Attica, it's no more than a ferry-crossing. You can live on the estate, and just go over for the festivals to show what you can do. If this is another fellow who's only for flattery and fancy-boys, never mind; you'll have seen Athens, which sounds to me worth seeing. I don't see how you can lose."

"Prokles asked me to be his guest, and said he'd show me the city. But I thought, then, that to be another tyrant's suppliant would be too much."

"Well, you'll be nobody's suppliant now. All you need

is to be civil to the father. You'll be no suppliant there; he needs it as much as you do." He did not add, "But of course he will not say so." Such things were our inheritance.

We were about to walk home, when I looked back at the midden. One of the pups we had drowned in the tub had come to life again, and was mewling and wriggling. I looked at Theas. He picked it up and put it to the dam, and it nuzzled to the dug, sucking strongly. We laughed, and went away.

3

THERE WAS MUCH to keep me on Keos. In two months, Theas was to be married. The girl he'd been betrothed to in childhood had died from fever a year or so before; and being now a man, he had claimed the right to choose this time. The maid, though not so well-dowered as our parents would have liked, was wellborn and not too poor, so they had given way with a good grace. When I was presented to her, she murmured a few shy words about my victory, eager to please any kin of his. I saw her eyes stray to him, wondering that he could be my brother and still so beautiful.

Everyone now thought I'd stay on till the wedding. I promised to be there with a wedding song, in time to teach the bridesmaids; but first I must go to Samos to see my master. He was alone, and I owed him everything.

Theas scratched his beard. It was now quite shapely, reminding me how long I'd been here. "Well, yes. It's true you ought to care for him, now he's old and past his best. But the father won't be well pleased. He meant to take you to Euboia, to see the farm."

"O Zeus!" I cried. "I *must* go. Can't I breathe without doing him some injury?"

"Come, come," said Theas. He thought this passion unbecoming; but offered comfort, just as when I'd squalled in infancy. "Things can be managed. Tell him it will dishonor the family if you neglect a benefactor. Say the old fellow is dying, and it will bring you into reproach if you're not there."

I made the averting sign, but did as he said. While I was a boy and feared my father, a stubborn pride had kept me from lying to save my skin. Now I was a man and afraid no longer, it came easily, and seemed mere good manners. After all, when I was born he could have put me out on the mountain.

Autumn was setting in; I had a rough crossing, and was glad to get into harbor. There was no one I knew on the mole, so I went straight to our lodging. The lyre-maker was at work in his shop below. At the sight of me he got up from his bench, putting his work aside. He was a cheerful man, as a rule.

"Ah, my dear Simonides, they said you would certainly be coming, and I never doubted it. He left you his goods, of course, and spoke especially of his kithara, which you have in keeping. Had he kin living, and do you know where they are? Is there anyone who ought to have his ashes, now his own city has fallen? Everyone said you would be sure to know."

After a while he said, "But you have not heard, then? I am sorry, indeed. I thought you had come to settle his affairs."

"I came to bring him home with me. When did he die?"

"Why, it would be the day you sailed he first took to his bed, or maybe the day after; and then it was four days, or maybe five."

"When I left, then, he had it on him."

"Don't take it to heart, Simonides. He said to me, and even to the wife when she brought him a sup to eat, 'I can lie up now like a lord. I told the boy it was nothing, or he'd have stayed and missed his chance.'"

I could not say to this kindly man, "I left him to die alone." I just asked if anyone had come to visit him.

"I doubt if many knew that he was sick. There was that philosopher, though, that he used to see while you were at your singing; he teaches mathematics and such. He came most days; was with him at the end, and saw to the funeral. You'll be wanting to see him; he has the urn in keeping."

"Yes; who is he?"

"He's a son of old Mnesarchos, who was a famous gem-cutter in his day. You'll find his house up the hill, just under the acropolis."

I climbed the steep way to the ancient walls, remembering how Kleobis had said he would make an offering for my victory. He had offered his lonely death, while I was being welcomed in my own city without a care. People turned their heads now and then to see me weeping; but I had nowhere to go, and had to make the best of it. When the houses thinned, I sat awhile on a hillside boulder, and covered my face to have my grief out.

Even before I left, our paths had been dividing, mine to the Victory, his to the fallen lords, and only one thing had done it: poverty. Theas had been right. If either of us had had a steady livelihood, I would not be here now, seeking a stranger who had tended and buried my friend. If he reproaches me, I thought, I must bear even that.

I wiped my eyes and set off, and stopped some men on the road to ask the way. They pointed, but looked at me strangely. Next time I had to ask, the passer-by spat and made the evil-eye sign. "Oh, mad Pythagoras. His house is just over there."

It was an old one, built of the mountain stone; not fancy-trimmed like the city ones, but cool and roomy. The court-yard door was opened by a Thracian slave, big-boned and red-haired, with a blue tattoo on his forehead. It surprised me that he did not speak in the slave-talk, but in excellent Greek. "Sir, you are Simonides of Keos? Please come inside, my master is expecting you."

Courteous, not servile, he led me through a herb garden, aromatic in the autumn sun; there was a round pavement with an upright pole in its center, and figures carved round its edge. A long measuring-cord came down from the top of the pole and was wound about a cleat; I had seen such things among the Ephesian mathematicians, who claim they can measure mountains with them, or some such matter. The slave paused a moment to see where the shadow of the pole was falling. He was plainly dressed, but in a good fine cloth. In Keos, one could have worn such stuff oneself.

He scratched at a door and opened it. "Here is Simonides, sir, the friend of Kleobis."

The room went right across the ground floor, and was full of things: shelves of books and scrolls and writing-tablets; tables of mathematicians' toys, cubes and cones and spheres and cylinders. One wall was whitened, and drawn all over with figures, and with squares and triangles made of blocks of numbers. There was a stand with a great astrolabe upon it; and in the middle, getting the best light, a long table laden with musical instruments, at which a man was sitting tuning a lyre. He laid it aside, and rose.

He was very tall, his black hair and beard hardly touched with grey. Under his heavy brows were large eyes with brilliant whites showing all round the iris. One could not look away from them. I should think I could have counted ten while he stood there without a word, fixing me with these strange eyes; then suddenly he came around his work-table, and embraced me as if we were old friends meeting after many years. I remembered the man on the road, but could not feel that he was dangerous.

"Come, rest; we can talk when you have eaten." I had taken no breakfast, in my haste to be off the ship, and nothing since, but had not known I was hungry. I took the chair he offered. His lyre was a fine old one of polished tortoiseshell, with arms of slender horn and a bridge of ivory. The slave, uncalled, brought wine and raisin-cakes; my host took them and served them to me himself.

"Rest," he said again, and picking up the lyre played on it softly. The intervals were new to me, and strange, yet soothing. Presently he laid it down. "We often talked of you, Kleobis and I. Now that I see you, I no longer doubt that you were his son. A good son, too. You have no memory of it?"

I now saw why they thought him mad. "Certainly," I said to humor him, "he gave me a father's care." He had suffered enough, I thought, without a lunatic to trouble his last hours.

"No matter. The Sight is rare. But the bonds of souls are for all men, as for every creature. Leave, when you can, your honorable grief. I foresee that you will live long. Even before your soul departs its present habitation, his in its new one may return, and you can repay your debt to him, as he, you may be sure, repaid to you some ancient kindness. In such ways we lift each other towards the light."

I began to understand him. At the tavern I'd heard of such beliefs, though only by way of joking. I just said that the landlord had spoken of his goodness to my master, for which I would be forever in his debt.

"It was a new bond to me. But now it is tied, the threads

will cross again. I shall be the better for it, and I hope he also."

"I was told, sir, that you have his ashes. It troubles me that the barbarians have his city, and I cannot give him a tomb among his kindred."

"It does not trouble him, you may be sure. But take for friendship's sake, if you wish, what remains of his outworn garment. He himself will have come already before the Judges, and heard their counsel; and knowing his soul's needs will have chosen his next life."

"He must be honored somewhere with a tomb. You have more right than I to bury him; do you wish to do it?"

"No, for his tomb would be untended here, which would cause you sorrow. I am leaving Samos, and shall not return; at least, not in this body."

I asked if Polykrates had exiled him. "That would have come, I think. Till lately, the Tyrant hasn't troubled himself about mad Pythagoras." For the first time he smiled. "But now he begins to hear that I and my friends are studying harmony."

"So? But he prides himself on being a patron of the arts."

"Not ours. We look for music, first in the heavens"—he pointed to the astrolabe—"then on earth in the laws of its creatures, chiefly in man; in himself, in his dealings with his fellows, in his body politic. That is as displeasing to tyrants as a doctor's advice to a drunkard. Well, we have work to do, which we need to pursue in peace. There is a piece of coastal land in Italy, good land unused; I traveled there to find it. My students are coming with me. He will be glad to see us go."

"That's a long way." It seemed to me the further edge of the world.

"This is an age of tyrants. They warn each other about men like me. In Kroton they will not trouble us."

"But, if you are founding a colony, what will you do for women?"

"Why, bring my students; there will be enough of each kind. The women have been men and will be men again, as you and I have been women. What is that, but a station along the way?"

"If you are selling up," I said, "and want a buyer for your slave, I shall be glad to hear your price. Don't fear I shall give him rough work, I can see he is above that. I promise to treat him well."

"That I do not doubt. But I am giving Zamolxis his freedom, to return to his own people. He has been a good pupil; it is time he began to teach. Besides, it is in my mind that his time of penance is over."

His eyes had fixed in his head, the white gleaming round the iris; bright eyes, not blind, and yet unseeing. With any other man, I should have thought it was a fit, and called for help. As it was, I would have gone away quietly, but had not been given the urn. I waited, wondering how long these turns might last with him, and whether I should tell the slave, so that he could be looked after. I was afraid to wake him myself. However, the shadows on the floor had hardly moved, before he came calmly to himself, and smiled at me.

"Forgive me. The Sight chooses its own time. When the door opens, even on the same day of the same life, there is always something new. Just now I tasted the food he shared with me."

He paused, and I was afraid he would go off again. "Yes?" I said.

"I mean Zamolxis. That is one of my strongest bonds. I was an Egyptian, a child—I know Egypt in this life, and much came back to me. My father took me on his ship to trade in Tyre. We were seized by pirates; Zamolxis was the captain. My father fought and was killed, escaping slavery;

they threw him dying overboard. I ran to the one man I saw taking no part in this, not knowing that only his rank prevented him. I clasped his knees and begged him to save me. He was pitiful, and chose me for part of his spoils; for his pleasure, the others thought, but he did no harm to me. Once, in a calm, I taught him the common writing, and once in a storm he comforted me. In the end he put me ashore, in a place that is now unknown to me, where I had kindred. Someday I may come upon it.

"Well, that is the cause of his present life. For the blood he had shed and the people he had enslaved, he had to make reparation; he was enslaved as a boy, to a hard master in these parts. I passed by—not by chance, you can be sure, although it seemed so—and heard him crying under the whip; and the Sight came to me, and I knew my debt. For ten years he has shared my studies; I took him to Egypt with me, when I went to the temple schools. He knows the motions of the stars, and the properties of plants. In all these years, he has not shed the blood of a living creature; he knows they are souls which have been men, or will be. Now he shall go to the Getai, from whom he came, in the country north of the Ister. As in his former life he brought death and darkness, in this he will bring life and light."

I thought to myself that he talked like a poet, and wondered what he sang. As to his tale, I could tell that he believed in it; but it seemed a waste of a good slave. He'll just be one more cattle-raiding tribesman, I thought, within half a year.

However, I replied as I thought he'd wish; and shortly after, he gave me the funeral urn; a beautiful piece, Corinthian, painted with lions and flowers. Later, I made a tomb for it in Euboia, carved with this epitaph: *I was Kleobis of Ephesos, till my city was possessed by the long-haired Mede. But my songs remain, and will abide his going.*

From time to time, I heard news of Pythagoras and his

school in Italy. Lately, when I was traveling to Syracuse, my ship put in at Kroton. He was dead by then, but I talked to some citizens, who honor him next the gods and keep all his laws. They live more plainly even than Keans, but from devotion rather than harshness; to me they were very courteous, and brought me to some old men who had known the founder well. I asked whether they'd ever heard anything of a freed slave called Zamolxis. Yes indeed, they said; he was still alive, and honored by the Getai as their greatest sage. Two kings in turn had appointed him prophet and counselor to the people. He lived in a cave, keeping his master's laws and preaching his philosophy. The Getai, who had been great hunters, now killed no living thing, and were known to the tribes around as Milk-Eaters.

ATHENS

1

I LIVED THREE or four years in Euboia, before my father died.

Every month or so, I used to cross over to show him the farm accounts: so many horses sold in Attica, the yield of olives or oil or barley. The steward told me, and I wrote it down; my memory is for words, not numbers. I would bring my father his half-share, and give him the mainland news; and, if he asked me, would tell him where I had performed.

I came, if I could, to the chief Kean festivals, and the games. One year I had my wish, and made Theas a victory song when he won the wrestling. At first I was still just Leoprepes' son, home on a visit. Later, things began to change. He let it be seen that I no longer disgraced the family; but I don't remember his ever praising a song.

The farm had had a wing thrown out, for Theas and his wife and their two handsome children, boy and girl. Philomache and her Midylos were still childless. His father Bacchylides, who had been a great athlete in his day, fretted about it more than he did. "We're both young yet," he said. "I don't believe she's barren." He had too much courtesy to tell her brother that he'd sired healthy bastards himself. "And even if she were, I'd sooner have a woman

who pleases me than a fool farrowing fools." She had a
bloom on her, and it seemed he suited her too.

Each year I traveled to the greater festivals as they fell
due, the Isthmia, or the Olympics, the Nemea, the Panathenaia; sang in the contests, and sometimes hymned the
victors. I have always enjoyed the challenge of a victory
hymn. One can't know beforehand who the victor will
be of any event, nor which victor is going to hire one.
Besides which, only one bard can win a singing contest, and
one may have one's work for nothing but applause; but a
victory ode means money.

The rest of the year I shared between Euboia, where I
had my house, and Athens, where I had my hopes.

In these first years, it was Euboia mostly. It is a god-
frequented land, with woody gorges and chestnut-shaded
hills. In the mountain villages, or along the shore away
from the big harbors, old men will tell you tales which
Achilles may well have heard at Cheiron's knee. They have
that smell of great age one can't mistake, like old green
bronze. I made my Lament of Danae there, because of a
song I heard a woman sing as she turned the quern.

The land had been in our family time out of mind. We
had been Euboians, till two generations back, when my
great-grandfather was on the losing side in the Lelantine
War. He'd been a great landowner down in the plain; when
that was gone he retired to Keos, and lived on the place
which had been his Kean wife's dowry, and where I was
born. My father used to say the Euboian land I farmed
was just a smallholding, compared with the ancient glories.
But I wanted a living, not a fortune, which I hoped to find
for myself; and I lived there very well.

The farm is in the hills near Dystos, east of Swallow
Lake, on a slope that faces Attica. It's a short ride down
to the coast, where any boatman will run you across to

Rhamnos. From there it's an easy journey to Athens, between the heights of Parnes and Hymettos. I used to keep
a mule stabled with a Rhamnos farmer; starting early, I
could be in Athens by noon.

Old Phileas, the steward, was worth his weight in gold.
He set me free. When I first came, he made me about as
welcome as a conquering Mede. He was a square, slow-
moving countryman, full of grumbles, straight out of
Hesiod. I soon saw his sullenness did not come from fear
of having petty misdeeds found out; he was afraid I'd spoil
his good work with ignorant meddling. The land was
tended, the slaves were well trained and fed, the horses
sleek. I saw what this would mean to me, and took more
trouble to sweeten him than I've done with many a prince;
rode round the estate with him, praised this or that (it was
wonderful how my boyhood lore came back to me) and
told him my father had advised me to lean on his ex-
perience. He softened; though he grumbled still that the
master would have nothing changed from his own father's
day, and if the horse-pasture was put under corn it would
bring in as much again. However, I was now his audience
and not his theme.

He found me a good maid to cook for me and keep house,
a freewoman, cheerful, black-haired and ruddy, who, when
she sang about the place, did it in tune. One day, when he
came with his morning business, he looked about at the
room, remarked on the well-kept furniture, and, gazing at
the sideboard, said, "That Dorothea, she's a rare admiration for you."

I pricked an ear. Noting he had a kindness for her, I took
it they were bedmates, and had not presumed on bright
smiles and dainty cooking.

"She's a good girl; whose daughter is she?"

He scratched his ear. "Well, sir, that's a question. She's

known as Smikros the pilot's daughter, but he claimed he'd
been a two-month at sea when she was got. Then he
drowned in a squall off Rhenaia, so it was all one to
him. But it's stood in her way, and the offers she's had
weren't fit for her. She reckons she's well placed where she
is."

His eye enlightened me. "Well," I said, "I daresay she's
not been without a father's care, whoever he may be. I
think she and I will get on well together."

I was right in this. Of course I was not the first; she took
it easily, as something we had both been expecting. Her
cheerful friendliness went on much the same; she felt that
she was now in her proper place, and could manage things
more to my advantage. When I offered to buy a slave for
her, she said she liked things done her own way, and would
never have the patience to stand over some clumsy slut.
She was the best-natured of girls, teaching me her old work
songs, but always quiet when I was making a song myself.
She bore no bastards—the women of the island have their
ways—and it startled me when one night, as she was taking
off her gown, she asked me whom I was betrothed to.

"Why, to no one. I would never have lived with you, and
kept such a thing to myself."

"Wouldn't you, Sim? One never knows with the gentry.
Every time you've been over to Keos, I've wondered if you'd
come back with a bride."

She did not mean it. She well knew I'd have told her;
she just liked to hear it said. But, though I could say it,
there were other things best said, too.

"My little quail, I'm not only not betrothed, I left home
just to avoid it. But . . ."

"Oh, you will." She had folded her gown, and stood up
with her hands on her firm white hips. "You'll want a son
to leave the place to, and then you'll do it. Don't make me

promises, or I might not take it so well." She was smiling; she had her pride.

"Get into bed, or you'll come out in gooseflesh. I'm not one for promises. Anything can happen to anyone; I saw that in Ionia. Men born in riches have ended up washing a Persian's floors. But long ago I made my mind up not to marry, and I don't expect to change it. You're all I need in a woman, my honeycomb. I wish I were all you need in a man."

She laughed and reached her hand out; but I took it in mine. "No, wait. Poets are traveling men. And I've barely begun my travels."

"Why, for sure you must travel, Sim. I know that. It's like seeing the great cities myself, to hear you come back and tell of them. While you're gone I can get the cheeses made, and the house turned out, and set something up on the loom."

"Like Penelope," I said. I wanted her to understand.

"Oh no, Sim. No hangers-on for me. My father would soon see *them* to rights."

"Penelope had a long time to wait. That's what I meant." Her hand fell quiet. I said, "Once a poet has made a name, he looks for a patron. And a patron wants his favored poet to be his house-guest most of the year."

"I've heard of that." She was thoughtful, not angry. "But this is good land. *You'll* never need to eat another man's bread."

"Not from want, no. That's why this land was given me. But I must go where I'll be heard."

"Yes, Sim," she said, and lay thinking. I blamed myself for not having talked of all this before. Most people I met needed no telling.

"Praise-singing is like love," I said. "You do it from the heart, or you're a whore. If a man I despise invites me, I can say no, and wait for someone better. But one day it will come. If you feel it's no life for you here alone, waiting for me to visit when I can, then I'll give you a dower, and find some old grannie to keep the house for me."

"You'll keep the place? You'll not sell it?" She was her father's child, both feet firm on the ground.

"No indeed; it's family land."

"Why then, what kind of fool do you take me for? I've a good home and a good man; and what's more, I'm respected now. You don't know how it was sometimes in the village. But now, there's many women married to sailors, or men who've gone off to fight for pay in foreign wars, would be glad to change with me. They've the cold bed, and hunger with it; and mostly their man won't make a name to bring them credit. If you've kept from marrying so that no one can blame you for being long away, that's fair dealing. You'll get no scolding here, Sim. We're folk who fill each other's needs."

Ah well. I'm glad I can bring back those old Euboian days, and Dorothea when she was young. As for Athens, that comes back like yesterday.

It has all gone, now. Oh yes, they will be making it very fine. By the time they're done, *my* Athens will be nothing to it. At one time, they were vowing they'd keep the High City just as the Medes had left it, to witness their impiety. They soon got tired of that, as who would not; but one learns not to talk sense to men at such a time. When they came round, they resolved at least not to mend what the barbarians had defiled with blood and fire. It can all go for rubble, to fill in the new foundations or raise the bastions up. Then they will build their victory ode in marble. Well, they have the right.

Aischylos was in Sicily a few years back—turned fifty, which I can hardly credit yet—and said to me over a jar of Etna wine, "It was you, Simonides, who first opened my ear to song. But it was those days that taught me tragedy."

I could not keep from smiling. "If you mean what I think, son of Euphorion, in those days you were ten years old."

"True, master of memory. And what I saw has mixed with what I've heard, most of all from you; and those again with what my mind's eye has made of them. It's all one cloth now, I shall never tease out the threads. But it taught me tragedy, all the same."

"Yes. I can understand it. You grew up knowing the end, as your audience knows when the play begins that it will end with Agamemnon dead. But when you were ten I was forty; when I first saw Athens, your father was hardly born. The end came to us from a bright noon sky."

He sat staring out through the porch towards the harbor, knitting his fair thick brows above his beaky nose; a strong man still, whose greatest pride is that he fought at Marathon. I could see him setting the ancient tale to his own sonorous music. No, he never knew the lyric years.

There was building then, too. I suppose it is all forgotten now. The new High City is to be for the gods alone; no human ruler shall have a stronghold there any more. It will be a dedication of the people, a pledge of freedom from Medes and tyrants. A great conception. I shan't live to see even the first stones laid. It's half ruin still, half builders' yard.

The Medes burned the gatehouse. By the time they'd cleared the fallen timbers, it was just as I remembered it when I first set foot there; a gap in the oldest wall, that the old men called King Theseus' Gate. Like enough he would have had one there. The stones were dark with time, mottled with lichen, and with ancient stains which they used to call the blood of the Amazons. The threshold was sunny, and lizards lived there.

From this dark entry, you came out into gleaming light.
(The Mysteries teach us the power of that.) Much was
brand-new, but everything seemed to be, it was kept so
bright, the bronzes shining like gold, the paint on the
marble never left to fade. Yet in all the splendor there was
something welcoming, homelike; nothing on the great
hubristic Samos scale. There were the comings and goings
of a great house, not a palace; though the Athenians always
said that the Palace of Erechtheus used to stand on that
very site where the Archon built.

He was always called *The* Archon. Polykrates, who lived
close to Asia, never made any bones about being Tyrant.
But Pisistratos was all Athenian; he respected custom and
the form of law. There were still nine Archons, even though
most were his kin and all of them his supporters. His big
old house next the Erechthid shrine, though very handsome inside, made no outward show of opulence. It took
me two years to get through the door.

They were pleasant years, though, visiting other cities, or
staying with Athenian guest-friends such as Prokles and
people I'd met through him. When the lyre went round
with the wine, I would have some little thing ready, a lyric,
or a skolion on events. Those lyres! Never in tune, passed
on by some man whose hands were calloused with the
bridle or the disk. Not that anyone cared, it was the song
they wanted, and it would have been conceited in a young
foreign guest to bring his own instrument along. After a
while, though, the lyres improved, because I began to be
handed them first, before they had been ill-treated.

Then at the Feast of Athene—the yearly one, not the
Great—I entered the contest for the choral odes.

In Keos, men do not sing at supper; it is better to choose
one's choir from boys who can still be taught. But in
Athens, men sing from their youth and keep it up. I used
men that first time, and have done there ever since.

We put on our fresh white robes and our wreaths of
wool and olive-sprays, and went up to the High City in the
late summer heat to wait in the temple forecourt. Before
our turn came, I looked at the seats of honor. In the midst
sat the Priestess of Athene on the highest throne, between
the priests of Zeus and of Apollo. Then came the priests
of the other gods, and next to them the Archons.

Pisistratos had the right-hand place, with a small respectful space around his chair; but one could have picked him
out without it. He was already past seventy, and Theodoros
could have carved him for a Zeus. Tall and still straight,
fresh-faced, with hair and beard of a pure shining silver,
and bright unfaded blue eyes, he was handsome even now,
and must have been remarkable when he was young. He
had a festal wreath on, of gold leaves with a few real ones
stuck in for modesty; and his white robe had a gold border,
but not too much. I compared this regal dignity with Polykrates' new-rich showiness, and could see why the Archon
had never been without a following, whether he was in or
out. He was listening, I noticed, to the present singers, like
a man who knows what he is hearing.

Our turn came. I stepped up between the spotted lions
by the terrace steps. My choir knew their order and moved
into it neatly. One expects that nowadays; then, one often
saw choirs jostling about, even arguing aloud about where
to stand. I bowed to the High Priestess—here was no
Polykrates who'd expect to be noticed first—took in the
other hierophants with a general reverence, and made the
Archon my homage. He responded gravely; I was reminded
of Zeus in the *Iliad*, shaking his ambrosial locks to a slight
sound of thunder. Yet it never quite lost a human courtesy.
I lifted my wand to the flautist (one must always praise
Athene with the flute, which was her own invention) and
began to sing.

The ode was about Athene's help to Perseus when he

killed the Gorgon; how she borrowed for him Hermes'
winged sandals and his sword, and Hades' hood of in-
visibility, and set him on his way. For all this I praised her;
but I ended praising Perseus, because when he became a
king, still owning Medusa's deadly head, he hid it underground, making a dedication of his power to justice.

No doubt the Archon had had plenty of such tributes; in
his long career it was agreed he had deserved them. One
look had told me he had too much dignity to let compliments decide a contest for him; on the other hand, my choir
had sung clearly and in tune, and I thought my ode was
better than the others. As it turned out, he and the other
judges thought so too. I was awarded a fine bronze tripod
with gilded rings for handles, and a white bull with gilded
horns. The Priestess of Athene declared me winner; the
victory chariot was led up, and the men of my choir, as
they pulled me around the precinct, sang me a paean.

Later, I got to know that painted chariot like my own
chair at home. I have stood in it some fifty times. The
Medes burned it, of course. I have a ring from its yoke-pole,
bent with heat, which someone picked up among the ruins
and gave me for a memento, saying I had ridden it oftener
than anyone else. Yet I can still recall the wonder of that
first time, and how I said to myself, not that I had pleased
the Archon—I had forgotten even that—but that I was at
last a victor in Athens.

After my sacred ride, I was led back to Pisistratos, who
said what he had doubtless said a hundred times before
with equal graciousness. He added that he hoped it would
not be long before he and his friends had the pleasure of
hearing me again.

The man next him said a few words of assent, which
surprised me till I saw the likeness. This must be Hippias,
the eldest son. He was then a little over forty. Beside his

father, he put one in mind of a famous statue, copied by a sculptor not quite so good. I said what one ought, wondering, as I went, whether the words about hearing me again were spoken every time, or whether they were worth something.

My prize beast was duly sacrificed at the altar before the porch, the priestesses' portion delivered to the temple servants, the rest of the meat carried to my host's house for the victory feast. For the first time I saw the trophy head of a victory bull, mine, hung in its garlands above the door.

My host was Prokles; he had asked everyone he knew. After having found me in Keos when nobody had heard of me, he was naturally pleased that he had backed a winner. The supper-couches went all around the wall; he had borrowed from half his guests.

All the Athenian poets had been invited. No doubt they said to each other what losers say of winners, some of which is sometimes true; but they were far more civil than I had hoped for, and, indeed, we had some very good talk about our craft. After the wine and the garlands had come in, guests wandered from couch to couch, greeting friends or getting acquainted with strangers. To me it was all delight; the first time in my life, I think, when I forgot that I was ugly.

The hour came when people drift in after leaving other parties, and a well-trained doorkeeper will tell unwanted ones that the drinking is over. Once or twice I heard the discordant singing going off down the street. Then suddenly there were laughing voices, the doorman was all civility, and my host got so swiftly to the door, one wondered how he did it without running.

Four or five men came in. The leader was a little over thirty, of middle height, graceful and slender, dressed with the greatest elegance in a robe of fine-combed wool dyed light green, and scarlet sandals buckled with gold. His hair was dressed in the latest style, bound round his head in two plaits, with a curled fringe combed down in front over the ends, as neat as if done in gold wire. His face, though it would not have inspired a sculptor, was comely, and seemed from liveliness handsomer than it was. He was clean-shaved, which you don't see today. Then, many young men of rank kept it up well into their thirties; it's a fashion which has disappeared, like others now thought to smack of aristocracy. His friends, though outshone by him, were very much in his style. Since my host, whose couch I had been sharing, had gone to greet him, I turned to my neighbor to ask who he might be.

He, and the next man, both fixed their eyes on me in wonder. It was as if I had pointed to the moon, and asked what was that light. "Why," said the nearer one, "that is Hipparchos"; and the other, seeing me still no wiser, added, "The Archon's second son."

He swept into the room with his little troop behind him, waving a greeting here and there. Unlike his elder brother, he had not their father's face; no doubt he took after the mother's side. Of course I had heard of him; no one could have been entertained in Athens even once without that. If my mind had not been on other things, I should not have been so slow. As it was, I had barely time to collect myself before he reached me.

"Ah!" he cried, embracing Prokles and me in a single smile, "we are still in time! I have been urging these fellows through the streets as though we were on a training run, to be here before the victor picks up the lyre."

I was presented, and he praised my ode. He was the first to mention the lines that I had liked best myself. (There is praise, after all, which makes one wonder what one did wrong, to have caught the fancy of such a fool.) A handsome laughing young fellow beside him, with dark hair hanging in long crimped lovelocks, said, "Don't forget Mother's message."

"I was coming to it, brother. She said the ode was very fine and made splendid music. I will add for myself, to spare their modesty, that my sisters said just the same. Thessalos expects me to forget everything I'm charged with, I don't know why."

Despite their different looks, there was a likeness in their movements and their way of speech, as if they were a good deal together. They and their friends were all found places on the couches; there was a sense of precedence, but without formality, which one could see was the style of their set. Fresh wreaths appeared for all; our host, provident man, must have been prepared for this visitation. The wine went round again. Then the cry began for a song.

I had known enough to be ready for this. At one's victory feast, one can sing whatever one chooses; and some people always expect something in the style of one's competition piece. But it is unwise to give it them. The solemn precinct, the great audience, the thought of the famous bards who have stood in that place before one, the men of one's choir all tuned like one's lyre to concert pitch: one can offer only a shadow of all this, singing solo in a private room. Part of our craft is a sense of the occasion.

There was a song I had made in Samos, and never had the heart to sing; not even to my master, for whom it would have gone too near the bone. It came from long brooding on the changefulness of human fortune, of fate and chance, and the folly of counting on anything beyond the moment. Now that the wheel had turned again for me and come bright side up, I knew that I could sing it.

> *The heroes too of old,*
> *   Sired by the gods our masters,*
> *Knew ere their days were told,*
> *   Their perils and disasters.*

All things are from the gods, I ended; when they send us joy, let us catch it as it flies, for who would choose life without it? Not even kings, not even the immortals.

The new guests made a very courteous audience. It must have been their second party that night, if not their third, and none of them were sober; but they listened quietly, applauded as if they knew what they had heard, and said some very graceful things. After that the lyre went round, and we all sang skolions. Though Hipparchos made himself lord of the revels and could almost have been the host, he was never insolent, and Prokles seemed flattered, rather than not.

A few places along, a man was sharing his couch with a handsome youth, with whom he had arrived. Between the songs, as people moved here and there, Thessalos went up, and asked the youth to move for a moment, as he had some news to give his friend. He got down, and was beginning to look about, when Hipparchos called, "Oh, my dear Kleinias, my brother wants a lesson. Come here and take his place, and let him find one where he can." The youth went over with a smile—he could have done nothing else, without looking surly—while Thessalos talked charmingly to the older friend. Hipparchos, laughing at first, grew serious and confiding. Once I saw the brothers catch each other's eye. It seemed they were loyal allies.

Prokles, returning to our couch from going among the guests, said in my ear, "He has paid you a great compliment, coming like this with the most select of his friends. As a rule, when he looks in at a party, he brings some flute-girls to play."

"No boys?" I asked, having used my eyes.

"Oh no. That matter he takes seriously."

I glanced that way. He did not look as if he pledged his soul in the cup; but I guessed what Prokles meant. "A matter between gentlemen?"

"Just so. A matter of pride, I fancy."

No need for more. The old nobility of Attica, like that of Sparta, looked back to the Sons of Homer. Women were for pastime; but your young friend must be someone you met in the gymnasium, not the whorehouse; someone whose father your father knew, who would lock shields with you or ride at your side in war. And no house went further back than the Pisistratids.

A few songs later, they left in a little breeze of gay goodbyes. Hipparchos took Prokles by both shoulders, and thanked him prettily for putting up with their invasion. "You must blame your own good company, and the gifted friends it brings you. Here's one whom I hope to share." He turned to me, with a boyish and modest grace. "I must put in my claim before all Athens gets ahead of me. Will you sup with us three days from now, and let us hear you sing again?"

I expect I accepted civilly as I'd been trained to do; when he had gone, I felt I must have stared at him like an oaf. Prokles rushed back from seeing him off to grasp my hand and cry, "You're made, my boy! You're made!"

He called for a toast to my success, and everyone drank, even the rival poets. There was only one silent man: the one whose supper-couch Thessalos had been sharing. He sat alone now; the handsome youth who had come with him was missing. But at any big Athenian party, trifles like that are no more than common form.

2

OFTEN, in those Athenian days, I asked myself, Why did I wait so long? I am twenty-five; I could have had all this much sooner. If I had gone to Keos when Kleobis first urged me to, and sung before my father, I could have won a crown there—I was good enough for that—and he'd have given me the Euboian farm. My master would not have wasted his health and hope in Samos; I would have gone to Athens, and found that the land was peaceful, and gone again. All I have now, I could have been heir to years ago.

I don't suppose I would have been crowned there any sooner; my work had ripened and that was all. But I could have been making friends, hearing songs, seeing the craft-work, sharing the talk, living the rich life of this city which put out the fruit of men's minds as an old vine gives its grapes in a good year.

From the day of that first supper in Hipparchos' house, I was Athenian in my heart, so far as a wanderer belongs to any city. All I had lost in Ionia was here, distilled and refined; the painted walls, the slender-legged tables, the couches with their fine embroidered cushions, the clean well-mannered boys who served food and wine; everywhere elegance, nowhere ostentation. No flaunting Samian gold-work; but, exquisitely painted, the first service in red-figure I'd ever seen. Or, for that matter, the Athenian diners either—yes, that would make men smile today! It was Hipparchos who had inspired it.

Answering our compliments, he said, "I was in Exekias' shop. He painted me that wine-cooler, which I don't think will displease me however fashions change. That day, however, I was there to order a small dedication to Eros." The handsome youth (a new one) who shared his couch, returned his glance with charm, but no vulgar simpering, and touched his wine-cup, doubtless inscribed with "The Beautiful" and his name. "I had attended to that, and was idling about the shop, when I heard the master roaring at a pupil who'd been working, it seemed, industriously in his corner. People say my curiosity will be the death of me someday." He turned on us his winning smile. "So I went over, in time to hear the culprit told that if he thought he had all day to spend in foolery, he had better make room for someone else who'd value his place. By now, I was craning over Exekias' shoulder. The young man was holding an oil-jar, on which he'd drawn a Greek and a Phrygian dueling. As you'll have guessed, he had amused himself by painting the background black, and reserving the figures. It was the very best Ilissos clay, that bakes a soft glowing red. Seeing Exekias just about to dash it to the ground, or maybe at his pupil's head, I caught back his arm, crying, 'Fire it! Fire it, my friend, and let us see. And don't have a brush laid on that cup I ordered, until I have had a look.'"

His friend toasted him in it, very tastefully; he was not merely presentable but exceedingly well-bred.

"And, after that, nothing would content me but to set something of the kind before all my friends. If you care for them, pay me the compliment of accepting them and taking them home."

Of course nothing else was talked of, as men showed their cups to one another. Thessalos's, which was lewd but witty, was passed right round the room. I am sure not a guest but was at a potter's next morning; in no time at all the young Psiax, whose fortune had been made in that one evening, had set up his own shop. My cup had Apollo on his tripod, playing the lyre; I kept it forty years, till some fool of a porter broke it.

Hipparchos was a host whom guests were eager to please. But he neither asked, nor got, the crude sycophancy of Samos. He had much more to confer than gold. Polykrates' courtiers grew rich, but were held in contempt and envy; Hipparchos could bestow esteem. His patronage was a prize to any artist, not just a living. Fashions he set were not seen later to have been foolish; when they came to be denounced, it was long after, for other reasons. Accepted by him, you were acceptable anywhere in Athens, as I quickly learned. When the wine-cups had been admired, he called on me to sing, making it seem that those trifles had been just an appetizer, this was the banquet.

I had never sung better than on that night, and knew it. The very images of the tale shone brighter in my head. The god-wrought armor of Achilles burned; the river-god he wrestled with was a great sinuous giant with transparent blue limbs and hair of stiff green rushes whose lice were silver fish. Much of it I improvised as my mind was quickened. Luckily I remembered it after.

Above all other talents, Hipparchos had the bright and perilous gift of making others shine. It was his paternal heritage, the only share he had been endowed with. For, of course, he could have possessed the graces of a god without getting where he was, if his father had not made his way secure.

It was my luck to be just in time for Pisistratos. I have always been glad not to have missed a man so remarkable and, as I still think, great. Soon after, as old age crept on him, he began to fail a little; but at that time, he was still what he had been, and one could understand how he had

done what he had. It was no lie when I sang of him that
he was a Perseus who had buried the Gorgon's head.

The first time he sent for me was soon after Hipparchos'
party. He did not keep late hours; as I went up, the orna-
ments on the temple roofs still caught a gleam of sun. The
stone house with its marble portico had an unforced
dignity, and some parts looked very old. Maybe it was true
that bits of King Theseus' palace had been taken into it.

There were no guards outside; he no longer needed them
as in his early days. The tale was that he got them by
trickery then, showing himself and his mule-team bleeding
from an ambush no one else saw, and asking the Council
for the right to protect himself. They only had clubs at
first, till his private army was ready and the spears came
out. I daresay it was true.

The house was spacious inside, and gravely rich, the
anteroom floored with yellow marble laid like a honeycomb.
There was a big Persian wall-hanging, and on a green marble
stand an old bronze lion, solid-cast, masterly. The chamberlain who placed us in the guest-room was well polished;
so were the couches and tables and sideboards, mellow with
beeswax and good slaves. It all looked, like its master, to
have been there a long time without getting frowsty. From
the way he greeted me, I could have been among the
highest-ranking of his guests. I thought of Samos. I suppose
from that moment he had my love.

The eight double couches made a big party, for him; he
liked to have each guest in talking reach. Dancers and flute-
girls and jugglers he never used, saying they were for men
without conversation. But he was a lover of the Muses and
good above all to poets. As I learned later, it was for my
sake he had filled up his room that night, to get me known
and make me feel myself valued. As a mark of honor, he
had put me on the couch of Hippias, his eldest son.

He was a grave and civil person, but the only one of the family without ease of manner; when he ran out of talk, he would include us in his father's, so that I heard a good deal of it. I should think, if he'd chosen, the old man could have been a poet. He had always the right word for everyone; and the poet who can improvise is always halfway to fortune. He could meet men on their own ground too, where they felt at home. I can even see him as one of those newfangled actors who go off masked as Hektor, to come back as sweet-voiced Helen. (The skill of those young men Aischylos brought along here!)

The gods, in kindness to mankind, have put in most men's hearts the wish to be loved and honored, even when they greatly wish for power. Power is the test. Some, once they have it, are content to buy the show of liking, and punish those who withhold it; then you have a despot. But some keep a true eye for how they seem to others, and care about it, which holds them back from much mischief. He was such a one. He had commanded men, and been admired by them; he had won the city's wars with them, and been admired by the Athenians. Long before that, it was said he'd been admired by Solon the Good himself, who in fact had been his lover. In a song I made later for his birthday, I likened him to a siren. He took it very well, though, as everyone knows, not every seaman who heard the sirens sing went safe home after.

That night, however, I gave him my Lament of Danae. I had been working a long time on it, but no one had heard it yet, except Dorothea. She was not given to easy tears, but it had made her cry; and, indeed, over the years I have seen that those who weep have not been always women. The sound works with the feeling, and seemed to come of itself, I don't know how. She sings it at sea, drifting in the chest with her god-got child. I have often wondered why it should be a chest; but I always respect tradition. *My child, in my grief you sleep, a gleam in the night . . .*

From respect to their host, they would have had to listen in silence. All the same, I soon knew that it was I who held them.

When we were leaving and paying our respects, the Archon said to me, "Simonides, you have painted the walls of my memory; I shall gaze often at your Danae. I should like to hear it again in a little while . . . A man like you, I expect, knows all of Homer?"

"Yes, sir. Since I was eighteen years old. I had a good teacher."

"Good. You shall help us rescue him. We will talk about it later."

Tall cressets lighted us down the steps, and each had his own linkboy to see him home. Not a word had been said about money; that came next morning, with a courteous message, and bettered my expectations. Whatever politicians say nowadays, that house was eupatrid as far as you could trace it back. They claimed to come down from Melanthos King of Athens, and through him from Nestor, and no one thought it absurd.

Before long he sent for me again, in the morning this time. He was sitting at a table of dark polished wood, set out with tablets and scrolls. Hipparchos was beside him; the first time I'd ever seen them together. There was a clerk at another table, with writing things.

Father and son smiled at me, and waved me to a chair. I felt at once that this was the son whose company was enjoyed the most, with whom the father felt easiest; yet with whom he was watchful, from a habit of ruling men.

"Hipparchos tells me," he said, "that your good memory is famous. I hope that you can help us. Next year is the Great Panathenaia, and we shall be holding the Rhetors'

Contest. It always takes time to choose which to invite, and find out where they are traveling, and get word to them to come."

I bowed gravely; or so I thought. Sometime later, Hipparchos told me that I looked down my nose. No poet has much time for rhetors; mere learners by rote, market-place reciters, who have their Hektor's Farewell, or Cave of Polyphemos, or Arming of Achilles, which they give each time, or sometimes two bits that they stitch together with lame frayed lines of their own devising.

"I should like you," he said, "to join my son as one of the judges."

"I am honored, sir." Which was true, as far as it went. "Are they to be judged for their declamation?"

"Well, we must take that into account, of course. But the reason we are offering a talent of silver as the prize is . . . but let Hipparchos tell you, since I can see him fidgeting to talk."

"It all began," he said, "when we were living in Thrace, after the Alkmaionids had broken with us and joined the enemy party, and we had to leave in a hurry." He lifted an eyebrow at me, to see if I knew the story, which he could hardly retail just now. Of course I did, old though it was; Pisistratos had sealed an alliance with this powerful clan by marrying the chief's daughter, had been polite in bed, but taken care not to get her pregnant. He'd wanted no rival heirs to his elder sons, especially from a family accursed for killing suppliants in sanctuary. In time the girl's mother asked her questions, the virgin bride was snatched back in outrage, and the feud began. I returned Hipparchos' glance discreetly, to tell him I'd heard all this.

"We were digging for gold," he said, "which Mount Pangaios is full of, and recruiting warriors, which Thrace is full of, and biding our time. Since none of us were digging with our own hands—the Thracians would always

sell us their tribal enemies—Father was often short of
pastime, and when a rhapsodist came our way he was glad
to hear of it. In Thrace, I can tell you, a dancing ape is an
event. The rhetors spread the news that we paid well, and
soon we were getting more of them . . . Well, you will
guess what is coming."

"Bad stitching," I said.

"Just so. Not only between the patches, but in them too.
They left out, and even put in; one would find all sorts of
things coming in from Macedon and Epiros and who knows
where. And these were the better sort, not strolling mountebanks. They had one great scene each, first garbled, then
ruined with their ranting, instead of letting the music tell
the tale. Then one day came an old, old man, who knew
the *Iliad* whole. My dear, it was like tasting wine after
grape-skin pressings. The exquisite treasures those swine
had passed over, or broken in their rooting . . . ! We feasted
the old man, clothed him and shod him like a lord, plied
him with gold, begged him to live as our honored guest;
but no. His pupil had been killed in a brawl, or gone off
with a woman, or some such calamity; he must travel to get
another, and teach him all he knew. He did not look fit
to stand another winter. At last, in our extremity, I cried
out, 'Let us get it written! I have a good scribe; I can even
write myself. Just stay here till it is done. Then it will live,
even if your next pupil fails you.' I can only say, Simonides,
that old man looked at me like some high priestess of noble
birth, offered well-paid work in a brothel. Can *you* understand it?"

I could; I was still under thirty. "Surely," I said, "it is
impossible Homer should perish. I myself have every word
of him."

"Long may you live, my friend; but no man lives forever. Believe me, Homer is in more danger than you know.
Nowadays, one can manage less and less without writing,

one is always getting some call for it. Onomakritos has his nose forever in his scrolls of oracles, and an oracle's brief enough. Hippias, who deals with Father's private letters, writes something nearly every day. And he keeps all his drafts upon the wax; left to himself, he couldn't quote you half of it. I've given it thought, and I tell you this: what men have written down, they have no need to remember. And soon they will feel no need to try. Then what's still unwritten will fade away."

Pisistratos gave his grave Zeus-like nod. "I believe that my son is right." He opened a coffer inlaid with ivory that stood by him on the table. "This is what we have so far."

The roll he took out was much joined and pasted together, but written clearly. He began to read me a passage; I think it was the Deeds of Diomedes. He must have had the tail of his eye on me, for he stopped and said, "Yes?"

"There are two lines missing there," I said, and gave them him. Hipparchos signed to the clerk to note them down on the wax. Pisistratos read on. He read very well, not performing at all, but giving each sound and stress its value. I wondered how much of it he had picked up from Solon. And then, with a shock, I heard a line quite new to me. Pure gold; it must be Homer; and I'd never been taught it, which meant that Kleobis had not known it either. If they saw me look up, they were both too polite to mention it. At all events, that reconciled me to the Rhapsodia. They don't hold it nowadays; but no matter, the work is done.

The Great Panathenaia is pretty well fixed by now. The Athenians would think it impious to put in anything new. But in those years, though it was very old already (they say King Theseus started it when he united the kingdom) the Archon was always thinking of something grander. That year I was leading a choir; four years before, I had been a sightseer, when the many-colored mass down in the Kerameikos uncoiled, like a bright serpent, into the procession: the knights in their crested helms and shining corselets (all fighting men wore their gear, the Archon had no fear of them); the hoplites marching with their blazoned shields; the garlanded beasts of sacrifice led by handsome athletes; and the Ship of the Goddess, drawn by its snow-white oxen, with her new robe hung from its mast and held out like a sail by two of the maidens who had embroidered it. The rest walked before it and behind, singing their hymn. The chorus leader had the right to dedicate her statue in the sanctuary, to stand there forever; or so she thought, before the Persians came. Never mind, it made them all happy then.

The Rhapsodia was held on the day after. Word of rich prizes had reached the artists—let us call them that—and they came in from near and far. We did find one who got a great deal of the *Iliad* right, and chanted it well, and gave him the first prize. Nobody went away without a gift. That year we added two new lines to the canon, and found sense in two more which till then had been incomprehensible; and the Archon was well content.

It would have been a time to stay on in Athens, and improve upon my success. But half a year before, I had promised the Keans that I would make them a dithyramb for the Delia, and I could not fail them. I would sooner have stayed; I thought about chances I might be missing; but my honor was engaged, and I said to myself that such things are arranged by fate.

I found time to visit Euboia, with some gifts for Dorothea: an Athenian gown with worked borders, a pair of gold earrings shaped like roses, and a bronze mirror engraved on the back with Aphrodite. I had seen her lean over the water-tub when she combed her hair.

She lifted them in her hands, and flew to kiss me. She was smiling; partly from pleasure, for she believed, like me, in never wasting what came her way; and partly because she guessed what this new wealth might mean, and wanted to show me that she kept her word. At the next women's festival, she would be the finest in the village. She could look forward to that—and would—when she saw me off.

I had not been there two nights, before Diagoras, the chief Archon of Eretria, sent his son over from the city, begging me to give a recital there. He's long dead now, these days they have a democracy; but they still look up to him there as a founding father. In his youth, he led the rebellion that put down the nobles. That was long before my time, but they must have been an insolent set, for it to have earned him so much gratitude. A maiden he had been betrothed to (for of course he was one of them himself) was offered by her father to a man of more wealth, who was to marry her out of hand. He raised his revolt and brought it off; and we would have said in those days that he was Tyrant, though not as men mean it now. He ruled with the hearty assent of the Euboians, and I myself lived on Eretrian land. I was glad to honor him.

He entertained me very pleasantly; a small vigorous man, still handsome, who had presence without arrogance, not aping the hubris he had put down. His wife ate with us in the old Ionian way, and had me to know she had cooked the dinner. She had been the prize of his valor, and was still paying it tribute, which he acknowledged by starting a little paunch. She, too, looked as if she liked her own good cooking. They both delighted me; next day I gave them the Winning of Hippodameia in my best heroic style, leaving no doubt of where it was aimed. The Eretrians loved it too, and voted me—for they had some share in government— a handsome fee. Then I went on to Keos.

It was all pretty much the same; except that now, each time I came, I found more people, of more consequence, asked to meet me. My father never remarked on this; but when I gave them the latest news from Athens, he did not

look displeased. Looking back, I see I had begun to think
of it as the civility one owes a patron. Well, it did nobody
any harm.

I picked the boys for my choir, and saw to it that they
kept their minds on their work. Not that I ever beat them;
just turned the slovens out, and got someone fonder of
music. If they wanted to go to Delos, they took care.

My pretty little Hermes had shot up like wheat, and had
a lovely alto; my Apollo was a young man now, training
for the boxing, not the chorus. In due course the ship with
its garlands and painted sail was ready, and the Kean
theoria set out for Delos: the priests, the herald, the
offering-bearers, the athletes, the choir and I, and some
leading citizens. One was my father; but this no longer
troubled me.

Delos, Delos! I have chosen Sicily to end my days in; I
gave my choice thought, and would not change it. Athens
I shall see no more; I'm an old summer cicada now, a bad
voyage would kill me. In any case, so much has altered
there, I would be a stranger. It is only when I think, Never
again the Delia, that a shadow falls on my heart.

Nothing much will have changed on Delos. The strong
cool young sun on the silver-sparkling rocks and the painted
marble; the old spotted lions sitting along the lake; the
bright Ionian crowds. It will have grown gayer, if not as
rich as before Ionia fell. But even Greeks from there who
have lost their cities save best clothes for the Delia. Friends
meet there after many years; youths and girls who were
children five years before exchange winged glances. If a
face is missing, not much is said: Apollo, who stands so
tall there staring at the sun, does not like clouds and rain.
It may be windy, it may be cold; but it is always fine for
the birthday of the god. Some Son of Homer sang that on
that day you might think the Ionians immortal, untouched
by age or time.

True, indeed. Since Apollo's healing shrines are in other places, and no one must pollute his birthplace by dying there, only those in their health and strength come to the Delia: old men with their beards combed smooth and their hair pinned with golden grasshoppers, their walking-staffs polished to show the grain; women fresh-bathed and scented with oil of violets; young men with hair flowing down over their shoulders, striding out in short tunics disdaining the sharp breeze; and the girls linked hand in hand, as they will be for their singing, in bright dresses with colored borders, green or saffron or blue, hearing each other their words for the choral odes, or giggling over their dialect songs poking fun at other cities; their mothers brooding over them, wary of the youths; the younger boys, whose voices will have broken before the next Delian feast, looking at the athletes and thinking about the games.

Spring was early that year. I don't recall a more radiant Delia, many as I've seen. It's not often the girls can find so many spring flowers for their hair, cyclamen and daffodil and hyacinth, nursed there in wet moss to keep them fresh. Mount Kythnos sparkled with little hill-flowers, and the glittering rocks were starred with them.

I have always liked to get to Delos early, before the crowds have trampled it, and try to see it when Leto came there first, to bear her child. She'd been delivered of the elder twin already; maiden Artemis could run beside her hunting the game, for the infancy of gods is brief. But Leto is still big with the younger, greater one; his light glows through her, like the sun through a rosy shell. His time is come; he commands her; she crouches by the palm tree and grasps it in her pangs; the shining babe slides down between her thighs; rests for a moment, turning his blue eyes to the sky; then the birth-cord falls from him; faster on his feet than a day-old colt, he runs to the lake to rinse off the birth-bloom; swims across and back; and striding ashore in his tall splendor, shakes the water from his golden hair. Before the crowds come, I can see all that; after, I can only tell it. That year, since I came on the state ship from Keos, they were there before me. The paean and the silence, one cannot have both at once.

Theas sailed with us; he had been chosen as an umpire in the games, and carried his stick of office. Our father's proud eyes followed him everywhere. His wife, eight months gone, had stayed behind, but he had brought his boy. No fear there of the Cretan strain appearing.

A little fleet from Keos followed the theoria. Most of our kin and friends were carried by Laertes, who had two ships now. I saw them arrive, but had to bring my boys to the precinct and rehearse their entrance.

I was with the Kean herald, talking about this, when he pointed past me at the harbor. "Look. The Athenians."

Yes, here was the state galley, the biggest yet. The sails were scarlet striped with blue; the whole vessel dazzled in the sun with gilding and polished bronze. The oars were painted white, so that as they rowed her in they flashed like wings. It was the grandest in the harbor, which had come to be expected; Pisistratos had seen to that.

They threw out their gangway. It was very broad, wider than a cattleship's. I saw movement within, and it came to me what they were doing; they meant to disembark in full order of procession. It's done now by many embassies; but that was the first time I know of. Being downwind, we could hear the flutes giving the note, and the paean beginning. At a stately pace, the procession crossed the gangway, to the admiration of the crowd. I approved whoever was getting them off so neatly from a cramped deck; but did not at once attend to the man who led the embassy, who I took it would be the priest of Apollo. Then something familiar struck my eye; it was Hippias. Standing in the prow, on the pilot's bridge, Hipparchos was directing the procession.

Often it's been my fortune that when I have done something to please myself, or satisfy my honor, against all seeming prudence, yet it has brought me luck. I'd left Athens when the scent of patronage hung in the air like the savor of roasting meat, rather than fail the Keans and disgrace my kin. And here was patronage, come to meet me.

The theoria marched singing to the temple; the herald cried, the offering-bearers came forward with their jars and baskets and wreathed bull; Hippias spoke the dedication, and poured on the altar a flask of precious incense, three times more costly since we lost the Asian cities. The Delian High Priest replied. Nothing could have been handsomer.

Important people would now be paying their respects. I let the brothers get to the Athenian lodge, and left them time for a rest and a drink, before I went to pay mine. I was here as a Kean, after all.

The lodge was handsome, built of stone by Pisistratos when he purified the island. There were still people about; but Hipparchos called out to me as soon as I was inside. Only he and Thessalos were there; the chair of state was empty.

"Come in, singer of heroes!" He shouted to a slave to bring another stool. Most of the guests were standing. "My brother has gone up Mount Kythnos to consult the oracle."

I said I hoped the answer would be favorable. I could hardly ask about the question, though I longed to know.

Hipparchos waved it away. "Oh, it will be favorable. He has nothing serious to ask it. Oracles are his study. Wherever one exists, it's the first thing he visits. They are all ready for him beforehand." He beckoned another slave to bring me wine.

Thessalos said, "He may get a surprise one day. Oracles are known for that."

"Not on Delos." He smiled. Everyone knew that even rich Polykrates had not been such a benefactor of the sanctuary as Pisistratos. I had had it in mind when I composed my dithyramb, never guessing his own sons would be in the audience. It must, I thought, be my lucky day.

"Onomakritos has gone up with him," Hipparchos said, "to write it all down, in case anything gets forgotten."

I stared at this. "Why, Onomakritos is a poet. Does he need to *write* it?" I had met the man and thought him a charlatan; but Hippias put great trust in him.

Hipparchos laughed. He knew well enough what I was thinking. "Well, he has charge of all the oracles from the time of Theseus down, or so he claims for them. I daresay it's a good deal to remember. He and Hippias go over them by the hour. They come to Father with them. Sometimes he even uses one, if it falls in pat just then."

"Especially Athene's," Thessalos put in.

This was sailing near the wind. I suppose there were a few very simple peasants who still believed Athene herself had escorted Pisistratos back from exile. From curiosity, I had gone myself to the home village of the tall girl who had put on the helmet and the aegis for him and mounted the chariot at his side. I was snubbed, however, whenever I asked the way. She was treated with great respect there, and shielded from vulgar eyes. I believe she married the first man of the place (not ill-dowered, you may be sure!) and bore him four tall sons. Ever since she put on Athene's armor, the people felt she was somehow god-touched. In Athens, of course, it had long since been a joke; people just admired its cleverness, though not as a rule out loud.

Lest I should feel awkward, Hipparchos sanctioned it this time with a smile. It was things like this that won him so many friends. I suppose it is no great wonder that men forget; but I am sorry, too.

The small guest-room of the lodge looked very festive, with its garlands and embroidered hangings, and the brothers' fresh bright clothes, dark Thessalos in yellow, fair Hipparchos in white bordered with scarlet. Pisistratos never put on purple, nor allowed his sons to do it. He knew what the Athenians would think of that. He always knew what they thought.

Some tedious people left, and the talk grew gayer; Hipparchos never expected artists he entertained to sing each time for their supper. After a while a shadow fell on the doorway, and soberness along with it. Hippias came in, with solemn Onomakritos. He really was carrying tablets, without any shame, like any palace clerk.

Hipparchos greeted them; I saw him take a second, keener look at Hippias' face. It certainly looked grave; but he was pious to the point of superstition. In any case, I took my leave almost at once, to let him talk with his brothers. I was short of time myself.

In the evening, my boys got in from rambling about the island, and crowded for their supper into the big room under the Kean lodge, where they would sleep in straw like puppies. I, like the kennel-man, would have my pallet there to keep an eye on them, and see they turned out next day without black eyes or bloodied noses.

Most of their parents were lodging at Rhenaia Island, close by, as people do when Delos is full. My own however were here, and I got up early to pay my respects before the procession began. To save time I put my robe and wreath on. As I came in, I saw the change in my father's face as he made out who it was. For a moment he'd thought it was someone of importance.

Even when he'd realized his mistake, he looked as if he had had some new thought about me; but whether welcome or not, I could not tell. My mother complained that the lodging was badly swept, and kept telling me to pick up my skirts, or I would not be fit to be seen. Theas, whom I passed conferring deeply with other umpires on the state of the wrestling-ground, waved and wished me luck.

It was a fine calm morning, with only the gentlest breeze; no need to tie one's wreath into one's hair. We marched to the forecourt of the temple (Pisistratos' gift, already looking mellow) singing our paeans, then stood in our order waiting for our turns. Mine came about halfway through.

I sang of the god's birth as I had conceived it, and how Delos is still suffused with his pure fire, which will not bear sickness, or death, or tears. The last part should always deal with things in the world of men; so I sang of the Purification.

I was little more than a boy when Pisistratos visited Delos as First Archon of Athens, instead of a simple worshipper. For many years it had been treated carelessly; there were graveyards in full sight of the precinct and the sacred cave. He had all the old bones given decent burial, with their own tombstones, at the far end of the island, and had the cleared places beautified. On one of them he built the temple. All this was in my ode.

I'd rehearsed my boys to turn their circle at a gentle pace, to save their breath for the song. There was no wind to carry the sound away; no one was fidgety with cold; the boys came in dead on time as my solo ended. We were well received. As we went off, I got a gracious smile from Hippias as well as from Hipparchos, and wondered if my father saw.

The Athenian choir came next. It was the first appearance of young Lasos, a most agreeable fellow whom I got to know well in later years. So far as music was concerned, his ear was better than mine; he used to say, as if it were quite natural, that he composed it first and thought later

about the words. This is why none of his words have lived
on after him. They were just part of the sound, like an
extra flute; he took pride in never using any word that had
an *s* in it, a sound that he thought harsh. He used all wood-
winds, no strings, and took it fast, the dance as well as
the singing. His choir was well trained, too. Though without any wish to copy him, I was spellbound by his mastery,
and was some time in noticing that someone was pulling
my robe.

Thinking that one of the boys wanted to go and relieve
himself, I said without turning, "Very well, but go quietly."
Then the tug got stronger, and I looked. It was Midylos,
my sister's husband. I saw with surprise that clinging to
his cloak was Theas' little boy. Our mother had been looking after him.

Midylos whispered, "Sim, I am sorry, but I think you
had better come. Your father is sick . . . They have taken
him to Rhenaia."

He glanced at me. There was no need to say more.

If one calls up one's youth to answer to one's age, one
must ask the truth from it. The truth is that I thought,
"Not *now!*"

Who would take care of the boys, and lead them in the
closing procession? The flute-player? I had never shown him
what to do, he had only to walk behind me. He could set
the note for the paean, but it ought to be sung, not played,
and he could no more sing than a frog; I did not trust the
boys not to burst out laughing. How would I get word to
the High Priest, now sitting in state and not to be approached, that I had to leave? Suppose the judges called
for me? What would the Pisistratids think?

All this rushed through my head; while young Lasos'
choir sang about half a line. "Yes," I said, "I will come."

I beckoned the flute-player; gave him some hasty instructions; chose the boy with the finest voice to start the

paean when the flute gave the note. I told the younger ones to behave themselves in the precinct, or I'd tell their fathers of them. I did everything as if my thoughts had been what they should.

As we edged through the press, I put my arm out to protect the kithara, still slung about my neck. How should I get it cared for? I would be crossing in a leaky ferryboat. After a salt drenching, it would never be the same again. It had been made by a master for a master; for his sake it was dear to me; it had spoken with his voice, and had come now to speak with mine; its beauty was closer to me than any woman's. Because of the fine weather, I had left its case at the Kean lodge.

The little boy said, "Uncle Midylos, why did they take Granddad away? Why couldn't he go to bed?"

Midylos said, "He has gone to see the doctor."

"What happened?" I asked. "He seemed quite well this morning."

"Yes, it was sudden; while you were singing. He leaned on me—Theas was still busy over the games—and said he felt giddy, and one of his legs was prickling. While we were leaving he fell down, and some men helped me carry him out of the crowd. He tried to speak, but the half of his face was numb. It sounded like 'Rhenaia,' and that seemed best. Theas has taken him over, and I came for you."

"Yes. Yes, let us go at once."

"Look, that's the way to the ferry. Only big ships are using the harbor now."

"I know. But there is something I must . . ." The kithara seemed to cling to me, like a frightened child. I forget how far I went out of our way towards the Kean lodge, before I found a man I knew and trusted, who promised he would get its case from the warden of the lodge, and put it in safekeeping. If I had not met him, perhaps I would have gone to the lodge myself. I cannot tell.

Most of the ferryboats were idle, waiting on the Delos side to take people back to their lodgings after the festival. I had never before been over to Rhenaia. Its living is mostly fish, between the festivals. Anyone who can afford it has built a room onto his house, to make something at the Delia and the summer Apollonia. Some rent their houses out and just sleep in their boats. We crossed where the channel is narrow, alongside the Chain of Polykrates. He had the notion of offering the whole island as a dedication to Delian Apollo, by tying it, so to speak, to his feet. It was just like Polykrates. Most of the chain was under water, hidden by weed; our boatman cursed it as a danger to the ships.

The feast had emptied the island. The jetty seemed forsaken. Theas' little boy said, "Uncle, where does the doctor live? Can I see Granddad?"

"When he is better." Midylos murmured to me, "He thinks the world of Leo." The child bore his name, and was Theas to the life as I first remembered him.

As we tied up, a boy got up from the shadow of a bollard, and limped towards us. "Is either of you gentlemen Simonides, Leoprepes of Iulis' son?"

"I am; where is he?"

The lad's face brightened. He did not look poor, just bored and lonely. "In the shelter, sir. I'll show you the way."

"What?" I said. He had used the word for a soldier's bivouac or shepherd's hut. I turned angrily to Midylos; but he laid finger on lip and shook his head. I understood. All the lodgings had been paid for, by people who would be back at night to sleep. To a sick man they might offer hospitality; not to a dead one, who would leave the place defiled. Rhenaia, it seemed, had a proper place for that.

The boy said, "Are you famous, sir? Your mother said so. And Melesias gave your father a new bed. This way,

sirs, it's not far." He led us on at a lurching trot. He was
clubfooted; I expect his kin had not cared to show him at
the feast.

The death-house was past the harbor, along the shore; a
stone-walled hut, with a roof of driftwood held down with
stones. No one was wailing, so I knew he was still alive.

A man was sitting outside upon a boulder. He looked
round at us; by the time we came up, he was grinning like a
pi-dog that scents meat. He was the man who had been ready
to stay away from Delos, in case anyone arrived to die.
Pythagoras' followers, as they told me when I visited their
city, do things like this as an offering to the gods. This
fellow was not one of them.

I suppose the plain dress of Keos had not promised well.
At the sight of my robes he almost dribbled. Anything he
could do for the poor old gentleman . . . not that it was
easy with so many folk away, but hospitality to the
stranger . . .

We walked past him. The doorway had no door. Only
the family was there, but there was barely room inside. I
could see my mother kneeling by my father, and hear his
heavy breathing. A cold, damp stink of old sickness and
death crept out. Little Leo did not ask again where Granddad was; he started to back away.

Philomache peered out. Midylos beckoned her, and she
took the child by the hand. "Come, let's look on the beach
for something pretty, to give to Grandpa when he's better."
He went with her silently, not deceived but thankful to
be gone.

Her leaving made room inside. My father lay with his
feet to the door, on his new bed. The boy had spoken truly;
the straw was fresh.

I stood by my mother and looked down. Theas' cloak was
rolled under his head for a pillow. Half his mouth had
dropped, so that he seemed to gaze at me with an angry

and sour disgust. In the prison of his face his eyes had moved, and were fixed on me. I knelt and took his hand. It felt cold and dead. The straw smelled of the urine his body could not contain.

"Father." What more? I was as dumb as the child had been. "I am sorry, Father." The good side of his mouth moved, and it seemed that he spoke my name.

"This won't do, Father," I said. "We must find you something better." Then I remembered that despite my splendid clothes, or rather because of them, I was the only man there who carried no coin at all. My money was at the Kean lodge, in the warden's keeping.

He could move his head a little. He turned his eyes towards a block of stone that served as the only table. There was a cup on it; my mother lifted it to his mouth, and raised his head. He swallowed some, though more was spilled; then he looked hard at her, and his eyes moved to me. I said, "He wants more"; but with every inch of face he could make work, he seemed to say, "You fool!" He looked at Theas, and his loose mouth mumbled again. I could not catch the words; but I saw Theas go white. He bent down and said, "You are my father. You know I cannot do it." He turned to me, his face telling me everything. "And nor can Sim, Father. You know that."

Indeed, I had been slow. This should have happened to him at home on Keos, where old custom met his need. He would have had no trouble there in getting what he wanted, and a friend to give it.

Theas said to me, "Sim, you know Delos. Would there be someone there?" He spoke quite simply; we were all Keans.

I shook my head. "Doctors, yes. But they're servants of Apollo. They have to take a vow never to give such things. 'Even if it is asked of me.' That's in their oath."

My father said, "Keoth." It was the best he could do, and clear enough.

"Yes, Father," Theas said. "Just rest now. We will take you home."

He shut his eyes. I expect that saying so much had been hard work. I went outside with Theas. The custodian came fawning up. I silenced Theas with a look—he had just got a buffet ready—and whispered, "You had better give him something. I came just as I was." The man spat on the copper piece and looked at me with scorn. The lame boy, who had stayed not for gain but because he had missed the festival, sat bright-eyed on a clump of sea-grass.

Theas and I looked at each other. Men from anywhere but Keos would have found much more to say. "No ship will leave Delos before tomorrow," he said. "But if that is too late, he will have had his wish."

"But now, today? He is lying here like a dog."

"That creature asked five drachmas for a bedstead. None of us had enough. He won't give credit. He charges for water, too."

"I'll go get my money from the lodge. Dressed like this, I expect some boatman will trust me."

"They burn the bed after, or so he claims . . . Yes, go, Sim." As I was turning, he added, "And don't take what Father said to heart. His mind's half gone, or he'd have known you couldn't do it."

"I know. Shall I see him first? No, tell him where I've gone, if he can understand."

I began to walk back along the foot-track towards the harbor. I was nearly there, when I heard a call, and saw the boy behind me, waving his arm. From pity for his deformity, I paused to let him come up. "Sir," he called, "I think your dad has died. I just heard the ladies wailing."

As he spoke, I saw Theas running to overtake me. The boy waited and watched. He had missed the feast, but in the end he had had his moment. As Aischylos told me, in most tragedies the Messenger is a much-sought role.

After a while, I remembered to take off my festal wreath. I wore one so often that I could forget it like my clothes. The boy picked it up from the ground, and, sitting down, teased out the braid from among the laurel.

We had not gone far before we could hear the women. I said, "After I left, did he speak again?"

"Not to make it out. I think once he said, 'Sim,' and I told him where you were. I don't know if he understood. Soon after that his breath rattled, and then he died."

The child was sitting where the boy had been. His eyes were great with terror; he looked at us without a word. Theas picked him up and held him firmly, saying, "We are all going home soon. Be good now, and I'll tell you about it later. Granddad is with the shades, where the heroes go." The child was still silent, but I saw his face was soothed. Theas ruffled his hair, and set him down. Then we went on towards the wailing.

They had closed his eyes, and bound up his jaw with Philomache's hair-ribbon. He looked his own man once more. His mouth was straight again, keeping its own counsel. Whether he judged the gods, or us, or himself, was a thing he did not confide. I remembered Pythagoras, and wondered what life he would choose next time, if a choice was offered him.

My mother and sister were beating their breasts as women do. Their wailing throbbed with the blows. I envied them. Had I been a barbarian, I too could have had my part. Women can float away upon lamentation, like birds upon the air, or fish in rivers. Later they must return and know their grief; but for a while they are freed, as the poet is by the song.

If I had gone back before I left for the ferry, I would have seen his death. He named me; perhaps it would have told me something. As it is, I ask myself, even now, why it was not until I came that he asked for hemlock. Was it just that I knew Delos, and might be able to find it? Or did he think I would give it more willingly than the rest? Or to be humbled before me, was that the last stroke, too much to bear?

We burned him at evening, on a platform near the death-house, whose stone is blackened with old fires. Shipmasters will not balk at carrying a funeral urn; but not even Laertes would have taken a corpse on board, his crew would have refused to sail. I went back to Delos to take off my choral robe, and put on what I had come in. We sheared our hair; even our traveling clothes were too gay for mourning, and we sprinkled them with dust.

I had brought oil and incense for the pyre; its driftwood and flotsam crackled and sparked with salt. The flames turned blue, and did not hide the blackening body; but they were fierce and quick. Before long the core of the pyre fell in, and he fell with it, sticks of bone among sticks of wood.

Something offended my nose, more than the burning. The warden of the death-house stood at my elbow. "If you have business to attend to, sirs, I can collect the ashes, and put them up for you nicely. The mourners before have always been very satisfied."

I must have whipped round on him like a snake, for he cringed away; then he yelped, as Theas got him in a wrestler's lock. "You carrion crow! If you lay one claw upon our father's pyre, I swear I'll rekindle it and throw you on." "With a rock on your belly," I put in, "to hold you down." As he went off, I divined that Theas had been as glad as I to drive out this scapegoat laden with our guilt. Theas had lived a blameless son, and his father's pride. I expect that his need was no less than mine, and maybe more.

When I went back to the Kean lodge, evening was falling, and the rocks of Delos glittered with sparks like fire. Theas was seeing to the urn, Midylos to the women and the child. Laertes would sail at first light, and I only went to gather my things together. I meant to sleep on board, rather than deal with scores of polite condolences. My boys would not know what to say, and my presence would spoil their holiday. The flute-player would look after them.

No one was about; Delian evenings are merry. I had found my kithara safe, and was on my way out with my things, when a man came up dressed for a party. Having heard the news, he apologized for this unseemliness. When all that was proper had been said, he told me that after the dithyrambs were over, he had been sent to look for me by Hipparchos, to ask me to supper at the Athenian lodge. He and Hippias had expressed great pleasure with my ode, and with its praise of their honored father.

"Please thank them for their kindness. Who won the contest?" He looked surprised. I said, "I have been on Rhenaia."

"Of course, of course; forgive me. As I heard, it would have been yourself; but you sent the judges word that you were obliged by piety to incur pollution. So they gave the prize to that young man, Lasos."

"They did well; he has a gift. I heard part of his piece and would have liked to hear it all. Wish him well from me, if I should not see him."

As I learned later, he got the message and was pleased. Nothing looks more foolish than a petulant loser.

The man went back to his party. He must have had a friend among the judges, to hear that I could have won. I said in my heart, "He has wronged me, even in his death."

I walked towards Laertes' ship, thinking how I might have gone home in the state galley, crowned with victory.

As I walked along the jetty towards the mooring, an oldish man approached me. I thought, Another fool with whom I must exchange civilities; but I put on a good face, and waited for him.

"My dear Sim!" I recognized the Kean accent. "I hear the good Leoprepes is dead. Give my sorrowful respects to your excellent mother, and all the family. You have lost an upright man, as I can myself bear witness. It was ten years ago, or maybe fifteen; at any rate, it was the year of the sheep-sickness. Before the start, I had bought fifty from your father; and when some thirty died, I was at my wits' end. I had counted on the lambs, to pay off a loan; it seemed I would have to pledge myself in bondage. Then your father's steward came. He brought word that fifty of your father's flock had died, and he had no doubt that those he had sold me must have had the sickness on them. He would take back those that were left, and return me the price of them all. Then and there, his man paid it me. He did not even demand to see the hides of the dead beasts. Just the silver, paid in full. My luck turned soon after, and now we do pretty well. But I have often thought that but for your father, I should be a thrall today . . . Did he never tell you this?"

"No," I said. "Never a word."

"Well, well. I am glad I met with you. To think of that; never a word. He thought his uprightness not worth boasting of, because it was his habit."

I went on my way. I remembered the sheep-sickness; I had been still a shepherd. When the first few died, he had beaten me for letting them eat black hellebore. Later, when he knew the truth, he said, "Well, Sim, it seems you were not to blame." I was angry that he said it so unwillingly, never counting the cost to his pride in saying it at all. This man had done him more justice. I had often been ashamed that he was known for a hard man; that he had never been known for a crooked one, I had not considered; just taken it for granted, as he had brought me up to do. All in all, I thought, I had best stop pitying myself over the choral prize. The judges had thought me the best, and I should be content to know it.

So I went to my mattress on the ship, with some bread and cheese bought on the way, and bedded down for the night. Some sailors were working late, shouting and hammering, so I lay awake. About midnight, I heard singing, coming along the waterside, and threw my blanket round me and went up on deck to look.

It was a komos of revelers, waving torches, and singing a skolion to which they dance-stepped along. They were not far away, and I could see Hipparchos leading them. He had one arm over the shoulders of the youth to whom he had given the painted wine-cup. They made a handsome group, like Dionysos with a young satyr.

The sound faded away; the sailors had turned in, and so did I. It had been a long day. As men count great events, nothing much had happened. The Delia had been celebrated; an old man had died in the way of nature, and his sons had put him on the pyre. Yet it had been a full day for me.

It is a strange thing to recall; but as I fell asleep, I was wondering how it might feel to be courted for one's beauty. I expect Pythagoras would have told me that in some past life, as youth or woman, I had been cruel to my lovers, and had chosen to make amends. In my time I have talked with many philosophers, who have expounded to me the ways of the gods with men. Out of them all, Pythagoras' belief seems to me the most just, supposing it is true. But then, if it is, and all these things befall us, unless we have the Sight we shall never know.

3

WE GAVE OUR FATHER the very best funeral the laws of Keos allow. No wailing, even by wife or daughter; one lamb and one goat to offer at the tomb; no incense. They measure even the libations of wine and oil. Had we had his body, his grave-clothes must have been as simple as in life, and his grave-wreath only of origan. We draped his urn with fillets of fine wool, and tied our hair into his mourning-wreath. (But for Midylos, Theas and I would have left our shearings forgotten on Rhenaia.) We put the urn on a bier hung with a linen cloth; and Theas and I carried it to the tomb in the silence the laws prescribe.

Later, to the scandal of half Iulis, we had a small carving done on his grave-stele, in the Athenian style, by an artist from that city. Of course he had never seen our father; but that is usual. He just asked his age and how he wore his hair and beard. He was done leaning on a staff, with Theas bidding him farewell. He, at least, was there to be copied.

To the very end of the rites, Theas was just what he had always been, the eldest son of Leoprepes. It was as though our father was still watching, as Homer tells it, on the hither shore of Styx, awaiting his rite of passage. After the offerings at the tomb came the funeral feast, given in the Kean style he would have approved. After that, if Patroklos' ghost spoke truly to Achilles, Leoprepes son of Theasides, of Iulis, had made the crossing.

We went home, and slept; next morning the sun was shining, and the birds sang their spring songs. Our mother went briskly about the house, with well-water and hyssop. Theas rode into town, saying he had business there; and came back clean-shaved.

"I'd have as soon kept it up after that time in Samos," he said quite coolly, "but the father would never have stood it. Athenian dandies—you know what he used to say."

So that was how the sculptor did him on the grave-stele, standing with our father. He forgot to mention it, and once the outline was chiseled, it was too late to change. I kept quiet about it, and so did he.

Looking back, I can't think why I was so surprised at the change in Theas. If I had been less taken up with myself, I could have expected it. I, the unwanted one, had long since had my freedom. Theas, the beloved, respected, cherished, had never been free at all. Now he was like a vine that bursts with green shoots in a single day of sun.

Not that he plunged into riot and revelry, like some heirs of strict fathers. That was never his style. But when next Laertes put to sea, with a cargo for Sidon and Naukratis, Theas was with him. He wanted to learn the trade of ship-master; then he would hire a good pilot, and buy a ship.

Nowadays, men of good birth seem to think sea-trading beneath them. It was different when I was young. Laertes had inherited a big estate, grew his own grapes for wine and raisins, pressed his own olive oil, and pastured the flocks whose wool he sold. But he never gave up the sea till he was past sixty and his joints got stiff, though by then he was one of the chief men of Iulis. When Theas joined him, he was in his prime: had traded as far north as the Euxine, for furs and corn and Hyperborean amber; south down to Naukratis for faience and alabaster jars and ivory and in-

cense; and bought purple in Tyre to sell in Athens. The
Ionian ports were open to trade again under their Persian
satraps; once more in Miletos you could get lapis and em-
broideries from Sardis. Laertes had started out, like many
another landowner's son, just selling his father's spare pro-
duce; now he was richer from trade than land. For years,
as I might have guessed, Theas had been dying with envy.
It had never soured their friendship; Theas had been born
without sourness in him; but I remembered, now, how he'd
told me in my boyhood Laertes' sailor tales, dwelling on
the fights with pirates.

He finished all this business before he said a word; when
he came back from Koressia harbor, he was like a boy again.
Our mother was much dismayed; she had never thought,
she cried, that *he* would be a wanderer. He replied that she
had plenty of kin in Iulis, and Midylos close at hand. He
was kind, but firm as rock.

When we were alone, I said to him, "Theas, what would
you have done if Father had lived to fourscore?"

He looked a little surprised, either at my asking, or not
having asked before. "I'm thirty-three. I was giving it two
more years. Half a man's life, and the best half, I reckon
is all one owes."

"That's fair," I said. "But I prophesy the best is still to
come." I was right in that. But I thought, too, that it would
have destroyed our father; and that after all he had had a
lucky death.

Remembering the knife Theas gave me when I left home,
I went to Khalkis, whose swordsmiths were famous then as
now, and bought him the best short sword that I could find.
He was delighted with it; in after years he told me it served
him well, though before they got to close quarters he had
done pretty well with javelins. I expect that in all those
years when he had exercised with them at home, he had
dreamed of using them in battle. At any rate, before he

was thirty-five—the age when he'd planned to claim his freedom—he had picked off the captain of a Cretan pirate, and sailed on to Naukratis with the captured ship, and his own cargo of Corinthian helmets for the Greek soldiers in Pharaoh's pay.

As for me, I went back to my land in Euboia, now truly mine. No one could say my father had been a harsh landlord. He did not like my absences, but kept to his word and never told me so. If he grumbled at my accounts, it was not from avarice—he might do it in a good year—but because I had altered something on the farm. It was true that since old Phileas knew the work so well, I had begun to give him his head. His changes were for the better; the farm ran smoothly; he did not take free men in thrall for debt, or ill-treat the slaves; so, my mind at rest, I was free to walk out in the woods and hills and by the shore, following the rise and fall of words as one might chase a bright bird that teases one by flying out of view or perching in hidden branches, then of a sudden comes swooping in perfect plunge, its colors flashing, the whole curve of its path clear to enraptured eyes.

I trusted Phileas, and he did not betray me. If he kept a few pickings for himself, which would have been only human, he never exceeded. I think he feared Dorothea more than me. She was a personage in the village now, and took a pride in it; even if my ship came early into port, I always found things just so.

All in all I had been living very well; it had been foolish to let my accounting to my father hang over me for a month beforehand. He had a way of fidgeting while I spoke, so that I felt something was coming without knowing what. I had sometimes lied to him, but only about small things for the sake of peace; and to his profit, not his loss. Yet these trifles had oppressed me, almost as if I were a boy who could still be beaten, even when I had just come from

Athens with gold in my belt and praise in my ears. I went home after the funeral feeling as if a heavy mortgage had been paid off.

But now in Athens a long day was ending, which had dawned in storm and fitful sun and returning gales, then passed into a fine untroubled afternoon and a mild evening. Now twilight was here and it would soon be dusk.

Not, like my father, with a single stroke, but little by little every day, the strong old master was failing. Often in those days he sent for me, or Hipparchos sent me to him, saying my songs refreshed him when he was tired. He was getting to be like ancient Nestor, who used to dwell on the days before Agamemnon was born, let alone Achilles. I would sing to him from the Sons of Homer, or sometimes make a song for him myself, about his early deeds in the Salaminian War. There, when he had thanked me with his regal courtesy, he would often set me right; he was not silly, just clearest in his memory about the past, as I am getting to be. About the present, he was apt to be forgetful. Sometimes when a man had been acquitted in his own court, he would order his arrest, not from injustice, but because the judgment had slipped his mind. No harm was done; Hippias would always oversee his orders and put things right. He did not even need to conceal it; Pisistratos, when reminded of the mistake, would thank him kindly, and praise the gods for giving him a good son to prop his age.

One night he had a few friends to supper, old men like himself who had been in his party since early days. He asked me too, because he had meant that I should sing. I was well prepared for his forgetting all about it, as in fact he did. It was a kind of compliment, that I should seem to him like any one of his guests. I enjoyed the good food and wine, and did not put myself forward; but I could feel, as the meal went on, that the company had disappointed him. His mind was sharp still, if not his memory; most of the others were maundering on about old men's trivial concerns, or deploring the manners of the youth—which, I think, had never been so good as they were then, and certainly have not since. He tried to lead the talk, but it would fall away in trifles. He did not, as Polykrates would have done, get up and go to bed; but, when the eldest made his excuses, graciously included all the rest. I, of course, went up last. He made a gesture for me to stay.

When all had been ushered out, he turned to me smiling. "My dear boy, all we old fellows have been rambling on till past our bedtimes. It is their loss, that they have not heard you sing; but I hope it need not be mine. Will it be playing tyrant, if I keep you for a while, to please an audience of one?"

I said what was natural, adding that it would be something to remember; which, indeed, I found was true.

He motioned me to the supper-couch next his own, and beckoned the slave to bring me a clean wine-table. Seeing him pause above his cup to smell the bouquet, I ventured to praise the vintage. He looked up, like a man recalled from his thoughts. "The best year in ten. I am glad it pleases you. It was Solon who taught me to know wine. Will you sing me something of his?"

I was startled speechless. Solon's fame, as I knew it, was firstly for his laws; then for refusing a tyranny, and choosing exile instead; then, on returning to find Pisistratos in power, for urging the Athenians to resist him. When they would not, Solon left his old panoply outside his door in the street, and gave out that he had retired. I had only snatches of his songs; they were all political, and I pleaded my shortcomings with relief.

"Did you never hear this?" He put out his hand for my lyre—at these small parties I did not use the kithara—and tried the strings; then in his old cracked voice gave the first line of a charming love song. He stopped too soon; just as if he had been some poet met at a festival, I said, "Sir, will you teach it me?"

What is more, he did, and I have it to this day. It is not very long; it likens itself to a flower which will not die while the beloved wears it. When I had sung it back to him, he said smiling, "Yes, it deserves to be worn longer, and you are young. I bequeath it you."

Even in his age, you could trace the bones of old beauty. He had all his teeth, and his mouth was still finely carved. Faint gold shone in his hair. When he was not looking, I half shut my eyes, and could trace the brave keen face, a sculptor's delight had the art of those days been good enough; listening to his lover, learning the thoughts of manhood. What other would Solon choose?

He had our cups refilled with the cold pale wine. We drank; I waited. "He loved me to the end. And I him. I loved him when he warned the city of me, and begged them to throw me off before it was too late. He would not have been Solon, if he had not done it. He was the best man of our age. When he did it he loved me still. It was partly for my sake too, for fear of power corrupting me . . . Do you know, people went to him, after that speech of his (part was in verse; I will teach it you one day when it is not so late); they went to him, and urged him to fly before I killed him. Dear man, he laughed. He said his old age would protect him—he was ten years younger than I am now. Again and again, after all that, I went to him for advice, never in vain. He was like a fine olive tree, which when its roots are checked one way will put them out another. Summer or winter, storm or calm, his soul sought justice and the end of wrong. He worked as he could, with what he had; first with the people, then with me . . . Kleon, fill up."

The slaves had gone, the butler was there alone. He shook his head like an old nurse, then lovingly filled the cups.

"There was no one like him. Everyone knew it; or why did they go to him when the state was like a knot of vipers? They begged him to give them laws, because he was in no blood-feud, and was the only man fit to do it. The lords, the knights, the merchants, the commons, all swore before the gods to keep whatever laws he made for them. And so they do. They keep them to this day . . . I see to that."

I gazed with fascination at that grim smile. Now I could picture him in his prime, while I was an urchin tending my first sheep, weeping from loneliness on the mountain; and he was lord of Brauron in the north, teaching his hill-men to fight.

"He had promised them justice, and that he gave. He took from every man the right to wrong another. He freed the debt-thralls. He canceled the mortgages, and had the debt-stones broken in the fields. I was with him often, when he was at work on it. I was young then. I saw he had removed oppression, but had not gratified envy or revenge. He seemed to me like a god. I said, 'If there is any justice in men, they will set you up a hero shrine.' He brushed that aside; but I think it was what he hoped for. From public office he never made one drachma, though ever since his fool of a father went broke, he'd had to shift for himself with trade. He was a fine soldier; but at home he would never grasp at power, he wanted nothing not given him by free consent. But what man does not covet honor?"

"What man," I said, "or what god, for that matter? But he has it, surely? The Athenians call him Solon the Wise."

"Now they do. I hope, where he is, it reaches him. They have lived with his laws and liked them, now that they have me, who could have given them laws they would have liked much less, but for my oath and honor, as well they know. Oh yes, they thank him now. Did they thank him then? Not they, not when it could have warmed his living heart."

His fingers tightened round the wine-cup's stem. I think he might have broken it, if it had not been made of gold. I asked, "How was it then, sir?"

"Then?" He looked at me, saw me young, and suddenly looked old again. "*Then* he gave out his laws, and had them carved on the wooden tablets you can see today, set up in the King Archon's colonnade. All sorts of men— lords, knights, merchants, commons—praised him for his laws and found them admirable. Except, each of them found, for just one thing. He had satisfied none of them. That shows you how just he was. So, therefore, each of them wanted a thumb upon the scales, just a tilt their way. *Then* they would truly honor him . . . Kleon, fill up."

The butler came softly with the jug. He had put in more water, when his master was not looking.

"He was a man of honor, and believed the same of his friends. Well, perhaps he was right; let us say they were not all men of discretion. Somehow, before his laws were proclaimed, one or two men learned that he meant to cancel mortgages. So they bought land on mortgages, for which they could not have paid. And mean-minded men, whose greed he had not satisfied, put it about that he had advised it."

He set down his cup. He had truly returned there. I saw that his hand was shaking.

"In my youth, I was not without some beauty. It was all I had to offer him in his trouble. Every day they bickered and complained; and always what they wanted had to be taken unjustly from some other man. He had a steady soul —that was why they'd gone to him in the first place—but he began to lose his sleep. Still, he had true friends who had never tried to use him. They told him his laws were just, and should be enforced. They urged him to accept a tyranny; they said he would be backed by all moderate men. They offered him gold of their own, to hire Thracian soldiers—excellent advice, as I have found. I was a boy still; I begged him to consent, as though he would do for my young face what was not in him to do at all. He was kind to me. Solon was always kind. 'Tyranny, my dear, is like one of those mountain climbs which take one up, but not down. One can only fall. They have sworn their oaths to me; if they fear the gods, they will have to keep them. And they cannot harry me to change my laws, if I am not there.' He was gone ten years, trading his way, seeing the world. I stayed, and became a man . . . He'd known I was old enough to think; he thought that because I loved him I would think like him. Indeed I loved him. Indeed he was my teacher. But what he taught me was not what he supposed."

I murmured some assent. I did not want to remind him of who I was, in case he had forgotten. I felt like Orpheus, visiting the shades.

"Few men are wise enough to know themselves, as Pythian Apollo commands us. He was. He had done what he could, and knew what he could not do . . . When he sailed, he gave me his dog, a young harrier, liver and white, that he'd been rearing. One can't do with a dog on shipboard, he could not keep him, so he gave him me. I reared and trained him; he was the best dog I've had. His name was Bia: Strength. I was young, but I knew it was an omen."

The old butler, who'd looked as if he wanted to get him off to bed, had stopped fidgeting and drawn near to listen.

"He grew old here without bitterness. It was as if he drained all of it in one draught and threw the cup away. When he came back to find they'd made me First Archon, he sang the Athenians one of his poems, telling them not to blame the gods if they thought better of it later. Someday I will teach it to you; but I expect you know those lines. Everyone does."

He was right, of course. He saw it with a smile.

"He retired from all public life, just as he'd said. But he knew how to live without being busy. He had traveled the world, meeting the sages and the kings; he knew the gods' names among foreign peoples, and their rites of worship. At Sais, the temple priests had told him Egypt's history back for six thousand years, and how the anger of Poseidon destroyed Atlantis. He had known and seen more than Odysseus . . ."

I wonder if, like old Argos, the dog Bia had known his master on his return. But then, Argos had been left masterless.

"He had known pleasure too, choosing the best like wine. All in all, he had enough stored up in himself to last him another lifetime. He lived between his town house and his farm, enjoying the seasons and his friends. People thought I made much of him for the sake of policy. It was no matter what they thought. We understood each other."

He picked up his mint-scented napkin, wiped his mouth and set aside his wine-cup. The butler prepared to show me out, I prepared my thanks. Then he said, "A good man will gather good men round him, and know too little of evil. A bad one will gather his like, and do nothing good. Ruling men, it seems, must be like this wine we have drunk tonight: strong enough, sweet enough, but with a fleck of mold upon the grape, which comes once in a way and makes it what it is. *And never drunk neat* . . . Ah well, it grows late. Thank you, my dear boy, for the pleasure of your conversation, and for your charming songs. We were all delighted. A very good night to you."

Eight or ten days later, he invited me again to sing; but while I was dressing, a messenger brought me his regrets. He was indisposed that evening, but hoped for the pleasure shortly. So I did not ride back to Euboia; at first, because I waited to hear from him; then, because I waited as all the city was waiting.

First, he had caught a cold; then, it had gone to his chest, with fever; then, his mind was wandering, and with his sons by his bed he had asked to see his children; then, he was sinking fast. As news came in, there began to be a hush all over Athens; at any sound in the street, everyone would pause to listen. The Acropolis, when I went up, was full of silent people, watching the house. When sunset came, the guards did not close the gates, and anyone stayed who wished. As the dark deepened, some went off to bed. I waited. It was a calm, warm night; and I knew the hour at which Hermes the Guide comes oftenest for his travelers. A little before the dawn, a woman cried; then we heard the household lamenting.

Around me, in the dark, women began to wail. In those days they went about more freely than in Athens now, and not a few had kept the death-watch. For some time they keened, their mantles flung over their heads; men stood still, talking in low voices, as people do when there is nothing left to stay for, yet they cannot make up their minds to go. As dawn was breaking, we saw the tall jar of purification set by the door, for those leaving the house to asperse themselves clean of death. In little knots the crowd drifted away.

I walked in half-awakened streets in the faint light. Doors opened, people looked out to ask for news. When they heard it, they seemed not so much grieved as dazed. For days it had been expected everywhere; yet now they could not quite believe it, nor see beyond. He had been there so long. He had put his style on everything, like Exekias who both shaped his vases and painted them. Like Exekias he kept up the old grand manner. He had been tyrant, but never upstart; he was the Old Archon now, head of the family. It was as if they had waked that morning, and found the Acropolis gone.

Next day he was laid out in state, and anyone he had ever received as guest came to do him honor. He lay in the hallway with its honeycomb marble floor, his bier draped with an old embroidered pall, maybe an heirloom from King Nestor's day. They had clothed him in pure white wool, and spread fine linen over him, and laid fringed fillets across him. He was crowned with a wreath of gold, twined with parsley and origan. His three lawful sons stood gravely by to greet us; his daughters and daughters-in-law and granddaughters keened for him, but decently, as Solon's laws required, without loud outcries or rending their hair and clothes. Nothing was in excess, nothing hubristic; but he looked in death what he had long been in all but name —last of the Athenian kings.

Before dawn next morning they took him to his grave in the Kerameikos, his menfolk walking before, the women behind wailing softly to the sound of a single flute. They needed no slaves to carry him; at every rest-halt there was a little crowd of Athenians waiting, in silence, to take the bier. Silently they did their stint, and silently stood back after, asking no recompense for the pollution; men came forward, even, to lower him into the grave. They laid on the coffin his old panoply, the two-winged helmet, the javelins and the spear, the gold-hilted sword, the shield with its serpent blazon. A wavering torchlight shone down into the vault; the shadows of the helmet-crests flickered like black bats. The kindred came forward with their gifts, pots of spices and scented oil, vases from Egypt, grave-flasks painted by masters of the art. Then the masons closed the slab, and so they left him, till the sculptors set up his stele. The mourners went home to take off their ashen clothes, comb their shorn hair, bathe and break their fast.

He did not stay long alone. Quietly, when the great had gone, the people came with their offerings. They brought

what they could, what they might have brought for their
own fathers: a basket of figs, a copper cloak-brooch, an
ancient vase long in the household, painted with checkers
and rings; a fillet stitched in the night; a little warrior
pinched out of clay with the colors fading; a dish of honey-
cakes. They laid them down, and went away with their
cloaks pulled over their faces.

Solon, I thought, now are you reconciled?

I turned towards my lodging to sleep. The streets were
waking, the stalls set up in the Agora; men met and greeted,
and everywhere one heard, "What now?"

On my way, I fell in with a man I knew, a certain
Proxenos, one of the first men of the Gephyriot clan. He
was as handsome as I am ugly, and pleased with it too; no
popinjay, however, but a noted horseman who had raced
his own chariot at the Isthmia. We walked on together;
he too had watched on the Acropolis. "And I would have
brought my son, if he were a few years older, so that he
would have had it to remember. Such things should be
handed on."

At his door, he asked me in to breakfast. Over the wheat
bread and warmed wine, I asked him what he foresaw for
the city now.

"Who knows?" He looked up frowning. "My father supported Solon, because the times were bad and the man was
honest. Everyone gave up something; my father said the
eupatrids gave up too much. To my mind he was right. But
we gave it for law, not tyranny."

It was the first time I'd heard that word used in Athens,
except about other states. His family was a very old one.
"I'm a Kean, so it's not for me to say. But it seems to me
there is law here, and justice too."

"Truly. While the Tyrant consents. He is still a man
with a spear while we have none. Pisistratos seldom lifted

it, and I give him credit for that. But we are still disarmed; the spear is there; and as for the man who holds it now, I doubt he is better than any one of us whose forefathers played their part in affairs in former days . . . Forgive me; you are a guest-friend of the family. I have said too much."

I said smiling, "You would have done in Samos. But here in Athens, we are just two men talking of public business, and your only fear is lest you have offended me. That is something, we can both agree."

"You are right, although . . . No, you are right. We have seen the fate of other cities in stasis; we should know when we are well off. Hippias will be made First Archon without dissent. He has been his father's pupil; for that matter, he must have been governing, in all but name, for some time already. He is steady and past his youth. No doubt we could do worse."

"And Hipparchos," I said, thinking it my due to a generous patron, "he has done a good deal to adorn the city."

"Oh, yes. That is his part; I expect he'll keep to it and be content. A pleasant lightweight, who will be neither here nor there."

Just then his young son, of whom he'd spoken, came running into the room, having escaped somehow from the women. He must have been two or three years old. Proxenos picked him up, and pretended to scold him; but I could see, and he too no doubt, that his father was delighted to show him off. No wonder; he was as lovely as infant Apollo in my Delian ode. He clung about Proxenos' neck, telling of some nursery exploit. It was a pretty sight; I offered the hoped-for tribute, that the family looks had been passed on.

"That's to be seen," said Proxenos, proudly rumpling his golden hair. "Handsome is as handsome does—eh, young Harmodios?"

4

PISISTRATOS on his deathbed had desired that the power should be shared between his two eldest sons, with precedence for the first. Law-abiding in death as in later life, he had willed it should be voted on by the Areopagos, that venerable tribunal. Each member was a former archon. But the old man had been First Archon a long time; of the ex-archons who could still get their old bones up the sacred hill, almost all in their time had been Pisistratos' men. As for the Alkmaionids, they were still in exile. Hippias became First Archon without a vote against it, with Hipparchos next in rank. As Proxenos had foretold, it all went smoothly.

For some time the Old Archon had been, to most Athenians, part man part legend. Nothing now changed in the life around them. It must have seemed the old order would last forever.

For my part, I would get no work during the time of mourning. It was neither an Olympic nor a Pythian year, so I took myself home to Euboia. Summer was ending in a sweet ripe smell of good harvests. I had friendly neighbors, thanks to my steward's good sense. When the crops came in, we all took turns to help each other, gathering the vintage, or lending slaves, or sharing an olive-press.

Country festivals delight me, with their ancient work songs as the grapes are trodden, the oxen led round the threshing-floor or the millstone. They are simple, these songs, like the beat of the heart or the breath of life; and their sound mates with their meaning as simply as the beasts mate in spring. They were sung before there were bards or poets, and of them we were all begotten. They are still our kindred, if we know our craft. Pulse and breath set us our bounds, within which is found all mastery. Without pulse and breath the body dies; without their measures the poet. But within their limits are the startled or the tranquil or the eager heart; the breath of ecstasy, or calm, or tears, or terror. What a possession is ours! Eighty years I have wandered through it, and have never reached its furthest frontier yet.

I did not lack company, having many friends in Eretria; I had my songs to make, and Dorothea to warm the house and exchange her gossip for mine.

"That Hipparchos, by your account of him, he'll be kicking up his heels, now his old father's hand is off the bridle."

"Maybe," I said. "But his father trained him, and I think he knows where to stop." He and Pisistratos had always used their famous tact on one another. Hipparchos never used to present to his father anyone, however amusing, that he might not care to acknowledge in public; he, in return, never upbraided his son for his loose acquaintance, unless he picked up someone politically dangerous.

"That's often the way," she said over her shoulder, as she stirred the pot with our supper. There was a hare in it, and some cunning spices. "But it's wonderful the changes you see when the strong hand's gone. Look at your own brother. Not that he's changed for the worse, but he's changed, that's sure. Would you ever have looked for that?"

"No, but I should have done." He had visited here both before and after our father's death; each time treating her with as much respect as if she had been my wife. But the first time, in his plain clothes with his simple barbering he had looked every inch a Kean. Last time, he'd looked

every inch a gentleman-adventurer, as we knew them then.
To save trouble at sea he had grown his beard again, but
now it had a rakish point to it; he had cut off his long
plaits, and wore his hair short to the nape. He had a gold
earring, and sandals with silver studs. In his fighting
panoply, which he put on to show us, he looked good
enough for a vase-painter; his helmet's tall crest was inlaid
with blue enamel, and his leather corselet embossed with
stampwork.

"This is heavy," I said. "What if you have to swim for it?"

"No laces, all clasps. I can be out of this before a ship
can settle, even if she's rammed. As for falling overboard,
we make the other fellows do that." Theas, it seemed, was
enjoying every day of his youth; all the more, no doubt,
because he'd had to wait for it till he had turned thirty.

"Yes," I said to Dorothea, "he's changed, but all he is
now was there already. It's truer to say that he's become
himself."

She took the spoon from the simmering pot, blew on it,
licked it, nodded. "It'll be the same with Hipparchos, I
daresay."

Of course she had never set eyes on him, or even heard
of him from anyone but me. If her voice had an edge, I
well knew why. Some women can read things in their men,
like a diviner in a goat's liver. She knew what I was waiting
for. She knew why I kept quiet about it: not from deceit,
but from fear that counting on it would bring bad luck.
That did not make her like him any better.

I expected nothing yet. When a Pisistratos dies, his
sons don't start to make merry after the bare month of
mourning; especially when the heir is a man like Hippias.
I was content to wait.

Meantime, I crossed to Keos, mostly to see Philomache.
The year before, she had borne a healthy boy; Midylos,
and his father the ancient athlete, had been near dancing

with delight. But it was a hot dry summer; many babies died of the flux, and she lost him at two months old. When I saw her soon after, she looked to have aged ten years. Now she had been brought to bed again; I found her blooming, and doting on the new one, for all that it was a girl. Midylos was one of those men who like a daughter, and was only sorry for old Bacchylides, grumbling that he would die before he saw a grandson. "Though," said Midylos to me, "he's not much past sixty, and as tough as an old vinestock. If he'd give over watching the pot, it might boil sooner. But he craves an Olympic victor. I sorely disappointed him. Even here on Keos, Theas always beat me in the games." He laughed. He was a well-liked man with a good farm, and well content.

As for Theas, no doubt his wife did not see enough of him; but the house was prosperous, and his two young sons adored him. "When Daddy's ship comes" was their day of festival; their dream of manhood was to sail with him. Sometimes I felt regret that I had no children, to whom I could be the father I wished I'd had. But I would never be such a father, the head of a house, the stay of a home. One can bargain with one's concubine, one cannot with one's child. With Dorothea at least I had dealt as fairly as I knew how; and now came the time when I was glad of it.

I had not been a month back in Euboia, when I had a visitor from Athens: Onomakritos of the oracles, no less. He announced himself by a groom riding ahead. Even for a man so pompous, it looked rather like an embassy.

With equal ceremony, I set food and wine before him, and made solemn small-talk till the last replenishment had been declined. Having meantime satisfied his courteous interest in my health, my land, my harvest and my relatives, I was free to ask how things were going in Athens.

The aspect of the planets, he said, was most benign, and Athene's sacred olive had borne abundantly, sure omen of prosperous times; it was plain the gods remained well disposed to the city. There was much more like this, letting me know that all went splendidly in Athens, without slight to the illustrious dead.

Just as I was thinking he meant to leave his business till next day, he came to it. He had been sent by both the Archons (there were still nine, but we let that pass as usual) to tell me that the sculptor had almost finished Pisistratos' grave-stele; they awaited only the epitaph to carve on it, and a threnody to sing at its dedication. The Archons were sure it would have been their father's wish, as it was their own, that I should make them. After that, they hoped I would stay on as their guest in Athens, and make the city my home; a source of pride to the Athenians, and of delight to them.

Nothing could have been more graceful. I perceived the mark of Hipparchos' hand. It was of a piece with his usual tact, getting me invited by Hippias' cherished diviner, to prove that he too would welcome me. I accepted gratefully, adding that I was honored in the messenger.

He bowed, like a man with more to say, and got down from his supper-couch to open his traveling bundle. I'd wondered why he'd not let the slave take it upstairs. He dug about in it, but spilled out the wrong bag, sending a handful of divining-pebbles rolling about the floor. The boy serving the wine—a well-mannered young Karian, whom Theas had bought for me in Halikarnassos—put down his jug and went to pick them up; but Onomakritos checked him with a solemn hand, and stood over them brooding. After considering each, he gathered them himself. "Sir," said the boy in his halting Greek, "is two there by door." The sage bustled over, gazed at them deeply, and said, "So far!"

He had dropped his pomp as a man does a fine cloak when he has work to do. For the first time, he did not look like a charlatan. When he had pouched the pebbles, I asked if it was for me he had read the signs.

"Certainly it was. How not, when it was on your account I came to spill them? An unsought omen is never to be neglected."

"You said, 'So far!' Am I to travel, then?"

"Yes, on the earth, and further than you have yet. And through the years of mankind, also. And the furthest of both will meet."

I thanked him for his divination. Poor man, I am persuaded he had the Sight, but not often enough to sustain his pride. If he had kept from hubris and its follies, he would not have ended as he did, in exile, the lying sycophant of a barbarian king.

His pebble-bag stowed away, he now got out what he had first been looking for. The Archons knew well, he said, that to give them the pleasure of my company this time of year would certainly cause me loss. They were happy to send me something in recompense, and to promise that I would not lose by coming to Athens, now or in time to come.

The bag that came out this time was big as the first and looked as heavy. But this one chinked when he put it on the table. Half of it was full of good white silver drachmas, stamped with the Attic owl. The rest of the weight was gold.

5

THEY SAY THAT the Arabian phoenix dies in flame, and is
reborn from its ashes. This is certainly true of Athens, and
I wish only good to that strong and thrusting chick. But
now I am old, the unburned phoenix is the Athens of my
heart. It is the city I have carried westward with me, into
Greater Greece. When I look back, my years there seem
one long summer, with bitter winter coming in a single day.
I can scarcely believe that there were fourteen years of it.
That it was the core of my life, I know.

Besides the rest, it was there that I first grew rich. I've
heard that I have a name for liking money, and so I do.
Most people do, who have got away from Keos and are
allowed to spend it. Men like it still more, who have fled
with nothing from a fallen city, and lived hand to mouth,
and seen a dear friend and master bleed away his pride.
Yes, I like to have money. I have made a great deal, and
spent what I needed to live well, but never all of it; so I
was no man's sycophant when the bad times came. In my
way, I am still a son of Leoprepes. He liked money too,
but he never cheated for it; Theas liked it, but never robbed
a peaceful ship for it; I like it, but I have never lied for it.
Money buys many things, of which the best is freedom.
Samos taught me that.

When I crossed to Attica, I had the Lament for Pisistratos nearly done. An epitaph had been in my head already,
before the summons came. I have put it in my book, be-

cause the tombstone it was carved on has disappeared.
Angry men are unjust, and the dead have no voice to answer.
I had hoped that my words would save it, but they are
rubble now. I suppose they will fill in the ground under
some grand new temple. Well, they will find good company.

I went, then, to court in Athens, just turned thirty, my
head steaming with songs. I was in the city of which I'd
dreamed since boyhood; I had a patron more like a friend,
who expected no servility; I was doing what I had been
born to do; and for being so happy I was getting paid.
Sometimes I would bend over water to glimpse my face;
I reckoned it should keep the gods from getting too jealous.

I found the two brothers ruling in perfect harmony. If
Hippias enjoyed it less, that was not because Hipparchos
crossed him, or tried to exceed his due share of power. Far
otherwise; he found the business of government tedious,
and left to his elder all he could. Such public councils as
absolutely required him, he would attend, and assent or
dissent as Hippias had instructed. On such occasions he
would even stand up to speak. He did it well (or he'd never
have opened his mouth) and I know his words were his
own, for he tried them out on me. But for him it was a performance, nothing more. He did his duty by his kin, as he
would have done in attending some dull wedding. When
it was over, he went back to his own affairs.

It was another thing with the religious rites and the great
processions. For all Hippias' well-known piety, when the
city's gods were honored, Hipparchos reigned. I have often
thought, in later years, that he was born too soon, and too
high. If he were living now, a mere knight like Aischylos
son of Euphorion, he might be putting tragedies on the
stage to delight the people, and making them laugh with
satyr-plays, and be kept in balance by the contest with his
peers. Who can trace the gods' ways with men? All tragedy
needs a victim. He was a patron of poets, but he never knew

of his last and greatest gift to them. He gave them a theme: hubris and nemesis. The tragic poets have lived off it ever since.

In those days, I kept my pity for Hippias. Not that his power was shaky. He was even valued; but only as the hand of his dead father, keeping in trust his heritage of good rule. Any citizen, if asked, would have said that Pisistratos would have made two of him, but there seemed no harm in him, and for that we could all be thankful. Of course he knew it; men feel such a thing through flattery like a stone through a sandal sole. He would have liked to make his own mark and hoped to do it, but was too prudent to make any changes yet. He was no fool; he saw the Spartans getting stronger in the south, the barbarians in the east; he could foresee a time when he'd need be a better man than his father, to keep what his father won. But at Hippias' age, then, his father had been a bold adventurer. Hippias was a worrier. He had no wish at all to relinquish power, and willingly took the larger share of it; but he was less sure of himself, and put much faith in oracles and omens.

I saw all that for myself; he did not confide in me, it was Onomakritos who shared his counsels. I thought of the Old Archon's words about strength and sweetness and the fleck of mold on the grape. Where the strength lay now was still untested; where the sweetness was, I had no doubt.

No one, I am sure, ever made patronage more delightful than Hipparchos did. Here in warm Sicily, King Hieron makes it kind and dignified, and just what an old man needs. But in those years I was young, and my needs were different.

Hippias had moved into Pisistratos' stately house. There was room in plenty for his growing children, and he could have taken in unmarried Hipparchos, too. But he was well suited as he was, and had no wish to move in. Hippias altered nothing, except to fill a room with shelves and chests for his ancient scrolls of oracles. He was a man for getting early to bed, and liking his household to do the same.

Hipparchos' house had a fine prospect, looking north towards Mount Parnes. It carried his style as a song carries its maker's. The things one saw there were always changing, as a poet may make new songs; but the style was always there.

If he had just bought something handsome, he'd give a party to show it off. It might be a small bronze of Dionysos with gilded thyrsos-wand and wreath; or a big wine-bowl painted with Theseus among the Amazons. (It was all red-figure now, and to be noticed a piece must be finer than the rest.) Sometimes he'd bring in a troupe of young girls to play the flute and dance, and show their tinted breasts through fine Kos tissue. Their manners would be charming, they would sit on your couch and chat prettily and pour your wine; but it was understood that if you wished for more, you must arrange for it at home. He never let a party run to riot, unless he was in the mood.

He patronized, too, some beautiful boy acrobats, who performed naked; but it was seldom that one was invited to stay the night. Unless he was entertaining formally, he had a friend to share his supper-couch, and no doubt later his bed. These friends were chosen as carefully as his table-ware or his clothes; youths in their later teens, handsome, well born, well bred; amusing too, or they would not be seen twice. The chosen would reign for some months, or even as long as a year. I don't think false vows of eternal love were ever made to them, and they were always dismissed with grace. Some splendid gift, suited without offense to their rank and station—a horse perhaps, or a gold cup, or an inlaid parade helmet—would give the signal that the time had come to adorn the supper-couch with a new face. Meantime, the youth had been brought into fame and fashion, and had met everyone in Athens who was worth knowing. Those who were ambitious, and used their opportunities, came out of it very well.

Certainly, we poets had no cause to complain. Unlike the favorites, we were not displaced by newcomers. We were like bees in a hive, to which new honey was always coming.

Lasos of Hermione, the same young man who'd been crowned on Keos the day my father died, very soon arrived. We got on well together; each worked in his own way, and each was called upon for different occasions. Hipparchos always made it clear that there was room for both of us; neither of us was quarrelsome or vain enough to make trouble for a courteous patron.

One day, when I had been there about two years, Hipparchos said to me, "Simonides, dear friend; what could we do to get Anakreon here?"

The "we" was like him, telling me I need fear no rival and was above the thought of it. He had never spoken a word about my tavern stint in Samos, though he must have known. I said, "If you like, I will gladly go and ask him. As you know, Polykrates never took me up, and won't remember me. I could see Anakreon privately, and talk to him as a friend. I know he would be happy here. But Polykrates has done a great deal for him; I should think pretty well anything in Samos is his for the asking. If he says no, I hope you will forgive him."

"Forgive!" he exclaimed with his easy smile. "What a thing to say. With artists like you two, one does not demand, one petitions. But, surely, he has done that fat old pirate too much honor already. It's Polykrates should be grateful, not he. Yes, do see him. Tell him how we live in Athens now, and ask him to make one of us. I put my faith in you."

There was no resisting him when he chose; I said at once I would set out in the next few days. Keos would be on my

way, but I thought I would leave it till my homeward
journey. In case I failed, which I half expected, I could
linger and delay bad news. Hipparchos always inspired an
earnest hope that one would not disappoint him.

At least, if Anakreon said no, he could be trusted to do
it prettily, and it would be good to see him. Next morning
I went down to Piraeus to find a ship. I was getting knowl-
edgeable, for Theas put in every few months and sometimes
oftener; Athens was coming to rival Corinth as a city of
good craftsmen. Its painted pottery was wanted everywhere,
as well as its olive oil. So I saw a good deal of him and of his
friends, knew several good shipmasters, and had been
warned against the bad ones.

While asking about, I picked up what news I could from
Samos. Polykrates was richer and foxier than ever. He had
broken off his old alliance with the Pharaoh Amasis; as to
the reason, accounts were various and you could take your
pick. Kyros the Great was dead, succeeded by that son of
his, that vicious mad dog Kambyses. His father should have
put him down; but the call of the blood is strong. He was
planning to conquer Egypt; and Polykrates got word of it.
He compared the opposing forces, and decided he'd backed
the wrong side. So before Amasis had time to ask his help,
he declared the treaty broken. His tale, which I'll believe
when I see iron floating, was that his long good fortune had
made Amasis fear some great reversal, which might make
their friendship unlucky. As things fell out, half the world
has come to believe this story. It is the hand of Nemesis,
you might say.

The truth was that Polykrates had hastened to court
Kambyses. He even offered him forty war-triremes, with
soldiers to man them. But he was more cunning even than
this, for the soldiers he sent off all came from the old
houses whose loyalty he mistrusted. Many who'd been boys
when he seized power were now grown men, and ready to

avenge their fathers. As it turned out, he undervalued their
wits. At the fleet's first port of call, they all put their heads
together, added up the score and got it right. Polykrates had
sent word to Kambyses, kindly to see that none of them
came back.

So they put about ship next day, and invaded Samos
instead of Egypt. How many Samians might have rallied
to them, it's hard to say, because old Polykrates was too
quick for them. He sent out his mercenaries through the
city to round up the women and children, and lock them
in the great boathouses of the naval dockyard. These he
promised to set alight, if the menfolk gave any trouble. It
seems he was believed. Well, he was a pirate; who knows
what he'd done in his time. So the rebellion failed, and
those who could get away sailed off into exile.

I hoped all this might further my mission to Anakreon.
Kind as he'd been, it would have been presumptuous to
call myself his friend; but he would have heard something
of me by now, as he'd foretold. We would meet on more
equal terms, and I thought I knew him a little. There is a
certain threshold between a courtier and a sycophant;
nobody tells one when one crosses it, but one feels it in
oneself. I only feared to reach Samos and find him already
gone.

The first thing I saw there was that the great new
harbor mole was finished, shining with new-dressed stone
and gleaming bollards. We had trouble to find a mooring,
the port was so full of ships: Egyptian, Tyrian, Kypriot,
Sicilian; several from Rhodes, which Polykrates had conquered, putting his son there as governor. The galley-slips
before the boathouses held a small fleet of snub-nosed,
boar-headed Samian triremes and pentekonters. The whole
waterfront bustled and chattered with trade, every house a
shop; and the merchantmen tied up there had their wares

spread out on the quayside, shouting for custom with lungs of bronze.

I'd have liked to go shopping and sightseeing, after so long; but nothing is secret on a busy trade-road, and it seemed that my name had run before me. All kinds of people were on the quay to meet me, some of whom I had barely heard of; but there were old friends too from the Victory, and I was swept in there to give my news. The same host was still there, and gave me a beautiful Lakonian cup to drink his health in. I looked again, and said, "What's this? What will Theodoros say?"

"Why, Simonides, to think of your knowing it again after all these years. He would say he liked to see a good piece treated with respect. I do that in his memory. I keep it for the masters."

"His memory?" I said, looking up from the painted owl.

"Had you not heard, then? He died one day in the foundry. They were running the melted bronze into the mold; he felt the heat, they say, and got short of breath. But he kept on his feet till the mold was filled, shouting at them all, you know his way; then he caught at his breast and fell down, and was dead before the doctor came. His prentices said that right till the last, while he could catch his breath he was telling them how to finish the statue when the mold was broken. Sophilos had no use in his right hand for a week, from Theodoros gripping it at the end."

I remembered his great fingers, so light on this very cup.

"It's Anakreon now," said the host, "who has his own." He took it from the shelf to show me. "A love-gift you can be sure, though he never tells. You remember his song about the girl with the colored slippers."

There she was, in elegant red-figure touched up with purple, tossing her ball. Round the outer curve of the bowl was a whole frieze of girls, playing with a ball, or with one another; the painter had made it plain that they came, like the girl in the song, from the well-built city of Lesbos. I admired the work, and asked where I would find the poet.

"Why, here. Just let me fill your cup. He'll have heard by now of your coming."

This was taking too much for granted, and I told him so. But the words were hardly out of my mouth, when heads turned to the doorway, and Anakreon came in with out-stretched hands. The crowd parted for him with as much respect as if he'd been Polykrates, but more cheerfully. His red hair was fading, but he had kept his thin fine-boned grace; he felt as light as a fawn when he ran up and clasped me.

In life as in song, he never used an unneeded word. He had claimed me as a brother, after which all other compliments would have fallen short. He just talked, as though we'd met only a few months back instead of years, and as if I had had a name as long as he had. Since the Old Archon died, I'd thought him the only man on earth who could really awe me; but now, in his presence, I felt only delight at being here. I had even forgotten my errand, when he said that of course I must put up at his house.

It was close by the Palace, in the best Samian style, with a carved doorframe, and a columned porch of rose-red Samian marble. Inside it was as handsome as Hipparchos's; smaller, but with everything in scale, as delicate as his songs: chairs inlaid with ivory, a carpet from Egypt, silver cups with gold insets, upon an ebony sideboard; a big wine-cooler painted with Meleager's boar-hunt. He had sent orders ahead to have bath-water warmed for me; and I was waited on by a beautiful young slave, whose polished manner I doubt the presence of a king could have dis-composed. He must have been as costly as the inlaid wine-cups; Persians nowadays were hard to come by. One thing was certain: not even Hipparchos could offer Anakreon more than he already had.

Still, I had to try. Soon after an excellent supper of sturgeon cooked with herbs, the youth was kindly dismissed to eat his share, leaving the wine between us. When I complimented him on so excellent a servant, he said he had been a real pleasure to train, having been bought from some vulgar fool on whom he had been quite wasted. "Now that I've taught him to think well of himself, he is so proud that he can afford to be gracious."

"Like to like. It's not every man to whom good fortune gives good grace." And I led round the talk to the pleasures of life in Athens, the good company, the Archons' open hands, and so on. Before I'd half done, his green eyes slanted round at me, and he began to laugh.

"Stop, dear man!" He leaned from his supper-couch to grasp my shoulder. "Enough! I can take the next verse myself. I was to have come to Athens, and said all this to *you*. 'Anakreon, my dear fellow, can't you persuade Simonides?' What collectors these autarchs are."

"Me!" I said, too startled to join the laughter. "But I thought—"

"Oh, that. I don't think he even knows you've been here before. No one has liked to tell him what he missed. A good deal was happening in those days, you know, a host of people passing through. He first learned of you from Athens. Now you're a treasure he's panting to acquire. You'd have heard from him by now, but as it happens he's in Naxos, visiting his old friend Lygdamis. Only just before he left, he urged me to go and bid for you."

This time I laughed too; then I said, "But you didn't come."

"No." He pushed his hair back, tilting his rose-wreath drunkenly. He was sober enough, though. "I put him off; I'm not sure why. Mostly from a feel in my skin, that all this"—he waved his hand towards the window and the spread of the town below—"can't last much longer. No reasons; or too many. When the fruit is sweetest, it falls. One can't tell the day."

I looked round the beautiful room, and at the window above the teeming harbor, the shops full of foreign luxuries, the well-dressed crowds. Just across the strait were the hills of Persian-held Ionia, so near it seemed one could shout across and be heard. But that had been so for many years.

"He didn't press me," Anakreon said. "He thought that I might be jealous."

"Do not tempt me into hubris, son of Apollo. Or your father will be after me."

He laughed, and lifted his wine-cup. Then he grew serious. "Hubris. That's what they are saying about the Tyrant. Well, yes and no. You know, he would never have burned those hostages. He gambled with them, and won. He always wins. The fruit hangs down full of juice, riper and heavier . . ." He dipped the rhyton into the masterpiece of a wine-cooler, wiped it with a drawn-thread napkin, and filled my cup. "But I ask myself, am I getting some warning from a god, or just feeling my skin too tight, like a sloughing snake? Does it concern any man but me?"

"Indeed. It concerns me, I can promise you."

"Yes, we have been concerned for one another. Now, as I see it, if you go back and say that Anakreon feels beholden to his patron, but will be honored to visit Athens as your guest, just to pay his respects—that won't set you back at court, will it? Then we can see."

"Why, I shall be the happiest of men. Will you really come?"

"How not, when Simonides invites me? I shall come to Athens and say all I've been told to say, which you have not yet heard the half of." He straightened his wreath, making a solemn face.

"But," I said, "you have heard my piece; and what do you say to *me*?"

"Oh, once I'm in Athens, I suppose Hipparchos will do his business with me himself. Then my refusal will come from me, not you, and cast no shadow on you. After all, you did persuade me to come."

"Refusal!" I felt as if I'd seen one of my father's best sheep fall down a cliff, and I expect I showed it. "I thought you were saying yes."

"I am sorry," he said, with a smile that would have softened bronze. "I thought so too, until just this moment. No, it won't do. He has been very good to me, you know. And in return I have offered praise which I can't recant without dishonor."

There is never an answer to that. I tried none. He pushed at his wreath, and it tilted over again.

"And then, of course, I'm in love."

"Again?" Disappointment had made me cross.

"Come, come, my dear. A furnace is no cooler for last year's fire . . . *Maiden-faced boy, heedless of my pursuing, And all unknowing my soul's charioteer.* That is no longer *quite* true. But he would never leave his ancestral home for me, why should he? Yes, well, I've a good-healing heart, as soldiers tell you they have good-healing flesh. I could go now, and know I had left my patron at his height of fortune, not waited like a ship-rat to smell the leaky plank. And yet, and yet . . . Bear with me, my dear. Ionia was my world, and only this is left of it. I think I will see it out."

There was no answer to that, either. I was not fool enough to spoil the rest of the evening. We drank and talked and drank and sang, and dawn was near when he

lit me to my bed, having long since sent off the gracious
Persian to get his beauty sleep.

Next day he asked some very pleasant people to meet me.
My presence was never explained; it was enough, it seemed,
that Simonides was visiting Anakreon. The noble Samian,
his soul's charioteer, was not on view. "Only a fool," he
said to me in private, "will show a purse of gold to a ship-
load of pirates. I could tell you things . . ." It was a good
party, and next day I took ship for Athens.

Hipparchos was so charmed to hear of Anakreon's visit
that I got anxious, and warned him not to expect too much.
One never liked the thought of disappointing him. All I'd
managed to do, I said, was tempt Anakreon with the glory
and fame of Athens, so that he longed to visit it; and had
ventured to promise it would surpass his hopes.

This would ensure him a dazzling fee for his recital, a
small return for his help and kindness. Often I wonder that
bards will be so silly as to bicker with their peers, and lower
themselves with jealousy; when, if we are friends, we can
not only learn from one another, but do each other useful
good turns like this.

He came to Athens the next month. Everyone had a
triumph. He did: he performed at Hipparchos' house before
everyone worthy the privilege, enchanting our ears, melting
our hearts, and leading us at will from mirth to tears. I had
one: he thanked me publicly for having led him, like a
guiding Hermes from Olympos, to the delights of this
splendid city. Even Hipparchos had one: Anakreon told him
that the graces of his court (with its famous ornament, the
great Simonides) made a singer who had failed to visit it
seem only half a Greek. After their private interview, my
patron came to me in the sweetest of tempers, saying,
"Well, you did *your* part, my dear Simonides. He would
come, without a doubt, but for his obligations. He didn't
say that in so many words, but it was plain to *me*. Wasn't

it charming, the little song he made about Kallias at the hunt?" (Kallias, a dashing horseman, was the current friend, as I'd remembered to tell Anakreon.) "I shan't repeat all his praise of you, it would make you too proud to live with. Mark my words, we shall see him in Athens yet."

Besides all this, it was a triumph for Polykrates, when his favorite poet returned to say how they'd tried in vain to steal him away to Athens, but Samos had his heart. I have lived a long time; but in the art of pleasing everyone while betraying no one, I have never met anyone to touch Anakreon.

6

I KEPT MY LAND, and cared for it. It was part of my freedom; and I felt its people my charge. I told Hipparchos at the outset that I had a family estate I should sometimes need to visit; one must start as one means to go on. He said with his easy good manners that of course I must look after my inheritance; hinting, just as politely, that he would rather it was not when he was giving an important party, or entertaining some foreign guest of honor. He gave me good notice of such things; one always knew where one was with him. I in turn would give good notice to Dorothea; now that I came less often, she liked to prepare a feast. It was coming to seem more her house than mine, and I would not spoil her hospitality by taking her unprepared.

Meantime, in Athens, I was a man with a man's desires.

The Archons had installed me in one of their guest-houses on the Acropolis, looking south to Phaleron and the sea. I ran it with my Karian boy and an old woman to cook. I never bought a slave-girl. I do not like the unwilling service of barbarians, with whom one cannot exchange a thought. I have never been a man who needs a woman every second night; I've had other things to save my vital spirits for. So when I did feel the need, I walked out to the Kerameikos.

It was a place, then as now, for the women of the middle sort, who liked to call themselves hetairas and not whores. This was a time when the great courtesans of Athens rivaled even the Corinthians, but I never thought of attempting *them.* They scared the ugly Kean shepherd who still lived on in me; I feared their mockery. Where I went, I was welcome enough. I had money, and was somebody from the court. It was an easygoing way of life; most of the time, at least.

Well, there was one girl . . . She was working for an old madam who'd been a beauty in her day, and ran a clean friendly house; not one of those where the girl's name and price are painted over the door of every room. The girls who were free would treat one like a guest, just catching one's eye and pulling their dresses tighter. All except this one girl. Thalatta was the youngest, I suppose about fifteen; a small face, triangular, a wide mouth and tilted nose; thin, with the air of having been betrayed by fortune, and taking it very bravely. She never displayed herself as the others did; just gave one a look and half a smile, as if saying, "We two could understand each other, if you did but know it."

I don't care for thin girls as a rule; the delight of the sculptor is also mine, I like the living marble. But she was clever, and her fragile body flattered a man's. "We two," she could say without a spoken word, "we have our secrets from all those fools." At first she did not talk much; after a while, she told me she came from Naxos, and that her father had pledged her for a debt. The truth, as I later learned, was that she'd run off from there with a sailor, and was no one's thrall, but kept a third of her takings. She used to tell me—never whining, she was too clever for that —that she was saving to buy her freedom, but lived in dread that her mistress would sell her first. Two or three men were offering to buy her. She would hint at dreadful things about them, always as if making light of it to spare my feelings. Sometimes she would point one out, if someone gross or drunken should be leaving as I came in.

"Oh," she would say, "one can put up with them now and then, that's only the luck of the trade, there are far worse houses than this one. But to be shut up alone with a man like that, always at his bidding, never to see a friend again—never *you* again, the only one who has understood me . . . ! Oh, I think I should kill myself before long."

Of course, I would always slip her something extra to save towards her freedom; and, of course, the time duly came when she was to be sold that very month. The buyer (a fat man with scrofula) would have the money soon. True, the mistress would wait till she saw his silver; but it was just a matter of days.

Well, she pleased me in bed, and I liked the thought of having her to myself; but most of all it was because, as it seemed, she had only me to care for her, that made me say I would be there with the money first. She embraced me, and warned me to say nothing yet to the mistress; the other man was rich, and if he knew, would raise his offer. It would be best if I gave her the money, not at the brothel, but at my house. I can't think how I swallowed that; I daresay because she was too clever to make excuses. Presently she led me out to the common guest-room and saw me off with a tender kiss. I was still on the threshold when I remembered I'd left my walking-stick inside the door, and turned back to get it. She was looking towards another girl who was sitting there, a painted Egyptian; and though she'd not had time even to open her mouth, her face said louder than words, "What did I tell you? The fool will pay." The other girl saw me first, and grimaced to warn her. That killed my last doubt, even before she saw me and tried to face it out. There was no need to say anything, and I went away.

For a while, this brought me back to my prentice days in Ionia. It was lucky that at least I remembered Hipponax, and did not spoil my work with tedious scoldings. She was not Women, but one girl, as Hipponax was one man, by whom one must not judge others. My pride was not so tender to blows as in those old days, and a visit to Dorothea healed its bruises. Presently, feeling cured, I pulled the scab off my wound by making a good story of it for Hipparchos, one evening when I was sharing his supper-couch.

When I had done, he cried, "My dear fellow! Wherever have you been wasting yourself? A man like you, in Athens, to be making do with a common trull! Tell me, what price did she set on herself, this little vixen?"

"A hundred drachmas. But then, there were the other bidders."

"You must be joking. Why, you could buy a good dog for that. Well, she has played that game for the last time. I'll see to it."

"By all means," I said, "if you know of any other fish she is playing on the line, give them a word of warning."

"We shall see. My dear Simonides, I blame myself for all this. I have been a selfish host; I don't invite enough women here. A man of your worth should not have to go foraging. People will think I don't look after you . . . Come to supper—yes—three nights from now. I shall try to make amends."

When the night came, it was clear that he'd taken

trouble. The room was garlanded, smelling of roses and
rich spiced food. The other men, of whom one was
Thessalos, were all distinguished; and the women did not
appear with the wine and wreaths, like common flute-girls
or dancers. They were to share the meal. After our host
had greeted us, and each man had been shown to a couch
with room for two, an inner door was thrown open with a
flourish, and in they came.

I wondered, indeed, where I'd been wasting my time.
They walked with the dignity of ladies bringing offerings to
a temple, but much more gracefully; their paint, if they
wore any, was as delicate as nature; their gowns in clear
bright colors were thin, but not tight, so that their bodies
were just glimpsed softly as they moved; their hair was put
up into embroidered snoods, as the fashion was just then;
and from their softly hennaed ear-lobes dangled worked
gold. They brought in the scents of a rose garden, planted
here and there with aromatics.

Hipparchos stepped down from his supper-couch to greet
them, just as if they'd been men; and I understood the
nature of this occasion. These were the royalty of their
calling. No lesser man could have brought them into one
room together. Certainly, he took on nothing he did not
mean to do well.

I don't know how they were allotted among the guests, it
flowed so naturally. I do know that from the moment they
came in, one had especially dazzled me: a young woman
with that brilliant fairness which art can never counterfeit,
and large deep blue eyes. It's a coloring that often goes
with silliness; when you see wit and sense there, it can seem
almost divine. Her gown was deep blue, sewn all over with
small gold stars, and starry clusters hung from her ears. I
was wondering who would have the god-sent luck to get
her, when she walked towards my couch, and said, like a
queen being gracious to a worthy subject, "Greetings,

Simonides, and good health to you. Why have you never called on me?"

I made room for her, with some confused reply. She settled her gown, smoothing out its embroidered borders, and said smiling, "I don't believe you even know who I am. I am Lyra."

Just so, on the slopes of Ida, might Aphrodite have declared herself to the young Anchises, simply, without fuss.

I must collect myself, before she thought me an oaf. "I have heard of Lyra, as I have heard of Helen. But I've neither the beauty of Paris, nor Menelaos' rank." (Nor his wealth, I thought.) "Fear of presumption kept me from your door."

"Foolish man," she said lightly. "Do you think that Helen would have shut her door to Homer?"

"Beautiful Lyra, but I am not Homer."

"Sweet-tongued Simonides, but I am not Helen. So we're quits. And because you have never deigned to attend my parties, I've had to sing your songs to the guests myself. Of course everyone said, 'But where is the poet?' And what could I reply?"

"Why, that the crow should stay in hiding, if he can have his song sung by the nightingale."

Her blue eyes changed and grew soft. "They wanted the Lament of Danae. I know every word, but I dared not. It always makes me cry."

She laid her hand on mine, and pressed it gently. I lifted and kissed it; the fingers were long and delicate, with faintly tinted tips. Even the slave with the jug and finger-bowl had seemed to rinse them with reverence. I recalled with shame the coarse grasping hands of Thalatta.

The first tables came in and were set beside us. You don't get such meals any more in Athens. (Here in Sicily, yes, if I could still digest them.) She ate with an elegance I'd not seen since I left Ionia. Now and then she would take up some choice bit and dip it in sauce and feed it to me, with a gay subtle glance that said, "This will be good, but some things are more delicious."

She leaned on her cushions just near enough for me to feel her scented warmth. Though she roused desire, she gave off too a sense of ease and harmony, both promise and present pleasure. Her skin was flowerlike however close one looked. I said, "Tonight for the first time I rejoice that I am not Homer. They say that he was blind."

"He is dead, too." She put a shelled shrimp into my mouth. "But don't lie to me, poet. To be Homer you would forfeit me, and him up there, and all that he can give you. Even your eyes. Your life, maybe. Not so?"

"I thought so once. He is for all time, yes. But only his own time could have begotten him. He is a god to me, yet my own time made me otherwise; and time has taught me that I have my own things to say."

"When will you come and say them to me, Simonides? I don't eat men, like Odysseus' sirens."

"Ah, but those who dare the current can still be drowned."

"Put your toe in the water, much-enduring voyager, and come to one of my parties. My friends only pay their share of the feast, you know. Sometimes we sing and amuse each other till dawn. Or sometimes we have a little contest of some kind; and then, of course, there is a prize." The lamplight shadowed a laughing-crease beside her mouth.

"I should have got someone to bind me to the mast. It is too late now; I have heard the music from the island. Yes, I will come."

The second tables came in, and she began to gossip about the guests, with a little salt but no vinegar. I remarked that our host's chosen companion was well past her prime. "Oh," she said, "Peitho will amuse him all the same. She has known everyone. His father too . . . well, of course he must know that. They say she was matchless in her day; she spent one fortune and saved another. Even now that she's put away her mirror, she still gets rich. Some old lover tells her what ships to take a venture in; she has a cargo now with Theasides . . . Oh, you know him! He comes from your part of the world."

"He's my brother. Is he so well known in Athens?"

"He's well known wherever he goes." Maybe I was wrong, but I thought she sleeked herself a little, like a cat that has almost purred. "He doesn't visit us very often; I think he prefers Corinthians. He tells *us* that he comes to Athens to see his brother. I might have known!"

"Most people say they never would have guessed it."

"Oh, there's a look. Men who both know what they can do. A style." She nodded, and glanced round the room again. Her fine brows drew together. "But *why* has our host put Antenor with Phylinna? I wish he would not do those things."

"It doesn't seem that Antenor is complaining."

"Oh no. That girl will get him and keep him, now. But everyone knows about him and Milto, he has been her friend so long. Poor girl; now when she's been ill and can't look her best, it really was not kind."

Milto, with too much paint on a face that should have had distinction, was doing her best to look as if her supper partner delighted her. I said, "I don't suppose he meant it. Parties like this he gives to please his friends; I doubt he knows much about such things himself."

She glanced up from the bread she was cleaning her fingers with, looked round at me and seemed about to speak; but just dropped the crust to a little dog under the table, and started to talk about her own pet dog at home.

The tables were cleared, the wine and the wreaths came in; a pretty boy and girl danced naked, Herakles and Antiope, which made everyone laugh; then a couple of flute-girls who had played for them played on, a screen of sound for talk. There was a good deal of merriment, and calling from couch to couch. Lyra did her share; but would drop her voice to talk to me again, as if she found it better. She will take me, I thought, when I have courted her in the way she will expect. I must ask Theas to buy me a Persian necklace. She would like lapis. When will her next party be? The warmth of the wine brought out the scent she was wearing. My hope of possessing her was only a part of my pleasure; it was almost enough that a creature of such loveliness was here, contented, in my company.

The dancers had gone; the flute-girls now made their bow; there was the pause that expects departure. Lyra pushed back a feather of hair into her snood. Her soft lips brushed mine like a whispered promise; she spread out her skirt to step down with grace. Then her head turned sharply, so that I followed her glance.

The women were not gathering to leave together, as they had entered. Their partners had got down with them. The first pair was already before Hipparchos, holding hands; I could half hear, and clearly see, the complicit thanks, the answering smile of felicitation. Only now it came to me that the party had been just the appetizer of Hipparchos' feast. The main course would be enjoyed in private. He had bought for each guest a night with one of the first hetairas in Athens. It was his little joke. He had done it mainly for me.

I don't know how I saw so quickly that something was wrong. Since I was a man, I'd been used to seeing men leave parties with women they had picked up there, dancers or flute-girls or hetairas. It had been expected by everyone, the host, the guests, the woman. In late years I'd done it my-self, if a girl made it clear enough that she was willing; I still half feared the disgrace of being refused in public. One made one's own arrangement, said thanks to the host, and collected the girl as one left; she might wave to friends, one's own friends might shout good wishes. But this was different. This girl with her grace and pride had not been fooling, playing the game of courtship when already bought. She'd believed she was free to choose.

Her head was turned away; she was watching Milto's face, as Antenor led away laughing Phylinna. I said quietly, "You were not warned of this."

She did not look round. "Were you?"

"No. Could you not tell?"

"Yes. I am sorry." She was very angry, though, and I felt the burn from it. Her long fingers were clenched on the gold-starred border of her overdress. Half to herself as she watched the room, she said, "The fee was high. But it was not that kind of message . . . Some of them knew. Phylinna did. Not Milto . . . Look, he is amused."

Well, I thought, a host who gives a surprise treat at a party is bound to look amused; no doubt he meant it for the best. I was more concerned with myself. I could feel the heat of shame crawling all over me.

"If I had been asked," I said, "I would have told him I never yet forced an unwilling woman. I am not to everyone's taste; I know it, and so should he. Don't fear I'll do anything to spoil your evening. I daresay we had better leave together. Or would you rather show them all that you do just as you wish?"

We should soon be the last to move. She turned to look straight at me with her large blue eyes; then suddenly she laughed, very sweetly, like a good singer going into a song, and slid an arm round my neck. Laying her head on my shoulder, she whispered in my ear, "What are you thinking of? Look happy, kiss me, do you want to offend him? Quickly! Now! We can talk as you see me home."

From her face, she could have been crooning me endearments. I kissed her and she clung to me. It was hard to

let her go; but I did not want her to think I was for taking
my present after all. We went up to the Archon's couch,
where he and his old hetaira were dismissing each couple
wittily. Lyra stepped up gaily, swinging our joined hands.

"Well, Simonides, my friend," he said with his most
charming smile, "have I made up at last for my neglect of
you?"

I was inspired to answer that he had given me the theme
for a thousand songs, and no poet could ask for more.

"And a lyre, I hope, which will answer sweetly to the
hand." For a moment his eyes moved round to her.

She bent her knee, spreading her glittering gown in her
right hand, and said lightly, "Oh yes, my lord, there will
be music." Then we were out, with the linkboy waiting.

He walked before us at a decent distance, being well
trained. I gave her my arm because the path was steep, and
because of the linkboy. Presently she said, "Did you mean
it, that if I'd chosen, you'd have let me walk out alone?"

"Certainly; it was your right. Thank you for sparing my
pride."

"Your *pride?*" Her voice had risen; quickly she brought
it down. "You never thought that was all? You must be
mad. He would never have forgiven you."

"Oh, he meant it for a joke. One never knows what he
will think of next. Thanks to you my face was saved."

"And you thought the joke was on you? You should
think better of yourself, my friend."

"But on whom else?"

"On us, of course. Milto once displeased a friend of his;
he doesn't quickly forget. As for me . . . perhaps he thinks
I need taking down a little. He doesn't like women much,
you know."

"I never heard him say so. Why should he care about
them one way or the other? He does without them very
happily."

"Why indeed? But a man need not scold like a Hipponax, for one to know."

"Hipponax! You must know the poets well."

"Oh, enough to converse with my guests, I hope. Besides, any man who wants a curse to throw at a woman has heard of *him*. I don't know what they would do without him."

"Well, his fame his outlived him. He would be glad of that."

"Would you rather live on by cursing, or be beloved and die?"

"The second, but I hope to avoid the choice."

"If you knew Hipponax, you must have known Ionia." I began to tell her about it, when, too soon, the linkboy stopped at her house. I paused only to bid her good night; but she drew me near and whispered, "He might tell tales. You had better come in awhile, if you don't mind walking home without a torch."

"I shall have starlight." I gave the man something and dismissed him. A lamp was burning inside, with scented oil. It was a guest-room which Anakreon himself would have approved. Four supper-couches of pale polished pearwood, a sideboard with a fine wine-cooler and red-figured cups, a little gilt Aphrodite on a marble stand. Everything was light and cool, no whore's trimmings at all; even the wine-cooler was painted with a scene of decent revelry. A curtain of patterned loomwork hid the room beyond.

"Stay a little," she said, "to be sure he's gone. He may have been told to wait and see."

"Yes, indeed." I did not yet presume even to smile. "He might go round the corner and come back."

"A cup of wine, then. Try this. A friend of mine ships it in from Samos."

It was excellent, just as good as what Theas brought me. "Tell me more," she said, "about Ionia. I shall never go there, now. Some women do, and I hear some of them prosper; but the Greeks who govern for the Persians do what they like with people like us, and I could not be at anyone's bidding. Tonight I should have known better; I was luckier than I deserve."

When the cups were empty, I made half a move to go, just to show I was taking nothing for granted. Our eyes met smiling. She took up the lamp; but it was not to the outer door that she lit my way.

Beautiful Lyra! Like the zenith moon, more lovely when the robe of stars was shed; like the moon, making no false vows that her light was for one alone. In the years I loved her, I can't pretend that I was ever free from jealousy; but I was never mocked, never betrayed or cheated. She had handsomer lovers—you could say that for most of them!— and richer, and higher-born; but when she said, "Simonides, you are my truest friend," I knew I was the only one to hear those words from her. Indeed, she was as good a friend as a lover, which is saying much for her friendship.

I made many songs for her; first to praise, and later to amuse her. They are sung in Athens still. It is hardly ten years since she died. When she had put away her mirror, as the saying is—not that she ever really did it!—we were dear friends still. As I said to her, "If you like, turn the young men away. But you are still ten years younger than I, and very much better-favored." Not that I had her to myself, even in those days. She was the kind of woman old lovers always come to with their troubles, or to talk about the past.

When I knew her first, she dazzled Athens, and great men sent gifts to her door. She accepted their flowers and garlands and their presents of fruit and game, but never took jewels from men she had not slept with. She did not like, she said, to live in debt; and besides, she liked it known who her chosen friends were. Indeed, men would brag even about having been asked to one of her parties, and she charged a good deal for the privilege; but she never let anyone buy himself in if he was boorish or tedious or made jealous scenes. She set her style. It was no wonder she aroused envy in women; and, as I'd learned at Hipparchos' party, also in men.

As for the contests she'd told me of, they were of various kinds, as the whim took her, or sometimes the need of money. Then, having ensured that no one she disliked was there, she just put herself up to auction. I was never present on such nights. Though well off for a poet, I was poor as her lovers went; and, besides taking thought for my feelings, she liked to see a sporting run. When wealthy rivals were there, the bidding went high, and there might be no such contest again for several months. She spent a great deal of money, having, as she said, very simple tastes. She hated clutter and tawdriness and mess; all she asked were a few good things, standing where she could see them; things that were plain and tasteful, like Egyptian alabaster or heavy gold.

Most of her contests, however, were for her own amusement and her guests'. Some were absurd, and the outcome left quite to chance; I remember she once had a bath brought in full of live fish, which we had to catch one-handed. The prize was always the same; so the contests were very eager. Some of them went by favor, for her poorer lovers. There was a young athlete well known for his straight eye with a javelin, who could hit the bowl just as straight at kottabos, and could have won with both eyes shut. Very soon after I knew her, she held a contest for a song.

She called me last. After the skolions and catches, I gave her something new, a hymn to violet-eyed Aphrodite. Then I was king of the feast, till it broke up soon after. It was understood on such nights that the victor would be waiting to enjoy the prize.

No pleasure comes free. On the night of the javelin-thrower I lay awake; he was a handsome fellow, whom I knew she'd wanted; I guessed he was learning more about the management of his javelin than he'd ever known. Well, it is all gone by. Aphrodite herself could not raise my old spear now, and I can scarcely recall the rage of that wakeful night. Yet her beauty lives for me as clear as ever, her room with its treasures, her laugh, her friendship. Often, still, I find myself thinking, I must tell Lyra that.

We were gossips from the first, exchanging my court news for hers from the city. Between Hippias' gravity and Hipparchos' boys, courtesans scarcely passed the doors of either Archon. It had been different, old men said, in Pisistratos' prime. Only performers and musicians were hired for the suppers now, and it was seldom that even dancing-girls were asked to sit with the guests. So Lyra valued my fresh bits of news, more than some of her costlier presents. I was glad therefore to bring her word that Onomakritos had been exiled, a scandal that shook the court for days.

As guardian of the oracles, he had great consequence with Hippias, who never so much as received a foreign envoy without consulting him first. He and his scrolls had been moved to the temple of Athene, and he was made free of the inner sanctuary as if he were a priest. This suited him well; he was a solemn man. Most of us got used to him; but not the young poet, Lasos of Hermione. It was his nature to dislike pomposity, and he let it show. So, when he had offered to present a dithyramb in honor of Theseus' victorious return from Crete, and it had been accepted, Onomakritos produced some ancient oracle which said the day should not be honored by any ruler; it was most un-lucky, King Aigeus having taken his death-leap then, on seeing his son's black sail.

The feast was called off, and Lasos was enraged; he had

already rehearsed his chorus. He came bursting into my house at breakfast-time, burning with his wrongs. I shared my food and wine with him—he had been too angry to sleep or eat—and said, to calm him, that between us we could surely get the piece put on to celebrate some other deed of Theseus. In respect of Aigeus' death, the oracle did make a kind of sense.

"What kind of sense?" He ran his fingers through his fair hair; he was a stocky, pink-faced Argive. "It was a lucky day for Theseus, it made him King. And for Athens too, he was a better king than his father. No, it was spite, Simonides. It's my belief that old fraud makes half his oracles up."

"I've seen the scrolls; they look a hundred years old to me."

"They look dirty, you mean. From old inscriptions I've seen, a few generations back they had a different way of writing, more like Phoenician. They're hard to read. Not his. He makes them up, I swear."

It was true that those I'd seen, I'd had no trouble in reading. "All the same," I said, "you might find yourself well out of it after all. Suppose you sang your dithyramb, and by chance some piece of bad luck did happen. Or Hippias got some notion stuck in his mind, about rulers being put out of the way. Then, if anyone were ever mad enough to try such a thing, your song would have an unhappy echo." I put this carefully; it was the fruit of Lyra's gossip.

After some thought, he said I might be right, but if so it was the fault of that old dog-face, and it was time he was shown up. When, on the day he would have sung his dithyramb, we had an untimely hailstorm, I said that Onomakritos did seem to have smelled out an unfavorable day. But I might as well have saved my breath.

I was surprised when he began professing to Hippias a

keen interest in ancient oracles; it seemed he had taken on
a contest against a master. Most people took it for mere
sycophancy, and I got a number of unsought compliments
for not having stooped to it. I had my own suspicions, so
thought it better to hold my peace, for Lasos' sake.
Onomakritos was far from a bad poet, if rather portentous
as a man; and stood well not only with Hippias, but with
Hipparchos too, having composed a whole Dionysiac rite
for him with action, music and words. If he'd stayed in
Athens, I shouldn't wonder if he would have gone on to
tragedy. He was a dangerous enemy; and I feared that Lasos,
whom I liked upon the whole, would get the worst of it.

However, Hippias received very well his modest seekings,
and at last was so pleased with his new pupil that he took
him to the sanctuary to see the oracular scrolls. From there
he rushed panting to my house, crying in the doorway, "I
knew it, Simonides! I knew it!"

As it happened, I had just got half of a good line, and
had had the rest almost in reach before he scattered my
thoughts. I felt like telling him to jump off the Rock, but
resigned myself to listen.

"You were right, some of those scrolls are old: the
Pythians, the Orphics, the Mousaios. I asked to look at
them; but no one's to look at them any more, in case they
crumble. Only Onomakritos, and guess why. Because he's
recopying them!"

Keeping my patience, I said that it seemed best, if they
were to be read by men to come.

"Copying, *he* says. Hippias read me some of the
Mousaios. Why, the old charlatan's style is stamped all over
it! The very plod of his feet. Listen to this."

He had a sound memory, did Lasos. (How seldom one
finds it now!) He had kept a dozen lines from a single hearing. They were very gnomic, about a lightning-flash from
Macedon which would burn the Great King's throne. I had

to admit that, apart from their being nonsense, they did have an Onomakritan sound.

"Oh, some were crazier still. About Atlantis rising in the west, and aspiring to rule the moon, sending up heroes in flying chariots. And a thunderbolt that burned a whole city of men. I can't give you above two lines of that, but they have his mark. He must be plotting something, just working up to it."

"So what will you do? Tell Hippias?"

"No use. He has the ear of a cow. And I expect the old scrolls have all been tampered with to match. Never mind. From now on I see my way." On which he took leave of me, and I tried to make a flying bird from the shed feathers of my shot-down song.

I had no quarrel of my own with Onomakritos; we had been judges together in one of the Homer contests, and worked on the recension. So I minded my own business. The Isthmian Games came on soon after; and the boxing was won by the son of one of my own tenants, young Glaukos of Karystos. His father found out by chance how strong he was; told him to fit a plowshare to the shaft, and came on him hammering it in with his naked fist. I'd encouraged him to enter; he was a sweet-natured boy whom I'd known from childhood, had never used his strength for bullying, had trained hard for the games, and looked almost godlike in the glow of victory. I made him an ode as a gift; I still think it is one of my best. After all this, Lasos' feud slipped my mind; and the war was over before I knew it.

The inner shrine of Athene's temple, before the Medes burned it down, was pretty full, and looked like an ancient lumber-room. It was less than thirty years old; but besides the sacred scrolls, it had all the goddess's old clothes, discarded when the maidens rerobed her; any number of ritual vessels and emblems for processions; and a great scrap-heap of old iron and bronze, battle-trophies offered in thanksgiving. Nowadays they build treasuries to house such things, but then they were heaped up halfway to the roof, ships' beaks and shields and helmets and so forth, from the Megarian and Salaminian wars. Behind all this stuff, it seems, Lasos had made himself a lair with a spyhole in it. He had seen Onomakritos visiting the place at daybreak, early enough to need a lamp, and bringing a fire-pot to kindle it. Lasos got up still earlier, feeling his way to his ambush in the dark.

Why do men do such things? Maybe, like dogs, they hate each other's smell and ask no reason. Lasos had lost nothing much through Onomakritos—in the end his dithyramb had been put on another day—his place at court and his stipend had never been threatened. He had lost some face, which certain men feel more than others. Or, it may be he was just possessed with a love of truth.

Came at last the long-awaited morning. Onomakritos kindled his lamp, and brought forth his own new copy of the Mousaios oracles. He did not unroll the old one. He took a wax tablet from his breast, and began to copy from that.

It was Lasos' moment. He sprang from his ambush, dislodging a heap of shields which crashed down with a noise like thunder. While Onomakritos sprang up open-mouthed, thinking no doubt that it was an earthquake, Lasos snatched the scroll from his nerveless hand, grabbed up the tablet, and ran straight to Hippias' house.

The Archon rose early for his devotions. He had just poured the libation when Lasos came rushing up. The ink was still wet on the scroll, indeed had smudged in the scramble; and the wax of the tablet was soft and fresh.

I had thought Hippias a much milder man than his father. I had been wrong. Pisistratos' hardness was a kind of tool, like a craftsman's hammer. He used it when the work required, skillfully, and then he put it away. With

Hippias, it was a thing you came upon; and so, I think, did the man himself. No Pisistratid ever took kindly to being made a fool of. Lasos told me later that when, for a moment, he wondered if he could have been wrong, it brought him out in a cold sweat.

What proved his case was simply his being alone. No injured seer had come after him to accuse him of impiety. Hippias sent for his brother; they scanned the scroll; went to the sanctuary, untenanted but for an acolyte clearing up the mess (unless you count the goddess, who one assumes had witnessed everything); compared the ancient writing with the new. A messenger, sent to Onomakritos' house, found him already packing.

Lasos was present when he was brought before the Archons. All he could find to say in his own defense was that these visions had come to him, sent him by some god; and that he wished them to be read by men to come. He was told to be over the Attic border by nightfall; an order he obeyed so fast that he never bade me goodbye.

Lasos came to me to report his triumph; and I asked him what oracle the man had been forging, when he was caught. A prophecy, Lasos said, that the islands off Lemnos would one day sink into the sea.

"What madness," I said, "to lose a good living for. I've sailed by Lemnos, and those islets hardly serve for fishermen to put in overnight. I doubt more than a couple have water. What possessed the man?"

"I can tell you that. He was possessed with a belief that these things would really happen."

"You mean he really took himself for a prophet?"

"I believe so, now." He sat back in my guest-chair, quite limp. I called my boy to bring him a cup of wine. He had had his moment; now the flame had sunk in him, leaving him chilled. "Yes, I think that he really thought so. I never saw a man more earnest. He could have fudged up some

story; but he never tried. He said he had sought no glory
for himself; he'd been content to give Mousaios all the
credit; he only wanted his predictions kept safe."

The wine was good, but he swallowed it down untasted.
"He was mad, of course. Not fit to be in charge of anything sacred. What could I do but say so? . . . Do you know,
Simonides, I wish I'd let it alone. I wish I'd never found
out."

Perhaps he wished wisely. I shall never know. While I
knew Onomakritos, I never found him base. His songs have
lived; even some he made in Persian-held Ionia, when he'd
sold himself to the Great King. In the end, he had sold
everything: his new master, his old one, and any gift the
gods had given him. All to buy him a recall to Athens,
though she were enslaved. I wonder what happened to him
after Salamis, that false prophet of Xerxes' victory. And I
ask myself even now: if he had stayed in Athens undis-
covered, among his forged scrolls, would he have grown
so base?

But there, he was mad. I suppose one day we would have
found him raving. After all, he never foretold the fate of
Samos.

7

I WAS IN KEOS, visiting Philomache for the naming of her
third boy. She had borne her second son four or five years
before, delighting the heart of the old grandfather Bacchy-

lides, after whom of course he had been named. I had heard great tales of the celebrations, but had had to miss them for the Olympic Games. She had let me know that this was preferring the lesser to the greater. I was resolved not to fail twice.

I found a big baby with red hair and a carrying yell; built on Bacchylides' pattern, I daresay. Indeed, when I got there, the ancient victor had him naked in his lap, jogging him and admiring his sturdy limbs. "Big babes, tall men," he said. The infant kicked agreement, and made a puddle in his robe.

The dark elder son stood by, watching in silence. It was clear by now that *he* would never make the weight for the pankration. Even so, he had been, all his life, the wished-for heir, spoiled by his sisters, sole lord of his small estate. Though his parents were too kind to blow cold towards him, no one had much time for him just then. His throne had passed to another, and he saw it.

I admired the new tyrant, spoke good-luck words and offered gifts. But I was glad that when shopping I had remembered the fallen ruler. I had brought him a little flute, stopped for the Lokrian mode. It was ivory with a gold band; it's never too soon to learn that music is precious. I saw his parents look sideways; some people think the aulos is no instrument for a gentleman. But he was too young for the lyre, and when he was only three I'd seen him beating time to songs. At all events, he was enraptured, tooted diligently, and was puzzled that he made no music. I took him outside and showed him how to finger it, and in no time he was picking out a tune. After that, he hardly glanced at the usurper's court.

One thing clouded the feast: Theas had not come. He knew when the birth was due, had sworn to be at the naming, and had a short run to make, no further than from Samos. The sea was calm; but sudden squalls come down

from the heights of Mykale, that can wreck a squadron
when ships a mile off can barely fill their sails.

However, his ship was descried not long after the naming;
and he rode up on a hired mule a little before sunset, when
the feasting was still lively. Keos has laws against costly
naming-feasts, as against all other extravagance; but Kean
wine, if not up to Chian or Lesbian, is very drinkable, and
at least there is no law telling guests when to go home.

As always, he appeared like some god of plenty, leading
a pack-ass laden with spices and Samian wine, a lapis necklace for Philomache, and a handful of gold luck-charms to
hang upon the child. After he had embraced us all and
asked us how we did and praised the baby, he said, "Forgive me for being late. I waited in Samos till I was sure of
the news. Well, it's true. Polykrates is dead. Murdered in
Sardis."

There was a moment's dead hush, then a clamor of questions. Most seamen are good at news-telling, from being so
often first with it. Theas took a swallow from his wine-cup,
and pitched his voice to carry. "He was lured over the strait
by Oroites, the Satrap there, who wanted to buy Kambyses'
favor. He sent word over to Samos that Kambyses wanted
him dead, and he planned to fly. Well, after all that madman's killings, it sounded likely enough. So, would Polykrates take him in, if he brought all his wealth along? He
had gold enough to make Samos master of the seas, just
like old Minos' Crete. If Polykrates would come across
the strait and swear a peace with him, he could see the gold
for himself."

"And he went?" I said. "Had he lost his wits?"

"No, he was too clever by half. He sent an envoy to view
the gold. The man was shown chests and chests of it, so he
said. Spread thin over pebbles, I daresay, it's a trick as old
as the hills. At any rate, he reported this great hoard; so
then Polykrates went."

"But, if he was satisfied, why not have sent the Persian a safe-conduct under his seal, and a ship to carry him? He claimed he was living in fear. Why should Polykrates go to Sardis?"

"He was taken when he stepped ashore at Ephesos. Don't ask me why he went; I asked in vain. Of course I met no one from the Palace, where I expect they were all running mad. But they said in the harbor that half his friends followed him down to his galley, begging him to change his mind. Even that daughter of his, crying out like Kassandra and telling her bad-luck dream. He told her to shut her mouth or he'd never get her a husband; and she called on the gods to grant her even that, if he came home safe again. And that was the last they saw of him."

I did not pretend to mourn; I had too much to remember. While everyone was talking, I was thinking my own thoughts. Presently I said to Theas, "Will this have reached Athens yet?"

He looked round sharply. He saw what I was at. "I doubt it. The ship that brought it from Miletos was going on to Rhodes, to take word to young Polykrates; and no other shipmaster was ready to put out. What do you say, Sim? Shall we go and tell your Archons?"

"It could do neither of us harm. How soon could you sail?"

"Now, if I make it worth my fellows' while. A good moon; the wind's right; and my pilot knows that passage as well as he knows his wife's. If he's drunk by now, I can take the helm myself."

He went over to his own wife, who was sitting among the women, and hoping no doubt for a night with him. But she was used to such things by now; and he'd brought her some earrings set with Arabian pearls. Kean dress laws were getting dented, since Laertes and Theas went into trade.

Down in Koressia we found the pilot nearly sober, only

two seamen helpless, and two Keans on the dock ready to
take their places. The cargo had been off-loaded, and we
sailed at once. For some time Theas had no time to spare
for me; but after a while he came aft and said, "It must be
chaos and old night by now in Samos. I hope you have no
friends there."

As if a snake had bitten me, I cried out, "Anakreon!"
Being with the family, I suppose, had put it out of my mind.
"He must be there."

"Who?" Theas went to the side to peer at the steeps of
Sounion, black against a shimmering sea. Its fickle winds
were quiet; he spoke to the pilot and came back. "Is that
the poet fellow, the Tyrant's sycophant?"

"Poet yes, sycophant no. He is Anakreon . . . Well, never
mind. I'm his guest-friend, Theas. He was good to me when
I was poor and unknown, and he a great man already."

"Oh," said Theas at once, "that's different. Then you
must do whatever you can for him. Let's see when you get
to Athens."

Between oars and sail, we made Piraeus by noon, and
rode straight to Athens on the fastest beasts we could hire.
Hippias saw us without delay (I had never wasted his time
with trivialities) and sent at once for Hipparchos.

Theas told his tale. He was quite at ease before the
Pisistratids. As Lyra had said, he was well known in many
cities. At the outset I could see them comparing his looks
with mine, and wondering which of us was the bastard; but
we were used to that, and they soon had other things to
think about. It was even plainer to them than it had been
to us that the whole of Hellas, its balance and counterpoise
with the Great King's empire, would be changed if Samos
fell.

All over Greece, the Pisistratids had allies, guest-friends,
envoys and secret agents, who must be advised or warned;
enemies too, who must be kept in the dark. This early news

was worth gold to them; and with gold they paid for it. They were never cheeseparers. From what they gave Theas, he built himself a warehouse on Piraeus. He thanked them with unfeigned warmth—he had hugely enjoyed the whole adventure—saying with his open smile, "All this good fortune I owe to my young brother, who dragged me from a feast when I had only downed one cupful, telling me you must be the first to know."

At this they turned to me and started all over again. But now Theas was taken care of, there was no more time to waste. The first time they paused for breath, I turned to Hipparchos. "Sir, as always you are too kind. But first let me say that when my brother left Samos, Anakreon was still there. What will become of him?"

Hipparchos started, much as I had done before. "What? By Herakles, Anakreon! Even that had been driven from my mind! Hippias, did you hear? Anakreon is still in Samos. We must get him out. Hippias, we must send a warship."

"Let me go," Theas said. "A small return to such princely givers. It will be a pleasure." Hippias looked inclined to accept; chiefly I think to get the business out of the way; but Hipparchos cried out that Persians would be everywhere, if Samos no longer held the straits, and he would not repay Simonides' gallant brother by making him their prey. Besides, a trader would be too slow. Without getting consent from Hippias, a thing never seen before, he summoned an officer of his guard, and sealed an order to take command of a naval pentekonter; let it be the fastest in the fleet, with the strongest rowers.

"Sir," I said, "may I ask a favor? Let me go with the ship. I should be honored to fetch Anakreon here."

At first he did not like it. (Hippias had gone, to attend to more important matters.) Putting out all his charm, he said, "We should all be poorer for Anakreon's loss; but he

at least is not an old and dear friend, as you are. To lose
you would be insupportable."

"I don't think, sir, I shall be in danger. I've never taken
part in Samian faction. But I do know a great many people
there; and even if Anakreon has left already, I might be
able to learn things that you would find useful." This
tempted him; and he let me go, ordering the captain not
to put me ashore if he found the city in stasis, for no one
was safe in a civil war. We sailed from Munychia at dawn
next day.

I had never before traveled by warship, or guessed what
speed is like on those long snaky galleys with twenty-five
oars a side, helping the sail. The wind had changed, and
again was in our favor. The rising sun glittered laughing
along the sea; the plash and creak of the oars kept time to
the chanty-man's bawdy song (these were crack rowers, not
to be spoiled with the whip); and I felt a new song of my
own twining around the beat, like a vine upon a trellis.

I was glad to be going; even though, with all these
soldiers, Anakreon would have no need of me to save his
life. I had other reasons. He and I were friends, and sharing a patron would not alter it—not that in itself. Athens
had room for both of us; we could only gain from each
other's company and the lift of each other's art. What I
feared were the fools about the court and city who, measur-
ing us by their own mean minds, would from the first
expect us to be rivals. In my life here and there, I've seen
poets who would never have wished each other harm, or
envied each other's honor, set almost at each other's
throats through base men's expectations. So I was resolved
his first welcome should come from me, to cut such things
at the root.

We met no Persians; the soldiers played knucklebones in
the waist. As we neared Samos, trade looked to be much

as usual. The harbor, when we rowed in, was full of men gathered to talk; which, as I have found in my many travels, means trouble, but not the worst; then there will be men in arms, or nobody in sight. There could be no stasis yet. But the captain had been so hammered with orders to keep me safe, he'd have bound me to a thwart if I'd tried to go ashore before news had come back to him. This was brought at last by the pilot, who had not hurried, having found some old friends to drink with. They had all told him there was still law in Samos, no Persian fleet in sight; the city was being governed by the regent whom the Tyrant had left behind when he crossed the strait, one Maiandrios. I demanded my freedom, went ashore, and, avoiding any place where people might keep me talking, made straight for Anakreon's house.

The door stood open; but when I tapped with my stick, nobody came. He must have fled already, I thought; I should find the place forsaken; so, without ceremony, I walked in.

The room was in confusion; stuffs thrown about, vases and scrolls tumbled upon the table; an open chest with a blanket half out of it, and the wall-hanging inside. Had he been murdered, then? But the place would have been looted. The street was noisy outside; and it was only now that I heard a moan, or a whimper, from the room beyond. I ran in. It was a dog that had been crying, a little white one, the kind they breed in Melita. It was standing on tiptoe to paw the knees of Anakreon, who sat on the bed with his head clasped in his hands, his fingers buried in his uncombed hair. As I looked, he picked the dog up blindly into his arms, like a distraught mother with a wailing baby. He was weeping himself.

"Anakreon!" I cried. He sat up looking desperate, as if the entrance of any stranger must portend something dreadful; yet not as if frightened for himself. When he saw who

it was, he cried out my name, even then remembering to
put the dog down gently, and came running to me. While I
tried to soothe him, the first words I could hear from him
were, "So horrible! Oh, horrible, horrible! Is he dead,
Simonides? Tell me he is dead!"

I guided him to a chair in the outer room, found wine—
it was plain the disorder had been no one's work but his
own—and gave him some. He threw it down like water,
and, starting to command himself, begged me to drink too.
The little dog, beseeching with its dark child's eyes, jumped
into his lap and licked his tear-stained face.

"Poor Blossom," he said, and looked about him as if seeing the place for the first time. "Simonides, what are you
doing here?" Without giving me time to answer, he ran
on like a man in fever, "I am ashamed of the house. I am
packing, you see, Simonides, that's what it is. I would put
you up, my dear, but it's better not to stop here, if I were
you I should go away at once. We might find a ship together. Let me get you something to eat; I know where
everything is, it won't take a moment. The cakes were
here . . ." He went scurrying about, picking things up and
putting them down, rather like some flustered dame whose
daughter is giving birth before the time. Blossom ran busily
to and fro behind him. "I don't even know where I shall be
going. Ah, here they are." He brought the crock, and started
looking for a place on the littered table.

I took it from him and put it down, and laid my hands
on his shoulders. "I can tell you, my dear friend, where you
are going. You're coming with me to Athens, where the
Archons will beg you to be their guest for life. Our ship is
in harbor, waiting just for you. It's true, Anakreon. I'm
telling you, you are the first poet for whom a king ever
sent a warship. I don't think even for Orpheus anyone
did that."

He quietened and looked at me. There crossed his face,

drawn though it was with sleeplessness, the shadow of his charming smile. The life he knew had come in sight on the skyline, and he began to be Anakreon once again. He even said something pretty about my coming to fetch him, and the pleasure he would have in being my neighbor.

"But," I said, "didn't you know all along you could come to Athens? We tried hard enough to get you there."

"I know. I know. It has been like the whole world ending . . . horrible! I can't tell you now. You don't know yet, do you? I'll tell you, but not now. I must put a few things together."

I began to help him wrap his precious vases, and asked where his servant was. "I let him go. He came to me scared to death, saying the Samians would tear any Persian they saw to pieces. Poor boy. I daresay some would. I gave him some journey money; I suppose he has found a ship. Oh, don't trouble with all that, this is all I need, and a change of clothes, that's all. Then we can be going. Blossom, be quiet."

"No, take your time. You can't throw such good things away. The streets are quiet, so far as I could see. Presently I'll find some porters."

"I only want to be gone from here. When you come back I'll be ready."

I did not protest; the bitch's shrill yelping hurt my ears, as she jumped from one to the other; she had the nose of her kind for catastrophe and change. I left them together, and found porters without trouble at the harbor; already ships were avoiding it. When I came with them, Anakreon had strapped up his baggage. He put Blossom under his arm, and we went down to the ship.

Meantime, some of the soldiers had been let ashore to the taverns and came back with the latest news; by the time we cast off, I knew what had been done to Polykrates. They would have liked Anakreon to fill out the tale for them, and were disappointed that he sat silent, muffled in his cloak, in the darkest part of the deck-house.

As it happened, the wind turned contrary, and the nearest harbor was Koressia. So I brought him up, the two of us soaked with spray, to Theas' house. It was plain, before we reached the door, that he'd asked in some friends to celebrate his good fortune. I saw Anakreon wince when he heard the singing. It could not be helped that Theas greeted us with a shout of pleasure, and bade us change our wet clothes quickly, and drink level with the rest. However, he had never been thick-headed. When he'd heard Anakreon's name, and taken a second look at him, he said he must be tired out with the journey and the gale, and would want to eat supper in quiet.

It was a big house now, our father's old place run together with Theas' new one; Anakreon's room had the women's quarters between it and the feast. I left him awhile to meet my brother's friends, all eager to hear the news. Few were much moved at Polykrates' fate; such things happened in Persia. As soon as I could, I went back to Anakreon. He had fed Blossom, but scarcely touched food himself. I'd brought him a warm posset with a little poppy, which one of the women had brewed for him, and begged him to eat something with it, to help him sleep. He picked up a morsel, but put it back on the plate. "Did they know down there, did anyone tell you, whether he is dead?"

"No. Nobody here knew that."

The little dog crept into his lap, and nestled there softly, gazing up with its liquid eyes. I remembered hearing somewhere that these lamblike dogs of Melita have the power to take away pain.

He said, "Did you ever see it, Simonides?"

"No. My old master saw it once. I think it was in Karia." I put the lid on the posset-bowl. It was time he talked, if he was to get any sleep that night. "Have you seen it, then?"

"In Phrygia. Fifteen, twenty years back. One could travel about in those days. The man had offended the Satrap, I don't know how. I didn't see it being done. We came by two days after. Two days he had been sitting there, on that iron ring, at the top of the mast. The vultures were coming; one lighted on his head, you know they go first for the eyes; then it squarked and flapped off again, and I saw that his hand had moved. And the bird came back . . ." He was shaking all over; the dog in his lap gave a little whine, and patted him with one paw. I too put a hand on his shoulder; he seemed glad of a living touch. Presently he said, "They used to set them up beside the road. There would be one every stade or so, the old skeleton sitting on the iron wheel, up in the air. And when the birds had picked them clean, you could see the spike up the middle. It's the spike, you see, that holds them there so long."

I could hear his teeth chattering, and pulled up the blanket round his shoulders. "You can be sure," I said, "that by this time he is dead."

"He was strong." He rubbed the dog's ears to quiet it. "He never exercised, but he was as strong as an ox. Nothing ever ailed him."

"It's the lean man lives long. Believe me, he is dead."

He sat looking before him, like a sick man weak from a fever that is leaving him. "Come, eat," I said, "or my brother's wife will be on at me. 'What was wrong with the supper, Sim, that the great Anakreon wouldn't touch it?' "

A smile flickered on his face. "Sim? Do they truly call you that at home? Do they truly dare?" After that he picked at the food; before long I got most of it into him, and the posset too. In the end he grew quite garrulous, as men do sometimes after a shock.

"His fate, Simonides, what an implacable fate! It was resolved to have him. It had marked him down, as the hunter marks the deer with the longest horns, because he has the shell for a lyre and is impatient to finish it. What drove him? What madness, to trust that man. He had even insulted him already; I know, I was there. He had sent an envoy to Samos, some business about ships. The man behaved like an envoy from king to king. Well, Polykrates had done things in his day, we all know that; but he looked as pure as lilies, anywhere near Oroites. The man stank, and had done for years. The greed of a crocodile, murder for any whim, oppression; cruelty most of all. Well, he may pay for it yet, now that Kambyses is dying."

"*What?*" I cried, jumping nearly out of my skin. "The Great King, dying? No one has heard a word of it. Is it true?"

He passed a hand across his forehead. "I am sorry. Didn't I tell you? I've hardly known what I'm saying these last two days. I daresay it's true. Sikinnos told me before he left. My gracious Persian, you used to call him. He always knew everything, I don't know how. 'The Great King's wound has mortified,' he said."

"What wound?" This news would have made the day for Theas and his friends, and only now I heard it.

"I don't know." He pushed the heels of his hands against his eyes. "He didn't say, or perhaps I wasn't attending. I'd only just heard the other thing. What were we talking about just now?"

"Oroites' insolent envoy."

"Oh, yes. It happened we were on our own that evening. I'd been singing something he wanted to hear again. Bathyllos had been playing for me—you remember him? His flute-playing improved as his looks went off. When this envoy was announced, and we could hear him outside, demanding audience at once, Polykrates said . . . What's that noise?"

He had gone paler, if that could be. Poor man, he was at the end of his tether. "It's some dog out there," I said. "It's nothing, the house must have a dozen."

It did seem, as I listened, that there were four or five outside. I could hear snufflings from tenor down to bass. So could Blossom. She had leaped from her master's lap, and, squeaking softly, was pressing her pitch-black nose to the crack under the door. Now that I thought of it, some Samian dogs had trailed us down to the harbor.

"Anakreon," I said, "you don't think that bitch of yours . . . ?"

"Oh, *no!*" He sounded quite like himself again. "It can't be half a year . . . Oh, Herakles!"

"Not Herakles, I fear, but Aphrodite." A huge deep bark sounded outside. Kean shepherd dogs are as big as wolf-hounds. Blossom scrabbled eagerly at the door; she had done her duty faithfully, and thought she had a right to something for herself. Two dogs started snapping at each other; Kean watchdogs are fierce. "If I open this door," I said, "we shall have them all in here. Can't you pick her up?"

He grabbed her, wriggling, and reproaching his ingratitude with her melting eyes. The suitors stayed, however, and we should have been besieged all night, if they had not started to do battle for right of precedence. This drew the kennel-man, who had to get help before he could whip them off.

I looked round for the Helen who had caused the war. Like the first one, she had gone home again, and was curled at Anakreon's side. What with sorrow and weariness and poppy-juice, sleep had at last caught up with him. He never stirred when I covered them both with the blanket.

After that, I went down to tell my brother, and anyone else who was still there, that the Great King was said to be dying. I remembered that Kambyses, who had killed so many men, had not begotten any. His only brother he had already murdered. He had no heir. Had he been a king in Homer, one would have foreseen great contests at his funeral games.

8

FOR SOME TIME, all eyes in Greece were turned on Persia. First we heard that Kambyses' brother had after all survived, and assumed the throne. He passed many welcome laws, remitted taxes, and was well thought of, except that no-body ever saw him. After some months, he turned out to be a pretender. It was revealed by a concubine, and con-firmed by the man who knew it best of all; he had cut the real brother's throat on Kambyses' orders. Having declared this, he leaped off the citadel wall, leaving Persia an anarchy. This is not a state which commends itself to Persians. Several lords made a pact together, first to kill the pretender, then to choose a king from among themselves by seeking a sign from heaven. They got into the Palace and did the deed, after which, as the world knows, Darius got the sign. It was to be that the chosen man's horse would be the first to neigh after sunrise. So they all rode eastward together; and if Darius was the only one of them with horse-sense enough to know that a stallion will whinny when he scents his favorite mare, I should think the Persians were lucky not to get one of the others.

With all this, rumor had not much time for Samos; on

the other hand, news came in faster from there. It appeared that the island was still being ruled by Polykrates' regent whom he'd left behind to do it; and this was the same man, Maiandrios, who had been his envoy beforehand, to view Oroites' promised gold.

Anakreon said to me, "I saw something of this. All we knew at first was that Polykrates was dead. So much we'd feared and half expected. I didn't spend those first days in the state you found me in, when I'd just learned *how* he died. Before that I looked about. Maiandrios started with a great flourish about putting an end to tyranny; talked about setting up an altar to Zeus the Liberator. But I don't remember any word about elections."

Certainly none were held; in fact, when the opposition looked dangerous, Maiandrios invited its leaders to a conference, and chained them up in the castle dungeons. Then he moved into the fort himself, which Polykrates had never needed to do, and set about getting rid of anyone still at large whom he distrusted.

"Do you know what I think?" said Anakreon when this news came in. "He was in it from the beginning. Whose word did we have but his, about all this deceitful treasure? It's my belief the only gold he ever saw in Sardis was what Oroites bought him with. I hope some god makes them both pay." Maybe one did; for Darius was not long on the throne before he got rid of Oroites. Maiandrios did not rule long either; but while his tyranny lasted, the Samians looked back on Polykrates' reign as a carefree summer.

Poets, musicians, sculptors, painters and potters were soon in flight before he had time to murder them; arriving mostly at Piraeus. Nearly all the talent from Polykrates' court attached itself to the Archons'. Athens seemed to grow more splendid every day.

Ibykos got away by the skin of his teeth. He'd believed in Maiandrios at first, but, thinking it unseemly to court a new patron in the house of a murdered benefactor, had lived privately and not come forward with any praise. It was not long before he had word the Tyrant's men were looking for him as a man suspected of treason; so he got off on a fishing-boat that night.

Hipparchos received him civilly, but did not ask him to remain. In the past he'd been a long time in Sikyon, down in the Argolid, a guest of the house of Kleisthenes; and ever since they'd married into the Alkmaionids, the Archons had counted them enemies. That was an undying feud, and poor old Ibykos had got himself mixed up in it.

Anakreon greeted him as a friend, and was sad to part with him. He'd long forgiven him for his first, sycophantic song in Samos; as he said to me, "My dear, it was just that it was so *bad*, and nobody dared to say so." Since then, he had made a whole garland of fine songs, love songs mostly, to please himself. I buried my private grudge, which he had never known of, and joined the party to see him off at Piraeus. "One can forgive him anything," said Anakreon going home, "for the sake of that song that likens the lover to an old chariot-horse, trembling when it is yoked for another race."

I don't think he had any great wish to stay in Athens. His tall frame was bent under its costly robe, his gold-pinned hair was snow-white; he was at the time of life when many men will crave for familiar things. He went first to Syracuse, where I don't doubt they made him welcome; but soon crossed to Italy, and ended in Rhegium where he was born. No doubt he did well there; one day when he was crossing the hills, some robbers thought it worth while to kill him. That's a hazard of our calling; Apollo has no friends among barbarians.

For some time we talked of him, and sang each other the new songs he'd brought; but there was so much talent in the city, even so great a man could pass by and be not long missed. Those years were rich and sweet, and I shall say so still. One must not renege upon the Muses.

Artists and craftsmen prospered; and the countrymen were still safe under Solon's laws. No man could distrain another for a debt. Hippias did the rounds of Attica to judge causes, just as his father had done. People missed the old man's presence, but the verdicts were pretty fair, if not quite so wise. Hipparchos supported his brother when required, pursued the joys of life, and furthered the arts. Hippias' children were growing up; it seemed, in those days, the dynasty might last a century.

Attic potters were famous now from Sicily to the Euxine. The sculptors came closer every year to that marriage of flesh and mind that their sons achieved. Just to walk through the city would lift your heart. For that matter, they are doing great things now and will do greater, if they only know where to stop. Well, if they don't I shall never see it.

Hippias entertained many foreign rulers and statesmen, and leading Athenians who had supported his father's faction. Thinking Anakreon too frivolous, he often called on me for a hero song; King Theseus was his favorite theme. These evenings, I thought of as rehearsals. Politicians will always prefer the useful to the true; and beauty will hardly tickle their hairy ears. Most of my best I gave at Hipparchos' parties; but the best of all, I think, at Lyra's. Disdaining base lovers, and choosing those who could offer her worthy praise, she had flowed into the images the artists made of her and the poets sang. Whatever graces we assigned to her, she took on; and not skin-deep, either. Though I never got as much of her as I wanted, it was more than enough to spoil my taste for coarser fare. She left you nothing you needed to seek elsewhere, beauty or wit or the crafts of Aphrodite. All one wanted was more; and not to know that next night was another man's.

However, rare bliss does make for restlessness. There were one or two old companions who made me feel at home and knew my ways. As for Thalatta, for years I never entered the street where her place had been.

One evening, I went with Theas to Piraeus. He had to spend the night on board, for some reason to do with cargo. We ate at his favorite inn, and parted at the door. I was unhitching my mule to go home, when I heard a woman cursing. That's nothing much in Piraeus. Then I heard my name.

She came from the waterfront into the dim light of a window. Somewhere behind her, the cresset on a moored ship flickered and danced. But for her voice, I would not have know her. She had thickened, and was painted like a Lydian, black round the eyes and a scarlet mouth; her bracelets were of copper and glass beads. She was tousled and dirty; she looked like the lowest of dockside drabs, the kind who will go on board and be passed round among the rowers. I stared at her wordless, my chief disgust for myself. She stood there cursing me in the thieves' cant of the wharfside, as if I had made her what she was. I took it she must be drunk.

I ought to have mounted and ridden off; but she had revived my anger. "Yes," I said, "I know I spoiled your game. Was I really the first who was not ashamed to tell? It was just by chance I had a good friend to listen."

"A *friend!*" She screamed it; I drew back from her dirty nails. "A *friend!*" She swung round with her back to me, and dropped her coarse patched robe. I exclaimed with horror. She was ribbed with old whip-scars; her back was like a Phoenician galley-slave's.

Resentment followed shock. "If you made off with some sailor's wages," I said, "what has that to do with me?"

Her look of bitterness pierced me despite myself. I had come from a good meal with good company; she must be living in some wretched kennel, if she had a roof at all. I took a few drachmas from my belt-bag. "Well, we had what we had. Take this for old times' sake." She snatched it from me, her eyes still cursing. I rode off quickly, in case she worked with a robber.

It was not a tale to entertain one's friends with; but then, one evening, I was sitting alone with Hipparchos. I remember, we were planning that year's theoria to Delos. Winter hanging on late that year, he called for some spiced wine while we broke off business. A brazier in the corner; a pale cold sky; little clouds edged with blue enamel. He wore a robe of cream combed wool with a yellow border, the end trailing beside his deer-footed chair. He pushed the tablets and scrolls aside, to talk, and told me some current joke about a greedy hetaira. It reminded me that I had confided in him before; so I told him how the tale had ended.

He gave a wise, kindly smile. "Well, well. That was her destined fate. She had a mean sense of her calling. True artists, like our Lyra, will take ten times as much, and a man will thank them for the privilege."

I did not much want to talk about Lyra; so I answered, "Yes. But this girl—whatever possessed her to blame *me*? She showed me her back as if she were accusing me."

He put his head on one side, as if thinking better of something he'd meant to say. I looked at him.

"My dear friend. I see I had better tell you. Neither of us is to blame; but I suppose she could not know it. Now it all comes back to me. When first I heard how you had been treated, I told the story—of course, without using names—to a certain man we know, whose name I won't use either. He was much moved, and begged, almost demanded, the woman's name. I was willing to tell him so much for his good. He was so enraged that I knew what he would say, before he could get it out. Yes, fooled just like you. I have seldom seen a man so angry. He said that my other friend, whoever he was, had been too forbearing. Now I know what he meant. My dear Simonides, I am sorry you had so ugly an encounter. But even if he paid off your score too, I can assure you she deserved it."

That was enough. I could picture her pointing me out to this second victim—or the tenth, maybe—as the ugly man who was threatening to buy her, unless she was rescued first. The whole thing hung so well together, that I never questioned it. Indeed, even to this day I have no certainty.

9

NEXT YEAR was an Olympic one. The sixty-fourth, it must have been. Why do the Olympics never stale? The last I went to was the seventy-fifth; but it seemed as fresh as ever.

There is the ancient beauty with its changes: the oaks of Kronos may shade one from heat or shelter one from rain; the Alpheus may chuckle low on its pebbles, or rush down in spate; the women across the water may be sunning themselves with straw hats and fans, or huddled in their scented tents; it may be sweet and balmy or grilling hot, the athletes plastered with dust and sweat like clay.

There is always something new; a dedication in the Altis, new craftsmen showing work; the horse-copers' pitches down the road to tempt chariot lords, the bloodstock and handsome mules. I bought a mule that year myself, a sweet

grey mare with the smooth pace that feels a part of one.
Dear Leuko, she helped me to many a song.

There are new faces, and altered ones: the young wrestler
who just held his own last time, now sheathed in bronze
muscle in his pride of strength, victor of the pankration;
some new poet from Further Greece; a philosopher from
Ionia, who'd once have recited his theory in Ephesos or
Miletos; a lord who inherited since last time, and is entering a chariot team; boys become youths, youths become
men. And the shift of politics between city and city, nowhere to be studied so well as here.

Always I rejoice most in the athletes, dedicating body
and spirit to the god: ambitious, emulous, passionate to
win; and yet, making their offering. It is nearly always a
joy to hymn their victories. There can be bad winners, as
there are bad losers, but they are few, after their long training at Olympia itself, when the spirit of the place seeps
into them. There are always ways of hymning a man who
has won fairly, but whom one does not much like. One
goes off into digressions about his ancestors or his city or
the family's patron god. They never notice, if the song goes
well; and one has earned one's fee without telling lies. Other
poets know, but that is our private mystery.

Head and heart of the games is the athlete. You could
say of the chariot-race that it is a rich man's toy, a contest
whose prize goes to one who did nothing but spend his
gold. Yet, like all the rest, I am its captive. After all, in
Homer, godlike Achilles put it first, and one can't argue
with that.

Though the owners don't mount their chariots, there is
no event where you see more endurance, courage or skill.
When I was young and poor, and had no one to command
a seat for me, I used to spread my blanket overnight on the
slope beside the track, stretched out full-length to keep
a place for my master, so that he could sleep under cover

and come down next day. The last two times, the boy did it for me. I daresay he won't need to again.

That year, though, I got a seat and even an awning. The Archons had brought a large company, with many men of rank. It overflowed the Athenian placings, and but for Hipparchos, we three poets would have had to take our chance on the slopes; it is not every patron will displace minor nobles for bards. Chairs at Olympia are for the great alone; but we had a bench with cushions, were well up the bank, and had a good view of the walk-past.

For the honor of the house, Hippias had entered a chariot. He had barely seen it, leaving everything to Hipparchos; so it was gorgeous, with the Race of Pelops in gilt relief. The horses were good Thessalians, and the driver, who had come with the team, was Thracian. He looked strong, but was rather big; your first-class driver can manage without weight, because he gets the team to think along with him. Such men are rare, however, and we all cheered the chariot on its way.

"Here's Kimon's," said Anakreon, and gave me a nudge.

Kimon son of Stesagoras sat in the row below the Archons; a man getting on in years, high-colored and hawk-nosed. His faded yellow hair was clubbed into a net in the old-fashioned style, and the pins that fixed it were headed with golden grasshoppers, meaning that his Attic ancestry went back forever. He looked a perfect type of the old oligarchs who in their great days had been little lords accountable to no one, ever since the line of High Kings died out. Moreover he was a Philead, and even the Alkmaionids ranked no higher, besides the Phileads having incurred no family curse. At one time they had been at open war with the Pisistratids; most were in exile; and how Kimon, alone of them all, came to be in the seats of honor was already an Olympic legend.

Anakreon, who had kept his eyes on the chariot, suddenly

grabbed my arm. "By Zeus, look! It's the same team again!"

For some reason, this was Lasos' first visit to the Olympics. He was short-sighted, which always made him fretful at the races. "The same as what?" he said.

Anakreon and I started together to enlighten him. "Those mares. He won the last two Olympics with that same team." "They must be now—what—ten years old at least, that's if they were two-year-olds the first time." Just then the charioteer raised his arm to salute the owner. "He's the same too," Anakreon said. "That little dark Sicilian." "They look in good shape," I said. "Mares are clever, if they can stay well." Then both of us said together, "What if they win?"

"What if they do?" said Lasos curiously. "Will it be a record?"

"No, it's been done by a Spartan once. But don't you know what happened last time; why Kimon is sitting here?"

"Don't tease the poor boy, Simonides. What happened, my dear, was that Kimon proclaimed the victory in Pisistratos' name, instead of his own. He *gave* it to him, an Olympic chariot crown. He might nearly as well have presented him with a city. So the Old Archon shook hands on it, and invited him back from exile. That's why he's here, instead of over there."

He pointed along the course, to where the Alkmaionids were gathered. It was only at times like this that one ever saw them; and then, if you had sense, it was at a distance.

"Well," I said, "I doubt he could ever have won with two-year-olds; they seldom stay the distance. They may even be eleven by now or even twelve."

"Eleven. They were three-year-olds, he told me so at the time." Out of the three of us, only Anakreon had been eminent enough, eight whole years back, to talk with Kimon. "They'll never do it again," I said. "It's just a fancy the man has taken."

It was a big entry that year; thirty quadrigas, no less. It seemed to take half the day getting them into the starting-stalls, after the place-lots had been drawn. Each four had a pair of grooms to lead it and help the charioteer; but there were more than the usual run of tangles and bickerings. No owner of sense will run stallions where mares are running, but the horses were excited as always by the crowds, and some charioteers are not above a sly flick of the whip at another team, if the umpire is not looking.

I've never envied those umpires. If the teams were to start from a level line, they'd be in heaps before they were under way; so they have this stepped-back order, one couple of chariots side by side at the apex, the next couple a length behind on each side, and so on outward, like a huge arrow-head. The umpires have to see the gates opened in proper order, the back ones on the outside first, and so on to the foremost that start the last; and I never saw a race yet where some driver did not complain that his gate was slow.

This time it seemed fair enough. The bronze dolphin came clanging down, the bronze eagle was hoisted on its pole over the altar; up went the gates and out went the chariots; the thunder began, and the pale dust rose billowing till it clotted our noses and tongues.

It was a good race that year. I am not one of those who value the event by the number of crashes, and sit near the turn to see them. For me, that is like giving a music prize for loudness. Besides which, I do not like the spectacle; I can picture the death of the blameless hero Hippolytos without seeing it enacted before my eyes. A chariot collision can butcher a good man and a gallant team as bloodily as a god-sent bull from the sea. Most drivers hitch the reins around them for extra grip, and though they wear sharp knives to cut themselves free if they fall, with a broken arm or a kicked head they don't get a chance to use them. Even if the driver escapes alive, it's not often the team gets off without one or all being dragged off the course and slaughtered. It was not for this that Poseidon gave to mankind a creature of such beauty. It is the horse at his godlike best that I love to watch.

It was a dry year; the dust was almost a fog, with people muffling their faces up to the eyes. From our good seats we would see the start and the finish, and all the turns at our end; the further turnpost was invisible in the murk. One saw only a turbulent mass like driftwood in a swirling river, heard the cheers of the crowd, the shouts and neighing that meant a crash or a foul. One chariot at our end had a wheel wrenched off on purpose by another; the charioteer, a fine driver, got his car and horses somehow off the course, and the man who'd fouled him was disqualified. He must have hoped that the dust would hide it. At the far end, we learned later, two teams tangled their yoke-poles and a man was killed. There were one or two other crashes from which men and horses were dragged out with broken bones, the men to race again, the beasts to die.

However, near a turnpost one does not only see disasters; one sees all the skill. All up the straight they have been working and weaving for places inside the turn; but many a driver has taken it too close and wrecked his car on the column. The man who can cut it fine and skim past is a winner, but he needs clever horses, all of whom know him and each other well. All this is as true as when prosy old Nestor instructed his son, who no doubt knew it all already, at Patroklos' funeral games.

The Athenian chariot was running a steady, well-judged race, neither fouling nor being fouled, getting the most from the team, coming fairly close in without collisions. But at each turn one saw, on the outside, a flash of bright yellow swinging round, the outside taken by choice, trusting in speed and in horses who knew their work. The driver in yellow was Kimon's; he showed up well, even after the sixth lap when the pale dust was cloaking horses and men alike. His team knew the track of old; he had no need to whip the outside horse or check the inmost, to get them turning as cleanly as a wheel. You could not have asked better of cavalry chargers with knights on their back to guide them.

At last came the twelfth, last lap. The ancient fever rose; the crowds roaring, the drivers cracking their whips and giving their shrill yells; the horses screaming as they had the last ounce flogged out of them. One team swerved across the course into another still running the lap before, so that they crashed head on; the frightful din of shouts and squeals hardly seemed to increase an uproar that was splitting one's ears already.

Only fifteen chariots finished, about the usual number. The Athenian team came fourth, which was creditable at least. But leading by half a length came Kimon's team with its yellow-robed charioteer and the neat-footed mares, their chestnut sides dappled with foam, their nostrils flaring scarlet, but game to the last, stepping off from the finishing post as prettily as deer.

We turned round to acclaim the owner. He stood up smiling, and lifted an arm to the cheers. In the thrill of the race, I had lost all thought of politics, which are made by men, while beauty and bravery are from the gods. It was not till Anakreon poked me in the ribs that I remembered.

The chief of the judges mounted the platform with the herald. At Olympia, the herald himself is the victor of a heralds' contest held beforehand. This one was a first-class trumpeter with a ringing voice. "In the name of Olympian Zeus, the winner of the four-horse chariot race is Kimon, son of Stesagoras, of Athens."

This time, Kimon of the god-descended Philead clan had claimed his victory for himself.

The chariot drew up before the podium, the mares jingling their harness as they got the air back into their lungs. Above them stood the wiry dark Sicilian, in the stillness this moment demands. He had been through it twice before; from where I sat I could see his eye already stealing down to the foam-flecked mares, with the fondness of a father, longing for all this to be over, waiting to caress them, to give them the little drink they must have before the deep one; to see them rubbed down, and put into their blankets. But he was only the charioteer, and must await the crowning of the victor.

Even at Olympia, I have seldom heard such cheering. People were standing on their seats, tearing the wreaths from their heads to fling flowers and oak-sprays at the podium. In the whole long history of the games, over the centuries, it had only been done once before, three victories running with the same team. It would become a legend.

And when that thought came to me, I saw what else it meant. The legend would be Kimon's, and his alone. Whatever had been proclaimed at the games last time, whoever had worn the crown, it would be forgotten. Men would talk forever of Kimon's triple victory. At that moment, he was bending his head for the olive crown.

In so much commotion, it was quite safe to look round. But if there had been anything to see, we had already missed it. Hippias and Hipparchos were sitting in quiet talk, like any two lords whose rank restrains them from vulgar acclamations.

Anakreon said, "They are taking it very well."

"Of course. They know how to behave in public."

Lasos was still in ecstasy from the race. It took him a moment to follow us. Then he cried in his headlong way, "It was an epic! No one, no man born of woman upon this earth, could be asked to give *that* away!"

"No," I said. "It would have been policy, of course; but policy has its limits."

Anakreon said softly in my ear, "Policy? Well, my dear, that depends upon what he wants."

Neither of us turned to share this thought with Lasos. He was quick-witted, but indiscreet. Before long, he would think for himself what an Olympic chariot crown can mean to a man who aspires to power; power that his forebears held for generations and never surrendered willingly—on sufferance to Solon, to Pisistratos not even that. Let Lasos think for himself, said Anakreon's sidelong eye. When the crowds were breaking up we slipped away from him and strolled off past the Hera temple to the shady slopes of Kronos' oak wood. Of course there were people all about, but one need not be overheard.

Anakreon said, "How much do you think it means?"

"Hard to say. Maybe no more than Lasos sees in it. He took the gift of the god, thinking he'd done enough last time for the Pisistratids, or not thinking about it at all. He could have counted on nothing beforehand. Think of the odds."

"Someone might have murmured to him how acceptable such a thing would be, if the long chance came off."

I said, "His family call him Simple Kimon, because he won't play politics. He lives for his horses and his land; he must have missed them badly in exile. That gift to Pisistratos got him home, which he wanted more than a second victory. On the other hand, he's a Philead, and he may not be so simple after all."

Anakreon picked up a green acorn, and turned it in his hand to admire the gloss. "Isn't his half-brother a petty king somewhere up north?"

"Miltiades? Indeed, and not so petty, sitting there in the Thracian Chersonese on the throat of the Euxine corn-run. You should ask my brother, who's had to pay his tolls. He's been a chariot victor too, it's in the family."

"Then so is money. How did he get among the Thracians?"

"He exiled himself in the Old Archon's time, and was asked by the Dolonkians to command a war for them, because of some oracle they'd had."

"Ah yes, I heard of that in Abydos. They're forever at war. They were grateful and made him King. Could that, too, be in the family?"

"I doubt it's come down to Kimon. He got tarred with the Philead brush, and had to go; you have to take care with a house that goes back to Ajax. But I'd be surprised if he's thinking now of anything much but his crown and his triple victory and his mares. Didn't you see him beaming from ear to ear? Simple Kimon, I thought, and none the worse for that. I should like to make him a praise song, if only for the mares' sake. But I suppose it wouldn't do."

"What I should like would be to be at his party tonight. *That* should be a good one. But I daresay that might not do either . . . *Look*, my dear, at that boy. The curly-haired one. Do you know, he is entered for the *boxing*? How can he do it? He will be ruined in five years."

"He's an Alkmaionid, so if you want to sing about him, leave out his name . . . Anakreon, do you ever wish yourself back in the days when you were an unknown name and a passing face, and could come and go like the breeze?"

"Of course, my dear. As both of us are doing now. But not if I had to pay for it."

I thought of my shepherd days; of my master dead in his poor Samian room, without help from me; of the girls I had feared to speak to. "No," I said. "Not if I had to pay."

We agreed together, therefore, that it had better not get about Olympia, however good Kimon's party might be, that it had been graced with the presence of Anakreon and Simonides. Meantime we paid our respects at our own

Archons' pavilion. We had delayed long enough already.

It stood up among the lesser tents like a trireme among fishing-boats. Even the Sicilians had brought nothing finer; it must have needed a train of ox-carts to heave it up from the harbor. The canvas was stitched in stripes of yellow and blue. It was far more splendid than in the Old Archon's day; the hand of Hipparchos showed all over it. From a gilded mast heading the tent-pole flew the trident banner of Poseidon, the crest of their god-born ancestor, Neleus of Pylos.

The Archons were in their chairs of state, receiving guests. We joined in compliments on the good run of their chariot. Of course, nobody mentioned Kimon's. It is all very well for the friends of boxers and wrestlers to taunt the losers; but among the chariotry, politer customs rule.

As we went away, I said, "They've got over it, it seems. The odds were too heavy against that victory; it's with things looked forward to that disappointment bites. They were just as usual, Hippias dignified and Hipparchos charming."

"Oh, indeed . . . But did you notice, with the sun coming through the canvas stripes, that Hippias looked blue and Hipparchos yellow?"

We laughed, and went our separate ways; Anakreon had a host of friends awaiting him, and I had not a few myself. For a while I looked at the stream of Alpheus, and across at the women's side. She would be there, she had told me so; she had even told me the colors of her tent, rose and light blue. But she knew I would not be coming, unless at the end of the games to exchange our gossip. She would be entertaining victors, strong young boxers and wrestlers and hurlers of the disk and javelin, who had said to themselves for months, "If I win, and my city makes me the victory gift, it would buy me a night with Lyra." Perhaps Kimon would visit her. Not tonight; he had his feast to see to, and could not ask her across the river to the Altis shore, sacred to men from the beginning.

I was shouldering off through the crowds, when a little dark hand grabbed my arm; and there was Neko, her Egyptian slave-boy, wearing new gold earrings. She spoiled him dreadfully; he was a saucy brat, but at least he was devoted to her. Naturally she had brought him to Olympia, where a girl could run her no errands across the stream.

"Big trouble find you, sir!" he said in his lilting Greek. "My madam she say, nice party tonight, special for friends, you come? Madam say, if you don't come, party no good. I tell her you come, yes?"

"Yes," I said, noting how gay and cheerful was the scene around me, and wondering why I'd been thinking it a tiresome crowd. "Take this to spend at the fair; and don't forget to tell her."

For me, this was the first Olympic since I'd known her; for her, it was only the second in her career. Already she knew what was due to her, and began her reign there in style, by holding court.

I think, if there had been room, her rose and blue tent would have held as many men of rank as the Archons'. However, it held fifteen at most, packed in right up to the flaps. She had hand-picked us, and let us know it. Little Neko, who served the wine, could hardly find room to put down his slender feet. It was a splendid party; the night was warm, the tent pegged open, and chosen latecomers were allowed to overflow outside. When it grew late, one or two people came on from Kimon's victory feast, still in the mood for singing. I had something in my head about his gallant mares, and, discreet or not, when the lyre came my way I sang it. The thought of those beautiful creatures, pouring all their virtue into victory, aroused my love of heroes. Surely swift Boreas, from whom all great horses are descended, swept to them in the race and bore them on. As I sang, I saw Lyra look at me under her lashes; but I only threw her a smile. A man must do what he was born to do; and not only when he is hired to do it.

A little later, she said it was unbecoming for a woman to put on contests at Olympia; but Neko should take the omens for her. She bandaged his eyes, not very tightly, and spun him round, and left him to turn again. He came to rest pointing at me, and pulled off the blindfold grinning. I thought it was because of the present I'd given him, till I saw her smile when everyone had gone.

It was the first Olympic night I'd ever spent on the women's side. The Alpheus, low that year, tinkled and gurgled among its pebbles; owls hooted in the sacred oak wood; from the men's side came distant singing, the whinny of a restless horse. A nightjar called. All around us, set to this music, were the voices of Aphrodite, murmurs and laughter and little grunts and squeals. Presently, quite near, came the soft sound of an Egyptian harp. She whispered, "The boy has a great deal of feeling." I don't know if it was he or we who first fell asleep.

The sun was up when we woke; when we had breakfasted, I was already late to get a good place for the pentathlon. Crowds had closed around the Archons' party; I made do near the top of the slope, among a press of Corinthians. None of them knew me, and they talked on among themselves. The Corinthian chariot was one that had not finished the course; it had crashed at the turn in the fifth lap, and they argued about it hotly, Corinthians being great racing men, even if they don't own as much as a donkey. "He should have kept out of the press; that's how Kimon won."

"He won because no one else was trying it. Well, it seems he was too lucky to please some god or other."

"God?" said a sharp dark young man who had not spoken before. "I hope some god is after the men who did it."

I was all ears now, but did not want to be noticed, and waited for someone else to ask the questions. But I had overslept; they had been asked already.

"In the very precinct!" said an older man. "What times we live in. Cutpurses, sneak-thieves round the tents, cheats in the market, that one expects, with riffraff coming in from everywhere. But to strike down a crowned victor, in the Sacred Truce! I live here in Elis, I've seen the Games since I was six, and in all my years I've known nothing like it."

A Corinthian said, "To give a great feast like that in a foreign city, he'd need to be carrying gold, with something to spare. It's a dark corner, round by the Council Hall; and he'll hardly have been sober, after the party. Well, you can be sure that by now they're far away."

The dark man said, "That's a thing I should like to be sure of."

People looked round, some questioning, some knowingly. The old Elian asked roundly what he meant. He had got as far as, "From what I hear . . ." when the trumpet sounded, and the athletes came marching in.

It was a middling pentathlon that year, the only notable feat a mighty discus-throw by a man from Argos. The first I knew of it was the cheering, and the umpire running out to peg the throw.

I stayed to the end, looking on or thinking, but thinking mostly. When it was over, and shadows began to fall, I threaded the loosening crowd, all talking by now of nothing but the games, and peered about for the red head of Anakreon. He, at least, would not have spent last night over the river.

He was with a crowd when I sighted him. As soon as he saw me, he shed the others with graceful ease, and hurried up to me, saying out of breath, "Wherever have you been? I've been looking all day for you, I thought you'd gone."

"Gone? Where? I was on the women's side."

"Oh, is that all? I wish I'd known."

His face looked quite drawn. I said, "But what did you think? That I'd left Olympia?" He said nothing. "I was all night with Lyra. All I've heard is rumor in the crowd. Are things really so bad? What are they saying? Where can we talk?"

We were by the old Hera temple; there was a quiet corner in its peristyle of black ancient timber. "Anakreon, the Archons cannot have done this thing. Don't tell me you believe it?"

He gave me a long look, and sighed. "My dear, I don't know. I have seen so much evil in my time, there's little I can't believe. You've known them longer. I was hoping that you'd tell *me*."

"Let's walk," I said. We went up into the dusky oak wood. There was an ancient tree split by a thunderbolt, by Zeus in the Titan War as like as not. Half still stood, half was felled, the fire-marks long washed with rain. No one was in earshot, and we sat down.

I said, "My mind's been on it all through the pentathlon. I don't even know who won the foot-race—four years to the next, and by then one may be dead . . . Well, I've thought, and I can't believe it. If it was done, it must have been by Hippias; he's sole ruler in all but name. And he's the most god-fearing man I ever knew; he wakes and sleeps by it. Can you see him violating a sacred precinct *and* a sacred truce, in one stroke? He'd as soon dance naked through the Kerameikos."

"I think so, too." He pulled a piece of pale lichen off the log, shook out the grubs, and peered at it. His short sight hid from him many imperfections; it gave him, I daresay, as much pleasure as it took away. Close to, he could count the veins on a fly's wing. "Exquisite. Like Thessalian gold-work . . . Sometimes I've thought there might be more in Hipparchos than meets the eye. Power does not much concern him. But a slight, I've noticed, concerns him a good deal."

"Hipparchos!" I gazed at him amazed. But then, it was true he had seen much evil. "He'd never be a man for a knife in the dark. I suppose like anyone he'd avenge an insult; but he's not had one. Kimon was his father's bene-factor, and that's the end of it. He owed nothing to the sons, and he could have promised nothing. It wasn't in his power."

Anakreon's face lightened. He had been through bad times, and did not want to think they could come again. I could understand it. I went on, "Kimon and Hipparchos can barely know each other. Kimon's a real country squire; the arts mean nothing to him. As for Hipparchos, he likes the graces. He takes nothing very seriously, even love."

"Fortunate man!" He sighed and lifted his eyes. "My dear, you have lifted a load from me. If you'd known my need of you, you'd have lain less easy last night."

I laughed; we brushed the bark from us, and, ready for supper, strolled down among the trees. In the open glade, touched with the yellow light of sunset, people were stroll-ing in twos and threes. "You were saying, my dear, that you missed the winner of the foot-race. Look, there he is. An Athenian, too. The Archons made him a present."

The young man was dark-haired and dark-eyed, walking lightly, with the springy step of a runner, still wearing the ribbons tied by his friends round his head and arm. "It comes back to me now," I said. "He ran a good race and used his head; but I missed his name."

"I heard it. It will come to me in a moment. Oh, yes. Aristogeiton, son of Theotimos."

10

KIMON'S MURDERERS were never found. His son, who had
come with him to the games, soon made it clear that he
did not suspect the Archons. I was there when he accepted
their sympathy as that of friends, and said that he blamed
himself more than anyone. Like me, he had spent the night
on the women's side. Not that his father had opposed it;
he had laughed and wished him joy; but if they had been
together, he might be still alive. This young Miltiades was
no fool, as he proved, when the Medes came, to everyone's
satisfaction; he knew the court and both the Archons well,
and what satisfied him has always been good enough for
me. But even he could think of no enemies his father could
have had. He wondered if one of the losers could have killed
him out of envy. Such things are rare, but not quite
unknown.

However, if Kimon had no enemies, the Pisistratids had
them. Olympia buzzed with Alkmaionids, like a wasp-nest
poked with a stick.

If an exile meets a man from his former city, what is
more natural than a talk to ask for news? Olympia seemed
quite full of Alkmaionids and friends, always just out of
earshot.

Next day was Full Moon, when the contests are only for
boys, because the great procession, and the Hundred-Ox
Sacrifice, take up all the morning. All the Hellene cities
send their embassies to carry offerings; and all Hellas had

come to expect that the one from Athens would be the finest. I had made the song for the choir to sing. I had not, of course, been asked to walk in the procession. People on show for their city have to be well-favored. I felt some remorse towards Anakreon, who I was sure would have been invited, had Hipparchos not feared it would seem like a slight to me.

Athens excelled all other cities. Yet it was surpassed; and by the Alkmaionids.

They were men without a city; but anyone who thought they'd be stopped by that never knew the family. When, sounding with flutes and lyres and sweet trained voices, heralded by trumpets, and carrying precious spices, the sacred theoria from Delphi came pacing in, it was Alkmaionid in all but name.

Nobody was surprised, who'd been at the last Pythian Games. It was in my father's day that Apollo's temple at Delphi was burned down. When I first saw it as a boy, there was just a makeshift shelter over the sanctuary; nothing had been left but the Pythia's cave below. That comes of thatch and timber; for decades all Hellas had been sending offerings to house the god decently in stone. Then the splendid Alkmaionids offered to complete the building at their own cost. When they had finished the work in stone, they faced it all with marble. Apollo, it is true, had always been the patron god of their house. At any rate, thenceforth they were as welcome to him—at least, to his priests and prophetess—as the swallows in the temple eaves. I never yet heard of an Alkmaionid getting a bad oracle at Delphi.

They were richer even than the Pisistratids. Everyone knows how old Alkmaion founded their fortunes. Kroisos, that golden king, befriended him, and, like a generous host, offered him as much gold as he could carry by himself out of the treasury, thinking he'd come out with both hands full. Alkmaion bound his girdle tight round his hips, and put on wide-topped boots; filled everything he wore with gold, and came out like a waddling moneybag. Kroisos, they say, when he'd got his breath back enjoyed the joke; he had plenty more, as Kyros discovered later, when he took it all. For the Alkmaionids, that was just the beginning. They had married into money far and wide, they owned the best land in the Attic plains; and Pisistratos, when he told them there was not room in Attica both for him and them, never took away their estates. The income still reached them; they still entered chariots at the games; and Hippias, from policy or discretion, had let them and their money be. They had too many offshoots and fellow clansmen still in Attica; their power in exile was a less evil than war or stasis. It was to be reckoned with, however. A great lord in exile will not be content with owning land that he cannot tread, even though he can live on it like a prince elsewhere. He wants the house of his fathers; their tombs, where he should offer sacrifice; and, above all, their former rank there, in the days when their word was law. Even those born in exile sucked in all this with their mothers' milk. They were bitter; and Kimon's murder was meat and drink to them. They put it about all over Hellas that the Archons did it, and thousands believe it still. I never have, though I could have profited by saying so in later years.

When the games were over, the two noble Elians who were that year's judges decreed that Kimon should be given a public funeral, and a tomb at the city's cost by the Valley Road. Thus they honored his triple victory, appeased his ghost, and denounced his murderers, whoever they might be.

The big crowds had left by then; those who stayed for the funeral were mostly Elians, living near, and friends or clansmen of the dead. The Archons and their party had left for Athens the day before, which was wise; and Anakreon

went too, saying he'd had enough of mourning. However,
I was known by now for a man who would go off on his
own affairs; and I stayed, from respect for quality. Kimon
was to have a funeral offering in the grand, heroic style. His
whole chariot team was to be sacrificed at his tomb, and
have its own monument, facing his across the highway.

He was lowered into his grave, handsomely robed and
wearing his wreath of victory. Precious offerings, some of
them from the Elian treasury, were laid beside him. The
slab was closed and the earth thrown over, and incense was
burned upon the altar before the sacrifice.

The four mares had stood good as gold, decked in their
garlands, tossing their graceful heads now and again, or
flicking their tails against the flies. The lean dark charioteer
was with them, patting their necks or stroking their noses
if they began to fidget. His face was drawn, but grave looks
become a burial.

When the libations had been poured, and the sacrificer
came for the first of them, she stepped up prettily to the
altar, taking him no doubt for a new groom. As the cleaver
swung home into the throat, I saw the amazement in the
creature's eyes before she drowned in her blood and
foundered.

The other three still stood. The charioteer had turned
them sideways from the altar. They had raced three times
at Olympia; they did not take fright at the smell of blood
or the screams of wounded horses. When the second was
led away, the two that were left grew restive; but he gentled
them, and they calmed under his hand. The man in the
grave was nothing to them; this was their master, who had
steered them through the race-track's clash and fury, always
safe to the goal. When the third was fetched, she backed a
little, but did not rear. An Olympic charioteer, though he
never drugged a horse in his life before, still knows how it
is done.

Now only one mare was left; and, drugged or not, she knew that she had smelled death. When they came to her she dragged and reared, and gave a shrill frightened neigh. He pulled down her forelegs, and laid his face a moment against her neck; and I could see the sacrificer asking him to help lead her to the altar; but he shook his head. She knew herself betrayed, and there was nothing he could say to her. He handed over her bridle and turned away, the mare looking after him with terror-whitened eyes; and when the killing was over, he was not to be seen.

Priests, judges, mourners and onlookers departed for the city. It was a fine day, not too hot, and I walked the other way by the murmuring water, following the Valley Road.

The dust lay thick on it and my feet fell quietly. A few stades along, I heard the sound of weeping, fierce and desolate, and saw lying out from a clump of bushes a yellow fold. He had worn his racing colors for the ceremony. I paused; but there was nothing mortal man could do for such grief as that. When Priam was lamenting his fallen sons, if Homer himself had come and promised they should live on in the *Iliad*, I don't suppose their father would even have lifted his head. So I did not stay to ask the names of his lost children. For that matter, I have never learned his own.

By the time I came back, people were strolling to take the air by the green waterside. A tall man greeted me; it was the handsome Proxenos, the Attic lord who had given me breakfast after the Old Archon's death-watch. We were friendly, courteous and careful with one another, found empty and pious things to say of Kimon, and agreed it was sad to see the immolation of so fine a team, but they would soon have been past their best.

There was a rustle in the myrtle grove, and out came his young son, with a green branch in his hand. He had been pretty before, but now seemed almost radiant. If he kept those looks after his bones took form, I thought, he would set the city by the ears; already he would have inspired Anakreon's lyre.

He ran up and grasped his father's hand. It seemed he had come to join our conversation. Turning to me, he said, "He won the crown three times."

"First say, 'Good evening, sir,' " his father told him. "Where have your manners gone?"

"Good evening, sir. He won the crown three times, and so did the horses."

"They were brave beasts," I said. "Let's hope they have had brave children."

He planted his beautiful brown feet in the yellow dust, and frowned. His brows were like gilded bronze, and his eyes summer-sea blue. He said, "Those bad men killed him."

There was no quarreling with such true words. But his father said quickly, "That is enough, Harmodios. You are interrupting your elders. Go back now to your play."

The boy gave him a quick look; he was used, I could see, to picking up a warning. Watched by his father—partly from love and partly not to meet my eyes—he went off into the myrtle grove.

THE SACRED WAY

1

○━○━━━━━○━○━━━━━○━○

THE YEARS SAILED ON, swiftly with fair winds; the wine-dark
sea lapped softly on the reef ahead, as if on a raft of
spindrift, which the prow will cleave easily upon its way.

The sons of Pisistratos still kept the goodwill their father
won. Sometimes it seemed he had divided himself in two,
Hippias having his public gravity, Hipparchos his private
wit. They were not emulous; each was content to be valued
for what he was. Hippias was praised for keeping up his
father's traveling court of justice. There were long memories
of the days when all causes had to go to the local lord. If
good, he was excellent, from knowing all parties well. If not
so good, he might have taken you in dislike or your enemy
in favor; or your case might be against him, himself, which
was as good as no case, before Solon made the laws and
Pisistratos got them obeyed.

No peasant or small farmer wanted to see those days
again; nor did the city craftsmen and merchants; nor, even,
did most of the lesser gentry. But the great lords and their
factions still felt the anger of the dispossessed; and not all
of them were in exile.

With all this we lived by custom, as one lives with
weather. I had my own concerns. I was singing well and
often; I was in my prime of vigor, wiry and strong; long

journeys were pastime to me, not fatigue. I went to all the festivals, at Olympia, Delphi, Nemea, Corinth, Delos, and sang at their victors' feasts; at Athens, there were the sacred rites of the gods, and the great festivals of Athene and Dionysos. With all this, I still found time to visit my kin on Keos; and it was there that I found my son.

I found him and he found me. I took him in peace, doing no wrong to anyone. Each time I saw him again, he had become more mine, and everyone knew it, he himself most of all.

Philomache's third boy had fulfilled his infant promise. Solid and strong, he looked a pankratiast already; if old Bacchylides did not live to see him crowned, at least he could die assured of it. But my boy favored me; it was as if some friendly god had thought better of my face, and made it over to what it should have looked like. He was small like me; like me, dark-haired and dark-eyed; but his features were neat as a girl's, though with much more firmness. His eyebrows were already thick, and joined in the middle; in that we are still alike.

He was never shy of me, as I'd first been of my teacher, a stranger I held in awe. Me he had known since he could remember, crowing to my songs while still in arms. His nurse would hush him, but he came in on the beat. By the time he was six, he was making songs of his own, and would sing me them with no more ado than a bird. When I began to teach him, he did not know it, thinking we were still at play. At bedtime he'd ask a song from me, as a prize for being good; and twice heard he'd have it all.

He left them no peace, his mother used to tell me, asking when Uncle Sim would be coming to stay again. Best of all, he loved me more for the music's sake than he loved the music for mine. By that I knew which god had given him to me. So, when he was old enough to travel, I asked his father's leave, and took him to Delos, to present him to Apollo.

He was entranced with the island, and cried out that the rocks were full of silver stars. (I didn't steal that, I knew he would use it later.) When in the porch of Pisistratos' temple he offered his little votive of a gilded dolphin, and the young priest bent smiling down to take it, he said, "This is for Apollo's birthday. Will you wish him long life from me?" Yet, as he told me long after, he had a sense of what we were both about.

So far, so good. But when I was away he was learning nothing, and his faults would be settling in. Most songs he heard would be from the peasants and the women; well enough, like bread, but not as one's only food. He went to school in Iulis to learn the lyre, but had a dull fool for a teacher, fit only to teach other fools by rote. He would soon have come to dislike it; no wonder, for he knew better himself. From being forever held back he had grown troublesome, and was always in hot water. All this I watched, fretting, till he was nearly nine; and then I talked to his parents.

His mother said, "But who will make him change his clothes when he gets wet?"

His father said, "You only see him when he's showing off to you. I warn you, Sim, he can be as mischievous as an ape. I'm telling you for your good. He'll plague you."

"If he does I'll send him back. I can afford him a steady pedagogue; I won't let him run wild."

"Why not wait a few years, till he's steadier himself?"

"No. I can't afford that, and nor can he."

"But you are so much away!" cried Philomache.

"Oh, I shall take him with me. He's tough as a nut. The road's a great place for poets to learn the trade."

She looked at her husband pleadingly. What she was

pleading for, as I guessed, was his consent. The boy had been a handful at home, and getting worse.

Midylos said, "He'll surely be in your way. You're guest-friend to high-ranking men, these days."

"He's quick. He'll take to the life faster than I did, and I was quick myself. Don't be afraid, he's ready."

The end of it was, he came; on trial, they said, to see how it would answer.

He had been noisy enough on Keos; on the ship, the mate gave him a clip for climbing up the rigging; but once landed at Piraeus, he was as silent as a sponge. He had no time even to ask questions, lest he should be missing something. Riding on the pack-ass towards the city, he found his voice; by the time I'd told him all he wanted to know, I was in danger of losing mine. He had been nowhere, except that once to Delos in the quiet season. When we met some Nubians he was alarmed; he had never heard that men can be born black, and thought they were from the realm of Hades. I showed him they were carrying elephants' teeth, which lasted him some time, until he saw his first horse. Horses are forbidden under Kean law; but he knew what it was, and shared it with me in one enraptured glance.

I lost no time in buying him a pedagogue; a man of Illyrian race, slave-born in a good house, and speaking very fair Greek. Brought up in Athens, he knew where the boy could safely go, and where not; he had done the same work before, and had been sold when his charge outgrew him. He took the boy to school and back, and taught him to look after himself. I would not have him waited on, for I seldom travel with servants; a good mule and pack-ass are less trouble and of more use. This man, Philemon, was honest and kindly, and I took care to treat him well. It made him too easygoing, as we found when his charge slipped off to Piraeus, and was nearly stolen by a Tyrian slaver. He would have walked on board—"to be shown the ship"—but for the luck of an acquaintance knowing who he was. He would never have been seen again, and for his good I beat him; but even so, he begged me not to beat Philemon, to whom he'd lied when asked where he was going. I rejoiced that he had justice in his soul, but this was no time to praise it.

As a rule, to keep him well behaved one had only to threaten him with missing the next procession or choral sacrifice, or his next piece of Homer. He never ailed, except once from eating green figs; though he had not lived as hard as I'd done at his age, on Keos no one is pampered. I knew he would be a good boy for the road.

By the time he was ten, he was traveling with me. Even then he was not a burden; over the years, he's done far more for me than ever I did for him. Where we were guests, he would shake down among the family boys, or lay his pallet by mine. Like me, he could drink the water in most places without getting a flux. Once a scorpion bit him; he was weeping with pain, but would let no one touch it, only asking for me. He was right, in that ignorant village; I nicked the wound and sucked it, and bound it with a cloth wrung out in hot water mixed with myrrh, as a Euboian herb-wife had taught me. When the pain was gone, he said it was a pity Philoktetes had not had me there to heal his wounded foot; I might even have cured Achilles. To this day, he has the white scar of my knife upon his ankle-bone.

On the road he'd make his songs, as I used to do; I had to remind myself that I'd been five years older. I got on with my thoughts, and asked no questions; sometimes he'd read one in my eye, and say, "It's not finished yet." Sometimes it never was; he would say, "It didn't come out right." I hoped he'd not thrown away something better than he knew; though it is my faith that such things return to one, when their time has come to be born. So I let him alone, unless he was short of a word and came to me for it.

I had a great shock to come, though. I suppose I'm hardly yet over it. Coming in from the city, and by chance entering quietly, I heard his voice, and looked around the door. He was cross-legged on a stool, bent over a wax writing-tablet, chanting softly to himself; so taken up with his task that he did not hear me. I was surprised; as a rule he'd had enough of school when lessons were over. He gazed at the wax with his stylos poised, and hummed the same phrase two or three times over; then again with a different word. On that he rubbed at the wax, and wrote something. It was only then that I knew what he was doing. It shook me to my roots.

"Bacchylides!" I said. "What are you writing there?"

He jumped nearly out of his skin. He could not have looked more guilty if he had been caught robbing my money-chest.

And so he should, I thought. I could hardly believe what I'd heard and seen. I took a deep breath, to prepare my words. How could he ever become a bard, if he rotted his memory with writing, instead of printing his songs inside his skull? It was an offense to the Muse; if it took on, it would be the death of poetry. If he could not remember his Homer or his Sappho or his Anakreon, he must come to his teacher, as it was a pupil's duty to do.

I had it ready, but I never said it. I saw in his eye that, before I started, he could have given me every word. He looked back at me, full of his answers, hopeless. It took me back. I could remember how it felt. After all I just quoted Achilles: "*Come, tell me, then we shall both know.*"

He smiled, but anxiously still. He had folded his diptych together, and was hugging it in his arms. After swallowing hard, and gazing at me in something near desperation, he said, "I'm not remembering, Uncle Sim. I'm *making* it."

"I don't know" I said, "whether that is better or worse."

"I'll remember it afterwards, I promise I will." His face got quite red, not with shame but effort. "I can do it in my head, the first piece of it. That always comes."

"Always, yes. It's the finishing is the work."

"Yes, I know. And when I'm doing that, and I'm stuck, I want to see the shape of the sound. Then I get it, like I did just now."

"Ah. But just on that piece of wax. Not in your head."

He laid the folded tablet down, and gave it me word for word. "That's as far as I've got," he said. "Look if you like."

Without doubt, it was the best thing he'd done. Boy's stuff still, of course, and full of echoes; but echoes are the heritage of us all, and he was learning how to make new music with them. He knew it, and if I denied it he'd lose trust in me; or in himself, which would be worse. So I praised ungrudgingly, and saw his face lighten as if reprieved from prison. "I do learn it," he said. "I go over and over it. I learn it better this way."

"Well," I said, giving it weight, "take care it is your staff and not your crutch." He nodded gravely. Then my mind went back and I could not keep from laughing. "Did they ever tell you at home that when my master and I had to leave Ephesos, I sang in a tavern for my keep?" I saw they'd cautioned him never to breathe a word. "My master was distraught and thought it would be my ruin. But I found it an education. There are plenty of paths to Helikon. Just don't lose sight of the top."

After that, I took him out to the Agora and bought him a pet quail, which I knew he longed for, and he went happy to bed. Though he never let me see him writing if he could help, it was understood there would be no more questions. He was getting his Homer well enough; already he had the Departure of Hektor word for word.

"Why," he asked me once, "did Andromache say their

little boy would starve, if his father died? He was King Priam's grandson."

"I have often wondered. My guess is that Homer had learned that piece from his master or some great bard, and liked it so well that he had to work on it, and keep it. So he put it there, although it doesn't fit."

"It's so sad. What really happened to the little boy?"

"He was the heir of Troy. So the Greeks threw him off the walls."

"Poor little boy . . . It's much sadder in Homer. Where the orphan comes to the feast and the other boys chase him away, that's really sad."

I remembered—though I doubt if he did—the naming-feast of his young brother. He was happy enough at school, his quick wit being admired there, even though he did not go much to the gymnasium. He thought it wasted his time, and I had to agree.

Although I told everyone the truth, that he was my nephew, it soon got rumored that he was my bastard son; as he could have been, from his looks. I denied the charge, but not with too much heat; partly because I felt it almost true, but mostly because I was not sorry to have it believed at court. The boy was no great beauty; you would never see his name inscribed in wine-cups; yet he was comely and bright enough to catch a roving eye. I wanted it known that I took a father's care of him, and would not have him meddled with till he was old enough to decide such things for himself.

In the last few years, Hipparchos had grown less choice in his pleasures than when I knew him first. There were parties now that I was not asked to, and I guessed why. Anakreon was invited for some time longer, but began to be dropped as well. He told me this with relief.

"I had been wondering, my dear, how it could be managed. After all, Athens is my home now, body and mind, as well as my living. Even so, one has one's pride. However, it was just a matter of choosing the right moment, when one was seen, and looking round here and there, and raising an eyebrow. It made its mark; more from me, of course, than you. He's thought *you* proper for some time. Well, he does know now that I like my company to have a little more style. That kind of hint gets home to him, you know."

Though the next commission for a choral ode was given to Lasos ("So unfair, my dear; he is never asked because he's a deadweight at *any* party") Anakreon was soon back in favor, and invited with more discretion. One thing did not change at Hipparchos' court: there was always the reigning favorite, from a good house and quite presentable. Anakreon, whose task it was to celebrate each in song, confided that one could usually do so without disgust. This indeed was true, and the rewards were generous. All the same, I was not sorry to have made my name by treating of other themes. Like every poet, I have sold my praises, in the sense that I've been paid for them; but, like Lyra with her lovers, I want freedom to pick and choose. Praising excellence, one serves the god within it; and false praise insults him, it has always seemed to me. The only worse thing is detraction of the good.

So I got on with my own work, which at that time of year was a song for the young virgins, when they came to Athene's temple with their offerings. It was a year of the lesser festival; but still, it meant a great deal to the girls, and it was a pleasure to train them. Some of them would be chosen later for the Great Year, the Panathenaia. One year in four, it meant as much to the wellborn maids of Athens as Olympia to the boys. Their chorus leader would have the right to dedicate her statue in the precinct, in memory of her triumph. For none of them would there be a Great

Year again. Last time, they had been children; next time they would be married. There was always a glow and bloom on them in the Great Year. They could have been young goddesses, and sometimes the sculptors caught it. I don't know what has become of those marble maidens, since the place was cleared after the Medes. It will all be very grand and new; they will not keep anything that is in their way. Yet I remember those quiet smiles, as if the girls had been lifted to Olympos, where trouble and grief could never touch them more.

Grief comes, though, to human kind, as surely as night comes, or winter rain. Handsome Proxenos had ridden for the last time in the knights' procession. A ship from Naukratis brought to Piraeus some fever out of Africa; it ran about the city, and overtook other ships after they had sailed. Theas took it, and went down with it at Andros, his next port of call. He was on the mend before I knew he was sick, but it left him weak, and he was a full month picking up. Proxenos, I was told, rode to the port to see off some friend upon a journey. He sickened within two days, and in seven was dead.

I went to the house to condole. He lay in state, crowned with parsley and strewn with sweet herbs; he had died too quickly to lose his looks, and made a stately corpse. His widow and a young girl, with shorn hair and ash-streaked faces, were wailing over him. His father, a bent old man too crippled to leave his chair, was acting host, and I made my call brief so as not to tire him.

When I praised his son for virtue, valor and beauty, he said, "Fate is the master of all things, even the gods. Four sons I had, and only one grew to manhood. Now he is gone in his prime, when I had looked to him to bury me. Well, he has left me a grandson in whom he will live again, his very image at just that age. But he is young to lose a father.

He looked to Proxenos for everything, not to a dried old reed like me. What changes I have seen, and never for the better! Now my time comes near, and he will be left head of the family, and he no more than a boy."

Next evening I went to the funeral, from respect. Proxenos had had some of the old nobles' faults, but rather more of their virtues. Had he had their power, he would have used it justly; though you might not always have thought so, to hear him talk.

The cortege was a long one, mostly made up of the dead man's fellow Gephyriots. The tribe came to Attica long ago from Tanagra, and will tell you they were Phoenicians once. They don't look Phoenician; I daresay they were Greek colonists whom the Phoenicians drove out. Not more of them are dark today than you find among Ionians anywhere. Six of them carried Proxenos on his bier. The friends walked before, the hired mourners keened behind to the sound of flutes. Close round the bier walked the near kindred, and then you saw how small the family really was. The old granddad had stayed at home; a man nearly as old, doubtless his brother, walked in the place of honor, the only adult male, alongside Proxenos' young son.

When I had called at the house, he had not been in the room; I saw him now for the first time in seven or eight years. As I approached I thought, Is that the little Harmodios? Can he really have grown so tall? How our lives fly past!

He must then have been about fifteen, the awkward age between boyhood's grace and the ephebe's firmer beauty. He had achieved the best of both. With close-cropped hair, black-clad, his face drawn with grief, even so he shone.

Fair as his father, with the same straight carriage, and, yes, already, his father's pride but deeper, bred in bone, the calm pride that thinks insolence beneath it, as calm courage need not stoop to bragging. It was graven into him, while he thought only of his loss and his new load of care; a part of his beauty, though such a face would have lent beauty to all its changes, laughter, or grief, or anger. His grandfather had spoken truly; Proxenos had left his monument on earth.

At the burial-place, we left our offerings to sustain his journey. The boy got into the grave, to set them about the corpse. When the slab was closed and the earth thrown over, he took up the family grave-wreath. The mourning locks of hair hung from it: white, grey or grizzled, but for two strands of gold shining among the bay leaves. Two? Then I remembered the girl, weeping beside the widow. She had drawn her dark veil, and I could not see her face.

The boy stooped with the wreath, gravely concerned to set it upright against the post which would serve until the masons brought the stone. I don't know what prompted me to look, just then, at the people standing by. Something in the air, a note of silent music.

I seldom forget the face of a victor. There stood the dark-haired runner, Aristogeiton, whom Anakreon had pointed out at Olympia. He had stepped out from the crowd, to watch the rite.

All the others were watching too, and I suppose it made him careless. His eyes told a tale that could have been no clearer if he'd sung it out to the lyre. He would have poured out his own blood as a libation, if that could have given comfort to the wreath-layer. Henceforth, he would be ready at a word.

The boy straightened up from his task. As he lifted his head, he glanced that way, as though someone had called his name. The blue and the dark eyes met. It was not for long; but something was offered, something accepted, something understood.

To this day, I do not know if that was their first avowal.

2

MOST OF THE NEXT YEAR was fortunate. I won a tripod at the Dionysia; my dithyramb had a dialogue between the god and Herakles, telling of their wanderings in turn. All the poets were growing venturesome; and drawing closer to tragedy, though, as Aischylos said to me lately, without knowing it. Never mind, much that we made in those days is living still.

At the year's end, without warning, Dorothea died. They told me that in the kitchen she dropped an old knife upon her foot, and the wound swelled up, with fever. Though the doctor purged her, she died within four days. She had been so hale and strong, that she and everyone supposed she would recover; and when at last her father sent me word, I was too late to close her eyes. The house was in perfect order. The days were long past when she'd refused a maidservant; she'd had the girls running to her for their orders up to the day before she died; the last she gave them was to make up a bed, to be ready when I came.

It was she, more than anything, who had bound me still to Euboia. From then on, Phileas managed the place till he grew too old, when I bought him a piece of land and got Midylos to find me someone else. Only Athens held me.

A few years turned Bacchylides from a charming son to a gifted pupil. Which was just as it ought to be; for he was not my son, and not in search of a father. If I'd really begotten him, maybe we'd have fallen out; a father's expectations can fret a boy like a chain. But we had freely chosen one another, each for his own good; our bond was close, but easy. Maybe that's why he has always cared for me like a son.

He was the best of companions, at home and on the road; lively, sturdy and shrewd. A quick keen learner, he soon had his Anakreon and Sappho and Stesichoros; his Simonides, too; built what he learned into himself, and turned it into his own music. He still composed on the wax; would laugh to me about it, and never failed to have the finished things word-perfect in his head. He has them still . . . those he learned as a boy. Already, getting into his middle years, his memory is nowhere near so good as mine at fourscore and three. Anything new he does, he'd lose if he didn't write it. He's a fine poet nonetheless. If that's the only way he could come at it, so much the worse; but not so much the worse as if he had never written.

By twelve or thirteen, he'd lost what little boyish prettiness he'd had, and was getting the look of Saturn that draws women: heavy brows, meeting; firm mouth framed between lines. Meantime, he was what passed in Athens as an ugly boy, and would be troubled with no suitors from the court. I was heartily glad of this. He had no feeling for it, thought it absurd, and was likely, if wooed by some man of rank, to laugh out loud instead of showing virtuous modesty. This would have disturbed the harmonies, as Hipparchos like to hear them. He thought of his fellowship as a singing-grove of Eros.

I had not suffered from this. He was still a discerning patron, who would no more have called on me for a serenade than on Anakreon for a hero ode. All the same, it was good to have no one in my house whom he or his friends might covet. A story was going about of a boy he'd as good as kidnapped, under cover of an evening frolic, and whom he entertained for three nights before his father, a man of no great estate, could get him back. And there had been a Macedonian slave-boy whom his master never got back at all; just a handsome present of gold, which was supposed to close the matter. The master had not cared to make trouble, but was known to be fond of the lad, who was said to be devoted to him. Since then, when Hipparchos was entertained to supper, favorites of the host no longer served the wine.

None of this talk reached the city commoners or country peasants. As always, Hipparchos sought diversion among people of fashion and rank. In public he remained a gracious presence; dignified but never stiff, always with the ready word or smile which shy Hippias could not manage; and, as a rule, if he'd promised someone a good turn, remembering to have it done. This was no false mask; to be liked was pleasant to him; he had learned the knack from his father, and knew just what little kindnesses mean most from a great man to a humble one. Hippias inspired respect, Hipparchos affection. The Pisistratids had come to power as the people's friends; and they seemed so to the Athenians almost to the end. That's why it took the Spartans, as well as the Alkmaionids, to get them out at last. Left to themselves, the Athenians would never have done it. The old nobility wished it still; but they had given up hope.

In those days, like most Athenians who could spare the time and still eat bread, I never missed the Isthmian Games. Athens to Corinth is nothing of a journey; the summer heat has not started; Athenians are welcome guests. True, the games have not the Olympic greatness; but one sees athletes of promise working their way to that, and proven victors trying for the climax of a fourfold crown: Pythian, Nemean, Isthmian, Olympic. I was still young enough to enjoy the sideshows, market and fair, and the boy, of course, was entranced with them.

Nowadays I find all the bustle too much, and leave it

to young Pindar, who has taken up the victor's song where I laid it down. That's well. Some men don't like to see another excel in their own art; I am only angry if anyone debases it. I can't take it with me to the grave; but, like a house where I have been happy, I want to leave it well cared for, and to see a good heir coming on. Well, but I suppose in the year I'm thinking of, young Pindar was not born.

The Isthmian race-track is nothing like as gruelling as Olympia's; some owners even race their own chariots there. As for the riding-race, in those days it was all owners up, no jockeys at all.

Hipparchos sat with a party, in the seats the Corinthians set aside for their ancient allies. I could have joined them, but had made some excuse because of the boy. Hippias was not there. He scarcely ever went to the Isthmia, which he thought frivolous and vulgar, and not what its founder Theseus would ever have approved.

The riders entered, and paced round before the stands. I was greeting someone I knew, when the boy touched my arm. "Look there, Uncle Sim. How do you think it must feel to look like *that*?"

I saw the approaching rider, on a big sorrel with blond mane and tail. He must be sixteen, now.

The boy was saying, "They all do in the songs, but you never really see it. He must be famous. Who is he?"

"Harmodios, son of Proxenos. A Gephyriot."

"Isn't he famous? He looks as if he were."

I knew what he meant. That serene pride had grown unaware of itself. I said, "His father's dead. I daresay he's more on the estate than in the city. That family never cared to be much at court."

"I know now what he's like. Achilles at Aulis, before the war began. That's it." I agreed that the hero would have been just about that age.

Each generation has its own dream of beauty. I have lived long enough to watch it change. Just then, he was what all sculptors were reaching after, and only the great achieved. Naked he sat his barebacked horse, brown gold, his hair plaited up for the race and bound about his head. His skin was like brown marble, his horse's like polished bronze. Into its braided mane, ribbons had been worked as finely as embroidery, with small blue beads. A woman's work; I remembered the sister, covered with her veil.

The parade went by. Till now, each Athenian had saluted Hipparchos in his seat of honor; two had even made their horses caracole. I watched to see what Proxenos' son would do. He raised his right hand and turned his head. No courtesy could have been more formal: precise, not slovenly, the salute of a gentleman who, in a foreign town, will not discredit his city by uncouthness. All the others had smiled, in the spirit of Isthmian gaiety, and had their smiles returned. Harmodios' face was cool smooth marble.

He passed. The eyes of Hipparchos followed, till his face turned away from me and I could not read it. That boy has done his fortunes no good, I thought. But, after all, with the games ahead and all the Isthmian parties, I daresay it will be forgotten.

The riders paced their circuit before the stands, and came round towards the starting-gates. As Harmodios drew near, I saw him lift his arm high, greeting someone in the crowd. The marble warmed and glowed; the blue eyes shone, kindled by eyes I could not see. When he rode on the smile still lingered, as a single cloud can give back the light of Helios, after he has sunk beneath the sea.

Bacchylides said, "He must have seen his lover." He spoke quite respectfully; as a rule he would have grinned.

The race was won, as happens four times out of five, by one of those young Thessalian lords who ride before they can walk. Harmodios rode a well-judged course, however, and came in among the first four.

After the finish, the crowd broke up around me, letting me see him stroking the nose of his white-blazed sorrel, while the groom put its blanket on. He looked truly in his element as bird in air or fish in stream: an Athenian knight with his horse, the ancient companion, his forebears' sign of conquest and mark of rank, each of them tracing his line back to the Trojan War. Maybe he was dreaming of the day when he would race a chariot here; it would have pleased his father.

He looked round from the muzzle he was fondling, as someone shouldered over to him through the press. Dark-haired Aristogeiton stroked the horse's neck; they smiled; spoke a few words, as it seemed about the race; Harmodios gave the groom his orders and handed over the bridle. The two walked off together, greeting friends. It was clear they were established lovers, long past the stage of declarations.

Later that day, the victor's father asked me to supper at the house he had hired in Corinth. He was Skopas of Thessaly, whose breed of horses was famous everywhere, crossed with both Persian and Arabian blood-lines. He and his son were true Thessalians, big and swaggering, but without the insolence some of those houses have, and fond of laughter; their long legs bowed from riding all day before their bones had hardened. They invited me to their estate to make the young man a victory song and train a chorus.

I said I would make the song at home (some hosts will never leave a man alone to work) and then would come with pleasure. When I got there, I improved on it a little; it's the one where Perseus invites Bellerophon to a feast, and while they drink, winged Pegasos covers Perseus' mare. It is still sung in Thessaly, where, I'm told, a dozen horse-breeders claim it was made for them.

I spent ten pleasant days there, ending with the feast;

they kept nearly sober till I had sung, high respect in Thessaly. Some of them had ridden for miles over the hills to hear me. I gave them Homer, in whose world they were almost living still. At parting they made me princely guest-gifts, and told me that henceforward I must count their house as a second home.

I thanked them and rode away, never thinking that before long it would be my refuge; still less that I would live to sing a funeral dirge for all of them, father and sons and kin, all lost in one angry stamp of earth-shaking Poseidon. I lived when the house fell down, because two tall young men with a horse to sell came asking for me by name. I had no need of a horse; I had never seen them before; when all was over, they and their horse had gone. They were very tall, even for Thessalians. It is said that the Great Twin Brethren, Sons of the Swan, Leda's immortal children, will befriend wayfarers and ride away. At any rate, ever since then I have offered at their shrine.

Swift is the dragon-fly's darting; swifter is fortune's change. I never spoke a truer word than that.

3

ATHENS WAS QUIET when I got back there. Young Bacchylides, whom I had left behind to get on with his schooling, had made a skolion on the music master, sung it too loudly, and had a beating. I had to own that the verse was neat.

All was much as usual about the court, but for a certain

restlessness, hard to put a name to. Hipparchos' latest friend, who had reigned for three months or more and seemed settled for half a year, no longer shared the supper-couch. He had been given a horse worth the price of a small town house, but was foolish enough to sulk, and was soon snubbed in public; after which he had the wit to retire into the country. Hipparchos remarked to me that he had grown tiresome, but said nothing of a successor. At the informal suppers, the couch would be shared with people not to be taken seriously, just guests, such as myself. Such times had been known before, and I thought little about it, till, meeting Anakreon at a concert one night of early summer, I asked him home for a drink.

I told the slave to leave us the wine and go to bed; our gossip was never very discreet. As soon as the door was shut, Anakreon said at once, "Well, I've done *my* best. I prophesy you'll be the next one called on. I wish he'd gone to you first. Now I've not only failed, which has annoyed him; I've made the quarry wary, and spoiled the chase for you."

I asked what he was talking about. He looked astonished. "What? Wherever have you been? Oh yes, among the horse-tamers. But surely you've heard by now what is going on?"

"No, not a word."

"Our playful friend has been shot through the heart at last. Why is it that with people like him, it's always someone impossible?"

"All praise impossible? That's bad for us all. And him."

"Oh, my dear, much worse than that. Impossible to *get*."

Like a hen with one chick, my first foolish thought was of Bacchylides. We would have to go traveling.

"I have tried," Anakreon was saying, "to drag him down out of the clouds; but he is blind with dreams. I tell you, he had better wake up soon. If he does it too late, there will be trouble."

"Why, who is it?"

"I can't believe you don't know. Well, perhaps I can. But weren't you on the stand at the Isthmian horse-race?"

I knew then. It gave me a shock, like bad news; the room felt colder. We poets sometimes have divinations.

"It's Proxenos' son," I said.

"Harmodios, who hardly gave him good day. Who sucked in oligarchy with his mother's milk. Who venerates his father, a man resentful even of Pisistratos."

"And," I said, "there is a lover."

"Acknowledged before all the city. If you know any more, don't tell me; I shall believe it in advance."

"But how far has this gone? I don't see how Hipparchos would even get to know him."

"Oh, that was quite tastefully done at first. It was while you were away. The Athenians who had ridden at the Isthmus were asked to a parade and sacrifice for Ilissian Herakles. A mounted torch procession to the shrine; pleasant, a delightful spectacle, everyone on best behavior. After the rites, a supper at the riverside, with a little music. I sang."

"What, a new one, and I have not heard it? Come, give!" I pushed the lyre at him.

It was his lyric about the fair young horseman who is begged not to caracole too high, because he is carrying someone's heart and one more leap might break it. It is charming, and I told him so.

"Yes, I've done worse. The right song at the wrong time. Too soon. Not that he took it to himself, at first. But it was set in the wrong mode, it made him uneasy. Hipparchos should have sent for you, to sing about Perseus or Achilles; but he was impatient. He always was, but it's grown on him."

"And after the music, what?"

"The host mingled, of course, among the guests. It was

all informal, you understand, no set couches, just cushions on the grass. The nightingales were in good voice; the river murmured; aromatic torches stood here and there, to lend enchantment without too much light. There was no lack of agreeable employment, with all those little walks among the plane trees; and as soon as my duty was done I took care to be invisible. A failed conjurer is better out of sight."

"And a failed lover?"

"Ah. When I came back, and found they had both gone, I thought I'd been successful beyond my hopes. But it was worst, not best. They had not left together."

"The boy had better leave town. What did he say; did anyone overhear it?"

"I learned from those in earshot that, after some trivial chat, not a word was uttered. But, alas, I fear that far too much was spoken, on either side. There has been an echoing silence ever since, which I do not like at all."

"I knew his father. I could make some excuse to call. Only to see how things are, no more. The old grandfather's been ailing; that will serve."

Next day I took a jar of my best Euboian honey. Inside the courtyard, the first person I met was the young Harmodios, on his way out. Certainly, I thought, Anakreon had been right. I could see his hackles rise at the mere sight of somebody from the court. Taking no notice, I made my kind inquiries. His cool thanks put me in mind of that salute at the horse-race. At this rate, I thought, he will grow up a formidable man.

"You will find him rather weak, sir; but I am sure he will like to see you for a little while. The women will take you in to him. Please excuse me; I have to meet a friend." He stopped to give some order to a household slave, in the voice of one already used to authority; then he was gone.

The women, as he had said, received me. Proxenos' widow I had met once or twice while he was alive. She was a fragile anxious lady, brought up from childhood not to fidget or complain, and now looking overstretched; if you'd blown on her, she'd have thrummed like the strings of a lyre. However, it was clear that nothing was on her mind but her sick father-in-law and her upset house, for which she begged my pardon. One could be sure her son had confided nothing. He'd have thought it unbecoming; besides, he could be sure she'd be shocked to death, fall ill as like as not, and give him nothing but trouble. This was a woman who had always leaned on her menfolk. She was a part of his charge.

In me, she saw only a man of her own years who had known her husband, and treated me as a family friend, keeping the young daughter unveiled beside her. Her name, I now learned, was Delias; she was about fourteen, rather tall for her age, grey-eyed, with long fair hair falling nearly to her girdle, very much her father's child. Though I saw that she was shy, she greeted me with courtesy, and after that kept her eyes upon her mother; anxious for her, I thought, rather than modest for herself. Proxenos' children must be a close alliance. And yet, how much of his life must be unknown to her.

That was true indeed, and to her cost. But then, how much that would concern me was unknown to me.

I found the grandfather dozing. He roused himself feebly to say, "How kind, how kind," and to hope my wife and children were in good health. I could see he wanted to be rid of me, and creep back into the womb of sleep. He was shrunk as small as a ten-year child, turned ninety years old; I wish I could have talked with him before his memory failed. I slipped quietly off. He would die kindly; they would hardly know when he was gone.

I had half a mind, next time I supped with Hipparchos, to mention this visit, just to see what it would bring forth. All poets should be inquisitive. But the old man's name

was Harmodios, his grandson having been named for him
in the usual way, and I did not think I could carry that off
easily. Besides, I remembered Anakreon's saying that I
might be asked in my turn to woo, and I did not mean to
put myself in the way of it. I knew too much.

The old man died soon after. Once more I brought a
grave-gift to the house and heard its women wailing, this
time in kindness more than grief. He looked lost in his
bier, like a child in a grown man's bed; there had been
handsome bones, though, in that fragile skull. The great-
uncle was absent, sick or already dead. Harmodios was
doing the honors.

It was his first family rite, as sole head of the house. I
could see his sense of it, his resolve to perform it well. His
earnestness made one feel what a boy he was, straining after
manhood. Well, I thought, that will come to him soon
enough. Poets don't always have the gift of divination.

No friend of the dead man's youth had survived to mourn
him. Many of his clansmen had come, and former friends
of Proxenos; but the guest I noticed most was Aristogeiton.
Several times, at the funeral feast, he gave the mother a
hand like a second son, and was so treated. It was only the
young Delias who would be quietly gone from any place he
came to. He was not yet thirty, and it would not have done
for them to stand talking in public, especially at such a
time; but there seemed more than that in her avoidance.
Maybe, I thought, Harmodios wants to marry his friend
into the family—that is often done—and she does not like
it. Or then, again, brother and sister must have been life-
long confidants, and now the secrets are told to someone
else. But I had done my duty by them all; I went back to
my own concerns and soon forgot her. Bacchylides, who
was now just about her age, gave me quite enough to
think of.

His inquiring mind took him rambling about the city and

the countryside, in what time he could spare from music; but I made him go to the gymnasium at least one day in two. He lived in Athens and must learn the carriage of a gentleman, whether or not he wished to become an athlete. He went obediently, and did his exercises; but, as he told me cheerfully, the best part of the palaestra was hearing all the gossip. Having no love affairs of his own he had no bashfulness, and chattered freely about those of his companions. I was amused by his mixture of shrewdness and simplicity; it made a good sauce to our midday meal.

"Harmodios was there today," he said, soaking his bread in soup. "He came without Aristogeiton."

"Why, have they parted?" I began to attend.

"Oh, no. Aristogeiton has to go out to his farm. Harmodios has more land, but he can afford a steward. And you know, Uncle Sim, if you can believe it, Hipparchos had another try at him?"

I nearly choked on my food. I don't know why I had expected the boy to have heard nothing; no one had longer ears; but I sometimes forgot his childhood was well behind him. "I never knew he had been so open. It is unlike him."

"Why, doesn't he talk to you about it? I made sure he would."

"No, indeed. I'm amazed that it's common knowledge."

"Well, I don't know about the city. But it is in the boys' palaestra. People would laugh, if it were anyone else. But I expect he could put us in prison."

"The gymnasiarch would make you sorry. But you don't mean to tell me the Archon pays his court on the wrestling-ground?"

"Well, almost. He stands staring. At first he used to just walk up and down with friends, only stealing glances; you know how, it always looks so silly. But now he stands and watches, as if he were a regular erastes waiting for his eromenos. Harmodios hates it. People look, you know.

Today when it started, he simply broke off his bout and left the other man standing, and walked out. And Hipparchos followed him." Seeing my startled face, and remembering I'd not been to school in Athens, he said, "Things like that often happen."

"Not to him. Bacchylides, don't gossip about this. I mean it. This is serious."

"Yes, I know." Indeed, his face had sobered. "I went to see."

"Did he see you?" I was surprised by my own alarm.

"No fear. I looked out of the privy window. Harmodios had to wash down before he dressed, so he went to the fountain. He'd come by himself with no one to sluice him down; and Hipparchos went and picked up the jug to do it. I couldn't hear all they said because of the fountain-spouts splashing. Harmodios said thank you, but it was too great an honor and he'd sooner do it himself. I couldn't hear Hipparchos, he spoke too quietly. But he stood the jug on the curbstone, and started to put his hand on him. Harmodios shook him off, like—like a spider. I really thought for a moment he was going to hit him. But he didn't; he snatched up the jug, and stood with it, ready to throw the water. So then Hipparchos went."

I was too shocked to speak. There are people to whom such things are never done; everyone knows it to be impossible.

"Don't worry, Uncle Sim. I didn't tell the others. Just for your sake I kept back this very good story, which you are the first to hear. It would have made a better one still, if Harmodios had emptied the jug on him. He had his hair in curls across the front, and a robe with three-color borders. I *would* have liked to see him all wet."

"I doubt you would."

"Well, maybe not. I saw his face, as it was . . . And Aristogeiton won't laugh, either."

"If Harmodios is wise, he will not tell him."

"He'll have to do that. For all he knows, someone saw. Like I did. If he doesn't tell, and Aristogeiton gets to hear, he might think he listened." He nodded gravely, a citizen of his world. "Look who Hipparchos is, and what he owns. Harmodios *must* tell . . . But he'd do it anyway."

"Yes. I fear that you are right."

I knew it, next time I saw the two together. They were going about the city upon their business; Harmodios had a kind of sparkle upon him, and I saw what the boy had meant, when he likened him to the young Achilles at Aulis. Aristogeiton looked darker. I thought, That man is afraid. What of? He never looked like a coward. Though it was not likely they would talk of it, I knew how gossip seeps down through the gymnasium from older to younger; so presently I remarked to Bacchylides that Aristogeiton seemed oftener in the city than he used to be.

He answered at once, "Oh yes, he is. He comes to watch over Harmodios."

"Well, there's sense in that. It would be better still to take him out of town."

"He'd never go. He's the head of the family. Uncle Sim, do you think the Archon would ever carry him off? I think that's what Aristogeiton is really frightened of."

"Carry him off?" I could hardly credit my ears. It was too absurd for anger; I simply laughed. "A man like Hipparchos doesn't run mad for love, like someone in a song. And he'd need be mad, to do that. Harmodios' family is one of the oldest in Athens."

"Yes, I know. But his father's dead, and he hasn't any brothers . . . They do say Hipparchos carried off a boy."

"Not for long. Except for the slave; and that was little more than a prank."

With his elbow on the table beside his bowl, he propped his chin on his hand and looked at me, thinking. I can still

see his eyes, under those dark brows which now are starting
to grey. Soft and thick they were, in those days.

"You are right," I said. "It was an act of hubris, and
unjust. You could say it was unworthy of a gentleman, let
alone a ruler. But things are less simple when you know
a man."

"And he's been good to you, too." He meant just what
he said, not more. He trusted me.

"That's so. We are eating his bread this moment. But
it's not his gold that keeps me here. I don't think we'd
come to want if we took the road. You'd enjoy it, I daresay;
at your age, I did."

"I'd have enjoyed Ionia, I know that. But it's gone, now.
In those days Athens was just one city; but now it's the
center of the earth."

In no time, I thought, he will be a man, and I'd best
remember it. "That's the root of the matter. Solon and
Pisistratos brought the Muses to Athens. But only one
man keeps them here. Without him, they'd fly away like
birds scared out of a field. It takes more than gold to whistle
them to your hand; more, even, than being a gracious giver.
To keep them, you must understand their song."

"Yes," he said gravely. "You're his friend; you really know
him, and I've only seen him when he's been making a fool
of himself. Plenty of other men do it too, over boys who
just make fun of them."

"But they can afford it better. Well, only the gods are
without a flaw. All one dares ask of any man is that he does
more good than evil. And that he does no evil of free
choice."

I could see him getting that by heart, like a song. From
loving the boy, I was beginning to love the man.

Presently he said, as he finished his watered wine, "It's
the Great Year. It will soon be the Panathenaia. I've only
seen one. What hymn will you be doing?"

"Two, as it's a Great Year. Men and girls. The men for a choral ode to Poseidon at the holy spring."

"You'll have to think of something new about Theseus, won't you? *Is* there anything?"

"Certainly. He's not yet been down to the underworld, to carry off Persephone."

"That's a dark tale, Uncle Sim. Do you think the Archons will like it?"

"That's with the god, who sent the song to me." I had asked myself the same question, but only as if asking whether it would rain tomorrow. This tale of the hero's hubris and nemesis had seized my mind, and I had no time for anything else. "Herakles shall rescue him at the end."

"And what about the girls?"

"That hymn is always joyful. It's for the maidens, who bring the offerings to Athene. Yes, I shall be busy. Hipparchos, too. He's been planning a full year for the Great Year. That will take his mind off his little folly."

A thought came to me then, and I said, "I don't think, this year, the city would grudge me the privilege of having my pupil carry my kithara. Just for the Presentation of the Maidens."

Before he found his voice, he looked almost beautiful. Never mind, I thought; he is in no danger now, and if he were he can well look after himself. I took him to a robe-maker to have something made up, a short tunic proper to his age, and a red shoulder-cloak.

A few days later, Hipparchos sent for me to discuss the festival. Of course I was one of many: high priests and generals, the engineers who had charge of the Sacred Ship, and that year were making a new one; the other poets, and the musicians. The heralds were there, to learn their stations and cries. The eldest of them plied back and forth with messages to the High Priestess of Athene, who was too holy to appear among men at all. Both Archons were

present; Thessalos too, who was to lead the youths' cavalcade, by reason of rank, for he was past the age. Hipparchos,
as usual, did almost all the business of the rite, and had a
good deal to say to me; but all day I never had speech with
him alone.

That I had expected; but I kept my eye on him, and what
I saw disturbed me. In the last few years he had been
thickening a little, till it threatened to spoil his looks; now
he was lean. He had lost flesh so quickly, I wondered if he
could have a wasting sickness. Men with a phthisis have
this burned-up look, till one day they cough blood and die.
But he did a great deal of talking that afternoon, and did
not cough even once.

When all the business was over, he did beckon me up. I
wondered if he wanted a private word, and didn't know if
I feared or wished it; it was a long time now since I had
known his mind. But it was only to say he would be sending for me shortly, to discuss the Maidens' Hymn.

Anakreon left with me, and we walked down the steps
together. I said, "Is Hipparchos sick, or has he had too many
late nights? The man looks raveled."

"Something has happened. I don't know what; nor does
anyone else—except one, maybe. A few days back he
passed me in the city within a yard, and never saw me or
heard me greet him. No, it wasn't meant; he might have
been alone upon Mount Parnes. He looked as if the Furies
were after him."

I remembered Bacchylides; but I had given him good
advice and meant to keep it myself. "Can it be love? I
thought he'd be cured by this time."

"He did not name his daimon. But it looked more like
hate to me."

"Or the terrible face of Eros, when he changes shape."

He gave me his sweet smile; like a wise young boy's,
though by then he was over fifty. "My dear, there is no

terrible face of Eros. There is just the one charming one, which he may decide to turn away. The Furies who follow him are all begotten by men."

That was his truth; and even in sad old age, when his smiling god had turned away forever, he did not renounce it. Happy Anakreon!

Next day, Hipparchos sent for me about the maidens' procession. I took my kithara to let him hear the hymn. This time, maybe I would be alone with him. But once more, no; Thessalos was sitting by him.

He at least was his usual self; a saffron robe, blue-bordered, gold clasps and studs on his sandals, an Egyptian girdle worked with ibises. His dark hair was cut to the nape in the very latest fashion, with an embroidered headband. He looked in high health and spirits. They waved me to sit at their writing-table. No clerk was there; Hipparchos wrote a very good hand himself.

Once again I wondered if he was sick. Beside his brother, glossy as a well-groomed horse, his lack of condition showed up. He was dressed with less than his usual care; his hair looked dull, and for the first time I was aware of grey in it; his cheeks were mottled, with broken veins, and when he held his stylos, I saw that he had a tremor. He spoke to me very civilly, but with only half his mind on me. It was Thessalos who saw my kithara, and jogged him into asking to hear the hymn.

I gave it, my own mind partly upon Thessalos himself. His concern with the maiden rite was something new. He was now about thirty, and might well be thinking of marriage. He was far from sharing his brother's dislike of women; and the great festivals are good times for choosing brides. Men can look the girls well over, before getting caught up with matchmakers and kinfolk. Wellborn girls are hard to get a sight of at other times.

Hipparchos roused himself when my noise had stopped,

and praised it as warmly as any man can who has not
listened. Thessalos, who was missing nothing today, picked
out one or two images for compliment. We went quickly
over the rite, which had only to be remembered from one
Great Year to the next. Thessalos said, "Was there anything else? Oh, yes, we never finished choosing the
girls."

He sounded too careless, and I was sure I had guessed
right. If so, his choice would be on the list already. As
usual, Hipparchos showed it me; sometimes I would ask
for some girl of middle station, whom I'd marked down at
a wedding or a feast, for her fine presence or sweet voice.
I had no one in mind today; he rolled it up, saying, "We
can finish it presently. Won't you take some wine before
you go?" I left the brothers with their heads together. He
had one friend at least, it seemed, in whom he could still
confide.

The maids were duly brought to the temple precinct, to
be taught the hymn and the order of the procession. Their
mothers led them proudly, dressed in their second best,
their new ones saved for the day; their hair just loosened
from the crimping-plaits, solemn-faced, too overawed even
to catch one another's eyes. Their mothers sat down on the
seats along the wall, appraising each other's daughters, and
looking at me to be sure I valued their own.

I have never desired young maids, preferring ripe fruit to
green; maybe it is because I feared their laughter when I
was a boy. But at the rites they always moved me: those
sure of their beauty, so ignorant of what Aphrodite may
send them when they have served Athene; the shy ones,
sure of nothing, except that this is their own Great Year,
which they will have to remember forever. They give no
trouble, as boys often do, who know they will find their
fates elsewhere and would sooner impress each other than

their teacher. The girls seek perfection before unknown eyes they have only seen in dreams.

It was the mother I noticed first, fanning herself, and condescending to the lady beside her. The girls stood in a clump, waiting for me to arrange them. There in the middle was the silver-gold hair of the young Delias.

I thought, Her name was not on the list; but it was not finished. He added her later, ashamed that I should see. And Anakreon says there is no terrible face of love! As surely as Dionysos, he can strike men mad. This poor wretch, who has had every gift he offered thrown back in his face, still hopes that by flattering the family he can buy his treasure. The girl is too young, hardly more than a child. Well, at least it will give *her* pleasure.

I felt a moment's surprise that she had been allowed to accept. But how not? It was her right by birth. Her mother would rejoice that the orphan had not been forgotten. Harmodios could not interfere, unless he told them everything; and why, after all, oppose it? It would bring her the chance of a better marriage. She had some of his beauty; indeed was becoming not unlike him. Young though she was, she was one of the tallest there. Like enough she would catch some young noble's eye.

With fifty girls to train, I had not much time to notice her. She was quiet and grave, and did not need to be told things twice. Though there were two or three girls more beautiful, she had the virgin candor of the young Athene herself, and the grace of a willow wand. The mother wafted her fan without a care. It was clear that Harmodios had kept his counsel.

I did not trouble the girls at first with their offering-baskets; highborn girls learn as young as peasants to balance loads on the head, ready for these occasions, and they could practice at home. But I had them pacing the precinct as they sang, to get the beat in their blood. There is the little ceremony some days before the great one, when the chosen girls are presented to the goddess and bring her offerings. I would have them ready for that.

Soon after this, I saw Aristogeiton walking across the Agora; and watched him with curiosity, after all I'd heard. I had lately seen one man scorching his soul to a crisp; here, by the look of him, went another. Since he was younger and much fitter, his sleepless nights had made him fine-drawn and handsome. But what would he know of that? An implacable god!

Just then he stopped a passing man, and they walked on talking. Soon he drew him out of the crowd, towards the stall of a pot-seller. She started pointing to her wares, and showing the price on her fingers. She was deaf and dumb.

They paid her no heed, and after talking there awhile went off together. I did not know the second man; he had a sharp discontented face, and did not look cheerful company. As they walked my way, I saw approaching a certain Charias, whom I did know; one of the lesser Alkmaionid clansmen, not of enough consequence to have been exiled. He used to say, rather too often, that he took no part in politics. He and Aristogeiton just lifted a hand in greeting as they passed; after which the young man spoke with great earnestness to his companion. When I came near, they became as dumb as the pot-seller.

I did not think much about it. Men with a grievance will go about getting sympathy from their friends; and if their complaint is against the great, everyone concerned will show a certain discretion.

As I walked on, I was wishing that I knew him as a friend, to quiet his fears; for, if Bacchylides had been right about them, they were quite absurd. Ah well, I thought, next year the boy will be a man with a stubble on his chin; and to both these poor fools, Archon and commoner, all this anguish will seem like a dream gone by. We are all children of Time, however much we may wish to kill our father. I walked on smiling, thinking how Anakreon could have contained it all in one short bitter-sweet song.

I rehearsed my girls each morning. The temple guard is there to keep out men, but some will always watch from beyond the walls. Bacchylides came most days. He had learned all his schoolmaster could teach him, and I'd let him leave; it was time he should study music as a man. The Maiden's Hymn, he had by heart the first day; as he still appeared, I took it he had begun to notice girls. Afterwards at our meal he would pass judgment on them, rather severely lest I should suspect him of it, but fairly on the whole.

"You can see at once which is Harmodios' sister, she's so like him. *She* gets everything right. He came to watch her today."

"He should be pleased with her. She holds herself very well. They must use their baskets tomorrow; the Presentation is in three days' time."

"Glaukos, Leagros' son, was standing next me. He hardly took his eyes off her. I think he's serious."

"That would be a good match," I said. It was an old house with wealth and reputation; Glaukos was the eldest son, an athlete of some distinction. It was just the marriage a family needed, so shorn of menfolk by death. I wished the girl luck with it.

Next day they carried their baskets. One girl had been too lazy to practice, and let hers wobble. I threatened that if she was not perfect by next day, I'd turn her out. It was only to scare her, for of course I could not do it; everyone would have thought her maidenhood was in question, and the scandal would have followed her for life. However, the silly girl was duly terrified, and performed without fault thereafter.

I was pleased with them all, on the day of the Presentation. The sky was bright; so were the girls, each in her festal dress, the peplos damp-pleated into tiny clinging folds, and fastened on the shoulders with gold brooches; the himation draped across, often an heirloom, with borders of six months' work; hair freshly washed and waved, combed down over back and breasts. Some had brushed their lips with the juice of geranium petals, but their faces needed no heightening. Rosy or pale, their light came from within.

They gathered in their order, on the terrace below the crowded precinct, looking up at the temple porch with the priests' and archons' thrones. Hipparchos was there, with Thessalos beside him. Hippias seldom came to these minor rites.

Bacchylides paced behind me, carrying the kithara. His hours at the palaestra had not been wasted; at his age I should have been glad of half his grace. At my signal he brought the instrument and held the sling for me. He had been well rehearsed, and did it without fumbling. I was about to sign for the flautist to begin, when I was aware of people turning, and saw that Hipparchos had lifted his hand, signaling me to wait.

I looked up, puzzled, trying to catch his eye. But it was fixed on the line of girls. I was not too far off to see where it had rested.

It's the likeness, I thought; I daresay it's the first time he's seen her. But what is the man about? He will never make a show of himself before all these people; he can't be so far gone as that.

To my surprise he turned to Thessalos, as if saying, "Is that the one?" His brother pointed, nodding. Hipparchos beckoned one of the sacred heralds, and said something; he came down the steps, looking grave as became his office, but also like a man who has been given a shock.

After saluting me respectfully, he said, "Sir, the Archon commands that the daughter of Proxenos must withdraw."

I stared at him, wondering if everyone had gone mad. Such a thing was unheard of. I just said, "Why?"

The man, who under his ritual dignity was clearly as shaken as I was, answered, "The Archon says the girl was never invited. She is not a proper person for the rite."

By this time my stare had become a glare; or so Bacchylides told me later. I said, "I know nothing of this. All these girls have rehearsed with me. Of course they have been invited."

"Sir," said the herald—an unhappy man if I ever saw one—"the Archon wishes to speak to you about it. Will you please go up to him?"

I looked round at the girls. Till just now, their happy whisperings had been like the hum of summer bees. What I'd heard was their silence. All their eyes were turned one way.

With a widening space around her, the young Delias stood still as a sculptor's block. Then her basket began to tremble on her head. She grabbed at it, wildly without grace, and stood holding it in her hands before her. In her face, which had gone chalk-white, I saw not guilt, but horror; and yet, a kind of knowledge, a little, even if not enough. She knew why this had been done to her.

The herald looked at me. I looked at the steps, and did not start to climb them. I was very angry, and wished to have it seen. The girl turned her desperate eyes on me, as if I had power to say, "Don't be afraid; I shall not allow it." She knew, as well as I, that I could do nothing. I was just the straw nearest her drowning clutch.

I got rid of my kithara, and went and laid my hand on her shoulder. "My child, I am sorry. Some great mistake has been made, we can be sure. But we must all obey the Archon for the present. It is better that you go home."

I looked round for the mother. Her neighbors were not struck dumb as the girls had been. Hissing whispers were everywhere; some were not even whispering. I beckoned her to come and take the girl away. As she got up, leaving her fan behind, I saw she was near fainting; but after all, she was not the widow of Proxenos for nothing. She kept on her feet, though the girl was holding her up as they went out. The women's chatter rose, mixed now with titters.

There was a stir by the gate. A man was shouldering through the crowd to them. I had never seen Proxenos transformed with anger; but it seemed that I saw him now. The rage in Harmodios' face was a boy's no longer.

He put an arm round his mother, who at once threw all her weight on him; here was the man of the family. The other hand he held out to his sister. She paused a moment, fumbling with her basket. He took it from her and threw it on the ground, and led them both away. I don't think that he looked at her.

I watched them go. Then I went up the steps to Hipparchos.

He was staring after them. When he became aware of me, he'd forgotten that I'd been summoned. His face was like a mask of clay, from which his bloodshot eyes asked how I dared accuse him.

"You sent for me." In public, I should have called him Sir.

That brought him partly to himself. I was supposed to have been told why the girl must be sent away, and to have gone back and dismissed her. I had saved him this trouble, a thing he could hardly complain of; but now I was here, he did not know what to do with me. It was a messenger he had wanted, not a judge.

He said, "We will speak about this later."

It was all I'd left him to say; but I had been in no hurry
to come, and now was in none to go. I stood and looked
at him. No, it would not be true to say I no longer knew
him. I had known him a long time. All I saw now I'd
known; but only as a man can know that his lynx kitten
is getting bigger, not really believing that its claws are
growing too. He had been much praised, much loved, and
much of it deservedly. His sense of his deserts had grown.
Now he was sure that what he desired, he deserved, and
anyone who denied it merited punishment.

Whatever he'd become, it was not a fool. He had read
me, as I'd read him. His bitter look said, Yes, I knew I
could tell *you* nothing.

I said, aloud, "I should have been told of this."

Thessalos leaned over. "How could we know she would
dare show her face?" Hipparchos lifted a hand at him. I
thought he'd brazen it out, but he fell silent.

Hipparchos said, without insolence or anything else one
could put a name to, "Simonides, you are a poet but not a
priest. This matter has been settled by those whose place
it is. We are here to serve a goddess. The High Priestess
is waiting. Let the rite proceed."

I looked past him at the altar beside the porch, wreathed
in its olive garlands, with the servers by it to take the
offerings laid on it. There indeed stood the Maiden's
Maiden, robed in pure white, waiting to bless each girl as
she did her reverence. A tall old lady, with a well-scrubbed,
innocent virgin's face, now looking severe as only innocence
can. What could she know of all this, except that it was
unseemly? Ever since she was a girl as young as these, she
had served Athene Parthenos. It was for others, who knew
the world, to see that the shrine was not polluted. Her
work was holiness, not justice.

I went down the steps, and beckoned my pupil for my
kithara. He slung it on me, his eyes begging that everything

should be well. I met them, and shook my head, and looked up towards the priestess. He understood. The goldsmith's apprentice knows that gold can burn; but there is always a first time for feeling it.

The girls were ready. They had closed the gap in their line. I signed to the flautist, and struck the first chord of the hymn. Their fresh voices rose, all together on the note, saluting the city's Guardian, who gave us the olive for our wealth, craftsmanship for our beauty, music for our joy, and justice to make us great. Gracefully they went up singing, carrying their pretty baskets to the altar.

However, the grey eyes of Athene do not miss much. She knew, that day, that she was an offering short. It seems she did not forget it.

4

WE WILL SPEAK of it later, he had said. Very well, let him send for me.

A day passed; then a second day; and I began to guess what it meant. He would never send for me, not about this. Time would go by, new things would happen in the city. Then one day he would send for me, and greet me as if none of it had ever been. In silence we were to agree that it was all forgotten.

I thought of Athens, the center of the world; of songs I'd made and would make, which foreigners would only half understand. I thought of Bacchylides, who now that Ionia was gone must be here, to hear the best. I thought of the victory chariot I'd become so used to mounting; of the tripod I had dedicated to Apollo. I thought of the man who had been my friend.

When next he sent for me, all the old charm would be back again—with just a feeling that it might be taken away, if one showed oneself ungrateful. I would drink and sing and talk with him, never speaking of what I knew; and when the next thing happened, I would have got into the way of it. Everything just the same; except that my friend would have become my master, with whom I must seem friendly to get my pay.

I had my men's chorus to rehearse. There were some fine voices that year; while they sang I could forget the rest. But only then.

Bacchylides was my pupil, which gave him all a son's right to know my mind. We were walking back from a rehearsal, which he'd come to hear, when I found myself saying, "After the festival, I shall have to see the man, whether he sends for me or not."

He looked at me across the kithara, which he was carrying home for me. He was in no doubt what it meant. "Everyone thinks you stood up to him very well."

"For me it was not enough."

"You didn't see yourself."

"Who's 'everyone'? The boys from the gymnasium? It will mean very little, you know, to most people in the city. The majority will take it that the Archon knew what he was about. Many will be glad to see an oligarch's daughter set down. Only a handful will know the truth. This is a matter between me and myself. And you."

I knew that by now he was feeling desolate; but he said stoutly, "I'll go wherever you go. Don't worry about me."

"Not even that. If I leave Athens, it won't be like traveling to the festivals. I can't sit down in Euboia and let my life go by. I shall take my chance in Thessaly. For a time, at least, you would have to go back to Keos. I owe that to your parents."

"To *Keos!*" He almost shouted it. People looked round. "Uncle, I promise you, on Keos I'd go mad."

"No, you would not. You would make some songs, to sing me when we meet again, and obey your parents, so that they think well of my instruction. As soon as I have a settled home, it will be yours wherever it is, as long as I live, or you want to share it. But I'm not taking you to a land without law like Thessaly."

He looked round. "You said 'if' at first. Now you're talking as if it were all settled."

"Perhaps I was. You were there; you saw it all; you know the girl was innocent. What do you think yourself that I ought to do?" I was not exhorting him; I really wanted to know.

He saw it, and paused in thought. "If you stayed, would it mean you had to tell lies?"

"In my songs, do you mean, or in my speech?"

"In the songs, of course."

"No. He has never asked me to flatter him. If the compliments stopped, he is still too proud to demand them."

"Uncle, you know that story about the man who was boasting of Corinth. And the Athenian said, 'But *we* have Simonides.' It's true, you know. You do belong to the Athenians, and their heroes and their gods. Hipparchos is just one man."

"True. And we could eat well without his bread. But if I go to him saying, 'You are no longer my patron,' I would have to leave the city."

"He might kill you, you mean? Could he do that?"

"No. He'd do nothing to me. Or for me, either. At the festivals he would just get other men to sing, and make sure I felt it."

"Then you *would* have to go, of course. But you know, I was there, I saw him. I think your friendship's over, Uncle Sim, whether you speak to him or not. As it is, it's a long time now since he asked you up to supper. But I think he'll still call on you to sing for the Athenians, because if he stopped they would be angry. And it's for them that you'll be singing."

"Yes, that might be. There's Hippias, too. He has no ear, but he thinks I am respectable and bring the city credit; and it's he who has the last word."

"Will Anakreon stay?" His mind often ran with my thought.

"I've not asked him, it would only give us pain. He will say it was all an unhappy business, but love is a lawless god. He's his own man, I am mine."

He walked on awhile in silence, then said, "Thank you for talking to me. I didn't like to ask. At any rate, it will all have to wait till after the Panathenaia. That *does* belong to the Athenians and their gods. It's only three days now, and you've a great deal to do. After all that, something may come to you; things do, when you've been thinking of something else. Or I've found that, with a song."

It was the first time in his life that I had leaned on the boy like this, and his strength surprised me; which itself surprises me now. On the other hand, I have never thought him a seer. That one time only, a god breathed in his ear.

5

I SPENT the next night with Lyra, a promise long since exchanged. After hard work, I sought the refreshment of her healing springs, more needed than ever now. We lay at sundown, Aphrodite's rites performed, watching the last light shine gold on the vine around the window, sharing a flask of Thracian wine cold from the well, lazily talking. She heard my story kindly, and told me I brooded on such things too much; though we both liked to choose our patrons, there were bound to be some misadventures here and there. She held up the wine-cup to my mouth, licked up what she'd spilled upon my shoulder, and added, "At least you tell me. There was a young man with me yesterday, who you'd have thought was having it for the last time in his life. I knew he'd be better for talking; but not a word. Some men don't know how often we hold our tongues."

"He was the loser." But Aphrodite was recalling me to her worship, and I had no wish to hear about other men.

Next day the city buzzed, preparing for the festival. Crowds stood to watch the banners and garlands go up along the Sacred Way, from Athene's temple down to the Kerameikos. I took my two choruses for last rehearsals, and was satisfied; in the presence of a watchful mother, I gave last advice to the leader of the maidens' chorus. I would be leading the men, and she the maidens, standing on the prow of the Sacred Ship. She was a plump sparrowlike girl, who would not have looked much in the procession, but had a sweet strong voice and perfect pitch.

In the evening Anakreon called, full of the day's gossip. As I'd guessed, he said nothing about the events at the Presentation. He had not been there, so had no need; and we understood each other. Our friendship was a thing neither of us would sacrifice, each knowing that the good in it far outweighed the rest. I have been glad ever since that we both felt it alike.

The day dawned perfect, sweet and balmy even before the sunrise, with a light breeze. The crowds were there already; in the Great Year, they come in from most cities in Greece, and from the islands. Bacchylides was away at cockcrow, to find his place in the dark; he had left a lamp kindled, for me to dress by, and beside it the kithara, groomed and polished like a race-horse. As I dipped my barley-cake in my breakfast wine, I gave myself to the day.

At this one festival, remembering all the heroes from Theseus on, Athenians of fighting age wore their arms. In their tribal groups, they were gathering all around the Kerameikos. They had made the best of their panoplies: leather corselets waxed and bronze ones burnished, helmets and spear-points gleaming. The cavalry, still more resplendent, were above within the city gate, wearing their scarlet cloaks. But Hippias himself was coming down to the Kerameikos, to lead the hoplites' march.

Further up, near the foot of the ramp to the Acropolis, the Ship of Athene stood on its tall car. At first light came its team of snow-white oxen; then the troop of girls, bearing its colored sail. It was the goddess' new robe, which they had all been embroidering to last her till next Great Year; two girls would hold it spread from the mast, to be seen by all the people. I wondered how many stitches the daughter of Proxenos had put into it, and with what hopes.

To be here, now, at the center of all this glory, making

the music to which its heart would beat: what more could a man wish for, what more could he offer to his god? I thought, How can I go? It was for this I was born, if I was born for anything. I have grown into this, as a fig tree grows to its fruiting, rooted in a city wall. How can I forsake it, and not desert Apollo too? If he would only send me a sign!

The girls were all gathered now. I went up through the crowds, to look at them in their beauty. Gowned and girdled and combed and crowned with flowers, by the hands of loving mothers and skillful slaves, they gave me grave smiles, too solemn now for laughter. I turned back downhill; the people who saw my kithara on its sling making way to give it room.

A little way on, I heard my name called from above. Bacchylides had been in time to secure his chosen place. He had swarmed up the column of my victory tripod, and, like the Pythia at Delphi, was sitting snugly in the bowl. He grinned, calling out that it had the best view in the city. I shook my fist at him, laughing.

Just below was the shrine of Leos' Daughters; it had a good-sized precinct, with a stone slab in the middle, on which stood Hipparchos, getting the procession into its starting order. From time to time he got down, to direct anyone who seemed confused. He was an expert at such things, and it was all going smoothly.

My chorus men were awaiting me; a fine tall troop, picked for presence as well as voice. (Once, I'd have feared to be laughed at, stepping out before men like these; now I thought nothing of it, and nor did the Athenians.) They had made themselves as handsome as they could, borrowing good panoplies from their kin if they did not own them; one had hired his, paying a whole sheep just for the day. I thanked them all for doing me so much credit. Hipparchos turned at my words, and called out cheerfully, "Are

your songbirds in good voice, Simonides?" I answered,
"And in spring feathers, sir." "So they are, as bright as
jays. But for you they will sing like nightingales. Down
there, please. My brother wants you to walk before the
horsemen."

"That's good," I answered. "No one sings better for
breathing cavalry dust." How easy it is, I thought, when
one can do it without thinking. But I shall have thought,
next time. We went down towards the Kerameikos.

I left my men standing outside the city gates till I had
got Hippias' own orders. He had a little platform, in the
middle of the potters' field. At times like these, he always
tried to put on his father's mantle, more from duty than
pride; when anyone came up to him he would smile, though
awkwardly; one could see him seeking a gracious word
or two.

All around him stood in their ranks the Athenian hoplites. The place was gay as a flower-bed with their painted
shields, boars and hawks and bulls and lions and serpents,
done black upon white or red or ochre, touched up with
purple here and there. The flower-thorns were their
bristling spears. Near me was the tribal band of the
Gephyriots, in its front rank Harmodios and Aristogeiton
side by side. Peaceful myrtle wreaths were bound about
their spears; but their faces were so set, one might have
thought them in the battle line, instead of at a festival.
Sometimes, when Hipparchos raised his voice, it carried
over to us, and I put it down to that.

Hippias was busy, and I had to wait; but there was still
plenty of time. The trumpet, which would signal the march
to start, caught the light on the temple roof. Higher up
the road, Bacchylides waved to me from his tripod.

Just when I saw my chance, another man was before me.
It was Charias the Alkmaionid about some business or
other, which I hoped was brief. It seemed Hippias hoped so

too; he made a signal to one of the bodyguard, who went over to make sure that his horse was ready. I began to fear it was too late to catch him; and he might well have forgotten all about me and my chorus. I pushed up nearer, thinking as I got close that in his panoply he looked a harder man than ever he did at court. After all, he had fought in most of his father's wars.

Charias had nearly done, when I was aware of movement in the rank near by. Two men in the Gephyriot troop had dropped their shields and spears, and were racing up the Sacred Way. From where I was now, I could not tell who they were, only that they were carrying green branches. People with messages were still running about, and I thought no more of it.

This time, Hippias had beckoned someone, so I had to wait again. At last I managed to speak to him. He asked if my flautist would be loud enough to be heard above the horses—he was always full of these small worries—then told me to get my men into their place. I said they were ready, and I would join them now. I had barely started, when a man on horseback came clattering through the gates—he looked like a troop commander—rode straight to Hippias, shoving everyone aside, jumped uninvited on the dais, and spoke quietly in the Archon's ear.

Hippias fixed his eyes upon his face, and asked him two short questions; then stood a moment in silent thought. His face hardly changed; yet I thought again, Yes, he has been a soldier, a hard one too. My memory brought back to me that grey-haired Mede who had ridden into fallen Ephesos.

Suddenly he beckoned up a trumpeter. The man mounted the platform, and blew the alert. The hum of talk from the hundreds of waiting men died like the hiss of beach pebbles when the wave has paused. Hippias signed for his horse, mounted, and rode over to the soldiers.

I was too far to hear his orders, till the officers passed them on to where I was. They were to gather by tribal bands, and stack their arms. This they all did, except the Archon's own bodyguard, which now moved up and closed around him. Now I saw them apart, I was surprised at how many they were.

More delay, I thought; whatever fuss has he thought of now? He was pointing the citizens to a place some little way off, towards the Hill of Kolonos. Did he want to address them, or what? At this rate, everything would drag on into the midday heat.

The men straggled off; inside the gate, the cavalry were getting restless. I had never seen such muddle at a public festival, even in a small town. Before going back to my chorus, I had better find out what we were supposed to be doing now.

The men of Hippias' guard had not followed the citizens, and nor had he. He kept some fifty round him, and pointed the rest towards the stacks of arms. These they gathered into one heap, over which a strong guard was posted. Then Hippias and the rest followed the Athenians.

All this on a peaceful day of festival made me wonder if the Archon had gone stark mad. I wished I were near enough to hear his speech. A crowd of sightseers were standing about staring; strangers from other cities, old men and boys from our own. The old men were looking surprised; the rest just waited patiently for the show to start.

I became aware that above, inside the gates, the cavalry horses were very noisy, and the men were shouting to each other. Horses quickly sense trouble from their masters. I thought, Those men know something I don't. I took a few steps that way; and came slap into Bacchylides, running towards me. I remember my first thought was that he might have broken the kithara.

He grabbed my arm, and stood still, gasping. His face

280 [*Mary Renault*

was grey, sweaty dust upon white. I cried, "What is it?" as if he were not fighting for breath to tell me.

"They've killed Hipparchos," he said.

I stood in silence, hardly feeling it yet, while all I had seen grew clear, from the moment when Hippias had had the news from the horseman. No wonder I'd remembered that he had been a soldier! I saw the whole pattern, the warp and weft of it—then my head grew light and cold, and my eyes felt empty of sight. I must have kept on my feet however, and just looked stupid; for Bacchylides said louder, as if to a child, "Uncle Sim! Hipparchos is *dead*."

I looked about me, as if I had just been put down in some foreign city. I was not so far wrong, at that. Presently I said, "Let us go home."

He took another look at me, lifted the kithara from my shoulder and hung it on his own. Then he put his hand under my arm. "Not now. They're running crazy up there. Somewhere quiet. Come down to the stream."

He led me towards the Eridanos with its ancient tombs. "Did you hear who did it?" I said.

"I saw it. Sit down somewhere and rest."

"I don't need rest. Don't treat me as if I were eighty." (Yes, I remember that!)

"Harmodios did it. He's dead too, they killed him."

We reached the stream with its leaning old grave-steles cropping out like rocks among the weeds. He guided me to a cracked, tilting marble slab, the tomb of some old-time lord, brushed off some plane leaves and set me down on it, then dusted a place for the kithara with his tunic hem.

As a man, well known to have witnessed the event, he is often asked for his account of it; it comes to me now in the voice of his manhood, not the hasty stammering of a shocked boy, though sometimes I hear that too in it, here and there. "I had been up in the dark to get my place, and then was disappointed with it, because I would not see the procession after it was formed. Hipparchos was standing just below, to halt each part as it came up and get it in order. It was him that I chiefly stared at, after all I'd heard. All I was near enough to see was that he performed his office very well.

"The boys with the oil-jars had been looked over, and sent on up the road; then came the sacrificial oxen. But the first of them refused its fate; there was a struggle and some shouting; the man who led it got some help from the crowd. And I thought, That's supposed to be a bad omen; but only perhaps when it happens at the altar. Well, it left an empty space around Hipparchos, and into this two men came running, with green branches in their hands. I supposed this was some rite I didn't know of; I had been a child at the last Great Year. I even still thought so when I saw who the runners were. A youth with Harmodios' beauty might always be singled out."

Here someone often interrupts to ask for a description, and he will say, "Like a young Apollo—but with the bow, not the lyre.

"As they reached Hipparchos they threw their branches away. I stared in amazement as they seemed to strike him with their fists. Then I saw that as he struggled, blood was flowing. They had carried daggers, hidden in the leaves.

"One of them must have struck quickly to the heart; he threw up his arms and fell. There was blood all over his face, from a gash upon his forehead . . . I had once seen a murdered corpse, when we were riding over the Isthmus. I had never seen murder done. I suppose the blood shocked me too; but I know that I thought, What dreadful faces. I dreamed of them for a long time after."

How easily men talk, how different is the acted deed. I recalled the man Charias, who had spoken to Hippias on his platform; the Alkmaionid who had exchanged a sign with Aristogeiton in the street. He must have been in the plot,

and had seemed to be betraying it. So they resolved to do
what they could, to make sure at least of Hipparchos, the
author of their wrongs, instead of falling on Hippias first
with their confederates, as they'd planned. Yet, from what
I saw, I am sure he was not giving the Archon warning—
more likely keeping him in talk to have him ready for them,
but without telling them first what he would do. Few men
can think such things through in the fearful time of action,
or remember to expect the unexpected.

Bacchylides said, "He was dead almost before I understood what was really happening. It was the same with
everyone, the people round, even the guards. There were
only one or two of them, not near him; they'd just been
keeping the precinct clear of crowds. While everyone was
still stunned, or milling about, Harmodios leaped on the
block where Hipparchos had been standing, and cried out,
'Athenians! Strike for freedom! Death to the tyrants!'
Aristogeiton took it up; but the people just stared, no one
came forward; then the guards rushed to Harmodios and
seized him.

"You know, in war" (it is the man who is speaking
now) "how they kill on the field, when the word is to give
no quarter. They wrenched the blood-stained dagger out
of his hand, pulled back his head by the hair and slit his
throat. He had long, fair hair, and the scarlet blood poured
into it. I stared in horror, and did not see how Aristogeiton
got away. Someone in the crowd must have let him through,
and after that he would be among people who knew
nothing yet."

Thus the man. The pale-faced boy, sitting by me on the
tomb, said, "But he avenged his honor. He did do that."
Then he flung himself down on the old green-stained
marble, shaken with weeping. I offered what comfort I
could till he had done.

Yes, I thought; it was as Achilles' heir that he must have

seen himself; inheritor of the ancient laws, which say a man
lives by his pride and shall defend it to the death:
Harmodios son of Proxenos son of Harmodios, and so on
back to some well-greaved Achaian at Troy. And Aristogeiton, to whom Bacchylides, concerned for his hero only,
had paid so little heed? The youth had killed for pride,
but the man for love: from anger at the hurt to his beloved, and that one man should have the power to do it;
from fear that he had power to take the beloved away. I
wondered if they had caught him yet, and guessed that
Harmodios would prove more fortunate. I thought of
Hippias' face.

I said to the boy, as his sobs quietened, "The anger of
Achilles. *Many brave men's souls it flung to the house of
Hades, and left the flesh of heroes to feast dogs and kites.*"

"*That the will of Zeus might be fulfilled?*" But I had
no answer. Nor have I now.

Great things came after; but the city I knew was already
great. In all men is evil sleeping; the good man is he who
will not awaken it, in himself or in other men. In Hippias
that day there had been a great awakening. So Aristogeiton
found in his hard dying. So the few men of his following
found, down in the Kerameikos, when the guards had
found they had had daggers as well as spears.

Courage and love; it is well that they should be honored,
even by men who have forgotten the truth, or never known
it, or have lied about it to serve a cause. Those proud young
oligarchs of my vanished city stand in the new one, cast in
immortal bronze, and the democrats do them honor.
Already people say that they set Athens free, though they
threw her into a reign of fear, and only the Spartans and
Alkmaionids broke it. They are even starting to say that
Hipparchos was First Archon and Pisistratos' heir; though
it seems to me like yesterday that Hippias, all else failing
him, crawled to the Medes to put him back in Athens as

their governor, and was flung back from the gallant shore of Marathon, and crept off with the Medes to die.

I sat by the boy, as he wiped away his tears and begged my pardon for them; I thought of the face of Hippias; and suddenly my roots were loosened from Athens' walls. As at Keos, as at Ephesos, as at Samos, it was time to go. We are wanderers all.

I said, "We must stay awhile, or the Archon will think we have some reason to run away. Let us go home now and sit in quiet. It's no time to be running about the city."

I stood up. Bacchylides slung the kithara on his shoulder, giving it a long look. It was just coming home to him that the wrath of Achilles had sent us both into exile. Yes; but before Achilles' anger had come the hubris of Agamemnon, King of Men. It is grief to see a hero go down to the house of Hades. It is bitter to lose a friend to evil, before one loses him to death.

But I had the boy to think of just now. I said, "We shall come back again. All that I know of Athens tells me so. A city is not as great as its rulers only. It is as great as its gods. I have served them most; and I think the city knows it."

"And its heroes," said the boy. "You have sung them too. Perhaps it was because of you that he died so bravely." He was feeling better now, and wanted to give some comfort back to me, in return for mine to him. "You sang it, and he did it. Have you thought of that?"

AUTHOR'S NOTE

If the lives of Greek poets in the latter half of the sixth century are to be understood, we must be aware more of contrasts than of parallels with the condition of writers today.

It was only on the very lowest level, that of the market-place entertainer, that the singer or reciter made his living from a public audience. Circulation of the written word was still unknown, and compositions were committed to writing only for personal reference, if at all. Many surviving fragments of the century's great lyric poets may have been recorded only after a long circulation by word of mouth. It is certain that the whole of Homer was so transmitted for some two centuries, and may incorporate material centuries older still, over a stretch of time during which the art of writing had entirely perished; Pisistratos' collation came just in time to rescue him for a literate society. During the Dark Age, and into the dawn of the archaic renaissance, the libraries of the bards were contained entirely within their heads.

Before the passing of the powerful aristocratic oligarchies, private means would assure both the poet's independence and an audience of his peers: Sappho, Alkaios,

Solon, had no need of patronage. This situation was changed by the advent of the "tyrants."

It is little understood today that nearly all the Greek tyrants were well to the left of the oligarchies they super-seded, and, though invariably of aristocratic birth them-selves, emerged as champions of underprivileged majorities. The term itself had originally a neutral connotation, like the word "dictator" in Rome. Its later meaning derived from the excesses of some tyrants, once all restraints on their exercise of power had been removed. The blanket generalization that "absolute power corrupts absolutely" is a historical absurdity (compare, for instance, Nero with Marcus Aurelius); and tyrants came in all shades of per-sonality from benign father-figures to sadistic monsters. What they had in common was that they were all heads of state, in whom resided the poet's only hope of public performance and recognition, even though he might be a man of property. Thus his situation was quite different from that of writers in other ages of patronage, such as Shakespeare or Samuel Johnson, who could pick up a living in time of need through the theater or the printing press.

Prose composition, dependent wholly on writing, had not yet begun; and neither, therefore, had history or biography. Anyone trying to piece together the lives and characters of the archaic poets must turn to the researches of scholars, among whom the late Sir Maurice Bowra has pride of place, who have collected from all kinds of scattered sources the fragments of their work, and references or quotations by other, often much later, classical authors. Thus the record of their lives is skeletal when it is even that; and their treatment in fiction leaves the novelist with many more lacunae to fill in than when dealing with a much-chronicled figure such as Alexander the Great.

Simonides is known to have been born in Keos (whose severe austerity laws are described by Strabo) and to have been so ugly that when he had composed a satire on the Corinthians, someone asked him how so ill-favored a man dared reproach a beautiful city. Nothing is known of his childhood, and I may have traduced a loving father who fostered his talent; but it seems that, once out of Keos, he felt no disposition to go back. It is not known whether he ever worked in Ionia before the Persian conquest, or in Samos either; but there is some evidence that at one time he lived in Euboia, before being invited to Athens by the Pisistratids.

His father's name is known; so are the names of his sister and her husband, because they were the parents of Bacchylides, himself a gifted poet, and his uncle's pupil and companion up to the time of his death in Sicily, at the age of eighty-eight. Theasides son of Leoprepes appears in Herodotos as a man of high repute among both the Spartans and the Aiginetans, who was allowed to arbitrate in a dispute between them, and thus averted a war. Unluckily his native city is not given; but Leoprepes, the name of Simonides' father, is an unusual one. I have made them brothers by pure guess.

One of the most striking features of Simonides' career is the respect with which he was welcomed back to Athens after the expulsion of Hippias, despite his long residence at the Pisistratid court. It seems probable that he left it after the murder of Hipparchos; the dates of his sojourn in Thessaly are not exactly known. Anakreon, who also found a refuge there, was also *persona grata* when he came back. It is probable that the Pisistratids were not so unpopular in Athens before the unforgivable defection of the exiled Hippias to Persia. It is also true that to the Greeks of the great age, good work was good work, and carried its own passport.

In the story of Harmodios and Aristogeiton, I have followed Thukydides' account in every particular that he

gives. The errors he corrects in the received tradition—
that the friends were democrats, and that they killed the
reigning tyrant—are the first known instance of distor-
tion of history for political ends.

The name of Harmodios' father is not known; but J. K.
Davies, in his indispensable *Athenian Propertied Families,
600–300 B.C.*, gives Proxenos as a family name.

The curious circumstance about Harmodios' father, as
with the dog in the Sherlock Holmes story, is that he did
nothing. Whether or not he knew of Hipparchos' attempts
upon his son, the public humiliation of his daughter would
have insulted him, as head of the family, more than any of
its other menfolk. I have therefore inferred that, in an
era when life-expectancy was short, he was already dead,
and that this place was held by Harmodios himself.

A bronze statue-group of the "liberators," set up in the
Agora, was taken as a trophy by Xerxes during the Persian
invasion, and carried back to Susa. The Athenians commis-
sioned another statue-group to take its place. In the fourth
century Susa fell to Alexander, who sent the original
statues back to Athens. For some centuries the two groups
stood in the Agora side by side.

CHRONOLOGY

SOME HISTORICAL EVENTS DURING THE
LIFETIME OF SIMONIDES

B.C.

556 Simonides born. Pisistratos expelled from Athens for second time.

550 Kyros establishes supremacy of Persians over Medes. Pisistratids in exile.

546 Kyros takes Sardis. Pisistratos returns to Athens.

540 Kyros conquers Babylon. Polykrates reigning in Samos.

530 Death of Kyros. Accession of Kambyses.

527 Death of Pisistratos. Hippias succeeds to the Tyranny.

525 Aischylos born.

522 Murder of Polykrates. Death of Kambyses. Darius succeeds. Pindar born.

514 Murder of Hipparchos by Harmodios and Aristogeiton.

510 Hippias expelled from Athens. Simonides in Thessaly.

499–494 Ionian revolt against Persia, ending in defeat.

496 Sophokles born. Herodotos born about this time.

495 Perikles born.

492 Persians invade Thrace. Simonides back in Athens about this time.

B.C.

490 Darius invades Greece. Battle of Thermopylai. Simonides composes epitaph of the fallen Spartans. Persians (with Hippias) defeated at Marathon.

486 Death of Darius. Accession of Xerxes.

480 Xerxes invades Greece. Athens evacuated. Greek naval victory at Salamis, retreat of Xerxes. Euripides born.

c.476 Simonides retires to Syracuse, accompanied by Bacchylides.

472 Aischylos' tragedy *The Persians* performed in Athens.

468 Death of Simonides.

About the Author

MARY RENAULT was born in London, where her father was a doctor. She first went to Oxford with the idea of teaching, but decided that she wanted to be a writer instead, and that after taking her degree she should broaden her knowledge of human life. She then trained for three years as a nurse, and wrote her first published novel, *Promise of Love*. Her next three novels were written during off-duty time when serving in World War II. One of them, *Return to Night*, received the MGM award. After the war, she went to South Africa and settled at the Cape. She has traveled considerably in Africa and has gone up the east coast to Zanzibar and Mombasa. But it was her trip to Greece, her visits to Corinth, Samos, Crete, Delos, Aegina, and other islands, as well as to Athens, Sounion, and Marathon, that resulted in her previous brilliant historical reconstructions of ancient Greece, *The Last of the Wine, The King Must Die, The Bull from the Sea, The Mask of Apollo, Fire from Heaven,* and *The Persian Boy*. In addition to the novels, she has written a biography of Alexander the Great, *The Nature of Alexander*.